INDIGENT

BRIANA N COX

PRAISE FOR INDIGENT

"Both a sharp indictment of the US healthcare system and a tightly plotted thriller, INDIGENT will invade your mind and body and not let go even after you have read the final page." —**Johanna van Veen, best-selling author of *Blood on Her Tongue***

"Picture Nick Cutter's The Troop adapted by Bong Joon Ho, where the acid-bath class struggle of Parasite intermingles with parasitic terror in Briana N Cox's slippery, slithering, symbiotically suffocating debut." —**Clay McLeod Chapman, author of *Wake Up and Open Your Eyes***

"Utterly engrossing. Briana N Cox takes what slips through the cracks and brings it into the light. An intricate and searing examination of how the medical system fails those most in need, INDIGENT is devastatingly timely." —**Erin E. Adams, author of *Jackal* & *One of You***

"With INDIGENT, Briana N Cox has crafted a scathing indictment of America's healthcare system wrapped in a tale that will creep under your skin... Not just because it's an excellently written tale of horror, but because it reads all too real." —**Markus Redmond, author of *Blood Slaves***

"With stunning, visceral prose and memorable characters, Briana N Cox deftly intertwines body horror and class consciousness to explore interconnection in its most terrifying expressions. INDIGENT writhes on the page and lingers wih the reader long after." —**Tiffany Morris, Shirely Jackson Award nominated author of *Green Fuse Burning***

"Briana N Cox has written Shivers for the Get Out generation with INDIGENT. A thoughtful, complex look at the intersection of gentrification and the ongoing opioid epidemic, as explored through the lens of a body-horror creature-feature phantasmagoria." —**Preston Fassel, author of *Our Lady of the Inferno* and *Landis: The Story of a Real Man on 42nd Street***

"In INDIGENT, debut author Briana N. Cox deftly weaves together an unsettling tale of body-snatching monsters with poignant commentary on gentrification, poverty, racial injustice, and the U.S. healthcare system. Blending hauntingly poetic prose with lose-your-lunch body horror, Cox's disturbing and timely novel is unflinching in its exploration of topics that are too often left in the dark. Like the squirming parasites infecting the residents of Leigh Pierce Estates, INDIGENT will wriggle its way into your brain and refuse to let go." —**Lauren Thoman, author of *You Shouldn't Be Here* and *I'll Stop the World***

CONTENT WARNING

Standard warnings for horror tropes (violence, death, murder) apply.

Other content warnings: medical trauma, graphic violence, ableism, classism, poverty, racism, sexism, use of slurs, disordered body thoughts, self-harm and addiction, allusions to suicide and miscarriage, religious trauma, domestic violence, police violence.

TABLE OF CONTENTS

*For James, Leah, and everyone else
who wanted a connection.*

CAM <3
JULY 17, 2011 — SUNDAY

The man who'd picked Camille up at the rest stop had introduced himself as Derrick, or Darren maybe. It didn't matter.

His eyes were on her like a pin pressed into her ribs, her breasts, jabbing at her as she rested her head against the window. She focused on watching the world fly by outside, street-lit patches of trees and stone cut out of the darkness, illuminated in warm patches of orange sodium vapor. The last time she'd looked at the clock, it was almost midnight. It was a new day by now.

How nice. She'd lived another day.

She wasn't planning on checking the time again. That would mean turning her head, making Derrick-or-Darren think she was looking at *him*, which she would never do. Not that way.

She knew what he expected the second he'd opened his mouth, rolling down the passenger's side window of his pickup to call out to her as she stood there feeling like an idiot, thumb outstretched.

What did she look like to him? Some stick bug girl in her daddy's jacket, barely old enough to drink and already strung-out, lit up in a stranger's headlights. Easy pickings.

"Hey, where ya headed?" he'd said. Casual. Like he picked up girls off the side of the road every night. *Lecherous, leech.* That smile trying its very best to be disarming. *Prurient.* That's the word she was looking for, the pervert.

Derrick-or-Darren took the backroads after leaving the rest stop at the Georgia state line, saying it would be quicker to get to Atlanta that way since the highways and main roads were a total clusterfuck no matter the time.

It could be true. Who knew? Definitely not her—she hadn't been to Georgia in years. It was certainly the quieter way to go, more isolated.

When was the last time she'd seen another car…?

She should've waited, stuck around for an old lady visiting her daughter down in Rome for the summer or a family driving back from white-water rafting in Chattanooga. Some beneficent person doing this out of the goodness of their heart. But she'd been impatient.

He wouldn't want her anyway, *not if he knew*. She considered telling him, out of curiosity more than anything else. She'd never done that before. Never hitchhiked, either. Maybe it would be easy, too, as easy as deciding to raise her thumb and get in the car. Maybe the hard part was just making the leap without getting cold feet.

INDIGENT

There wasn't much time for consequences anyway. She wasn't even hungry anymore. That had stopped days ago.

So who cared if he knew? **They** didn't. For the past few days, **they'd** been oddly quiet. **They** let her ask the man at the information kiosk for directions, let her sit next to someone on the packed bus from Nashville, not even stirring when she got caught and kicked out, left waiting at the terminal for nothing and no one.

She'd even been able to ask one of the girls at the ticket counter for a light with no problem. The girl had given her the cheap lighter at the bottom of her purse. An extra. A spare. Something worthless she could give away to someone pathetic to feel good about herself.

Camille closed her fingers around the lighter in her jacket pocket, thumb tracing over the spark wheel and the smooth, cool plastic. Last week, she wouldn't have let someone do that. *Look at her like that.* Ari was probably the last person she'd let feel sorry for her, and look how that turned out.

She still remembered it, even though everything else from that night had long receded into a loud, ugly blur.

"Are you okay?" His voice had been quiet, calming. Not wanting anything out of her. "Don't freak out. Just breathe. Breathe... You're okay..."

I'm not okay.

Her chest tightened. She didn't mind **them** leaving her alone for once. But she knew it wasn't anything good. **They** were leaving her alone because **they** didn't need her that way anymore. **They** were laying the groundwork to throw her away.

Each morning, her ribs stood out just a bit more, the bruise on her stomach spread deep purple across her skin like English violet petals, stretching over the protruding bones, raw to the touch. The last time she'd used the restroom, she urinated blood, dark red and thick.

I'm not even hungry anymore.

It was amazing, not to be hungry. But **they** were just giving her space. Space to find someone warm to curl up next to before she died, for **their** own sake. Not for hers. Nothing was ever for her.

"D'you mind if I smoke?" she asked, already taking out her lighter.

"Sure, no problem," Derrick-or-Darren said, tapping the steering wheel.

She lit a cigarette—last one, *dammit*—and cracked open the window. He eyed the pack, reading the label taped to its face: CAM <3.

"That you?"

She looked away. Mom loved her labels, sticking them on everything she could like they were kindergarteners heading out to school for the first time. Clothing tags: CAM <3. Lunchboxes: CAM <3. Cigarette cartons: CAM <3. She didn't notice them anymore.

"Yeah. Camille."

"Pretty."

She nodded, stayed quiet.

"We're 'bout an hour out," he said finally, once it was clear she wasn't up to talking.

Another nod. Head on a wire. Up and down.

The road wound downward through a ravine, surrounding them on either side with walls of slick rock. *Shale and limestone.*

Mom had told her that the last time they were here, always trying to teach her about the places they visited, quizzing them on the car ride over.

Georgia was mostly shale and limestone. Brittle. Full of caves. The ground underneath them eaten through with an intricate lace of tunnels, smoothed by acidic groundwater. Slowly dissolving in looping, interweaving shapes and reaching fingers.

"I was gonna stop at this motel 'bout thirty minutes away. Cheaper, ya know?" he said, an edge to his voice. Hopeful and desperate.

"I don't think I have enough to pay for a room."

"Not even a cheap one?"

"I never carry that much money with me."

He was quiet for a second. "You could stay with me if you want. Don't mind."

Of course you don't. He was looking at her. She could feel that pin pressing its way against her cheek, her legs. Dragging across the skin. She didn't know what was so appealing about them. They were like toothpicks by now, the skin pulled so tight over her knees and ankles that they ached, the bone threatening to rip its way through. Maybe he liked his girls like that, feather-light and frail, a pretty little bird whose neck he could wring.

"You really don't mind?" she said.

"'Course not."

Just tell him what he wants. When they got there, she'd say no and hide in the lobby with the secretary if she had to. But there were other ways it could go.

If he insisted, she could go along with it, and then she'd bite off his dick and wait for him to bleed out and drive the rest of the way herself. She could do it now, if she wanted. Save herself the trouble of having people see her at the motel. Bat her eyelashes and ask him to pull over.

She sucked down more smoke and blew it out of her nostrils. It was soothing. Like sitting too close to a bonfire, a delicious warmth—the world reduced to dancing orange and red and black shadows and the taste of burnt sugar and pine needles. Crumbling. Like rodents being scared out of their underground burrows. *Smoke them out.*

She should ask him for another cigarette. Or... she could *tell* him. That was an option.

She dared a sidelong glance while his eyes were on the road. Farmer's tan and monstrous hands with tendons staring out on the backs of them, stark, like they were whittled out of softwood. He was like that all over, vascular and stringy. That vein in his forehead, already bulging, would pop out like a cartoon if she told him the truth. The thought of the little pulsating 'X' in his temple, of his eyes, bug-wide and disgusted, taking up half his skull, made her want to laugh.

What would happen if she did? Would he laugh with her? Hit her? He didn't seem like the kind of guy who'd tolerate a woman—a girl—laughing at him. With how little of her was left, she didn't know if she'd be able to take a punch, not without her nose shattering or her jaw dislocating like a leaf of cardboard.

He was thankfully quiet after securing the promise of Camille going to a motel room with him. What were her options? Thirty minutes away from Atlanta didn't mean thirty minutes away from Leigh Pierce Estates.

Estates. A florid name, so it was definitely some shoddy apartment complex, or a trailer park. They'd stayed in plenty of places like that: *Beachland Groves, Washington Terrace.*

Ari hadn't been able to tell her much more than that. Now, he wasn't answering her at all. Dad was probably screening his calls, treating them like they were still stupid teenagers. *Hopefully.* It was better than the alternative.

He's done with you. The cigarette crumbled in her fingers, just a line of ash. *Dad doesn't have to take his phone every time you call because he's ignoring you all on his own. Dad always wanted a boy.*

She should've left sooner, with Ari. Then she wouldn't be in the middle of nowhere, sitting in a shitty pickup truck at 1 a.m. with some redneck slavering all over her, imagining her as a collection of holes that needed filling. The fucking pig. She would've been hungry again. Esurient. Together.

Or maybe he just never wanted a girl.

They should've left sooner. If she was being honest, they *should* have left years ago, but she was stupid. She'd told herself they needed to stay until Ari got used to things, but all that did was give her parents time to figure out that they liked having him around. It had only given them time to steal him, even though he was *hers.* Unequivocally.

He knew that, didn't he? He had to. That's why he'd told her where they were staying...

"So, what's in Atlanta?"

Camille jumped, stubbing out her cigarette in the ashtray, already reeking with old tobacco chew. What had him interested in that *now*?

With the motel getting close, it'd probably dawned on him to go through the motions. *Get to know her as a person.* She was going to be sick, nausea bubbling up, but the rest of her cigarettes were in her bag rolling around in the truck bed behind them.

"My boyfriend," she said finally. "*Zài dì yuàn wéi lián lǐzhī,*" Ari had whispered to her once—*I wish we could be two tree trunks, intertwined*—and she'd cried, so happy to have someone who'd understood, to have one need in two bodies.

But sure, "boyfriend."

"*Boyfriend?*" His voice pitched up, mocking. "Why didn't *he* pick you up, then?"

"We're... taking a break," she answered.

"I get it, I get it. My girl and me are havin' some downtime, too."

She closed her eyes. *Isn't that convenient?* She breathed out. *Good for her.*

"I'm sorry," she said instead.

"Not your fault. Just gets lonely sometimes, ya know?"

She nodded. It sounded ridiculous out loud. They'd "taken a break" a few years ago, too, back when Ari got fed up with her and her parents and left them—no warning, no note—at a Motel Six outside Indianapolis. *There was a warning.* She couldn't be mad about it. *An obvious one.* Besides, wasn't that what she did? Slipping some over-the-counter sleeping pills into their dinner and running—sprinting—away until the apartment was out of sight, her bag thudding against the back of her legs. Almost three weeks ago now.

There was plenty warning, you know that. You know why. The only difference between now and then was when Ari showed up at their door, tired and hungry and apologizing, Dad wasn't crazy. Things could be *salvaged*. Now, the only option was to grab him like she should've done the first time and leave on their own.

The truck pulled into a gravel parking lot, half-hidden by all the trees. The Peach Pit Motel. "Fresh Coffee, Free Wi-Fi." A smattering of cars parked around the square of low buildings, all dark except the main office, glowing a sickly, muddy orange through the windows. The kind of place her family would stay.

"Be right back."

He took the keys with him, bones cracking as he stretched, a build-up of acid in the joints, bubbling, releasing air. She watched him through the lace-curtained window, that bull-body leaning against the check-in desk. Then, she got out of the cab, climbing up to grab her backpack from the truck bed.

She could run now—

But there he was, Derrick-or-Darren ambling toward her with two Styrofoam cups, steam curling up and over his face and a bright yellow key tag dangling from his fingers.

The room was everything she expected. Antediluvian shag carpet, blankets that were white once on the single queen bed, a boxy TV resting on top of the dresser with its cord winding down, snaking into a hole in the exposed plaster. Camille heard *him* pissing in the bathroom, the water running. Getting ready. She took a breath to steady herself.

Smoke and sweat, mold and Pine-sol.

Without thinking, she took one of the pillows and dropped it on the floor next to the bed, where she and Ari would sleep while her parents took the mattress. When she was younger, she would sleep in the bed with them, arms and legs pinwheeled out between them. She couldn't remember when that had stopped. *Honor thy parents.* Once, when she was sick and miserable, they let her have the bed to herself for three days.

I want to kill them.

The thought came without warning, making her blink, redness creeping up her neck, into her cheeks. It was probably true, but there wasn't a lot to do about it now. Honoring them and wanting them gone weren't necessarily separate things. With her stomach quiet, she could hold space for two things at once. Maybe she'd feel different in the morning.

She poked at the pillow before picking it up, squeezing it to her chest as she stared at the watercolor painting hung over the headboard. A widemouth bass fighting for its life, fishhook lodged in its fleshy lower lip.

If Ari were here, he'd take a picture of it, add it to his collection of hundreds of other photos of motel watercolors and posters and kitschy inspirational wall art. Dad always hated that habit, but it never occurred to Camille to question it.

They all had something. Mom and her smiley family photos at every tourist trap they could find, Dad with his recipe book,

Camille's scraps of fabric and anything else she could tape smoothly into the pages of her journal. Some mutual need to prove that they were here with everybody else.

Dad hadn't tried out any new recipes all year. *Something's wrong with him. That's why I had to do it, why we have to go—*

Maybe she'd take a picture to show Ari when they met up? But no. That was his thing. Instead, she opened the drawer by the bedside table and found the dusty little pocket Bible, tearing the ribbon bookmark out of its spine. She held it in her fist. Better than fussing with her hair. The smallest bit of pressure made it fall out now.

That morning, she'd woken up with her hoodie full of dark blonde half-moons, the base of her neck almost bare.

She climbed up on the bed, curled on her side, on top of the sheets, waiting for the bed bugs to start crawling over her, legs clicking—fighting over her blood before they realized it was no good, before they realized something else had called dibs already.

Why would anyone want me...?

The bathroom door opened, wafting steam, the warmth prickling uncomfortably on her bare face. After a moment, she looked over, saw him sitting on the other side of the bed. Hair damp, wearing only underwear, that cloying smell of motel soap clinging to him. The bedsprings squeaked, moaning like a dying thing.

Now would be the time that **they** showed up, came squirming up her throat, trailing stomach acid, burning the pink of her insides until it was cracked and bleeding, digging out from underneath her teeth. Demanding. But nothing happened. **They** were too busy eating away at whatever was left under her ribs. **They** were leaving her alone.

Alone with this man. He stretched out his arm, draped it over her legs. Like he knew her. But his touch was empty, horrifically unresponsive against her skin. Did he think anything at all?

This was what **they** wanted, wasn't it? Someone strong, new. Someone empty. Were **they** just waiting for him to be on top of her? *Inside* her? She'd gone too long without doing her part, and now **they** were making sure she was miserable before **they** ended it.

Were **they** trying to be cruel? *I will direct my jealous anger against you, and they will deal with you in fury. They will cut off your noses and your ears.* Why would **they** even know what cruelty was, when **their** needs were so simple? Animals weren't cruel. Unless some part of her had rubbed off on **them**.

I will cut off my nose to spite my face—

"You doin' okay?" he asked, Adam's apple bobbing. *Lewd.*

She sprang to her feet. "I'm gonna go get a Coke," she said, grasping for an excuse.

"Thought you didn't have any money?" He shifted, lying with his back flat against the bed, grinning up at the ceiling. She gritted her teeth, staring at the droplets of water clinging to the hairs on his chest, shivering as he spoke.

"I don't have *room* money." She pulled on her jacket and slipped into her sneakers. Swimming in them, everything hanging off her bones. Before he could respond, she hurried outside.

The pavilion was deserted, nothing but two buzzing vending machines underneath a single bulb, mayflies drifting in and out of the circle of light. She trudged toward them, the night humid, her feet heavy. Mosquitos hovered by her legs, flitted maddeningly past her ear. More parasites.

They wouldn't touch her, she knew that. It was one of the few upsides. No more bug bites. Not on her skin, at least.

She watched the soda can fall into the bottom of the machine and fished it out, hoping the carbonation would calm her nerves. Clear soda for stomach aches, dark soda for energy, orange soda for fun. She got an orange soda and popped it open. A jolt of pain went through her hand, up into her arm.

Her thumbnail had cracked, blood oozing out dark and viscous.

Camille held back a sob, more at the shock of it than the pain, already subsiding into a dull discomfort. She sucked her thumb until it stopped bleeding, the taste sharp, familiar. When she pulled it away from her mouth, all she saw was an ugly line running down the center of the nail, the cuticle twisted like tree roots pushing up through concrete.

Her nails. Her hair. *Such a pretty girl, look at those curls.* Her body. Every part of her cracking, folding in on itself... *And those freckles. I can't believe you tried covering them up...*

She couldn't go back. **They**'d choose him instead. **They**'d be done with her. And there was no way she was leaving a piece of herself with *him,* letting him go on picking up girls on the side of the road—girls no one wanted, who he could dig into.

Her bag was in the room, but she had shoes. She had Dad's old Salvation Army jacket with her phone, a coin purse, and half a granola bar in the internal pocket. There was her lighter and her pack of cigarettes. And the book ribbon, crushed and wrinkled in her fist. Good enough.

She chugged her soda, almost able to make out the bright, citrus-sweet taste she remembered, the one she loved as a kid —the ghost of it. Then, she started walking...

Limestone. Shale. Lactic acid. Lewd, licentious. Ezekiel 23:25. Twenty miles to your destination. Just put one foot in front of the other...

Things could've gone differently.

Why hadn't she just asked him to drive on through, find a seedy motel within city limits if that's what he really wanted? Why did Mom put up with so much? Why hadn't she taken a hammer to Dad's head in his sleep to protect them? Why hadn't Camille done that herself before she'd left, like an adult, like someone who could take care of herself?

Why were **they** being cruel, after all she'd done for **them**? Why didn't she bring Ari with her? Why had he come back in the first place? For *her*, like she was worth it? He could've stayed gone.

And, worse than anything else, hanging unwanted in the front of her mind, was the thought she hadn't allowed herself for years. One she had no way of avoiding now as she slogged to Atlanta, glancing over her shoulder, on high alert for that red pickup—

She *could've* been a good person.

She could've left him out of this.

No tears. Her body didn't have enough water for that. But her chest heaved, lungs constricting, refusing to take in enough air. Camille stumbled, determined to stay moving.

Just breathe.

I'm sorry. I'm sorry, I'm sorry, I'm—

You're okay... Just breathe...

PART ONE

THE ESTATES

"Poverty made a sound like a wet cough in the shadows of the room."

Ray Bradbury

A PORTRAIT OF LEIGH PIERCE

Leigh Pierce Estates was always awake.

Sixty-three low-rise units spread across five stories—four above ground and then the basement. One hundred and twenty-six official tenants, though the actual number shifted wildly on the tides of temp jobs and familial theatrics and friends of friends from the southern coast waiting out hurricane season somewhere further inland.

Not that the owners cared much, as long as rent was paid. And rent was good. Cheap. As cheap as anybody could get without dipping into public housing, which—many of the residents would proudly say—Leigh Pierce *was not*. No handouts. They *worked* for their money here.

Construction on the estates began in 1972 and screeched to a halt thanks to the fuel shortages, a dark hole guarded by the crouching skeleton of plywood and rough lumber left sitting on the corner of Metro and Fulton. Gathering mold, filling up with flood water and run-off until it was bought up again for half the original lot price. The new construction crew cleared the burnt-out soda cans and needles from the would-be basement and got back to work—

Foundation. Plaster. Brick. Ticky-tacky.

The foreman had heard through the grapevine that lead paint would soon be banned and stick him with a hefty fine, so he directed the crew to cover the interiors of Leigh Pierce with a quick new layer of leadless eggshell white and called it a day, the insulation and popcorn ceilings packed with asbestos dust that wouldn't be banned for another decade.

By then, it was a new owner's problem—one she chose to ignore. This wasn't public housing. She didn't get a government check to bring in some wetback to gut the walls and give the tenants a reason to sue. Besides, how bad could it be? Probably just another pointless regulation (President Carter's fault somehow) there to make her life harder.

And so there was Leigh Pierce Estates, boasting on-site laundry and a choice between studio or one-bedroom apartments, just a short walk away from the city bus stop and a ten-minute drive from Grady Memorial. So popular that the basement storage was converted into eight more apartment units, prone to flooding in the spring and mold in the summer.

But they were warm in the winter. Cozy. Soaking in the heat that leaked from the laundry room across the hall. Warm and gloriously cheap, and available on a monthly lease. Perfect for anyone just passing through, which they *did*. Flooding in and out of the basement like the sand-flecked liquid bursting from the overtaxed water heater at the end of the hallway, slowly gurgling down the limescaled drainage grates.

The Estates stayed remarkably unchanged over the years. Its courtyard overgrown with crabgrass and crawling with aphids, occasionally sprouting a tomato vine or squash flowers from the neglected community garden.

Obstinate, it sat there as a tornado ripped through, uprooting the townhouses and liquor store down the street, leaving Leigh Pierce untouched. It sat there while the surrounding greenspaces were bulldozed, Section 8 rooms sprouting up from the gravel lots, then a plaza that cycled through mom n' pop places until finally landing on a nail parlor, a dollar store, and a food stamps office—burglar barred and paranoid. The line started up at 8 a.m. sharp and didn't settle down until closing.

Leigh Pierce watched the city swell. Payday loan offices turned to community centers turned to yoga studios and green juice shops. *This* was industry. Consumption and starvation and consumption again, twice as hungry on the come around. Twice as urgent.

101:

Anika Davis lived on the first floor of Leigh Pierce. She woke up at 4:30 every morning, creeping from her spot on the living room couch to the bedroom where her son slept, touching his hair—checking that he was still breathing.

Then, she would leave twenty dollars on the kitchen counter for the babysitter and head out to meet Deliyah Lucas and Miss Bill by the downstairs rent office. They walked together to the bus stop and took the southbound to the airport where they'd spend the next ten hours scrubbing toilets.

Once, Anika had found a girl hiding in the handicap stall, legs drawn up. Trembling. She'd stayed with the girl, talking with her in broken high school Spanish, waiting for security. That week, she'd got a fifty-dollar bonus on her paycheck and a certificate of thanks printed on thick paper that she hung up in her living room. Proud.

205:

Some nights, when his asshole coworkers phoned it in and he wound up working late, Anthony Howard from the second floor saw the three women walking to the bus stop, worry nipping at him. One had to be in her seventies, and one had a kid, he was pretty sure.

Anthony kept a single-action 9mm under his shirt ever since his last manager at the McDonald's took a bullet to the face during a robbery last year. They had a gun in the break room, but nobody was quick enough to grab it. Anthony had mopped the place up after and found a tooth, chipped and bloody, waiting under the cash register with clumps of dust and stale fries.

Sometimes, he daydreamed about driving up at just the right time to see some moron pointing a gun at those ladies. He'd pull up. Take care of it. He'd get his name in the paper and bring it up real casually at work, and finally get that general manager spot. But until then, all he cared about was getting back to his studio on time to crash for a few hours before his classes.

311:

Lan Cong left her third-floor apartment early every Monday and Wednesday to get to Atlanta Community College before traffic got too bad, where she sat behind Anthony in the 8:30 a.m. Financial Accounting Fundamentals course. She always noticed when he was late and whenever he smelled like stale grease or pot. She noticed a lot.

Her job at the Queen Nails—"Call me *Laura*," she'd say to the ladies who came in, simpering, acquiescent—as nothing but noticing. Sitting there invisible while she picked at their yellowing cuticles, listening to their gossip.

Of course, they always glared at her whenever she would say something to her coworkers in Vietnamese, assuming she was talking about them. Sometimes she was, but why did they care? *They* were the ones sitting in the salon chair, and she was the one with her head down, back slowly stiffening into a permanent hump, scraping fungus off their nails.

415:

Miss Inez would wake up as early as her body let her, riding down from the fourth floor to look after Anika Davis's boy. A few months ago, they'd had to open up the apartment down the hall from hers, water staining the ceiling of the apartment downstairs with stinking brown rings. They'd found the man who'd lived there decomposing. Dead for weeks. *Weeks.*

Inez had invited the maintenance man—till a boy, really—n for some ginger ale to calm down, and when he'd left, she'd made herself sick over it. After that, she made a point of knowing at least a few neighbors. Good thing, too. Anika kept her place clean, but her son needed a firmer hand.

One day, Inez had looked out the window to find him causing a ruckus in the parking lot, sitting in the basket of a shopping cart, his little bad influence of a friend leaning against the cart's handle-bar, passing him some reefer and yelling filth at whoever walked by. She'd hobbled out with her walker just on time to hear them shout "Chingchong dingdong!" at Lan, a nice enough girl who Inez let borrow her car for errands—nother contingency.

Inez had dragged him back inside and bent him over the sink to wash his mouth out with soap. Then, she'd sent the boy down to the basement with a load of laundry to get done before his mama got home. No discipline, that boy. None at all.

And further down...

Wholly unnoticed until they skittered through the eyeline of something larger, were the scavengers. Maggots ate their fill in the Dumpster by the basement entrance, tearing through food waste with their grasping face-parts. Soaking in sticky pools of refu^&se. Growing wings and burrowing into the roadkill run down at the four-way intersection. Silverfish curled up in sink drains and washing machine drums. Hiding in moldy AC units, worming snugly behind the uneven trim along a carpet's edge.

The springtails. The roaches. The rats...

And Rashon Wilkinson in his basement unit. B4. Pacing.

Pacing.

Pacing...

It was 2 a.m.

He hadn't slept in more than two days, and it wasn't even his fault. He hadn't taken anything—not a *single* goddamn upper—and he'd caved and taken a few Ambien only after the first day of no sleep. They were his last ones, and they didn't even work. It wasn't his fault... It *wasn't*. Nothing he could've done about it—

He went to the kitchenette and threw a frozen dinner into the microwave. There was nothing worse than sleeping pills on an empty stomach. He stood by, watching the plastic tray crackle and warp through the window, brown gravy bubbling over the edge and onto the glass.

When he was little, his grandmother had told him never to stand next to the microwave while it was going. *Boy, you gon' fry your brain.* He never listened to her. *Maybe that's why I turned out this way.*

He wrapped the container with a dishrag and carried it to the living room before the heat could leak through the carbonized fabric and burn his fingers, looking down at it. Salisbury steak, gravy flooded over into the creamed corn and burnt, poke-holed brownie. School food. Nursing home food. His stomach twisted.

Back to pacing, then. Pacing...

And figuring out what the hell to do now that Zion was dead.

He couldn't stay where he was. That was obvious. He'd heard them crack Zion's head open. It didn't matter that it was through a door, or that he'd never heard something like that in his life. Like when he'd found a brown recluse spider in his shoe. Never seen one. Still knew it was bad, that it was somehow worse than usual. He'd dumped it onto the carpet and crushed it underfoot, found out later its bite could make people's blood boil from the inside.

That sound—

Like a tree limb breaking.

Rashon glanced at the pictures he'd taped up on the cinderblock walls—prison walls—his sister's idea to lighten the place up. He had three of them. A calendar photo of a monster gar, six foot long, another of Lake Malawi, and a blurry picture of him and Alexis—Keisha's little girl, his niece—last year when he'd been almost clean and they'd gone fishing over at Lake Burton.

Keisha. He could call her. Apologize for being a fuck-up and hope she'd let him crash on her couch.

They haven't left. I heard them crack Zion's skull and drag him back. They still in there...

He'd just been minding his own business, getting his tackle box together. It had been late, or early, however you wanted to look at it. Around three in the morning. He couldn't sleep and had decided that, once the sun came up, he would go fishing at that little man-made pond by the Sam's Club. He would catch those tiny bluegills and throw them back and feed some geese. *That* had been the plan.

Then, he'd heard them outside his door.

Zion had his salesman voice on, the voice he only ever used when he was talking somebody into something stupid. It had to be someone new then, a guy who'd fall for his bs.

"I'm tellin' you, man. You ain't gon' find anything better for what you payin'..."

Liar.

Rashon had cracked open his door to have a look. Zion was almost to his apartment at the other end of the hall, yapping away at some meth-head looking Asian kid, nothing but skin and bones and nervous tics. *Get 'em young, get 'em young.* Then, he'd closed the door and gone back to his gear.

I minded my own damn business.

That's all he'd ever done. It wasn't his fault that Zion had shown up. Gurgling. Like a catfish breaching water.

"Shon!" Zion's voice had sounded rough, strangely quiet, like he'd been socked in the throat. "*Shon, let me in! Let me—*"

And then *that sound*. Then nothing. Zion's shadow still under the door. Until it wasn't.

Rashon hadn't moved, hardly breathed. He'd still been holding a lure in one hand, his fist closed over it. It'd taken him a minute to open it, wincing at the hook he'd driven into his palm. A little plastic minnow. Metal. Blood. He hadn't even felt it.

Did Zion feel it? His head splintering? Busting like a watermelon?

Rashon was now halfway through packing his gym bag when he noticed the blood on his hand. The hook hand. The bandage had disappeared and his palm was leaking, spotting all his T-shirts and sweats with red. He didn't care. Keisha had a washer and dryer at her place—*in* the apartment, too—so he wouldn't have to worry about anybody seeing.

He hadn't called her. *Fuck*, he still needed to call her—

There was a knock on his door.

But nobody ever came to see him. Maybe it was the cops. What was he gonna tell them? They wouldn't listen. He wasn't the kind of person cops listened to. They wouldn't care that it wasn't his fault.

They knocked again. Louder...

And again. Violence in that sound.

Violent like a branch snapping. Like a throat being punched—

It wasn't his fault.

CHAPTER TWO
CLOSTRIDIUM TETANI

Xavier held his breath, reaching into the kitchen sink to search for the drainplug, almost up to his elbow in brown water.

The garbage disposal whined, spit up half-dissolved scraps that floated up around his arm, bobbing, glancing off his skin. Rot hung in his nose. He flipped off the disposal with his free hand and plunged the other into the drain, fingers wrapping around something, slippery like a lump of algae.

A mouse.

Dead and waterlogged in his palm, nearly indistinguishable from the rotten vegetables now swirling around the drain. Its body was in one piece, but just barely, torn up in the disposal blades, insides trailing out.

He tossed it in the garbage before Miss Inez could see, didn't want to freak her out. She never would let him set out traps, said it was "too mean," whatever that meant. Like letting them drown themselves in her dirty dishwater was any nicer.

"How long it been backed up?" he asked, grease and food slime sticking to the sides of the sink as the water drained.

"Oh, just a few days," she said from the living room couch. "Want some breakfast while you here? I can get some coffee goin'."

She did this shit on purpose, let the place get bad just so he'd have to show up and talk to her. *Where the hell are her kids?* "Then you shoulda called a few days ago, Miss Inez."

"I didn't wanna bother you."

She'd been like this since Mr. Torres died. Parkinson's—had to stop his contracting job because of the tremor. He'd talked about it while Xavier dealt with his clicking toilet, and Xavier had shown him an exercise to cut down on the falls, something he learned from Uncle Rob.

Not that it'd helped. Torres had still taken a nosedive in the shower and wasn't found 'til the property manager got the water bill and nearly had an aneurism. Xavier had turned off the water, covered the bloated body, and let Miss Inez talk him into going to her place for some ginger ale and tequila—*Just a lil' somethin' somethin' to get through the morning, now*—and she'd been calling him up for something every week since.

He couldn't complain too much. Desai was always looking to fire somebody. It was the only way anybody took him seriously. But he couldn't fire Xavier if emergency maintenance kept getting calls. Let him try finding someone cheaper.

Xavier managed to leave without having to sit for breakfast, giving Miss Inez a one-armed hug and walking down the hallway to the emergency stairs. He put in his earbuds, pressing them in too hard. Time for Zion's place. Oldies rap, then. That's what Zion listened to in his house.

Zion's probably dead.

He walked the three flights down to the ground floor, getting the dolly and a stack of broken-down cardboard boxes from the janitor's closet. The rent office was locked, no light on underneath the door. *Be Back Soon!*

Good. He didn't want to be stuck in an elevator with Desai and his stupid fucking vape pen, even for a floor. Desai used to smoke pot like a normal person and be mostly tolerable, but he'd gotten a wild hair up his ass recently and started wearing cologne and button-up shirts. And vaping.

Maybe Zion just knew something I don't, ducked out while he still could.

The dolly squeaked along the cement basement floor as he stepped out of the elevator, one bad wheel turning uselessly. He heard Desai before he saw him, arguing in Tamil to someone on the other end of his cell. The new landlord probably—some Indian real estate guy who'd made the news a few months ago for buying up a shit ton of apartments across Georgia state.

Xavier'd never seen him. Neither had Desai. But they spoke the same language, so Desai got the property manager gig and promptly turned into a douchebag. Sure. That's how it always went. Money was a language, too.

Maybe that's why Zion left. He ditched us before things got worse.

Desai met him in the hall, sweating through his expensive shirt, the fabric of the collar sticking to his neck. Barely 6 a.m. and already ninety degrees outside. Set to get hotter. It was worse down here by the dryers and water heater.

"Right on time, dude," Desai called, leading the way to the apartment at the very end of the hall. Basement unit twelve.

B12. One of the two occupied units—*Only one occupied unit now*—which was definitely for the best. Two seconds out of the elevator, and Xavier was already boiling alive. How did anybody live down here?

"Thanks for getting this done. I called the movers, and they wanted to charge six hundred an hour. You believe that shit? The landlord pitched a bitch about it, you know."

When you're bein' sketchy as fuck, they can charge whatever they want, can't they?

Xavier made some noncommittal sound in the back of his throat as he opened the door wide on Zion's place. Quiet, all his stuff still here. No sign of him, though. And a *smell*. Something sharp and unpleasant underneath a heavy layer of bleach. It wafted into his eyes.

Desai shot him a look, worried. "It looks like a lot, but just put everything up against the wall, and—"

He took a step inside, his foot brushing a glue trap, dead rat and all. Desai flinched backward, hand to his nose. Xavier held back a laugh.

"And, *maybe*, if you find stuff that looks like it's worth anything... Might as well see what we can get before we inventory everything, right?" Desai finished, playing it cool.

Of course, Xavier kept his face blank. *He thinks Zion's dead, too. Everybody does.*

"What if he comes back?" Xavier asked, more for himself.

"If he wanted any of this shit, he'd've left with it."

"He don't have kids or a mom or nothin'?" Something hit him—*I don't know either.*

"They would've shown up by now if they cared," Desai said.

We were s'posed to be friends. Why don't I know...?

"Rent's pretty low for the basement units. If we cover it, you can have what's left, plus what I quoted you before. Like a bonus."

Xavier shoved his hands in his pockets, his face burning. He hated this, standing around Zion's apartment acting like they didn't know him. Like Desai didn't show up at this door every week, five-thirty on the dot, to beg for free weed—*Come on, man. I put a* roof *over your head*—before inevitably paying full price.

Acting like this was normal.

He sighed. There were still those textbooks he had to buy, and he hadn't found whatever apartment was hemorrhaging power, either, bumping up everybody's utility bill a solid twenty bucks. A communal burden. He'd just have to feel bad about it later.

"What d'you wanna sell?" Xavier sighed.

Desai relaxed. "Use your judgement. And don't worry about cleaning. Not worth it with—"

The manager stopped, turning instead to pick up the glue trap between two fingers and throw it in the garbage. The rat's body made a soft thud at the bottom. Xavier tried meeting his eyes, but he kept moving, pulling down the fly ribbons hung on the windowsill, trailing melted glue as he tossed them out.

"I know it's a fuckin' basement, but y'all could at least *try* to make it nice," Xavier said.

Desai stopped, chewing his bottom lip. He reached for his pocket, took a citrusy puff off his vape pen. "Look. You didn't hear it from me, okay?"

Xavier narrowed his eyes. *Zion was onto something.*

"You didn't hear from me. But this place isn't gonna be around long enough to care."

"What?" *He knew something no one else knew.*

Desai spread his arms wide, rocking back on his heels—Boom!

Xavier blinked. That couldn't be right. It *wasn't* right. "But... I *live* here?"

Desai skirted around him, lingering in the doorway with a nervous grin, and a childish, violent urge Xavier thought had been stomped out of him by now rose up. He was too tall and too dark to even think about getting angry, had been since fifth grade when Mom bought him those embarrassing, gaudy clothes to make him look younger.

They gon' think you grown.

He pushed the feeling down. Diaphragm raising and lowering, lungs going concave then convex again, full of fresh air.

"*You* live in the newest, most convenient location for personal, climate-controlled storage..." Desai explained. "It's a better investment with all the development going on. Apparently."

"Apparently," Xavier repeated.

Something hurt. His right molar aching. He breathed, his jaw clinched shut. *That can't be right.*

Xavier stared at him, watching the grin waver and finally drop. *Good, take this seriously.* Watching Desai's muscles tense, braced for a punch. For something.

That can't be right.

Xavier turned away, upping the volume on his phone until the bass from his earbuds drowned out everything. "No cleaning. Cool. Got it," he said, getting to work. Being productive.

His jaw hurt.

"Great! I'll, uh, I'll let you do that..." Desai took a step back, one foot out of the apartment. At least he had the grace to feel bad about how much he was fucking everyone over. "And, *hey*, former employees get a discount! So... if you ever need storage... Lucky, amiright—"

Xavier closed the door, locking it. Doorknob. Deadbolt. Chain lock. OutKast still rattling around in his eardrums. "What you *mean*, you ain't listened to 'ATLiens'?" Zion had asked once, the most offended Xavier had ever seen him. "'Elevators'? 'Extraterrestrial'? How you miss those? You live here! It's *about* here."

I live here.

He blinked, about to cry or hit something or scream. But that was something saved for when work was over with. For working hours, he'd just believe that Desai was wrong. Or lying.

Please, God, just let him be lying.

What should we do instead, Xav? His mother's voice, calm and redirecting in the back of his mind, a life raft to clamber onto. He leaned against the door, staring up at nothing, sure that, half-camouflaged between the bumps and shadows of the popcorn ceiling, he could make out a few stray drops of blood.

Zion had lived at Leigh Pierce for a year—a lifetime for someone in the basement. The units down there were glorified motel rooms, a revolving door of junkies and illegals and women with black eyes and nowhere else to stay. Xavier didn't mind any of them.

If they didn't clog the toilets with paper towels or stuff chicken bones down the garbage disposal and get confused when it wouldn't run, they were fine by him. They didn't usually do those things. Because that meant calling *him*, and calling him went against their instincts, ruined their quests to be left completely and totally *alone*.

Zion, though, was one of the rare basement tenants who talked to his neighbors, asking Xavier one morning as he messed around with a broken dryer in the laundry room if he wanted to make some extra cash.

And yes. Yes, he did.

A few hours later, Xavier had found himself driving to Atlanta Community College with an upcycled Wal-Mart bag hidden under the passenger seat and an extra hundred in his wallet.

Easy enough. Just drop the bag into one of the trashcans on campus and leave. Someone else would do the rest. Xavier had gotten it done quick and immediately felt like shit, could practically hear Mom needling him. *What in the hell you think you doin', boy?*

What am I doing?

He'd sat there on the bench outside the Communications building, watching people move in and out past the metal detectors. Smart people. Good people. What the *hell* was he doing...? He'd been certain one of the mall cops was trailing him, so he'd wandered over to the student office and picked up a few pamphlets, trying to look smart, to look good.

That night, Mom had seen the pamphlets that he'd thrown on the coffee table, and that was the end of it. Not like Georgia State was ever going to call him back after he flaked the first time.

Maybe it was good to get back on track. Finally. He had Zion to thank for that. Even if it was an accident. Even if Zion would've preferred he stayed put at Leigh Pierce, wallowing over shit he couldn't change and running his dirty errands. He deserved some credit.

Credit for keeping those dumbass high school kids from smoking in the laundry room, and for fixing the plaster himself after punching a hole in the wall—*Don't ask*—the job done so well that Xavier hardly noticed when he came over to watch anime on Zion's plasma screen. Xavier'd offered to vouch for him to the then-property manager, Anne. Get him a legit job. Zion had said no.

And now he was dead. *Only maybe dead.*

He could've offed himself. *Don't say that, don't even think that.* If Zion had gone out that way, though, he hadn't done it here, and there was no note that Xavier could find.

He could've told me... Or maybe he couldn't have. Maybe he didn't know Zion at all.

44

INDIGENT

Xavier went back to the spot on the ceiling, the only thing that hadn't been scrubbed into nothing. Standing on the coffee table, he took a closer look at it, the cheap wood creaking under his weight.

Blood. Or brown paint. Three drops.

He touched it, chipping away at the popcorn ceiling and dislodging some flecks of brown and white that fell into his face. *Shit.* He hadn't redone the ceilings down here. That old daytime commercial played back in his mind, droning on between the babysitter's soap operas and game shows:

If you or a loved one has been diagnosed with mesothelioma, you may be entitled to financial compensation...

Xavier thought of Zion and imagined pressing his face to the ceiling, breathing in the poisonous dust. Letting it seep through the mucous membranes and into his blood. Then, maybe, just *maybe*, he'd be entitled to enough money to cover rent and utilities and groceries and school, and he could finally take a fucking break.

Living room. Kitchen. Bathroom. Bedroom—the last leg of things.

Xavier went through the dresser and the closet, packing up jerseys, T-shirts, sweatpants and socks—all black, impossible to mismatch. The bed was made, the sheet ironed and tucked tightly under the mattress. *Something's wrong.* Xavier pulled some shoeboxes down from the closet shelf, overflowing with receipts and other papers.

"Should I call somebody?" he asked, voice raised, his cellphone resting a few feet away on the dresser as he dug through the boxes for anything worth keeping.

"Who? The police?" His mother's voice was loud, her bus rumbling in the background, hissing tires and pistons. It was raining where she was. He heard the wipers going.

"I mean, yeah. What if somethin' happened?"

"He the kinda boy shit happens *to*, ain't he?" Mom said, phone jostling. There it was again, that pain in his tooth. "If he don't wanna be found out, he don't wanna be found out."

His space.

"So. You okay?" she asked after a few seconds, softer. She didn't like Zion, last he checked, but she liked Xavier hanging out with somebody. *God, here he is,* she was probably thinking, *back to being a hermit. Back to being somebody I gotta worry about.*

"I'm good."

He could hear her taking a short breath, could practically see the look. Lips together, eyebrow raised. *Really?* Now, she was going to let him sit there with what he'd said, waiting for him to add something. To be more honest.

Instead, Xavier pulled down one last shoebox, its contents spilling out like guts onto the shelf. Off the shelf, over his feet—

Travel brochures, some cheesy paperweights. Fort Walton. Dolphin Beach. Miami. Orlando. There wasn't a shitty themed bar in the state Zion hadn't shelled out money to for a souvenir shot glass. And hidden underneath the souvenirs, porn.

Some new facts about Zion: he liked Florida. He liked abs. He liked tits more than ass, and—Xavier almost laughed at the stupidity of it, the second-hand embarrassment—he kept physical magazines. Like they didn't have anything better.

"They gon' get caught doing shady shit and say you stole everythin' to cover they asses. You watch," Mom was saying, the silent treatment not working nearly as well over the phone.

"Mom. The property manager's a pussy. He ain't gon' say nothing."

"Text him about it. Get it in *writing*, you hear me?"

"Got it..."

He reached above his eyeline on the closet shelf to get the rest of the lost souvenirs, the ones that had spilled out and over. The shadow of something was peeking out. He grabbed it—

"Shit!"

And jerked his right hand away, bleeding.

Three drops of blood on the ceiling. Dried. Soaked into the paint.

"Xav, what happened?"

There were three tiny punctures on his hand, one of them on the joint of his pointer finger. Well, that was never going to heal right.

"Just a second..." He grabbed his phone in his good hand, toggling on the flashlight to search the shelf. Finally, he saw something. A flash of scales and teeth.

"I got bit by an alligator," he said, reaching up much more carefully this time.

A gator. Just its head, unnaturally polished. Small enough to fit uncomfortably in the palm of his hand, staring at him with glassy marble eyes and pointed teeth. Grinning. It sat on a heavy wooden

base with a copper engraving—"ORLANDO TROPHY SHOP."
More Florida.

He never mentioned Florida.

"Don't play with me."

"I'm not. I'm gon' call him Lando."

He put the alligator head on the dresser, matching his cuts to its teeth. It had to be the first few, the ones clustered right under the nostrils. He flexed his fingers, blood outlining his calluses, the sting running up his arm.

"Who hides porn in a box of sharp shit..." he muttered, hoping she didn't hear.

"Hidin' *what*?" she said. Worth a try. *It's the thought that counts.* "Boy, you take that man's shame and get rid of it. *Now.* Being dead don't mean he ain't embarrassed."

"He might not be dead."

"Whatever you say," Mom's voice was further away. Distracted. "I gotta let you go."

Xavier hung up, separating out the souvenirs from the unmentionables. Fort Walton. *Honcho.* Dolphin Beach. *Penthouse...* He'd throw them out before he left today. When Mom was right, she was right.

With his hand cleaned up, off-brand Band-Aids already beginning to peel and leaving residue in the creases of his fingers, Xavier cleared out.

INDIGENT

He left the boxes against the wall for Desai to paw through and locked up Zion's place, a pit in his stomach. He'd found a rat half-alive underneath the bathroom sink, peeled it painstakingly from the glue trap it'd been stuck to. Now, it stared at him from the corner of a shoebox, feral and bloody and alive.

The basement exit was propped open with a brick. A major lease violation. Xavier kicked it away on his way out, the rat beginning to gnaw at the cardboard. "*Shit*, wait—"

He set the box down, tipping it over with his foot. The rat, covered in paper-dust, dashed into the sewer drain. So much for letting it out in the courtyard. It'd probably hate grass anyway—

Something twitched in his periphery.

Something at the top of the basement staircase. A pair of ratty shoes peeking out. Thin, pale legs. Whoever they belonged to was slouched behind the brick column at the top of the steps, against the wall. They shifted, leaning forward into view. Watching him. *For how long?*

Short blonde hair. Huge eyes, the skin pulled tight over their face—t*he orbital bone*—making them bulge out. A girl, probably. It was hard to tell.

Xavier shielded his eyes, trying to get a better look at her, but she ducked away. Just some ninety-pound junkie looking for shade away from the street. Another aneurysm for Desai if he found her out here.

Not *his* problem, though.

"Hey, man," he called. "This ain't a great place to hang out."

She inched closer, stiff, legs unmoving. *Something's wrong.* Closer. The sun hitting her face, the pterygoid muscle spasming under her skin, clearly visible even at a distance. A tremoring shadow moving along her jaw.

Xavier balked. Whatever was wrong with her, it was bad. Her mouth moved silently for a moment, finally pieced together, "D'you have a phone? My dad took mine."

"Nah, I—"

"Everybody has a phone," she interrupted, falling back against the wall. Her head thudded against the redbrick, one foot twitching mindlessly at the impact before going still again.

"Well, I don't, okay? Look, if the manager see you, he gon' call the cops, and that's bad for everybody…"

Xavier waited for a response, but she stayed quiet. He shrugged and started to head back inside. He'd have to get rid of that door prop.

Not our business.

One hand on the door handle, stopping. She was a neighbor, wasn't she? She was right now, at least. Inside, outside—soon, they'd pack the foundation with C4 and blow it all to hell, and there wouldn't even be a difference…

He walked back up the steps to get a better look. She was tiny, her body swimming in an oversized jacket, like a kid wearing her dad's clothes. No telling how old she was, though. Her small hands poked out of the sleeves, thin. Nails ringed with blood. A stubbed-out cigarette.

Something's wrong.

He'd seen worse, though. Told himself that as he worked to keep his face neutral.

"You got somebody who can pick you up?" he asked, unlocking his cellphone screen and handing it to her.

She smiled at him, the freckles across her nose crinkling. *My age maybe?* Her skin stretched so thin over the bones, thin like paper, lips cracked and gums pale, nearly gray. She was probably cute before... whatever this was.

She had the number memorized, dialed without hesitating. Nobody answered, and she tried again. Same number. Same waiting...

The left side of her face drooped downward, imperceptible at first, the eye seeming larger. A basset hound eye. She didn't react, didn't seem to even notice.

Facial paralysis. Stroke.

Xavier swiveled his head, found the parking lot at the end of the alleyway deserted. He needed someone's help, someone to stay with her and keep her head elevated while he ran to get the first aid kit in the office, the defibrillator that was probably expired by now—

Shit, no way this girl can afford an ambulance.

Her call dropped again. No answer. No voicemail. He took her hand, saw the veins standing out. Breakable. He had to keep her talking. Keep her talking.

"You know anyone around here?" he asked.

"My parents. They live here. Apartment B4."

B4. Rashon. Never bothering nobody, selling catfish—scaled and gutted and wrapped in parchment paper—out of the trunk of his car. "*Rashon Wilkinson* is your dad?"

"Yep."

He stopped, thrown off by the lie. How obvious it was. How fast. "Why you stuck out here if your dad's downstairs?"

She shrugged. Just one arm, the other one gone limp. "Got kicked out."

She pushed down on her knees. They didn't budge, perfectly rigid even under the pressure. On closer look, half-hidden by her sneakers, her ankles were purple and swollen.

"No one else is even mad at me," she said. "Just Dad. I just gotta call when he's not around..."

A wet sound started in the back of her throat. Then, something popped. A joint? A tendon? Something, somewhere. She looked at him, eyes wide. Scared. A question—

Did you hear that?

An image of Mom rolling over a stray cat in the parking lot, black fur invisible in the dark. Crunching. *Did you hear that?* Of Zion sitting at the foot of his bed smoking, shirtless and giggling. Someone knocking on the bathroom window, fast and conspiratorial. *Did you hear that?* This girl's body collapsing in on itself. *Did you hear that?*

Her right nostril flared, a line of blood running from it, down into her mouth as she started to convulse. Blood and saliva sputtering out of her lips.

Xavier sprang forward, cradling her head. Her hair tore from the roots like nothing, spread golden and light across his arms as he kept her head stationary, getting picked up in the breeze like pieces of wheat grass. Like fluff from a dandelion.

Her body jerked. Another *pop.*

Blood smeared his hands—

His shirt.

Flecks of red dotting his face. Wet and warm.

He finally got the phone as her fingers clenched, unclenched. Out of her control—

The ambulance didn't get there on time.

Xavier drove to the Greyhound station with the alligator head in the passenger's seat. Smiling at him. Pink gums pulled over teeth.

Her gums were gray.

He'd decided to keep it—a kind of memento—digging it out of the To-Sell souvenir box after Desai had told him to take the rest of the day off, strawberry kiwi vapors floating out of his nostrils in anxious huffs. Ranting.

"We only got approved 'cause this was s'posed to be a nice place. Oh, they built a Starbucks down the road! Fucking perfect! Just ignore the dead meth head outside, we promise there won't be any more of *those*! God, they're gonna renege, I know it..."

The douchebag. Xavier hadn't felt bad about leaving Desai with the EMTs. Let *him* explain that shit. Not like it would be hard, just more work—work he was getting paid to do.

The last time Xavier had dealt with anything like that was Uncle Rob—"God, another fatass. Getting our exercise in today, boys," Xavier had heard them say as they hauled Rob onto the stretcher. Gently. The actions didn't match the words. "I'm so sorry." The words didn't match the words, either. Not the ones said when they thought he wasn't listening. The bag closing over Rob's face.

A *thing*. A bulky, inanimate *thing*....

He wasn't going to do that again if he didn't have to. He wasn't about to talk to anyone else today either. Well, except Mom.

The alligator would be a good distraction, something to talk about instead of Zion, who hadn't texted him back. Or why he'd only picked up one value meal on the way to the station, his appetite nonexistent. Or why his favorite sweatshirt was stuffed in the trash. Or why he'd spent a half-hour scrubbing his face with cheap pink hand soap until there was no blood left.

Her blood had gotten in his mouth—*In his mouth!* Tomorrow, he'd go to urgent care and get tested. Every test they had. Just to be sure.

Xavier turned onto Forsyth Street, seeing Mom's bus stuck waiting at the next stoplight. He could just make her out through the windshield, leaning tiredly against the oversized steering wheel, and flashed his headlights at her. She noticed just in time to see him pulling into the Greyhound parking lot, pumping his fist. Grinning. Tomorrow's dinner was on her, then.

INDIGENT

At least *one* nice thing happened today.

By the time she finally clocked out at the bus station, he had the alligator set up nice and dramatic by her dinner in the passenger's seat.

She jogged to the car with her vest unbuttoned, tie stuffed in its front pocket. It was crazy they made her wear an outfit like that just to drive a fucking bus. Did she still like it?

Back when she'd first started, she'd been excited to move up from school buses and shitty tweenagers to more discerning, private patrons. Twirling to show off the new uniform, bragging on the little copper nametag. "Wouldn't it be better if *this* picked you up for school every morning?" she'd said. "The vest's how you know you *goin' somewhere*."

She didn't seem too excited now, stuffing the nametag into her purse and opening the car door with her free hand. She reached for the fast food bag, jerking back when she caught a glimpse of the scales and teeth.

"Holy shit!" she yelled, poking at the alligator. "Get that thing outta my car."

"You late!" he said, smirking. "And it's Lando, I told you." *The first Black gator in space.*

He moved the bag out of her way and put the alligator on the dashboard. It smiled at them, delirious and blank-eyed, just like everything from Florida.

She sat down. A passenger, finally.

"First off, I am not late. You *early*," she said, and buckled her seatbelt. "And why the hell is 'Lando' in my car?"

"Hey. Me and this guy shared blood, sweat, and tears, okay. He's pretty much my *son*."

She smiled, touching the alligator's snout. "The only grand-baby I'm gon' get."

Xavier gave an exaggerated wince, not taking it seriously. Like *she'd* want grandkids so soon. Did she even like kids?

He didn't think so.

"I'm workin' on it, okay?" he said. "I'm accruing value."

Step One—Every man needs to ask himself, "What is holding me back?" Eliminating those things from your life without prejudice is the first step to accruing value. Step Two—

Mom rolled her eyes. "Right. If you wanna 'accrue value' in a job that's worth shit, one of the ticket girls quit today. Twelve an hour." She started snacking on the fries, salt coating her fingers. "I'm thinking of askin' for it, too." Xavier tried not to look worried, not quite managing it. "What, you don't wanna eight-hour shift with your mama?"

She laughed. He didn't. "That's less than what you make now," he said.

"You been tellin' me to get a job that's better on my back."

Xavier bit his tongue. He couldn't tell her. Not right now. Not while they were trapped in the car together. "What if rent goes up?" he asked, voice quiet.

Mom shrugged, unbothered. "I'll figure it out."

She reached for the bag, her fries already gone, and Xavier handed her the paper-wrapped burger. His hand was bleeding again, those three little holes soaking through the useless Band-aids. He'd already replaced them twice.

INDIGENT

Mom noticed, gave him a hard look.

The urgent care parking lot was full, and the lobby was full, and the exam rooms were full, and two babies had been screaming for at least two hours. Non-stop.

Xavier leaned against the wall, tooth aching. Mom was already asleep beside him, standing up with her arms crossed. The woman could sleep anywhere. The crying got louder somehow, one on both sides, for both ears.

What could be wrong with them? A- asthma. B- bronchitis. C- colic. D- diarrhea. E- ear infection—

"Coates?"

He touched his mom's shoulder, and she blinked, still half asleep. "Be right back."

An exam table had been set up in the hallway—not enough observation rooms to go around—and Xavier sat on the edge of it, waiting. If he pressed his ear to the wall, he could hear the man on the other side moaning. Miserable and constant. At least he *got* a room. Lucky.

F- fever. G- GERD. H- hand, foot, and mouth.

Eventually, a nurse came by to inject his bad hand with a local anesthetic—three shots, one between each of his fingers. Xavier held his breath and looked away as the needles sank in, puncturing the skin, before the nurse broke out the stitches. A painless pressure of sutures drawn through flesh.

He kept his eyes on the poster tacked to the wall—"BUDGET NUTRITION FACT$". Cartoon smiley faces floating through cloud-like intestines. Plump and pink. *A happy gut is a happy you.* The nurse said the stitches were absorbable, no need to come back.

Absorbable stitches are made of intestinal lining. A pig's insides were being knit into his skin, a wave of queasiness washing over him as the nurse ran through her spiel. Lightning speed.

"Have you had any muscle spasms?"

"No."

"Upset stomach? Headache? Fever? Trouble swallowing?"

"I don't think so."

"Any changes in appetite?"

"Nope."

"Do you need to talk with a social worker about financing your visit today?"

Xavier chewed his lip. "I need a blood-borne pathogens test," he said, still staring at the poster, his hand numb, a disgusting taste in his mouth.

"I don't think that's necessary for what you got goin' on. I *do* wanna give you a tetanus shot, though."

"It's for somethin' else."

She sighed, like his potential AIDS was her problem. "What test you want?"

"I don't know. All of them?"

Another sigh. "Lemme get the phlebotomist, hon."

The phlebotomist was cute and around his age, and she stuck him six times before eventually finding the vein in his elbow, the butterfly needle resting against his skin. *The median cubital vein of the antecubital fossa* draped with little plastic wings. "Deep veins, sorry."

He didn't think she was cute anymore.

Xavier stood at the intake desk with a neon green bandage wrapped around his arm and vials of his blood being shipped off in a biohazard box. By the doors, Mom was still waiting, hardly having moved at all.

"Gonna be twenty-five dollars today."

He took out his wallet, relieved that the cost was only in the double-digits. Doable. And Mom materialized beside him, nudging him away with her purse. *Does she keep bricks in that thing?*

"He shouldn't have to pay nothin'. He on my insurance."

"There's a co-pay, Ma'am."

Xavier looked at her, realizing with a quick flash of panic that the receipt would go to her if she paid—the receipt with the blood test listed in its neat list of itemized prices. She'd see the test and freak out, think he was sleeping around like an idiot or sharing needles behind her back.

He insisted on paying, angling away from her as he fished around his wallet. Two tens, a five, a one, his EBT card, and his emergency debit card. Nothing else. *Why can't you pay for stitches with EBT?* He slid the cash across the desk and shoved the receipt in his pocket without looking. Not great, but better than telling her.

Not worth the look on her face—

One he'd seen before, running, excited to hand her the crumpled permission slip for his school's Christmas program, ready for his free night of shopping. No parents allowed, whatever his imagination and one-hundred and fifty dollars could get. So much money to him. She'd smiled, signed it. And he'd heard her crying in the bathroom before dinner, on the phone with Memaw. "I only get paid once a month, I just need somethin' 'til then. I'll pay it back. I wanna take Xav shoppin'…"

The next day, he'd looked for who else had been given a permission slip: some trailer trash girl and Trevor Yon, who'd been pulled aside one day and asked if his family was able to do laundry at home. *Charity case.*

"Ma, are we poor?" he'd asked her, watching her face fall. *That look.* And he'd had to watch that look, nothing else in his arsenal.

"No, we not poor," she'd said, and his stupid kid self couldn't just let it go.

"Okay, but do we live where poor people live?" Later, he'd stood behind Trevor in the cafeteria, plugging his nose—"God, man, when's the last time you took a shower?!"—and thrown away his permission slip.

That same day, he'd gotten sent to the nurse after hitting his head on the bleachers during gym class. Three times. Alleviating the pressure, something easier. Centralized. He said he'd slipped. Nobody'd bought it.

Do we live where poor people live?

Xavier closed his wallet, the screaming behind them louder, the baby's mother shushing and muttering.

I- impetigo. J- jaundice. K… Kyphosis? Kuru? Nothing that makes sense starts with 'K'.

Shanice tried to keep her feelings to herself, make like it was just the long workday, the exhaustion. Who knew if he bought it.

Xavier never talked to her. He'd always been terrible at lying, and he was lying now. Or leaving something big out, at least. *What was that blood test for?* Just a check-up? *Oh yeah, while I'm here...*

Diabetes ran in the family. Her mother had it, and her grandmother, and Shanice was planning on getting it, too, especially with how much this job had her sitting on her ass all day. Maybe she had it now. Was Xavier checking his blood sugar? Being smart.

He'd talked to Rob, hadn't he?

He did. He'd taken to Rob right away when she'd brought him, just five years old then, to visit his uncle at the Motel 6 where Rob stayed after leaving Barnesville for good. He hadn't planned it. Her brother never planned shit. And so—the motel. And the shopping spree for a brand-new wardrobe. The pool, the movies on the TV, the waffle maker at the breakfast bar. An amazing vacation for a kindergartener, all while she was working double time, making sure Xavier didn't run into any weirdos. Going to cry in her car after hearing Xavier and Rob at the pool. Arms flapping. Squeaking water wings.

"Catch me! Unc, catch me!" as he'd leapt into the water.

Screaming. Her boy, *screaming*.

Xavier had hardly made a sound as a baby. Not for attention. Not when he was hungry. He's watch her from thc playpen in the corner while she brushed out some girl's hair in the kitchen sink. Not a peep, even whenever the girls bitched about her pulling too hard. Shanice had dragged his crib out by her bed, worried that she'd never catch it on time if he was hurt, choking. Something.

He'd lay there, reaching for the farm animal mobile, looking at her with those giant eyes when she held the animal figures up to his face and made all the right sounds. "Moo. Baa. Neigh." Looking at her like she was crazy, not making a peep.

Just a late bloomer.

Until one day, Shanice was on the toilet. Hiding. Having gone to the bathroom to splash water on her face but staying in there for hours, just sitting. Brain turned off. Sleeping with her eyes and ears open. When suddenly—"Mama, where you at?" Five years old and the first words he'd said to her, knocking on the bathroom door with those tiny fists. The chubby fingers.

Mama, where you at? Asking for her.

But there he'd been, meeting her brother for the first time and *talking*. Screaming. With a practical stranger. So she'd cried in the car, alone. What else was she supposed to do? Yell at him for having a good time?

What about Rob was better? What made him *safe*?

Anika Davis's boy was on summer break, which mostly meant finding ways to be out of the house so old Miss Inez would get off his ass about everything.

When Ma found out he was being held back, she'd just said now he'd be bigger when he tried out for football in middle school. He didn't remember saying he wanted to play football, but if that made Ma feel better, he'd hide his glasses in his backpack and go to try-outs. Easy.

Miss Inez, though, went *crazy*, breaking out a stack of million-year-old workbooks, making him sit at the kitchen table all day reading boring-ass chapbooks and doing math, her sandal coming down whenever he complained. *What's a hundred twenty-three divided by thirty-four? I don't kn—* Thwack!

But *now* he had something. He had a video.

If he did his schoolwork, Miss Inez might be nice and drive him to the rec center, where he could show it off to the rich white kids who played basketball at the indoor court. *Hey, guys, wanna see a dead body?* He'd finally have their attention.

He'd noticed the drama just in time to get footage of some homeless-looking girl getting zipped up and wheeled off. Out of the alley and into the parking lot.

Now that he could get a closer look, it wasn't as exciting as he thought it'd be. Blood and garbage—a lot of the second one, just enough of the first for a little puddle and a smear against the brick wall by the Dumpster.

It was gummy, less like water than he expected. He filmed it, his toe leaving a little dent in its smooth edge, like he'd taken a bite out of it. Gross.

And something more than that, *moving*—

"Hey! What're you doing?"

The rent office guy was standing at the bottom of the stairs, holding a pressure washer tank and glaring at him.

"Get outta here before I tell your mom you've been snooping around."

Anika Davis's boy booked it down the alleyway and kept running, sprinting as fast as he'd ever gone. Maybe he *would* be good at football, and his glasses and asthma and the fact that letters always seemed to get flipped around in his brain wouldn't matter. He'd be a football star.

He slowed down by the Quik Stop, breathing hard, and took out his phone to watch the video. *Five bucks, and I'll show you a dead body! Wait, no, ten bucks. It's that good!* And it *was* that good. He wouldn't even be lying.

Standing in the shaded awning by the gas pumps, smoke and gasoline fumes wafting, he held his phone close to his face, trying to make out the smallest details. There was something in the video. That *movement* again, clear as day.

Hair-thin and see-through. A pulsing shadow. Barely seen...

Worms.

CHAPTER THREE
GORDIACEAN THANATOLOGY

Clock. *Zhōng*. Pillow. *Zhěntou*.

Mom. *Yuèmǔ*. Dad. *Yuèfù*.

Hammer. *Chuízi*. Temple... Shit.

What was it? *Tóu*... maybe *é'tóu*? No, that wasn't right either, was it?

Ari was losing it. With Cam gone, he didn't have any reason to speak Chinese anymore, not that she'd been any good. It was nice, being the most fluent one in the room for once. Being the *only* one didn't feel nearly as nice.

He stood by the bed, glaring at Cyril's sleeping body—*Dad, Yuèfù*—and took a breath, the hammer dangling loosely from his fingers. Heavy. *This is his fault.*

The one good thing about Cyril's stroke was that there was no waking him up once he was out. When Ari put the face of the hammer against the side of Cyril's head—against the *temple*—Cyril didn't move. He hardly breathed. Not a single twitch. Ari paused for a second then flipped the hammer so the claw touched the skin.

Better. He wanted blood, wanted him to really *feel* it. He tightened his fingers around the handle—

"Ari."

Leena's voice. Clear and tired. He glanced up, saw her propped on one arm on the other side of the bed beside Cyril, neck craning to look at him. Not asleep after all. She was as far away from Cyril as she could get, feet hanging off the mattress, not touching him. Of course she wasn't. Something was wrong with him. She had to know.

"Don't," she said, the same voice she used when she'd caught him sneaking food before dinner. *I'm not angry.* She wouldn't stop him. He could still get it over with. *I'm just disappointed.* "Please."

Ari took a step back, afraid to break eye contact. He put the hammer on the bedside table. Exhausted, stomach twisting. He hadn't eaten since Cam died, even when Cyril and Leena had sat in the kitchen tearing through the leftovers. Stress eating. And he hadn't eaten anything *good* for much longer.

This is my fault.

Leena got up, the mattress creaking under her weight. She hurried to him, cupping his face in her hands, and the world opened up. Senses intermingling, shared between **them** and making it that much more obvious—Leena's fullness compared to that yawning hole in his stomach.

"Are you mad at me?" he asked, the first thing that came to mind.

"Oh, sweetheart." Leena simpered.

She sat him down on the foot of the bed. Her hands moved to his shoulders as he buried his face in her hair, in the crook of her neck. Saying nothing, rocking... Swaying... crushing him against her. Breathing each other in. Cyril didn't move. Dead to the world, as always.

This is my fault.

Ari hadn't cried like this since his brother died. That had been his fault, too.

At least *then* he hadn't been so hungry.

The man who'd lived here before them liked fishing. Fishing and forgetting about life for a while. That was the impression Ari got, anyway.

There were two things in the hall closet—fishing poles, all adult-sized save for one that was short and pink, and downers. And it took him all of fifteen minutes to find even more. Kept in the bedside table, a random kitchen drawer, rolled underneath the living room couch. Under-the-table vallies and oxy and an actual prescription for hydromorphone, already half-gone.

For when all the other ones just aren't getting the job done, I guess.

He'd have to avoid the oxycodone like the plague, but that still left a few options. He'd never taken hydromorphone before. It could be fun. Or it'd be something to do.

Then there was the beer taking up most of the fridge, the TV dinners, and the cellphone with five contacts, none of whom had called or texted since they got here. It all painted the picture of "Wilkinson, Rashon" as a man who probably didn't mind being put out of his misery. And that no one else minded either. Whoever owned that pink fishing pole didn't seem to be coming around.

A daughter maybe?

The only family photo in the whole apartment had her in it. Ari had been careful to leave it out of frame as he went through his routine of documenting the other pictures. A fish and a lake. It was his thirty-fifth animal this year and his forty-first landscape—two of the most popular decorative themes in the American South, the cheapest parts of it, at least. A good distraction.

But now, Ari was starving.

That was the main thing on his mind as he wandered through Leigh Pierce Estates, avoiding Cyril and Leena.

"Leigh Pierce was a founding father, you know? 'William Leigh Pierce.' He had a failed export company, and he was *probably* from Georgia! Isn't that fun? Did you know that?" Leena had asked, sitting in the passenger's seat of their old car while Cyril napped in the back, Ari keeping an eye out for anyone who looked good.

She hadn't stopped rambling since Cam left, like she could talk enough for both of them. Ari had spent the last three weeks tuning it out. "Did you know that, honey?" she'd asked again, poking his arm.

"No, Mom, I didn't know that."

He'd spotted someone promising—a Black guy who'd spent all night moving between the parking lot and the basement staircase. Always alone.

"Oh. Well, now you do!" she'd said, slumping against the seat, side-eying him.

It'd been a bad choice. People were calling and texting the guy non-stop, blowing up the phone until Ari had finally just snapped the SIM card in half. And the bills showed that he paid rent *monthly*, no autopay, giving them hardly any time to stay there before the landlord got worried.

When he'd read that, Ari cursed so loudly that Cyril and Leena heard from the living room, their voices cutting in—"Language, young man!" Like he was a middle schooler.

In retrospect, he'd only picked that first guy—the dealer in B12—because it seemed good enough and he couldn't stand being in the car with the two of them anymore. Eight hours of pretending to tolerate each other and barely managing it.

Was Cam really the only thing making this work?

He was only wandering around now because he couldn't stand being stuck in an apartment with them either.

Did it even work when she was here?

The answer came quickly and honestly: *no.* But there'd been a symmetry to things, a precedent for what configurations worked best at what times, responsibilities and roles laid out. Then Cyril had to go and get sick and ruin it.

I should've gone with Cam. Stupid. I've always been so fucking stupid—

And hungry, his stomach bubbling.

Ari walked down the hallway, picking doors at random on the second floor, a plastic bag stuffed with old takeout containers he'd dug out of the garbage hanging from his wrist, the words on the bag flashing bright red in his periphery. *Thank you Thank you Thank you.* As good a disguise as any. Invisible.

He knocked on apartment 205. A man, tall and Black and wearing a McDonald's polo, appeared at the door. Eye crust, salt, and cooking oil. It didn't cover up the smell of pot as much as meld together, making Ari's stomach turn.

"I got an order for Johnson," he said, trying to keep down the nausea, looking past those gritty, red-rimmed eyeballs and into the apartment behind them.

"I ain't order no food," the guy said.

"You sure?"

Ari didn't get an answer, just a door shut in his face. Whatever. The glimpse he'd gotten had been promising. Pot and fries. A shitty bachelor pad—nothing but a futon with a laptop resting on the edge, fan whirring. Most importantly, it looked like he lived alone, and it looked like he was healthy. Healthy-ish.

That hand, fingers peaking over the doorframe, nails white and clean and round. Tendons below the skin, flexing, muscles below the fat—

Ari bit the inside of his lip—*snap out of it*—walking further down the hallway, counting the doors. *Liǎng bǎi qī, liǎng bǎi jiǔ, liǎng bǎi yīshíyī.*

The second floor was mostly off-limits. People with kids or dogs, heavy smokers who opened the door looking shriveled and gray, the smoke settled into their skin, their hair. *How? Cam never looked that bad.* But 205 was good. More than good. Ari could find a way back in today before Cyril and Leena even knew—

Snap. Out. Of it. God, you act like Mom never feeds you.

He took the stairs to the third floor, then the fourth, making a note of all the numbers that seemed safe. Salt-and-Pot living alone in 205. The girl in 311 who pretended to only speak Vietnamese even though her sharp American vowels were a dead giveaway. Two separate old ladies in 401 and 415 who admitted to not ordering any Chinese takeout but who were willing to pay for it anyway as long as it gave them an excuse to talk at him about inflation and the weather, Ari standing there staring. *Oh, it's allergies. It's not the heat, it's the humidity. They're both so bad this time of year.*

Disgusting.

He used to like talking to people. He used to have conversations with strangers while he waited for the train. Now, it was just noise, air wheezing in and out of their clogged-up nostrils.

Ari found his way to the roof, the door at the top of the emergency stairwell padlocked for show but easy to open with a strong enough push.

The view from fifty feet above-ground made his stomach drop. Not a bad feeling. It was like a rollercoaster, like lying next to Cam when she was asleep, his hands on her face, drifting in and out of a dream that was more hers than his. The twinge in his legs when she dreamed of running. His mouth watering when she dreamed about food.

A precipitous and satiating drop.

He watched the half-empty parking lot, the neighborhood seeming nice this far away. No homeless people posted outside gimmicky yoga studios. No trash rotting in abandoned garbage cans. No eyes turning to look at him, like he didn't notice. Like they *knew*. Waiting for him to give himself away.

We know. We know—

He took six Valiums from Wilkinson's stash—hopefully enough, he had too high of a tolerance for those things—and waited for them to kick in. To disconnect his brain from his stomach. From his whole body.

If he was better with people, he would sell them, get enough money for a motel and some new clothes. Even door-knocking had taken so much out of him, though. Nerves shot. So selling them was a non-starter, and after a while, he was where he wanted to be, splayed out on the gravel and smoking one of Cam's cigarettes. CAM <3 staring at him—*she'd kill you if you wasted them*—enjoying the warmth in his throat...

Too much to eat and not enough to do.

The memory was loud. The phrase, Chinese, too fast for him to catch, in a voice he didn't quite recognize. He remembered what people had said though, those kids from school and the old ladies they worked with, their sneering mouths. *Where are your people from?*

"What?" he'd said.

"It means 'Come help me,'" the woman had sighed, dragging him into the kitchen to wash dishes with her, smoke pouring out of her mouth as she took a drag from another cigarette. He could taste the smoke in the air, over the fry grease and Pink Stuff cleaner. It stuck in his throat.

I can tell where your people are from just from listening to you. Your Chinese sounds Russian.

She'd been angry, and he should've probably said sorry. A safe bet. But he couldn't make out her face. Just a smudge, blotted out by grease.

Why can't I see her face—

He blew out the smoke, let it pass. Breathed it in again...

"D'you have anymore cigarettes?" a voice had asked. New and familiar all at once.

Rain. It'd left the city clean and glassy, run-off sloshing underneath the concrete. Mist rolling in from off the lake. Water everywhere, water smearing the world around the edges. She'd taken a drag off her nearly gone cigarette. How did she manage to keep it lit? No umbrella in the rain.

They'd walked together to wait for the L-train.

"Nobody smokes anymore," he'd told her.

Wait. Had they walked together, or had she followed him? Or maybe she'd just appeared there on the platform beside him. *What a coincidence.* Smoke and light and water...

"I do. They're good for stress," she'd said, smiling at him. Awkward, like she'd never done it before. Every freckle, the drop of water shivering on the tip of her nose, perfectly clear.

The honest truth was that Leena hated cleaning, but it gave her hands something to do, and she was grateful for that.

Two cups cold water. A half cup of hydrogen peroxide and a spoonful of baking soda. Let sit. Scrub. Make sure all the suds are gone, then add one cup of water and a half cup of white vinegar. Let sit. Scrub. Never mix hydrogen peroxide and vinegar. *They'll make fumes that sting your eyes and get stuck in your throat.* Not deadly, but not nice either.

It was good to stay busy. The road trip from Louisville had been less than pleasant. Cy had spent the whole ride asleep, and Ari had just sat in the passenger seat, their hands barely touching on the center console, tapping her whenever he felt her getting too tired. She'd pull over, and he would go on driving. Never speaking. The silent treatment. He *knew* that would get to her.

Spiteful boy. Like she *wanted* this. Like she'd be cruel enough to plan it this way.

If it had been up to *her*, she would've picked somewhere closer to the country. A whole house, if they could find one far enough away from any neighbors. They had those here. Country folks loved their space. But it wasn't up to her.

Ari had been driving during the last leg of things, and he always gravitated toward cities, to those endless, crowded miles of gray. She couldn't be mad at him. They both just needed something familiar. Leigh Pierce Estates was one of the better places they'd stayed, at least.

It was better to think about chemicals, cleaning solutions—the best home-made combinations to remove blood from carpet. The best solutions for dried, cracked skin after hours of scrubbing. She hated it, how ugly her hands looked, those scaley lizard fingers.

INDIGENT

She went to bed wearing rubber gloves filled with Vaseline, re-doing her nails every morning. Light pink polish. Subtle. Modest. Lovely nails that made up for her thinning hair and bald patches, the skin hanging loose around her neck like a chicken gizzard. She had to keep *something* about her pretty. Her hands, then. Her nails—*ten* whole things about her that looked nice, however small.

Her poor hands were really being put to work this week. The boy from the first apartment had made a mess. Blood trailing out into the hall. Thank God no one had been up to see that. What would she even begin to say if someone came waltzing out of the elevator with a basket of laundry, seeing her on her hands and knees in the middle of the hallway, soaking up blood in a ratty old bath towel? They'd just been lucky the floor was cement and not carpet.

He's trying to get us caught. Her hands pressing hard, deep red soaking through the fibers and staining her fingerprints.

But this was no time to start accusing each other of anything. Yes, Ari was put out with them now, and for good reason. She would be angry, too. But he wasn't *that* angry, was he...?

Even better not to think about *that.*

For two days, she was up before the sun, staying awake long after both of her boys had gone to bed. Scrubbing, dusting, setting out traps for rats and flies. The horrible vermin, sneaking in where they didn't belong and weren't wanted. *It looks great, hon. Somebody should pay you.*

Then, they'd moved—again—to the apartment down the hall. B4. Identical in every way to the one they had just left, just frustratingly, maddeningly, regressed back into filth. A sad man living alone with no one to impress and no woman to keep him in line. So, of course, that was the state of things when Camille arrived. *Why couldn't she be here for the* nice *apartment?*

Cyril had dragged her out with that burst of energy he got when he was in one of his moods. Then, he'd come back, taking Leena's hands in their soothing gloves, massaging them gently in his fingers. *Let's go to bed, hon.* They'd had a snack to calm down, her mouth greasy and full of iron as she lay beside him, waiting for his breathing to even out.

Then back to work. Sleep not even an option. Camille had seen this pig stye.

It is in vain that you rise up early and go late to rest, eating the bread of anxious toil; for he gives to his beloved sleep.

Was she not beloved anymore? Had her abandonment of Camille cast her out as well? Lifting up layers of grime, leaving the paint so bright white it hurt her eyes. How it should be. How it *should've* been when Camille got there.

It distracted her from the twisting in her stomach, **their** unsatisfied churning. Vinegar, bleach, and Dawn. The smell put **them** off eating, stinging her nose and eyes, sitting chemical and sour on her tongue.

Camille had died the next afternoon.

Cyril had been asleep, and Ari had been helping her in the kitchen, sectioning everything out and wrapping the portions in parchment paper. She'd hoped to get him to eat finally. He'd hardly touched anything for the last few weeks. The silent treatment, a hunger strike. *Overdramatic.*

She'd worked straight through the night and gone right to prepping breakfast, her nails not even done. Shaky, her hands twitching all on their own. If she'd let it do that for long enough, maybe it would pop free of her wrist and go skittering. Leave her like everything else.

She could feel Ari's worry in brief snatches. *You need some sleep.*

And you *need to eat.* But he wouldn't. At a certain point, they had to be allowed to react to this situation however they saw fit. If Ari wanted to starve himself, fine. If she wanted to stay awake until her body popped into pieces, fine. If Cy wanted to go on letting them do that, fine.

She'd just focused on the food, not even tempted. She had a leg up on the boys that way, used to denying herself after a girlhood of her mother pinching the nonexistent fat on her hips. Tragic, really. If she'd known how things were going to turn out, she would've eaten all she wanted.

Ari had known something was wrong before she did. *How? Is it my fault? Am I a bad mother, after all this? Couldn't even keep an eye on my own little girl*—His hands shaking. The shoulders. His entire body. Like hypothermia, like his cells were combusting. *He loves her more than you.*

"What's wrong?! What's wrong?" And she'd taken his hand—

Heart valves stopped up. Blood crawling to a torturous halt. Stuck. Trapped inside shrinking veins. Dry veins. Help—

The world had *snapped* shut, some part of Leena's senses, some crucial, crucial part gone.

And they were on the floor, she and Ari. How? Had they collapsed? She couldn't remember. It smelled like peroxide and lemon. Nose touching the linoleum, her forehead pressed against her boy's while they'd laid there and breathed.

In and out.

In and out.

Blood in her mouth. She'd tongued the cut along the inside of her lip where she'd bitten down—bit hard—and the blood was flavorless. Water gone stale overnight. There'd been a sound in her ears, some after-shock she couldn't place, and she'd felt Ari move from underneath her hands, torn away, vaguely registering Cy's body over them. Huge and dark, his voice urgent.

"Quiet, quiet! Screaming like a goddamn woman—"

Screaming? *Them?*

And a slap. That couldn't be right. Cy would never hit any of them. Never.

Never...

Camille was dead. An absolute certainty. Her daughter had been just on the other side of the wall. Seeing and feeling, taking in the world, sharing it with them, however minutely.

Then she wasn't. She was gone...

Such a pretty girl, look at those curls. Looking her in the eyes, those big, scared eyes. A little doll. Terrified of her even though she didn't have to be. Camille never had to be afraid of her, not her baby.

And those freckles. I can't believe you tried covering them up... Holding the girl's face in her hands, pulling them away covered in clumped mascara and foundation, two shades too dark.

The poor thing didn't know anything at all about being a woman, about how to be feminine. No guidance.

Begging. No, persuading—*convincing*—Cy that life was precious. That this sweet girl was precious. Taking the girl in her arms as the struggling slowed and slowed and finally stopped. Watching with awe, like a sunset, like the aurora borealis, as the girl's mind opened wider. More every day. Enmeshed. *Her baby. Her baby...*

Leena sat at the kitchen table eating breakfast with Cy, the flavors still muted in her mouth. *The world is smaller.* Ari didn't join them.

After they were done eating, she stood by while Cy did his exercises, ready to catch him if—*when*—he lost his balance. He was so fragile now. In some ways. Trunk bends, three sets of ten. Sit-to-stands, one set of ten. Nice, even numbers.

She waited, her hands on his hips, on his shoulders, keeping him steady as his frustration boiled, thoughts hot and ashamed. *I used to be so much more.* He wouldn't let anyone else touch him like this. Vulnerability was good in a husband, but never in a father.

An old sensation flitted across her body. His arms around her. Shushing, patting her hair back...

"How're you feelin'?" she asked. Was this where they were now, her having to *ask* such a simple thing, like she was nothing more than decay in his bones?

But Cy was still doing his job. He still knew her, better than she knew herself.

"I'm alright, hon." He squeezed her hand. "We're gonna be okay. Don't worry."

"What'm I supposed to do all day, then?" she asked. A joke, but not really. She'd run out of cleaning, at least until somebody tracked in more dirt.

"Try to relax," he said, kissing her knuckles. Then, "Ari eat yet?"

"No," the word coming out strained from her scratched-up throat. Crying did that. She'd probably hurt her vocal cords, ripped them to shreds.

"Can't keep it up forever," Cy said, stretching his good arm. Unbothered. So sure.

Last night, he stood over you while you were sleeping, Leena wanted to say. *He was gonna bash your brain in.* "Hopefully, I'm worried," she said at last. *He was gonna get blood all over my nice, clean sheets.* "But you know that already."

By the time Cy was done with sit-to-stands, he was sweating profusely, shirt soaked through at the armpits. Trembling knees. She took his elbow and walked him to the bathroom, helping get his bad leg up into the tub after he undressed.

She was sweating, too—all the heat, the dead weight. Sweating and *glowing* with purpose. She wasn't an expert in these things, but she liked to think that the exercises helped, that Cy was more like himself in the hours after they were done, before he closed off again. A brick wall.

Is he even sad?

He'd only mentioned Camille once, the same day that she'd died. Leena had locked herself in the bedroom, the dresser against the door, wrapped up in the comforter even though it still smelled like algae and sweat after two rounds of washing, her lungs tearing out of her throat.

Ari's voice had been there for a while, but she hadn't answered. She'd just listened as it floated away and blended with Cy's. Hostile. Arguing. "You and Leena have no priorities, I swear to God."

No priorities. How was their daughter not a priority?

"Camille's gone. And it's her own damn fault. What're you gonna do? Spend the rest of your life bein' pissy with me 'cause I'm the only one who doesn't act like a fuckin' *child* every time somethin' bad happens?" he'd said.

She'd dragged herself out of bed, the comforter still around her shoulders, and went out to meet them. To break things up. Cy had hit him. *Hit* him!

He hit our boy. Our only one.

She'd found the two of them in the bathroom, pink-tinged water fanning across the floor, a plastic bucket overturned. Cyril had been sitting in the middle of it, Ari's chin cupped in his hand. Apologetic.

"Look at me. We can't let this throw us off. We've got to be a united front. We have to be *on the same page*. We are. Aren't we?" So desperate, that voice. So sorry when he got like that.

Leena'd interrupted them, brushing her fingertips across Ari's hair—letting him know all was forgiven—before heaving Cy back to his feet. As gentle as she could be, all five-foot-three of her lifting the six-foot-something of him. He deserved gentleness. They would talk about Camille later.

They were a united front, after all.

Ari always remembered more this way.

Bird. *Niǎo.* Cloud. *Yún.* Satellite dish. *Wèixīng tiānxiànpán.*

Who used satellite anymore?

Roadkill. *Lù shā.*

He'd been sitting on the floor, a patterned rug scrunched under his bare feet, a cardboard book in his lap. Animals. A hand had pointed to them, saying the names aloud—*māo, gǒu, lí, fù shǔ.* A voice unclear, waiting for him to repeat. To wrap his tongue around the sounds...

"Hey!" A high-pitched voice, a shoe in his ribs. "You gotta hang out somewhere else."

A kid. Elbows and knees and Coke-bottle glasses staring at him.

Ari got to his feet, Cam's cigarette gone, a pile of ash and the burnt-out fluff of the filter by his hand. A burn on his palm, unfelt and already half-healed, and a purple sky shot through with orange, his eyes adjusting to the dimming light. Head spinning.

"I do?" he asked, the kid bouncing from foot to foot. *Why aren't you on Adderall?*

"You gotta get permission. I can come up here's long as I check the meter on the water thing and scare away pigeons."

"Pigeons aren't allowed to live here?"

"They make everythin' super dirty. They got parasites."

Ari smiled. It might crack his face in half. "I'll let you take care of it, I guess."

Sunlight bounced off the boy's glasses, giving him giant animal eyes. Glowing. "Were you gonna jump?" he asked as Ari passed him—*creepy fucking kid*—and Ari ignored him, pulling open the door with hands that still didn't feel entirely like his own. A distant feeling of rust flakes biting into his palms. Downstairs. Outside...

Dumpster,

trashcans,

fire escape...

Color draining from the sky, sinking back into a deep blue-black expanse. No stars in the city. Every time he looked up, he lost his balance, set to fall backwards through the ground and straight out the other side. *Go back to China.* He snorted. But those half-strangers in Heilongjiang wouldn't want anything to do with him. They hardly did *before* and definitely wouldn't now.

He lit another cigarette, transfixed by the white center, spots in his eyes. Atoms freezing and wearing away at the world. Burning holes in it. Maybe things weren't so bad. He could go back to Cyril and Leena. He could act like nothing was wrong. Go on and on, all the way until he died, and **they** ate him from the inside out and left nothing for anybody to find.

As long as he had enough Valium. *That* was the issue.

And the eyes—

Sure even through the haze. Dead certain.

Someone was watching him. Calm, curious—not the panic he would've expected at the realization. Someone was watching him, and they were safe. Family.

Ari looked around, moving his head in slow arcs, ears ringing. No Cyril, no Leena. Just spots of light, cars moving down the road, headlights growing and shrinking in his eyeline like a sputtering candle.

Here comes a candle to light you to bed. A few of the apartment windows were lit, shadows moving behind the closed blinds. *And here comes a chopper to chop off your—*

There.

Above him, a window on the third floor. Someone was standing there, looking down at him, their eyes meeting for a second, less than that, before the blinds snapped back.

"Cam...?"

His voice died in the air, unanswered. Stupid, the pleasant high fizzling out into that heavy, familiar dullness. *But who else could it be?*

"Why does everybody keep hanging out here?"

Ari looked back at the man framed perfectly between the columns of brick, hair gel and cologne drifting toward him in the breeze.

"Look, the guy who sells... *stuff* moved out. He's not here anymore, so you can leave."

Ari tapped the ash off the end of his cigarette. *I'm hungry.* Watched the breeze pick it up. *Very hungry.* "I live here," he said.

"I've never seen you before in my life."

"I've never seen you either. Weird." Ari shrugged, staying put. If he moved now, something bad would happen.

"You know what? *Fine*. Whatever." The man rolled his eyes, leaving for the parking lot. Light played across his shirt, outlined the shoulders, the spine, in silk—

Ari's hand twitched to the boxcutter in his jacket pocket. **They** twisted under his tongue, and he pressed his teeth together.

Back to the third floor, counting the windows. Right side, third from the left. *Sānbǎi yī, sānbǎi sān, sānbǎi wǔ...* apartment 305. Maybe. He'd knocked on their door with no answer. *Cam would've answered.* Who was it then? *She wouldn't have left me...* He waited another moment, willing whoever it was to come to the window again. But nothing happened.

"Dinner!" Cyril said as soon as Ari opened the door to B4, waiting to ambush him. A trapdoor spider popping up out of nowhere. "Mom and I are insisting."

He put an arm around Ari's shoulders, drawing him in, and Ari tried not to flinch. Something was wrong—missing. Camille knew that.

Less than a year ago, she'd curled against him in the backseat of an old Nissan, sharing body warmth, the car heater busted. Leena had wanted to see Vermont in the fall. Beautiful and freezing. "Dad's gone crazy." Cam had used Chinese, of course. The only way to say something like that.

It couldn't have been long after the stroke, half of Cyril's reflected face still dropping in the rearview. *It made him crazy.*

Now, Cyril steered him down the hall towards the bathroom, hand on his neck. Resting there, skin against skin. Everything that he used to share, replaced by that cloying, suffocating blankness. Cyril was hungry, but not as hungry as he could be. That was all Ari could get.

"What you kids talkin' about back there?" Cyril had turned to look at them, him and Cam bundled together in the backseat, his half-frozen face unreadable.

"The leaves, look at all those colors. So pretty out here..." Cam had answered, smiling, innocent. Happier times...

She'd always been better at lying than him. More practice. Ari didn't even bother trying to hide his discomfort now, and Cyril never felt the need to explain himself.

"Get cleaned up. Fast. We've been waiting on you to eat. It's probably gone cold," he said, leaving Ari alone in the bathroom.

Ari didn't leave the bathroom until he had to, filling his palms with burning water as he listened to Leena's voice out in the kitchen.

"Why'd you have to upset your mother?" Cyril had accused, standing over him, the two of them listening to Leena on the other side of the bedroom door. Locked tight. *You knew this would happen, didn't you?*

Ari leaned against the sink, breathing in steam until he couldn't wait any longer, picturing one of **them** sitting inside his skull, a homunculus looking out his eye sockets, pulling a string—Straighten up. Pull. Right foot. Another pull. Left foot—

Dinner was already laid out, an extra plate left on the counter, staring at him from the kitchen as Leena took his hands. He knew she saw it, then: apartment 305. Cyril would ignore it, but not her.

86

She looked at him curiously, but she didn't ask. It would happen later, once Cyril was asleep.

Mealtime prayers were the only way to acknowledge what had happened without Cyril putting a stop to it. Leena had picked up on that fast enough, clasping her hands and praying about the role of family in forging ahead through adversity, about grief. Cyril nodded along. That was fine. Praise the Lord, amen.

They'd never asked if he was a Christian.

After wrapping up, Leena took a bite, hiding her grimace behind her hand, all politeness.

No room to complain about the little food they had left. Ari didn't pay much attention to the conversation, still riding on top of the last dying waves of Valium. It was easier to just eat, his dulled-down senses doing most of the legwork in making it edible.

"So hot out today." Bite. "Made a swamp cooler to use tonight, just in case." Ripping off a chunk with his canines. "Still too many fruit flies. I set out..." Grinding it between his molars, breaking it down—

"*Ari.*"

Blinking.

"See? Not even listenin'," Cyril said, waving a hand in front of his eyes.

"I was *saying*—" Leena started over. *Miss, we need to talk about your son.* "—that I understand being out of sorts right now. I do. But we should all be trying to be more productive with our time."

I think he needs more support at home to get through this.

"I went shopping today," Ari responded, tongue running along the ridge of his teeth.

"Good. That's good," Cyril said, still bent over his plate, shoving more into his mouth. His third helping, at least. Savoring it.

True to his word, the first thing Cyril had ever said to him: "This is a rule you live by now, son. Any food is good food."

"That's perfect, sweetheart. Thank you. We were running out..." Leena was saying.

Perfect. Thank you.

What she'd never say was that the last two meals he'd shopped for had been shit. It would've been a total waste if they hadn't gotten a place to stay out of it. B12 was a ticking time bomb. They'd opened the ribs and found his insides gawking at them, black-marbled and oily and tumorous. It was a miracle they'd gotten to him before his own body did. Barely edible. And even if they tried—and they *did* try—it came right back up.

B4 had hardly been any better, everything chemical-tasting and dangerous. Cyril's throat had closed up, poisoned viscera falling out of numb lips as Leena pounded him on the back, and Ari had lost feeling in his tongue, his mouth a senseless pit, like it'd been injected with lidocaine.

Two in a row. *Wasted.*

Nothing worse than waste. Nothing—

The realization had made Ari forget for a second that he hated Cyril. He'd let the old man touch him, trying to calm each other down.

Any food is good food.

"What d'you see that's blue?" someone had asked. Him or Cyril, no difference.

The couch, the blanket, the fibers in the carpet, the box of plastic spoons on the kitchen counter, a cup, the pause button on the TV remote. Blue was an easy color. They could go on like that for hours, back and forth, finding the smallest things to focus on, keeping back the hysteria threatening to boil up and over.

We're gonna starve to death. An animal panic.

Underneath it, though, had been relief. They'd abandoned Cam to starve. Fair was fair. Cyril had caught onto that—*ungrateful,* the word cutting through his usual blankness—and Ari had been left alone, unsure if the disgust he'd felt with himself was Cyril's or his own.

They'd spent the next day salvaging what they had, boiling it to hell and back until there was nothing left but a safe, wholly unsatisfying gray-brown slop.

Ari put the last forkful of it on his tongue, a pool of melted fat and salt slowly congealing on his plate. Teeth working through gristle. Squeaking.

Small twinges of pain as **their** bodies burrowed out from his gums, resting in the dark corners of his mouth like stray strands of cornsilk, absorbing **their** fill before it could even hit his stomach.

Cyril said goodnight, closing the bedroom door behind him while Leena stood at the sink, scrubbing and humming. Eighties songs—Cher, Peter Cetera—mom music.

Déjà vu. Same Leena, same song. Except Cam had been there, hadn't she? "Oh, this was one of Camille's favorites when she was little!" The B-52s cutting through daytime radio static, Cam burying her face against Ari's chest.

"That's one of *her* favorite songs," Cam had clarified later, when they were alone. "Not mine."

Not mine—

"Sweetheart, come help me with these so they're not sitting out all night," Leena asked from the kitchen, her voice soft over the running water.

He blinked, drifted over to help Leena. Should he try again tonight? Cracking Cyril's skull open? *Ungrateful.* Maybe he would.

Leena washed, he dried, and the pipes groaned under the counter.

"Three-oh-five, you think?" she asked after a few minutes of quiet.

He nodded and she touched his wrist, her fingers shriveled and warm, a silent agreement passing between them.

CHAPTER FOUR
DESIDERIUM

Scaphoid, lunate, triquetrum, pisiform, trapezium, trapezoid, capitate, hamate.

Xavier flexed his bad hand, sutured with pig parts, a rash spreading out from under the bandage. A bad reaction to something. *Their gloves are always shit. Should just buy my own.* He rotated his wrist, tracing over each bone and mouthing its name.

Uncle Rob would tease him about never getting it completely right, the only thing he could poke fun at on the technical side of things. "You a goddamn encyclopedia, you know that?" he would say, smiling wider and wider as he pointed to his legs, his side, his foot, and Xavier had rattled off the muscles and bones from memory.

A parlor trick. *A goddamn encyclopedia*—except for the hands.

"Wanna know a trick?" Rob had asked, standing over some little old lady from Bankhead Senior Living who'd been running through her forearm exercises. Rob had grinned at her, scandalized. "Some. Lovers. Try. Positions. That. They. Can't. Handle."

Scaphoid, lunate, triquetrum, pisiform, trapezium, trapezoid, capitate, hamate.

"That was not for your ears, Miss, you too precious for that," he'd said, winking, earning a misaligned-denture smile and ten reps of pendulum swings. No complaints.

That was Rob, getting the best out of people for fifteen minutes at a time, chargeable to most health insurance. That's where the rest of the teasing happened: the people part. Dirty looks and head shakes, people gaping at Xavier like he'd asked them to get up and run a marathon. Not a convincing bone in his body.

"Don't take it personal, Xav. Sick people are mean. Hurt people are meaner. It ain't ever about you," Rob had told him once. The gun in his glove compartment had probably helped him be more forgiving, but he hadn't mentioned that.

The nerves were getting to him as Xavier paced the living room, studying for next month's placement exam that would hope-fully let him skip the intro anatomy classes and go right to clinicals. He just had to trust that Rob had been right, that he was an *encyclo-pedia* who knew his shit.

Focus on other things...

Mom was frying something. Porkchops it smelled like, the apartment full of warmth and popping oil. Comfortable. He didn't want to ruin it by checking his community college account. Their tuition updates.

The email had come in that afternoon while he sweated behind an N-95 mask, locs pushed back, spraying down all the nooks of the fourth floor with a bleach solution that killed anything dumb or slow enough to touch it. Mold season.

It'd been sitting like a brick in his chest, unanswered, and he'd worked overtime to avoid it even more, finishing off the third floor before clocking out. The rent office was already dark, Desai steering clear of him ever since dropping the wonderful news.

Good, the douchebag.

Be reasonable, don't kill the messenger.

A few hours ago, he'd sat at Desai's desk, the dark room smelling like imported cigarettes and bad cologne, imagining what it'd be like if it was *his* name on that plastic nameplate. Would he sell everybody out? Would he watch Leigh Pierce go down, some impartial observer sipping a Coke, viewing the cloud of toxic dust through a pair of binoculars?

Nobody else to kill, though, so what now?

Xavier sighed, grabbing his laptop. He'd be too nervous to eat if he kept putting things off, and he wasn't about to miss out on real food. *Real* cooking—

But somebody was outside. A gut feeling. His ears burning.

"That mean somebody's talking about you," Mom had said once, tugging on his ear as a kid, smiling like she'd told a secret. Left ear burns for compliments, right ear burns for gossip. Or maybe the other way around. *What did both mean?*

Xavier went to the window, pulling down one of the blinds, a perfect view into the alley. To the square of concrete where that girl had died a few days ago. He'd been avoiding it, paying the Davis kid to take their garbage down to the Dumpster and taking other entrances to get in. It gave him a bad feeling.

Someone was standing by the Dumpster now. Smoking. Dark hair and dark jacket and a glowing spot of a cigarette illuminating a pale hand. A hand in the dark, disembodied. Floating. They glanced up—at *him?*—and Xavier pulled away, the blind snapping back into place, off-kilter. Like he'd seen a ghost.

His nerves were making him jumpy. Urgent care needed to call him back already.

Xavier sat down with his laptop and pulled up the community college website. "Don't be typin' with your bad hand. Those kinda things take forever to heal up if you keep moving them," Mom said from the kitchen.

"Shoulda told me that before I went to work all day."

He kept typing, and she tossed a dishrag at him—overshooting—the microfiber glancing off the top of his head. His eyes followed it as it landed on the coffee table next to Lando—an excellent junk mail paperweight—clinging, staticky, to the teeth. Fucking thing.

Then, back to his computer screen, to the updated tuition statement.

Something had to be wrong with it. Negative forty-five dollars. *Negative.* The cursor hovered over the balance sheet. "In-state Federal Aid Applied (First Semester): $2,300. Total Due: -$45." *Negative* forty-five.

Mom said something, the sound falling flat, unprocessed.

"You hear me?" Mom said, irritated, her footsteps getting closer, reading over his shoulder. "Oh my God. You gon' be a doctor!" Mom screamed, shaking his shoulders with every word, jostling his brain loose.

"A certified physical therapy assistant!"

Just as good, just as exciting.

She put her arms around him, squeezing. "*Certified*! Every time I know somebody who needs they back cracked, they getting sent to you, 'cause you a professional. *My baby's a professional*!" Voice so high it shorted out his already punch-drunk brain.

She kept her arms around him, her eyes going to their family picture, centered between his high school track medals. The two of them and Uncle Rob—Mom's hair and nails done, Rob in his one suit, and Xavier in his cap and gown, camera flash turning his sweaty forehead into a white-hot spot.

Three figures standing over his graduation cap, pristine and black inside its dusty shadowbox. *Shit, I should clean that*. Mom had insisted on buying the cap and gown, not renting. He'd left it in the plastic wrap until the day-of, not wanting to disturb it, thinking it'd be better if he didn't touch it at all.

Step Two—You get what you give. Demonstrate your inherent value to attract even more high-value opportunities.

"He'd be proud of you," Mom said quietly, kissing the top of his head, locs still damp and gross from his shift, but she didn't react to it, just sat beside him. Thinking. "I'm drivin' down to Miami on Monday. You should come," and pre-emptively, before he could say anything. "It won't be a long vacation or nothin', but..."

Zion liked Miami.

They could go to the beach, buy some gimmicky drinks on the boardwalk, get a little darker while all the white people burned up under the sun. They'd been there once, when he was a kid, wading in the ocean, surrounded by floating clumps of what looked like seaweed until he picked one up, saw the gelatinous animal-parts of its body. A sea slug leaking purple, staining his palms—

"I shouldn't. They been a pain at the office," Xavier said, the lightness fading. That ache back in his jaw. Right side.

She gave him his plate. Fried porkchops, greens, a slice of white toast with a knob of butter.

"Okay. I get it," she said, acrylic nails tapping against the table. "I'll make you a good dinner tomorrow, then. With a chess pie. That work?"

He smiled and sawed into the porkchop with extra enthusiasm—*clear the air*—taking a bite. "You know I ain't ever gon' be mad at food."

Xavier crouched outside the rent office, his tooth aching, trap music blaring from a cheap, crackling Bluetooth speaker while Anika Davis's kid pushed the floor buffer around the lobby. Impossible to filter out.

Whatever. The kid could listen to anything he wanted if it meant *something* got done while Xavier took a breather. This probably counted as child labor. Unpaid child labor. *Shit—*

But God, his head was killing him. He hardly got an hour of sleep last night. And he'd had a weird dream, too, once he'd finally drifted off.

Swimming in the ocean at night. Someone was on the shore, but he couldn't tell who, got the impression that they weren't waiting for him. That he could drown and they wouldn't notice. Rising waves, salt in his mouth. The next wave carried him so high that his head scraped against the sky.

No. The *ceiling*. A gray cinderblock room with water flowing smoothly through the grout of the far wall. Push and pull. Draining smoothly between the bricks. The wave swelled again, pressing his body against the ceiling. And held him there. *It must've been high tide.* Water in his nose, his ears. Building pressure—

Then he woke up upset, unnerved all morning, his head pounding. And it had only gotten worse. He'd spent the last two hours crouched by the windows, forehead pressed against the cool glass as he cleaned. Greasy scuffs and fingerprints dissolved under a layer of Windex and dripped down...

Down...

Spray and squeegee.

Spray and squeegee.

Spray...

and...

Through the streaks, Xavier saw a nice black car pull off at the curb. He saw a man step out. Spray-on tan and gray suit. Briefcase and clipboard. Not the landlord. A real estate agent? Or maybe some new social worker?

The man didn't look like a social worker, though. Long, quick steps carried him to the Leigh Pierce entrance, a guy who knew where he was. And wasn't happy about it.

Xavier watched him, the headache at the base of his skull radiating through his jaw, into his shoulders. Anika Davis's kid stopped the floor buffer to go open the door.

Desai appeared from the rent office, frowning at the music before readjusting his face into a rigid smile, waving. "Mr. Michaels! Thanks for stopping by. I'm so sorry to keep you waiting, it's good to see you. Really great..."

So that's what Desai sounded like when he was trying to be accommodating.

"Doctor," the man said, smiling right back.

"Sorry, sorry. Of course."

Xavier watched them out of the corner of his eye, invisible. Desai led *Doctor* Michaels to the office, still apologizing. *Something's wrong.* It'd be easy enough to eavesdrop—the walls were thin—but his head was killing him.

He set out a wet floor sign, shooed the Davis kid off, and went to the elevator. No stairs today, too worn out.

What's wrong with me...?

The more paranoid part of him wondered about the blood test. It could be that. Or the fact that this was his ninth day in a row at work, Desai's promise to hire more maintenance staff just smoke blown up his ass. It could have been that dead girl in the alley making any attempt to clean this place up seem especially useless. It could have been Atlanta Community College and the classes coming up in just a few months.

Just quit now. Just quit and relax. What's a few more shitty paychecks?

He could go to Miami. Go to that kitschy bar where Zion got his souvenir shot glass.

A lot.

He stepped into the elevator, metal grinding against metal, screeching behind the panels.

It's a lot when we need to find another house—

A hand shot out before the door could slide closed. Lan, his neighbor from 311 and one of Mom's favorite girls at the Queen Nails. The only one who remembered to massage her hands before the manicure.

She hurried into the elevator, huffing. She had new glasses, blue plastic rims, and one of her teeth was crooked. It poked out at an angle next to her canine. Cute.

"Good morning," he said. *Fuck, it's the afternoon. It's almost nighttime.*

"Good morning," she echoed, pressing the button for their floor.

Lan was studying accounting so she could buy a salon of her own. She'd told him so, going over the game plan while they'd shared a value meal over her lunch break. She ate her fries by tipping the container and shaking them right into her mouth, not wanting to get her hands greasy. "It sticks to you all day, and the ladies complain. Any excuse to leave a shit tip, you know," she'd explained, self-conscious.

The elevator *pinged*.

"You're still startin' classes next semester?" she asked, stepping out and waiting for him to follow. They walked together, not touching.

"Plannin' on it."

A smile as she readjusted her glasses, cleaned the smudged lenses. A happy one? Hopeful? Or just polite? Small talk—he could never tell.

"We could carpool, you know, if our schedules line up," she said.

"Okay. Cool," he said, and she left him at his door, her hips swaying.

If he didn't have a headache, he would've said something better. Smoother. That's all he had right now, though—*okay, cool.*

Zion had dragged him over to the Queen Nails a few months ago, flashing a roll of fives like he owned the place and insisted that Xavier got set up at Lan's station. "Look at how bad your cuticles are. You should come in more," she'd said, clipping away with a tiny pair of scissors.

"How often should I be doing that?" he'd asked, not sure if she did it on purpose—leaned in, pushing her tits together to make a perfect V, poking out the top of her T-shirt as she looked up at him.

"You should come in every week," she'd determined. And she *was* the authority on those things.

"So!" Zion'd said, loud enough for the girls to hear, already giggling. Xavier had known what was coming next, already mortified as Zion elbowed him, grinning. "You gon' hit that or what?"

INDIGENT

Shanice had hated her grandmother when she was younger. That mean-ass old woman who'd tugged on her nose every morning to stretch it out, make it less Black-looking. Though she'd never admit it, not if somebody tied her down and tortured her, she'd thought about killing Granny once.

Hair in ponytails and bobos, her bare feet covered in grass, tracking it inside where she'd found Granny asleep on the plastic-covered chaise lounge in the family room, a little metal fan going. Spinning and clicking. She could've put a pillow over the old woman's face and told everybody it was heat stroke. They already knew two old people who'd died from that over the summer.

Ungrateful, triflin' little girl.

"What's your Memaw like?" Xavier had asked her when he was little, strapped into his car seat in the back of her Corola while they drove back from visiting her parents for the first and last time.

Memaw. When'd her mama pick that name up? It'd sounded fake. But his cousins called her that, so Xavier did, too.

She'd looked in the rearview mirror. His eyes huge and probing. "She was a good cook," Shanice'd answered.

"Hmm. Okay." Deadly serious, his bottom lip jutting out. "I wish mine was."

And she hadn't been able to help but laugh.

It wasn't a lie. The family recipes were the one thing in Barnesville worth keeping. Black-eyed peas, sweet plantains, mac n' cheese, okra, catfish, chess pie. Sunday food from the potluck suppers after service, from weddings and funerals. Granny's wake had been delicious, if nothing else. If Xavier knew anything about that woman, it should be the food.

Shanice sweated through her lace front, trying to remember the best parts of it as she got Xavier's college dinner made. Not a regular meat-and-three. He deserved something *big*, something they only cooked when they celebrated life and death and God.

That was a nice thought two hours ago. But this pie was going to be the damn death of her.

If she had the recipes, it would have been easy. Her mother kept them all above the stove back home, a hundred warped, brown notecards in Granny's handwriting, filed away in the box with a white hen painted on top. *Rob did that painting.*

Wasted talent.

Shanice had thought about stealing the box when she'd left but decided it was better to leave that house and everything in it. Let it collapse into dust behind her for all she cared.

Pulling her first attempt at a pie out of the oven, she wished she would've been less proud and less dramatic. The pie's sugar filling was deflated to the bottom like caramel stained glass, and she tossed it, sweating. Good thing she'd picked up extra ingredients.

Xavier took another bite of chess pie. His fork sank into it, caramelized sugar crackling beautifully outward from the tines. The sweetness sat on his molars. Decadent.

With the dinner and the scholarship and Lan (maybe) wanting to see him more, Xavier's headache was letting up some, sinking into the haze of an oncoming food coma that would hopefully knock him out for good tonight. No insomnia, no weird-ass dreams.

He felt *rich*. Like he'd done something right.

"If I'm gon' fit in my uniform tomorrow, I better stop," Mom said, stretching. She readjusted her back brace before setting down her plate, her second piece of lemon meringue pie half-eaten.

"Yeah, everybody over here makin' fun of my job 'til you remember I'm the one who gets to go to work in sweats," Xavier said, patting his stomach. Bloated, but with just enough room for a bit more. A half-slice's worth of room. He reached over to get her plate—

And there was a knock on the door, Mom's smile shifting, lips pulled down over her teeth. It was probably one of their neighbors with an emergency—an exploded kitchen pipe, or a bat flying in through an open window like they sometimes did in the summer.

He'd have to dig his tennis racket out of the closet for that...

Mom went to answer it, and Xavier started to get up, searching for the notebook where he logged his overtime hours. But something kept him there, knees locked.

Don't move.

With her eye to the peephole, Mom went rigid. She spent a few seconds making herself presentable, pulling back her sweat-damp hair. *Don't move, don't make a sound.* She opened the door, the chain lock still secured, peering out.

Smart woman.

"Yes?"

"Hello, Ma'am. Are you Mrs. Coates?" A man's voice. Measured, tastefully white. It reminded him of Uncle Rob making calls to PCPs between clients. *Hello, this is Robert Coates calling from Serenity Home Health.* Light and inoffensive and fake.

"Ms. Coates, yes." Her voice matched his, not a trace of Barnesville, Georgia in it.

Xavier thought he'd be sick, catfish and collard greens and black-eyed peas and sweet tea and chess pie thrown up and out onto the floor. Wasted.

Don't move.

"Do you mind if I come in for a bit? We shouldn't get into the details out here, but I have a few questions for you and your son, if he's home."

Mom stood there, not looking back at him, not giving his presence away just yet. The man said something—lower and unintelligible—and she gave in, unlocking the door.

Xavier's legs jerked, the blood rushing back into his feet. *Run.* "Who is it, Mom?" he asked.

But he already knew. Michaels. *Doctor* Michaels from the lobby, passing by him like he was nothing, less than nothing. Finally done badgering Desai for a few hours and here to... to *what*?

Run—

Xavier stayed seated while Michaels introduced himself—"Dr. Brian Michaels from the health department, so nice to meet you both."—shaking his good hand. Mom fussed over him, offered a drink, a better chair, their IDs. *Anything you need.*

The doctor refused them all, sitting in the armchair across from the couch, Rob's old place. Nobody sat there. Mom settled on a getting him a slice of pie, putting it in front of him while Dr. Michaels dug through a file folder.

"Oh, thank you. Thank you," he said, not looking at it.

They watched Michaels silently as he took out a notebook and a pen, flipped to a blank page. "As for why I'm here..." he started, "The property manager, Mr. Desai, told me you're the one who called in the body of a young woman on the premises. Is that correct?"

Mom's nails dug into his shoulder, and Xavier shifted, hiding his injured hand.

"That was me, yeah."

Michaels perched the notebook on his knee, jotting something down. "Did you notice anything strange when you found her?"

Another squeeze. If Mom pressed any harder, her acrylics would snap right off. Go flying into Michaels's pie. "Well. She was dead."

"Besides that."

Xavier's jaw worked back and forth. "I don't know. She looked like she was on something. I just figured she ODed..."

"Happen a lot around here?" Michaels asked, not looking up. Still writing.

"It happens," Xavier answered. He thought his molars would crack. Michaels gave him another perfunctory nod.

"So... Xavier. Did you have any physical contact with the body when you found it?"

"Sir," Mom cut in. "Did he do something wrong?"

"Just covering all our bases." Finally looking up at them, searching the air, pen clicking. *Click, click.* "The Jane Doe your son found had an... infection we haven't really seen around here, so we want to stay on top of it."

Click. Click.

Run—

"You don't have to be alarmed. We just don't usually see it here," Dr. Michaels said with a shrug, a faux casualness that set Xavier's aching teeth on edge. "It *does* pop up sometimes in the…" He went back to studying the ceiling. "…the *urban* areas… *rural* areas. You know."

Xavier's mouth still tasted sweet. Sugar leaking down into the crevices. Into the cavities.

Do we live where poor people live?

"It gets in the water. Hell of a thing," Michaels said, taking an industrial paper-clipped stack of pamphlets from his briefcase and peeling one off the top. "It's just a good idea to keep an eye on it, ensure anyone who might've come in contact with it is doing fine?"

He gave Xavier a questioning look, expecting an answer. Smiling.

"I didn't touch anything. I feel okay," Xavier said. It sounded mechanical in his ears, an obvious lie, but the doctor didn't seem to mind.

"That's *great*! Really great. I have some pamphlets with all you need to know. And my card, just in case. If you need to call—I'm sure you're fine—but if you *do* call, we have a medical indigency plan if you're worried about financing any treatments…"

The papers were glossy, innocuous, like the pamphlets by the desk at urgent care. Like the poster of smiling cartoon intestines. *Eating well on a budget. Preventing diabetes at home.* Mom grabbed them first, reading the bold red font. "SO YOU'VE GOT A TAPE-WORM: Need-To-Know Taeniasis Facts."

Michaels gave them a sheepish smile, finally noticing the pie and taking an obligatory bite.

Better eat all of it, if you're gon' be here.

"Well. This is fantastic! You made this?" Michaels gushed, and Mom grinned at him, her eyes hard.

Michaels had woken up that morning in his Midtown Atlanta condo to a litany of emails from the IDPD, panicking about worms. *Worms*, for God's sake.

It was the South—every other redneck walking around the Wal-Mart probably had worms. Dealing with it was pennies out of the budget. You didn't even need a de-wormer prescription for *dogs*. For some reason, though, this was urgent, so he took the company car out to Leigh Pierce Estates with a stack of educational pamphlets, ready to get it over with.

The property manager was a high-strung young man named Arjun Desai who told him in fast, jerky bursts about the meth head who'd wandered onto the property—"very weird, never happens, this is, like, the first time"—before keeling over.

The maintenance worker, Mr. Coates, was young enough to still be on his mother's insurance, and he'd been even cagier. At least the property manager had given him some useful information. *Should've come in scrubs, suits always make people clam up.* The kid was closed off—"flat affect," he'd written in his notes—and was clearly lying about not touching the body. Probably went through the pockets before calling 911, took something, maybe. That would explain the nerves.

As though Michaels cared about petty theft. The same handful of twenties had probably been circulating between the tenants here for the past decade. Hardly even theft at that point.

God, these people hate me. Why'd they send me out here?

"We just really need someone with a higher clearance to get this done, someone who knows what they're doing,[1]" Madison had explained over the phone that morning. His boss' boss. No arguing.

"Just make first contact, do a write-up on the environment. Get a blueprint, saves us some trouble later. I'll send you the Cliff Notes, and Carter's set to meet up with you tomorrow to go over the actual details. Now, I'm just trying to keep this off the news. Fucking vultures, but if it bleeds, it leads, you know?"

"Okay... Anything else?" he'd asked.

"Wash your hands." A wink in her voice, and she'd hung up.

Nobody ever told him anything.

LEIGH PIERCE ESTATES — CASE OPEN

Subjective:
Location report—Four floors, one basement, one accessible rooftop. Three entrance points, handicap accessible with assistance only; two steps required to enter building, no ramps. One elevator and one set of interior emergency stairs. Railings on the exterior basement staircase only.

---

[1] Michaels, B. (2010, November 25–28). *A predictive model for micro-urbanization as a risk factor for communicable disease"* [Conference presentation abstract]. Twenty-eighth annual convention of Allied Epidemiology Institute, Pasadena, CA, United States.

INDIGENT

Case History—Subject expired on property, near secondary entrance. No health reports re: parasitic infection. Medical history could not be assessed.

Objective:
Spoke with property manager (AD) regarding property documentation, tenant count and histories, and circumstances of Subject death. Spoke with witness (XC) regarding circumstances of Subject death.

Assessment:
Recommendations include safety and hygiene precautions (pairs or group; environmental hazard protections, unsanitary environment)

Plan:
- Establish low-level surveillance of property by 7/21
- Maintain contact with AD
- Autopsy documentation review[2]

Anthony was late. Again.

In the middle of dinner rush, the new kid had ripped off her drive-thru headset and gone to the walk-in freezer "for a new bag of fries"—spent thirty minutes sitting there, thawing out a box of burger patties under her ass, pulling her hair out. She had a bald patch behind her ear by the time the manager dragged her out.

It's too much stress.

---

[2] Coroner, G. S. (2011). Inquest into the death of Unidentified Female (File no. S89097/2011n96a). Court of Atlanta, Georgia.

She was lucky he wasn't the manager. He would've fired her ass the second she disappeared in the middle of a fifteen-car backup and a full dining room. Actually, he never would've hired her at all. Flowers tattooed on the inside of both her wrists—the kind of cheap work people got to cover up something that would make them look worse. *Wonder what that's from?* Of course she'd flake out at the worst time.

Nearly two hours over tonight.

He didn't even remember driving home. Just *blink*—and there he was, pulling in close to the Dumpster so he could throw out the greasy clamshell boxes piled up on his floorboards.

The radio was flipped to 94.5, 4 a.m. silence filled with the droning rap and 808s that everybody and their mom was making now. His little cousin, too, so he couldn't say nothing. Maybe he'd catch their song eventually.

Another *blink*, and he was out of the car, taking the two steps to the Dumpster and tossing his trash. Another *blink*, another step. His eyes were burning.

He wiped them with the hem of his shirt, knew from experience that using his hands would do nothing but move around the grease that had settled into the whorls on his fingers and the lines of his face. Caked in. In the summertime, he thought it would cook him alive. He could lay out on the sidewalk at noon and start sizzling if he wanted to.

Fuck, he needed a shower—

"Excuse me?"

Blink.

A woman was standing next to his car, hand on the hood. An older white lady in a Denny's uniform, bad wig and drawn-on eyebrows. *Why they always do that? If you don't have eyebrows, you don't have eyebrows. Nobody cares.*

"Hi, I'm sorry... D'you have any jumper cables?" she asked.

Her voice reminded him of something, a connection sparking up in his sleep-deprived brain that he couldn't pin down. It took him a second to register what she'd said.

Another *blink*.

"My car won't start. I think the battery's dead," she added. "I'm s'posed to be at work in twenty minutes, and my car won't start."

Work. Another spark. That was part of where he recognized her. Something about *work*.

"I probably got some," he heard himself say. *Dammit.* Why couldn't he just let himself go to bed? *Yeah I'll pick up her shift no problem, yeah I got jumper cables.* He knew better than to mess with old white ladies anyway. They were always the ones who'd smile then call the manager from their car two seconds later, trying to get him fired for forgetting a straw.

"Thank you! Thank you so much!" She smiled. Her voice was warbly, like a bird.

Like *Snow White*. That was it—sitting in front of the TV as a kid, sorting through VHS tapes. *These new shows rot your brain.* Snow White with that high-pitched cartoon voice. Going to *work*. This lady even kinda looked like Snow White... if things hadn't worked out, and she was still working at a Denny's at sixty-five.

"No problem."

He closed the Dumpster, something scurrying inside and settling back down.

"Thank you, my car's just over here."

Anthony took a step, something hot on his neck. Dribbling down.

Blink.

He fell to his hands and knees, heaved up the fries and soda he'd been running on for the last five hours. Burning up and out of his throat. The vision in one of his eyes was blurry.

Blink.

Still blurry. Worse than before. Something cracked, and his arms gave out—

Anthony saw something underneath the Dumpster while he lay there, face pressed against concrete and puke, unable to move. Couldn't remember how. The smell down here was sour. Rancid.

What was looking at him...?

A raccoon or a cat. Something big and feral. Two bright silver-dollar eyes. Glowing. Watching him from its hiding spot, safe and snuffling.

Blink.

"You didn't tell me he had a gun."

Leena saw it as they carried the boy down the basement stairs, the pistol's handle tucked into his waistband. A lot of good it did him. But *still*. It could've gone very bad with one of those things involved.

"*Mom.*" Like she was crazy for even pointing it out. "Who's gonna pull a gun on you?"

Well. Not this boy.

Had anyone? Thirty years of this and how often had it happened...? Once? Twice, maybe, if she counted a toy pistol with little aluminum BBs? Never serious. Men never thought about those kinds of things. They all figured they'd be the next Clint Eastwood, knowing exactly when to quick-draw and shoot.

Save the day.

That was her blessing with this face, this body. A body no one ever looked twice at. Camille, pouting— "Why can't I actually help?" Always wanting to do a man's job even though she was built to be a distraction. *Such a pretty face—*

Leena dropped the legs, the boy's shoes banging against the stairs.

"You okay?"

"I'm fine, I'm fine. Just wait a second..."

She peeled off her cardigan, the fabric clingy and damp with sweat, covering her hands with it as she pulled out the gun. She held it away from her body, between two fingers—d*angerous thing, dirty thing*—lifted the Dumpster lid, and tossed it in.

It reminded her too much of Cy, him opening up his daddy's old break-barrel shotgun. "Where're the shells, hon?" They'd been in her purse, where they had been for weeks. It was her job to stop him from doing anything stupid. Always had been.

"You know I don't like guns in the house," she said briskly, taking up the legs again. And they moved down the stairs.

Through the door.

Across the hallway...

She counted on it being late enough for them to be alone, not as observant as she should be, admittedly. That last meal hadn't held up as long as she'd hoped. Might as well have been junk food with how much they'd had to cook it down.

Had she even called Cy to get the kitchen set up? The bed...? Didn't remember. Too late now.

Adrenaline pushed them on, making the two-hundred odd pounds balanced between them seem light. But not just adrenaline—a promise of full stomachs, the buzzing anticipation of a hunger soon to be sated, *really* sated for the first time in more than a month.

This was a good one. She knew it.

They knew it, already twisting out from under her pretty pink fingernails. Fanning across the dark, ashen skin over the anklebone. Burrowing in, morphing and kaleidoscopic, the transparent lines of **their** bodies shot through with the brightest, most brilliant red as **they** ate and ate with a suffusing warmth in her own gut.

It made her stumble, lightheaded.

But they kept going, finally back to apartment B4, to the tarp laid out on the kitchen floor, flat and clean and ready. Cy had done his job, thank God.

They arranged the body on the plastic, arms and legs out, a thin slice of white skull poking out from the gash in the sheered-down curls. Winking at her like a sliver of moon in the dark, dark sky. Clean.

What should she say? Something quick. Something she'd known since childhood.

"God is great. God is good," she breathed as she dragged the edge of her fabric scissors along the seams of his shirt, the cloth parting easily, as easy as paper. Cheap clothes. Always so cheap. The fabric was ripped away from underneath her hands before she could even think, showing the bare skin.

"Let us thank Him for our food." Hardly able to get the words out, throat constricting.

"By His hands we are... we are..."

Cy took the first bite, teeth rending the muscle of the upper arm, coming away with a chunk of meat. Red and luxurious. *Like red wine.* Her voice caught. *Like strawberries and fresh cherries.* He wasn't done chewing before bearing down on the arm again. Rip. Down to the white of the bone.

Her eyes darted. Rolling. To Ari's hands—black and red, pulling away something from the insides. Bright and smooth and shining. *Like a tomato, perfectly, perfectly ripe, the seeds waiting jewel-like and pale in its center—*

All fat is the Lord's.

And Leena fell on the body, skin splitting wonderfully under her teeth.

One life. *Humming.* Glutted.

One life, spread between three bodies. Three mouths tearing and chewing. The earliest imperatives, superseding all others: find shelter, find food. Three homes, warm and strong and *wanting*.

Three homes eating.

One life broiling in acidic stomachs, knotted together, climbing up and up through the esophagus, that expanding and contracting tube, that all-loving provider, up into the mouth.

Three stomachs packed with nourishment, a great white line splitting open along the seams, over-full. Waiting for those strands to start twining, interweaving. Repairing. Stronger than before. A lacework of scared flesh and **them**. Indistinguishable. Allowing for a full house. Allowing the bodies to eat. And eat—

And eat.

What else was a body for?

Eat. **They** twisted in deeper. *Eat*. Still so simple. An impulse. Repeated again and again.

Eat—

Xavier woke up with another headache. *A tension headache*, wrapped around his skull like a snake squeezing the life out of some unlucky rat. *The brain doesn't feel anything. It's all in your head.*

He ripped off his do-rag, but the pressure stayed put. Twinging. He lay there with his eyes closed, massaging the temporalis muscle, up from the corner of his jaw, around to the mastoid process protruding out behind the curve of his ear. It didn't help, the pressure building. *Pop.* The Eustachian tube between his ear and his nose flexed, contracted—forcing out pockets of air. *Pop pop pop.*

Eat something.

That was an idea. The temporalis muscle: attachment points at the temporal fossa and temporal lines of the skull, all the way down to the coronoid process of the jaw. Main function: mastication. *Chewing.*

If he wanted to work out the tension, he had to chew, which meant he had to eat. Simple as that. Then, he'd drown any pain left in Tylenol and hope the headache died down by the morning. Desai would have something to say about him slacking off all day, about the jobs piling up...

He staggered out to the kitchen, careful not to wake up Mom. She snored on the futon in the living room, nothing but her hair bonnet and the curves of her legs visible. Not a sound as he opened the fridge—icy blue-white light and leftovers from his celebration dinner—and picked something at random.

Eat.

Xavier stood there in the refrigerator light, working through the leftover plantains one by one. His teeth cracked through the pan-seared shell. Cold, jelly-like grease coated the inside of his mouth.

As he chewed, his jaw loosened, the pressure leaving his temples like a valve turning slowly down to zero. *One less thing to deal with.* He put the container back on the shelf... then grabbed it again. Rude to leave just a few pieces. Shutting the fridge, he sighed with an exhausted relief and took the midnight snack back to his room.

Eat first.

Then, come find us.

Make peace.

Break bread.

Just a part of a part of

A part of a part of a part of

a part of a part—

You must be lonely.

PART TWO

GORDACIA VALENTULUS

"Hunger has always been more or less at my elbow when I played, but now I began to wake up at night to find hunger standing at my bedside, staring at me gauntly."

Richard Wright

"So ya got money fo' duh bus, o' ya need me duh drop ya off at a sheltuh?"

It was the first thing the state trooper had said since picking her up. He'd flashed those panic-inducing lights at her about three hours after she'd ditched Derrick-or-Darren at the Peach Pit Motel, the sun just starting to crest over the trees.

Her feet had been aching, something sloshing around her shoes, between her skin and socks. Blister water. Blood? She hadn't looked.

Loose thy shoe from off thy foot; for the place whereon thou standest is holy.

"Get in!" he'd said from the window, pulling over to the shoulder. His nose was bandaged, lips swollen. He sounded like he was

120

speaking through a mouthful of tar. Maybe he'd been in an accident. Maybe someone'd beat his face in. Did he deserve it?

Was he asking for it?

"Get ya where ya need ta be."

Probably. That's how things worked—equal and opposite reactions. Consequences.

At least he wasn't like the ticket girl—pitying, in the mood for some self-serving act of charity. If anything, he'd picked her up to put the world right. *Get ya where ya need ta be.* Someone like her didn't belong on a backroad out in the sticks. Too weird. Unseemly. It made him ask questions.

She belonged under an overpass. On a street corner, forcing eye contact with drivers as they stopped at the intersection, her skeletal hand jerking off an imaginary cock, seeing if they were interested in the real thing. The real thing for cheap. He'd drop her off there, a place where he could see her and have no questions at all, no impetus to do anything about it. Then he'd leave, equilibrium re-established. Amen.

Camille looked out the window.

It was amazing how much she could think about when she wasn't hungry. She listened to the scratch of the tires on the road. The static of the police radio. The endless wet gurgling of the trooper pushing air in and out of his busted face.

I've been here before...

And she had—in the back of a cop car. She was little, nine or ten, at most. Her mom—the woman who had *been* her mother at the time—had caught her shoplifting at the K-Mart, and a bored deputy had shown up at their trailer during dinner to teach her a lesson, putting Camille in handcuffs and marching her out to the back of his car to sit her down and talk about the slippery slope of shoplifting, then drugs, then prostitution, then prison. All before she was old enough to drive. Mortifying. Thanks to that gross root beer lip gloss she'd palmed from an endcap while her mom was grabbing a slushie at the K-Café.

The second time she'd been caught, her mom skipped the cops and went straight for a belt. Camille remembered *that*. But it was so hard to bring up her face—the woman who had been her mother. What Camille recalled most were the hands, those stubby fingers and the butterfly tattoo on the wrist, blurry with age. She would look back over her shoulder, bent at the waist, staring at the butterfly of her mother's raised hand, wings flexing, about to take off from the skin. Bringing down a belt or an open palm.

Camille hadn't thought about that in a while, but there wasn't much else to do, sitting in the back of a cop car for the second time. Images rose in her mind of that first woman glimpsed through a crisscrossing metal partition and pollen-spotted windshield, standing there with hands on her hips, face an indistinct smear.

What was clear: She had a mother who was blonde. She had a mother who walked barefoot on gravel, no problem. She had a mother who took life out on her.

Where is she now?

Soon enough, the Atlanta skyline appeared, long shadows spilling over into the middle distance. The police cruiser merged onto the highway, joined the sea of cars. A stampede of snorting, honking animals all around her, behind smoke and glass and metal.

The trooper tapped on the partition with his knuckles, pointing at the city through the windshield and smiling like he'd made the whole damn thing.

"Home sweet home, yea?" he said, and she nodded, the sun in her eyes, already sweating.

She'd told him that she was from Atlanta, that she was trying to get home. "How ol' are ya, sweetheart?" he'd asked, garbled, chewing on the words. Grinding them down.

A twinge. *Sweetheart.* Mom's name for all the interchangeable pets who shared a place at the table, a place on the floor next to the bed where Mom and Dad slept.

"I'm twenty-four," she'd answered, really feeling the blisters. She had to keep moving.

Sweetheart.

Did his use of that word mean anything at all, or was it just this place? Just the South? She should've been used to it. She was from here, apparently. An old student ID—Double Glade Middle School in Alabama—a towheaded girl with heat-straightened hair, acne and freckles covered in spotty foundation.

Ari had shown her Mom's album one night, sneaking it out with Camille gripping his arm, leaving bruises. They both liked pictures, him and Mom. That's why she'd let him know about it in the first place. She'd *trusted* him.

There was something wrong about it, a violation that had made her want to curl up and die.

I have trusted in Your steadfast love; my heart shall rejoice—

"You don't remember your *name*, Cam," he'd said, and then he'd pried into Mom's life.

It was Emily. All that trouble just to figure out three syllables. Was that really *her* in the picture, though? The chubby cheeks? The ghost of a double chin? Had she ever had that much meat on her bones?

She didn't feel like an Emily, but there was something familiar about it—the subconscious shapes of letters long-memorized jotted down onto a piece of paper or a faraway voice hitting the right sounds for her to turn her head, like a friend calling out in a crowd.

You don't remember your name. She could recall the lip gloss. The butterfly tattoo. But all the bigger things—her name, the first woman's face—were gone.

What *did* she remember, then?

A ceiling with glow-in-the-dark stars clinging to it. Being embarrassed about that. Too kiddish. She remembered feeling mature. She remembered feeling solid ground underfoot, sharp-edged stones poking out of mud, gravel shifting under her weight. A confirmation that she was substantial, that the matter and mass of her body could displace the world around her, affect it somehow. Very definitely *real,* that girl. *Emily.*

She glanced at the GPS on the dashboard. Ten more minutes to Atlanta.

CHAPTER FIVE
VOYEURS

Michaels hadn't seen Greg Carter for a few years, not since Stockholm.[3] Climate health equity and spatiotemporal data analysis in the morning, Gamla Stan tours in the afternoon, and pub crawls once it got dark. Getting more confident in their broken Swedish with every pint of draft beer. *Skål!* they'd yell before clinking their glasses together.

Skål!, clink, chug. Over and over until the night turned into a black pit in their memory.

Things hadn't changed much. They met at West Lake Golf Course the next morning, Carter getting them in two hours before

____

[3] Michaels, B. & Carter, G. (2009, July 8–12). *A proposed policy agenda for prevention of airborne communicable disease across vulnerable age demographics in dense-population urban environments.* [Conference presentation and panel]. International Association of Public Health Officials, Stockholm, Sweden.

opening so they could have some privacy before the place became overrun with "yuppies and Republicans."

They got a very nice caddy who—Carter insisted—spoke just enough English to do the job and nothing more, then went to the green where Carter nursed a Bloody Mary and debriefed Michaels on *Gordacia valentulus*.

"A pretty antiquated name, isn't it? Why not *nematoda*?" Michaels asked.

Madison had sent him pictures. A vivisected worm in a petri dish, no thicker than a piece of angel hair pasta even with its skin splayed out and pinned back. Very much just a roundworm—unremarkable.

"It's an antiquated worm," Carter said, shrugging.

Michaels had worked overseas for a time dealing with an outbreak of Guinea worm. He'd monitored the dried-out parasitic husks protruding from dark ribcages and ankles, wrapped tightly around a piece of gauze, pulled a few centimeters out every day until it was finally removed.

He'd diagnosed it the handful of times it had appeared in the States as well, tweezing it from the skin of mortified backpackers newly returned from their spiritual journey abroad, ready to jump back into investment banking. *Gordacia valentulus,* though, was different.

"You know what 'valentulus' means? *Strong*," Carter explained. "Like roaches. Last outbreak was going on thirty fucking years ago—did everything shy of nuking the place, and some *still* got out.[4] And we're *still* dealing with them. Fucking bugs."

---

[4] *See*: Beryl Ridge, Missouri, Butler County Sheriff's Office case reports #0478-0542.

Michaels frowned. *Fucking bugs.* There had to be a more professional way to phrase that. But he'd given up a long time ago on changing Carter's language, that fundamental lack of decorum Carter wielded like a shotgun in every conference room he stepped foot in. It wasn't a realistic goal.

"Fucking hell," Carter spat, slicing his ball into the rough, and the caddy went to grab it without a word, wading into the grass.

Are there mites?

Parasites on the brain?

"For your situation, they're like roaches in another way. You see *one*, you know there's bound to be more somewhere else. Close."

"What're you thinking, a five-mile radius? More than that?" Michaels asked.

"I'd stick to five for now."

Michaels nodded and took his shot, landing it cleanly with a proud *whoop*. He still had it.

"Only getting better with age, huh? I was hoping it'd be the opposite," Carter said, swilling his drink as they climbed back into the golfcart, teeth tinged a watery red. "You ever seen *Texas Chainsaw*? That part where he picks the girl up and hangs her on a hook?"

"What's that have to do with anything?"

Carter gave him a shit-eating grin and spent the next thirty minutes regaling him about the time he'd come across *Gordacia valentulus* in a cheap bungalow out in Cheyenne. The uninfected homeowner had been found in the bathroom, hanging from the showerhead, blood draining from cut arteries into a plastic bucket and the organs emptied out and piled in the bathroom sink.

"Gutted like a pig," Carter said, shaking his fist for a touch more drama. For the *pathos*. Michaels fought back an eye roll.

The first infectee had blown her head off—"Worms moving in the brains splattered on the wall, even!"—and the second had tried to make a run for it, powering through a taser and a few rubber bullets before getting apprehended, kicking and screaming. They'd interviewed that one out of an isolated quarantine zone back in Carter's home state.

"I'll send you over the audio, if you want. Pumped him full of enough lithium to kill a horse and still nuttier than a sack of squirrel shit, swear to God. It goes after the brain first, we think, fucks them up *but good*," Carter said, chuckling at Michaels's reaction, leaning against his 9-iron with a thoughtful look. "Spooky, ain't it?"

Ari woke up first, his head resting on Leena's stomach and Cyril's arm draped across his back, arms and legs tangled. Overlapping.

He peeled Leena's shirt off the side of his face, the fabric tacky with not-quite-dried blood, then slid off the tarp that Cyril had thankfully remembered to put down on the bed yesterday.

The world slowly shrank as he freed skin from skin and dropped to the floor, his back against the bedframe. Coming back to himself, remembering what parts were *him* and what parts belonged to someone else. He held his breath and listened for the sound of Leena's breathing, waiting until they were off—out of sync—before he breathed out again.

My legs. *Wǒ de tuǐ.* My arms. *Wǒ de gēbó.* My eyes. *Wǒ de yǎnjīng.* Mine.

Leena's hand flopped down next to his face, red-caked nails reaching out, resting on his head, her fingers in his hair. Crunching. Dark red flakes peppered the carpet.

"Good morning," he managed, finding the muscles to speak, but she didn't answer, just kept snoring.

He got up. *This is the day the Lord made, try to do something with it,* Leena would say, sing-song, smiling.

His phone read 1 p.m. Monday. Eight hours—not too bad. They could pass out for a whole day after eating that much. But this wasn't a good place. **They** knew that. What would happen if someone found them? He imagined an alien hand groping him while he slept, his unconscious body reacting to their touch—drawing in on itself... popping like a tick—

My lungs. *Wǒ de fèi.* My heart. *Wǒ de xīnzàng.* My brain. *Wǒ de dànǎo...*

Time to check the apartment.

The damage wasn't too bad. Leena had tracked blood into the hallway before remembering to take off her shoes, the ratty white sneakers left by the bedroom door, soles stained red. Besides that, they'd managed to keep blood off the carpet.

He couldn't say the same for the kitchen floor. A watery-red puddle had formed under the fridge like leaking anti-freeze, everything else thrown in a plastic storage tote with a few bags of ice, taped closed. Even with the AC going on high all morning and an automatic air freshener spritzing lavender and honeysuckle every few minutes, the air smelled sour.

Unappealing. That was good. It meant he was full.

Full. Finally.

Had they shown up? That ghost from 305 made tangible just on time for a meal. But Ari would remember that, wouldn't he? The ghost was either eating alone or not eating at all, and Ari wasn't sure which one was worse.

He climbed in the shower, standing underneath a burning stream of water. What would he say when he found them? The one he'd seen through the blinds, the one who'd had to eat alone. Whoever they were.

Is it her? He wouldn't get his hopes up. *But who else could it be?*

Who else...? Nial? A few years older than him, the son of Cyril and Leena's old friend. He'd shown up a few years ago, all grown up and explaining in a Missouri drawl what he was doing in town. He'd talked with his hands. And there'd been Nial's partner, nervous, muttering a "Thank you" to Leena as she set down his plate.

Then, a few months later, Nial again, stubbly and balled up on a moldy Rust Belt sofa. Just Ari and Nial and some guy who they'd picked up outside a bar. "Got kicked out of the house," he'd said, looking for sympathy. "Just lookin' for a couch to surf on, ya know?" They'd offered their sympathies and their couch. He'd been a nice voice behind the bathroom door, singing over the running water.

"This always happens." Nial had looked up at Ari like it was his fault. "They always leave." And he'd lurched forward, kissing Ari on

the mouth, which he hadn't refused but hadn't reciprocated either. Impossible to hide.

"I thought you were 'taking a break'?" Nial had sighed, sinking back against the couch, too drunk for embarrassment. "That's not why you called?"

Like it hadn't been obvious. After leaving, who else did Ari have besides Nial—an acquaintance, some friend of a friend who he'd had dinner with once?

But that was important. Sharing food. It was all they had.

Nial had held Ari's face in his hands, thumb over his mouth, not letting him pull away. It'd been unsettling back then, a violation of privacy. Of space. "That's cute," Nial'd said, finally, before leaving Ari on the couch—head buried, hands over his ears—trying not to hear the singing man get his head caved in. Shower still running...

Washing away the blood, just like now...

So there was Nial, the only option with a name and a face. He stuck to familiar places, though, and Atlanta wasn't one of them. Probably not one of Nial's friends either. When they burned out, they did it *entirely*. No exceptions. There was no one else, not that Ari knew of, anyway.

It was someone *new*, then. Or Cam.

If it was Cam, what would he say? *I love you.* He watched dried specks of blood get pulled down the drain. Swallowed up. *I love you more than anything.* The water turned red, then pink. *Are you mad at me?* It finally ran clear, and he stepped out of the shower to dry off, wiping steam from the mirror.

If it wasn't her—*please let it be her*—he had no idea what he'd say. It'd been so long since he'd had anyone new to talk to. Really talk. But if they were in the same boat as him, hypothetically, things would fall right into place, like Nial picking him up from the bus station in Cleveland, hugging him at the terminal like they'd known each other for their entire lives. No questions.

Like the song, plucky guitar strings and metronomic clapping. *They were gonna be friends.*

Ari decided to hold off on the Valium, wanting to be as clear-headed as possible. He put the pills in his pocket with a touch of pride, a sweet sense of self-control. Cyril was up and getting ready for the day. Cooking it sounded like, an amazing bit of normality. Maybe Cyril was fine after all. *Just needs better supports at home.* He just needed time.

Ari left the bathroom, still humming.

Xavier called out sick that morning, hanging up before Desai could make any ultimatums. *Taking advantage of you.* When was the last time he'd asked for a sick day? Three years ago? Bronchitis. Lugging around a gallon of sweet tea and TheraFlu until he'd hacked up a painful glob of lung phlegm and blood and Mom had forced him to stay home. One day for antibiotics, then back to work.

To the bone, into the grave.

He'd felt like garbage ever since Michaels had shown up. That health department badge clipped to his suit collar. That man sitting uninvited in his house. *His house.* Not even a year ago, people had to twist the state's arm close to breaking before they did anything about their tap water running gray—in their *houses* with kids and old people and pets all having to drink it, bathe in it—but he was supposed to believe that good doctor Brian Michaels had anything helpful to say? Any skin in the game at all?

Coming into *his* house—

Xavier could take a day off. He'd accrued at least a few.

Step Three—Accruing value is all about patience. Do right by your responsibilities, always look for more. Responsibilities, and the respect you get from them, appreciate over time.

The morning wasn't going well, him hunched over the sink, waiting for his stomach to empty itself out. Food poisoning. Bad leftovers. Or maybe just too much of a good thing.

"Got the bloat," Uncle Rob had said once, standing by his cousin's bovine pen in Barnesville, the toe of his work boot touching a dead cow on the other side of the fence, its stomach grotesquely huge. "Can't even watch a cow. That's how you know your cousin ain't shit. He don't *listen* like you do."

I listen. I'm trying to.

Bloat. Or food poisoning. Or worms.

That pamphlet about tapeworms was still tucked underneath Lando's stupid grinning face. Xavier read it over three times and put it back exactly as he'd found it. Some of the symptoms lined up, but it couldn't be right.

Urgent care had left a voicemail saying his labs came back normal. No AIDS, no hepatitis. Worms would mean antibodies. Antibodies would mean a warning in bold red font, him getting called in to be poked and prodded at again for twenty-five more dollars.

No worms, then. He'd even checked his stool. *Sounds better than 'dug through shit.'* Nothing. Food poisoning, then, and Mom didn't need to know that after spending a good five hours in the kitchen cooking. For *him*. Her cooking couldn't make him sick.

But maybe it had, gut sounds bubbling in his inner ear, the vessels branching bone-dry around his skull... Without that excuse, though, he didn't have any reason not to go to Miami if he was shirking work, so he had to be at work. He held his head under the bathroom sink, drinking straight from the tap until he felt a little less dehydrated, then put on his sweats and headed out.

The stairwell was empty, the lights droning like a wasp by his ear. Footsteps compounding, telling people he was there. Xavier put in his earbuds to drown it out and hurried to the lobby.

There was Desai's face peeking through the rent office window.... And there was his hand, grabbing Xavier's arm—

"Dude, wait! I need you to keep quiet about the basement apartment. The landlord's gonna be on my ass about it—"

"Cool. You haven't paid me for that yet," Xavier interrupted, not in the mood. *Zion hasn't called me back. No one's called me back.* He turned away, but Desai followed him.

"What? You'll get paid as soon as I get everything sold. That was the agreement."

No, it wasn't.

What was Desai—five-ten, maybe? Xavier had an easy four inches on him. He'd only ever been in one fight—middle school, Marius Kilcrease, who'd picked on him every day until Xavier had finally worked up the nerve to hit him in the head with the hardcovered edge of an algebra book, striking gold. Marius, blood running down his face, then proceeded to beat the shit out of him. He'd lost that fight.

He wouldn't lose this one, though.

"You snitched on me," Xavier said, shoving Desai against the wall, his empty, pretentious head bouncing off the cinderblocks. "You snitched on me. Then some guy shows up to *my* house, flashing a badge and giving my mom a fuckin' heart attack. Fuck off!"

And he was gone. In the lobby one second, sitting in his car the next, stuck between horror and elation. *I just shoved my boss into a wall.*

A memory of Zion sighing as Desai finally fucked off with a dimebag of weed after thirty minutes of useless bargaining. Of Xavier laughing, hiccupping. Giggly, like a kid who tried smoking for the first time—a lightweight. He probably should've been embarrassed, but he hadn't been with Zion sitting beside him, their knees touching...

"Man, just tell me the next dumbass thing he says on the clock, and I'll punch him for you," Zion had laughed.

I did it for you. I did it.

Xavier started the car. It wasn't a punch, but close enough. Close enough for that fluttering panic to work away inside his chest. There hadn't been any blood, nothing to complain about.

Somebody was gon' tell him off eventually. Why not me?

He pulled onto the road. Then—

I'm gettin' fired. Fuck.

When he was younger, Xavier had tried to copy Uncle Rob's way of saying things, trying to reverse engineer whatever about his uncle that put people at ease. Xavier had never been any good at it. Jokes never hitting right, the same old white ladies who lined up to dance with Rob at the nursing home Christmas parties, shimmying their arthritic hips at him, looking at Xavier like they'd found a still-alive spider crunched under their house slipper.

"It just ain't where your strengths are. There's more to the job than that," Rob had said, sipping a beer in his Chevy on the way back to the Estates. Rob had taught Xavier how to drive in that truck. Then, he'd drunk too much and wrapped it around a light pole off I-75, miraculously unscathed.

The universe itself loved Rob—until it didn't.

But Rob had been good at this, unlike Xavier, who was always *almost* saying the right thing, *almost* understanding what people meant, being *almost* convincing. Unsure how to bridge the gap to the other side of finally having this shit figured out—where everyone else seemed to be. If not everyone, at least the white girls from GSU and Georgia Tech asking for observation hours. Pushing in, sitting between them in the Chevy. Automatically likeable, automatically confident.

It used to be worse. Xavier used to feel it with his whole body, make himself sick over the stupidest things. Memaw called them conniption fits. Rob called them panic attacks. Mom tried not to call them anything. *You just get so up in your own head sometimes, that's all.*

Uncle Rob's old textbooks helped, taught him that the body was just a machine with parts that could be isolated and worked on.

136

Hands clenching? That wasn't him; it was the lumbricalis muscles acting up, like a mysterious *clack* coming from a car engine.

Know the engine inside out, find which part was acting up, fix it, go on driving. Easy.

That feeling was back in full force today—the conniption, the panic attack, the nothing-at-all—him trying to relax his diaphragm and external intercostals in the middle of the Atlanta Community College Student Store.

Sticker shock. Textbooks, it turned out, were just as expensive now as they'd been a few years ago.

Xavier held a copy of *Clinical Anatomy Fundamentals* in his hands—two-hundred and three dollars and five cents, not including tax—paging through it with a desperate energy, looking for anything in it that he couldn't get from his phone in a pinch.

And you lost your job. How're you gon' pay for that when you lost your job, and someone's looking at you?

He closed the book, sliding it back in place on the Biological Sciences shelf, running his hand down the titles. Their *spines*, vertebrae made of stacking letters. *C1- C2- C3- C4...*

It calmed him down some, helped him refocus.

Someone's looking at you. Someone? Maybe Marius—*Really on your mind today, isn't he?*—Marius walking down the aisle with the rest of the basketball team to see Xavier having an episode. *Retard.* More fuel for the fire. Maybe the staff thought he was going to steal something. Keeping an eye on him just in case. Can't be too careful with *those* kinda people—

"Hey!"

Lan, familiar and nice. Lan, who never accused him of stealing even when he was in her bedroom, wrapping electrical tape around a burnt-out wire in her ceiling fan, her doing dishes out in the kitchen. Not watching him. Deliberately *not*. Lan in a faded T-shirt, hair down to her shoulders, walking toward him. "I didn't know you were off today."

"I'm sick. Don't tell my boss."

They walked together, close enough for him to see the single strand of hair caught in the hinge of her glasses. She talked about accounting, about her cousin being pregnant and that being a real problem, about how their neighbor Tony had been a no-show today for the first time in two semesters. And Xavier nodded and focused on not vomiting on his own shoes. When they got outside, he went to the trashcan—*Zion's drop-off spot*—and puked.

"Oh, you weren't kidding," Lan said, rubbing his back. "Don't breathe on me. If one person at the salon gets sick, we all do."

It was 3 p.m. by the time Leena got going for the day, yawning her way to the kitchen, where Billy Joel was crooning out of their portable radio (one of the best Goodwill finds they'd ever made). His voice crackled through the speakers, singing at her from the bottom of a bad lung.

She'd begged her mother to drive her out to St. Louis to see him, sweet with nostalgia, but didn't wind up convincing her. Her parents would never say yes to something like that.

A while later, she and a friend had taken her father's car all the way out to Chicago to see the Bay City Rollers. She hadn't asked—about the concert or the car. More exciting that way.

She'd wanted to do something *exciting*.

She'd got her lip split open and her bedroom door taken off its hinges over that. *You want privacy, you prove you can be trusted with privacy.* No tears. She'd anticipated it, driving with one arm hanging out the window on their way back to the Ozarks, "Bye Bye Baby" still ringing in her ears. Three encores. Wind pushing against her smooth, smooth skin. Things had been the same even back then. Better to live in the present.

The present...

Where the fibers under her feet sizzled with store-bought carpet cleaner and Cy—she wanted to cry just seeing it—was standing at the kitchen sink, humming along to "Uptown Girl."

She prolonged the moment, going to flip on the oven light. Marrow was bubbling in the center of split bones, finger-thin dishes of crème brulé. Cooking down low and slow.

"Mornin', Sleeping Beauty," Cy said, turning from the sink to give her a peck on the cheek. "Feeling productive today," he added, grinning.

He went back to work, running cold water through the intestines, fingers massaging the slick silver skin on their surface, coaxing out the bile. "I found a fish recipe behind the fridge while I was cleanin' up. It uses lard instead of eggs for the breading," he said. Small talk? Honest to God small talk.

"We should try it," she said, giddy.

"Camille would've liked this one. Give her an excuse to go fishing. Remember her out in Michigan—or was it Wisconsin? She'd be out in the water all day if we let her." A smile in his voice.

"Hm," Leena said, short, the name too much right now. "Never could stay clean, could she?"

Cyril didn't answer, just went back to the stove. She wanted to put her arms around him, rest her head between his shoulders while he cooked, like she used to do. But something about this seemed tenuous. A bubble. If she touched it, even for a moment, the entire world would shiver and pop. Best to just leave it be.

"Go get cleaned up, hon. *Relax.*"

With his permission, she let herself breathe easy. She was lapsing in her mourning, but she was full. She was full, and Ari was speaking to her again, and Cy was cooking. Camille would just have to forgive her.

In the shower, she didn't even feel disgusted at this body. Her body. The girls at First Glory would've killed for it: the collarbones, the wrists. A woman who existed off God and air. Just like Candy— *Was it ironic, her name being Candy?*—showing up to Bible study, thinner and thinner, asking Leena if she knew anybody who brought in skirts and things.

She'd looked good. And then she hadn't. Cancer, everyone'd thought.

Looking back now, Candy had probably known before all the rest of them. *Maybe she thought she deserved it. Or maybe she thought* we *did.* She'd always had it out for the other girls.

Leena had been pinning up art projects in the hallway, eavesdropping on the pastor in his office: "It's the chickens comin' home to roost," she'd heard, pushing a tack into the wall, the plaster giving under her finger. "Those boys of hers with a daddy—now this was told to me in confidence, so don't go blabbin'—" Fingerpainted blobs of flowers. "Their daddy out fucking every pervert of a 'man' he can find at every truck stop off I-44. And she's not doing a damn thing about it..."

The chickens comin' home to roost. But unlike Candy, Leena took care of her family just fine.

Camille's dead.

She scrubbed under her nails and repainted them. Three layers and a clear overcoat. *That doesn't mean she's gone.* Leena brushed out her wig, parting the synthetic black hair, satisfying and smooth. *Glued to this place like a ghost.* A flash from last night—her fingers in coarse black curls. Ripping them back.

She sniffed, her eyes watering. Kept brushing.

When someone knocked on the door a few minutes later, loud and insistent, she'd already reapplied her mascara and blush. A smudge of pink lipstick high on each cheekbone, blended in. Like pig skin, the hunks of meat she'd pick up for her parents from the butcher's when she walked home from school. Pink pores.

She waited for Cy to get out of sight, her gut telling her that this was in *her* basket, not his. *A bubble about to pop.* He shut himself up in the bedroom with the oven still going, and she cracked open the door. "Yes?"

A man and woman. Business casual suit and pencil skirt, plastic badges clipped to their collars. *Run.*

"Good afternoon, Ma'am. Do you mind speaking with us for a moment? We're taking a census of everyone living in this property for the public health office," the woman said. She was a girl, hardly older than Camille.

Run—

Leena had worked at the county clerk's as a young woman, her supervisor always leaning over her typewriter, bringing her out to tell people bad news. "Just sweet talk 'em. Help me smooth it over." He'd been shot at a traffic light when things started getting bad. Road rage. He couldn't smooth it over.

And it'd been a woman who'd shown up at her and Cy's door, the beginning of the end, trying to be less intimidating. She'd worn a pencil skirt, too, just like this little girl.

"Of course, that's fine," Leena said. She kept the chain lock secured, looked at them through the crack in the door. A few inches of dangerous, dangerous space. "I'm not sure if I'm the person you wanna talk to. Rashon's the one on the lease, and he's out fishin' with friends."

The woman nodded, marking her clipboard. *Rashon, the name they wanted to hear.* "That's okay, Ma'am. Do you live here as well?"

What would happen if she slammed the door on the girl's hand? Like her father had done when they needed a particular kind of discipline. One that *lasted*.

"Yes," Leena said, considering what would be best. "I just moved my things in a few weeks ago." She held her hand out for them to see, wedding ring glinting. Cy's mother's ring. A perfect fit. She hadn't even needed to resize it.

They gave their congratulations and left Leena with a glossy leaflet about handwashing, her heart threatening to beat out of her chest. Fear crystallized in the marrow of her bones, moved like oxygen in her blood as she watched them knock on B12. What would they do when they found it empty...?

And where's Ari?

"Nà shì yī míng jǐngchá."

"A cop? Really?"

"Yes, *really*. Dumbass."

Pieces are missing.

He'd had a drink, something cold and carbonated and tasteless. Sunspots glaring off the windshield. A faceless voice in a Northwestern hoodie. Peeling iron-on letters, sleeves frayed where the cheap sweat-shop seams had come apart. A Camry, a window that had been patched with garbage bags and duct tape, wind sucking against the plastic.

The jacket, the car. Answering in English even when he'd used Chinese, *trying* to be more discreet here. Drew, then. Had to be.

Drew panicking like what he'd needed didn't grow on trees around here. Adderall for oxies. Uppers for downers. Unfair, but someone would bite. Him saving his brother from bumbling into every plainclothes cop looking to entrap them. Again.

Fool me once—

Now, Ari sat on the edge of the roof, popping pills.

Shame on you.

There'd been plenty of *that*, Ma sitting there, face impossible to make out. He didn't have to see it to know she wasn't looking at him. She never did after what happened—only past him, around him, through him. Pretending he didn't exist. Good thing, too. Better that way.

Another pill. Past the teeth, down the throat.

Fool me twice—

He watched two men milling around the Leigh Pierce parking lot. White guys, strangers with camo jackets and brown-bagged cans of booze—what apparently passed for camouflage. But they didn't belong here.

He could tell what they were: Cops showing up to cut them into pieces, Cam leaving enough traces of herself to track them down.

Did she do it on purpose?

The night before she'd died, there was an image in the front of her mind. *She wanted us all dead. All of us.* They'd been right to throw her out. It wasn't just Cyril insisting—they'd been *right*. The cops were proof. It just didn't feel like it....

At least he had a good distraction, most of his afternoon spent trailing the woman from 305—older and Black and enviably heavy, someone who could eat and keep on the pounds. He'd browsed the rack of paperbacks at the dollar store—one for him and one for Leena—while the woman filled her cart, too much for just her.

Then, to the nail parlor where he had lingered outside, smoking, preoccupied with watching people filter through EBT. Their skin, the shape of their bodies. Short sleeves and shorts and sandals, nothing to imagine. Seeing who'd be good. *A full stomach is just an empty stomach, waiting.* Eyelid twitching as he'd tried to think about literally anything else.

He'd watched the woman from 305 eat a candy bar with no problem. *She's empty, then.* A waste of time. He'd started to accept the failure—*What would Leena do with another mom around anyway?*—ready to abandon this thread when he and the woman had been ambushed by suits in the Leigh Pierce lobby. She'd been cornered by the mailboxes while they'd herded him to the bench by the entrance.

Another pill.

Ari was still coming down from their talk, the remnants of adrenaline and fear and white-hot anger still buzzing through him. He must've said something to get them off his back, some bs excuse, but he didn't remember. Only air in the throat.

He'd been too focused on the suit's Adam's apple, on the *sweet* sound it would make if he sliced the skin open, revealed that little white ball of cartilage underneath like the meat of a lychee fruit... if he wedged a boxcutter underneath it...

Pop—

"Miss Shanice Coates. Apartment 305?" Cutting through the sound in his ears.

Miss Shanice Coates.

She lived here with her son, who worked for the complex. He was around here somewhere.

Around here somewhere.

With a flyer covered in cutesy cartoon germs crushed in his fist, Ari had headed back to the third floor, running into that Vietnamese girl who lived at the end of the hall. She suspected something. Not the right thing, but *something*. So he wound up on the roof, texting Leena and waiting for them to clear out, for everyone to *stop noticing him.*

He swallowed another Valium, imagined climbing up the water tower ladder, prying the tank open... He'd stick a finger down his throat, throw up blood and stomach acid and **them,** and let it fall into the water. **They** would get into the pipes. Into showers and pitchers of Kool-Aid. *Ninety degrees out today.* Give the cops something to find if they were so interested in looking.

Ari ripped the idea out of his head, horrified to even consider it, and took Valium number four. Enough to stamp out those intrusive thoughts and replace them with nothing at all while he watched them. The roaches.

But an image of Cyril walking in front of him in the woods imposed itself over them. Birches. White and papery against the snow, breaths pluming out of them as they lugged duffel bags of inedibles.

It would eventually be normal. But back then, this memory in the white trees, it was the first time they'd been alone together, and Ari had been sure that Cyril was getting rid of him—*I'm gonna die. I'm gonna die in* fucking *Indiana*—planning on drowning him in a half-frozen creek like the mistake he was before traipsing back to their motel. *"Bad news, girls. Sorry, sorry..."*

He'd kept Cyril in front of him, staring at the back of his head while the old man talked about what would happen if they were caught.

"You ever dissect any animals in science class?" he'd asked as they approached a slope, a sharp incline of mud and ice and grasping tree roots. All dead.

146

"A pig once, and a squid."

"Remember what you did with them when you were done?"

"I don't know. We just... threw them away."

"Well. There you go," Cyril had said, bracing himself against a root to climb up and over. "What d'you think your insides would look like once they cut you open, boy? A pig or a squid?"

"No one's gonna find out."

Cyril had smiled, leaning down to take his hand. Skin touching with a flash—confident that he'd be eaten up and spit out after a few weeks—*just like the first one.* Cyril begrudgingly impressed that Ari was tougher than that, at least. Worth the time. *You should probably call me "Dad" now, doncha think?*

Ari popped another Valium—the last one he had—watching the two men sit on the hood of a car as they took in the scenery. Did they have cameras? Mics?

What do your insides look like?

He could cut them open first, before they got to him, dislodge their stomachs from under the ribs. Pull them up, red tentacles of the esophagus and intestines dripping, attached at the edges. Trailing.

A pig or a squid?

Shanice waited outside the bathroom, fastening her necktie. "You know, I *paid* for groceries this week, so why'd I wake up today with my fridge half-empty?" she asked through the door.

All she heard was more retching and the wet *plop* of water on water. Maybe dinner had been too greasy. That always happened when she eyeballed it. *Dammit.*

She thought back, for just a second, to Dr. Michaels, to those people posted out in the lobby who wouldn't let her check her mail in peace. They'd kept her there for five minutes with a lecture about handwashing, like she was a goddamn child.

Tapeworms.

But Xavier would tell her if it was that bad.

He'd just made himself sick over that doctor showing up. Rich food and stress and too much work. He got worked up over less when he was younger, before he started studying harder—taking it seriously.

Xavier vomited again, sounding a little bit emptier. "That's what you *get* for eatin' everything at once! There's kids in Africa who have to save they food," she said, listening to the toilet flush and the sink running, holding in piss.

Xavier slunk out of the bathroom. Like she hadn't patted his back while he threw up into an old cooking pan every flu season when he was little. *Get it all out.* He didn't look as bad as she expected with how dramatic he was being. Still sick, though, washed out and sweating.

Should've picked up more water at the store.

Shanice checked his temperature with the back of her hand then closed the bathroom door behind her to do her business.

She was thrown off by that doctor showing up too, no lie. She'd held hands with Robbie when they were kids, some white woman from CPS talking down. *Are you happy here?* And those people out in the lobby who probably gave him shit today. Talking down. *Does your mom take care of you?* She'd been worried sick for days about having said something wrong, getting Mama in trouble. *Are you hungry?*

A sickness bubbling up, and Xavier had absorbed it like a sponge, like he always did.

She washed her hands, scrubbing underneath every nail. Light blue and French tipped, for Miami. What had those people asked her? "Do you wash your hands every time you go to the bathroom? How about before you cook?"

Shanice had been self-conscious when she'd first started going to the salon, having to sit there and watch them scrape lint and skin flakes from under the nails. Dirty, like she'd never even heard of a bath. Now, she was careful, clean. A good customer.

"Miss, do you know that washing your hands is one of the main things you can do to prevent the spread of pathogens?" they'd asked. Lord, she could slap them.

On the bright side, Xavier had been talking with the girl who usually did her nails—Lan, the same girl he'd been making eyes at for years, doing it behind her back like she didn't notice. Shanice had eavesdropped on them out in the hall while she was putting up groceries, before Xavier booked it to the bathroom without even saying hello. It had given her some time to act natural, pretend she hadn't been grinning her ears off.

It'd be a cute grandbaby if they got together, good hair and nice light skin and big eyes. Her dad would have something to say about it, but he always did. She could hear it now, him sitting in that rickety swing out front, ranting. *Squeak.* "I didn't go to fuckin' 'Nam for my grandbaby to fuck some goddamn gook." *Squeak.*

"Nobody calls them that, anymore, Daddy," she'd say, "not even racists." And he wouldn't care, would go on blabbering about shit he knew nothing about until he was blue in the face. *He didn't go to 'Nam* for his daughter to be dressing fast. *He didn't go to 'Nam* for them to bitch about hand-me-down school clothes.

Maybe if the bastards had sent him to 'Nam and given him a gun instead of sticking him in a mess hall making chili for four years, he wouldn't feel the need to bring it up every damn day. Wouldn't need to overcompensate.

Or maybe he'd be even worse. No telling.

A floating room. The tide coming in and out through hair-thin cracks in the grout.

There were differences. The water tasted like chlorine—the filter gurgling somewhere—and the person sitting on the shore was Shayna. Hair in vacation microbraids, towel wrap over her bathing suit. *That was the last time I saw her. Sitting by her parents' above-ground pool. Not looking at me.*

"I just don't know what you want," she said while he floated there. An echo.

He turned to the shore and started swimming toward her. To do what? Defend himself? Say she was right? They'd come a long way since those awkward make-outs in the Varsity parking lot, cold lips like orange crème, warming up. They were older, could have this talk.

What did I say back then?

"You just say, 'I got this, I can do this by myself.' Then you tell me you want attention. Then I give it to you. Then you tell me you wanna be left alone..."

Nothing. He hadn't said anything the first time.

"I can't read your mind, Xav. Is *that* what you want...?"

Xavier wasn't fired—inexplicably—clocking in the next morning without trouble. No breakfast. No appetite.

There's an explanation. He ran the floor cleaner along the first floor's central hallway. *You're cheap.* The tiles went from gray to white in front of him, the grime cut through in clean, even lines. *You're familiar.* Someone stood at the end of the hall, watching, their eyes on him, a shadowy reflection on the floor tiles like a patch of dirt he couldn't buff out. *There's an expiration date on the job anyway.*

The shadow laughed—*At me?*—and Xavier stopped the machine, faced burning, looking up in time to see a black shoe lifted midway. His legs twitched, a surety written in the track medals hung on his living room wall, in the practiced flex of his calves, that he'd be able to chase them down. Get an apology out of them—

What should we do instead, Xav?

Right. He took a deep breath. Diaphragm. Intercostals.

Contract.

Release.

His phone buzzed in his pocket, and he ignored it. Contract. Release. *Know the engine inside out, find which part was acting up, fix it, go on driving.* Contract. Release.

It didn't stop. When he finally answered the call, the buzzing driving him crazy after a few minutes, his voice was strained. *Jaw next. Relax your jaw, then the lungs, then hands, then neck.*

"Hello?"

"This is Atlanta Urgent Care," came the voice on the other end. A woman, robotic and pleasant. A Black girl trying to sound white. Obvious. *Why did they do that? Why did they* have to *do that?* "I'm calling to inform you of an unprocessed payment. I see we got the initial co-pay, but your bloodwork was processed at a separate location that wasn't covered by your insurance."

His teeth were grinding, the sound loud in his ears. *Jaw more than once. Jaw, then lungs, then jaw again, then hands, then neck.*

"Okay... How much is it?"

"It's four-hundred and thirty-two dollars in total."

His bad molar leaked tooth rot into his mouth. "I don't have that right now."

"We can discuss a payment plan if—"

He hung up, wanted to throw his phone against the wall so no one would be able to bother him—not urgent care, not Desai, not the guys harassing people out in the lobby, not his neighbors finding new and interesting ways to clog their garbage disposal, not the community college's automated voice telling him to sign up for classes. No one.

His arm tensed—

Mom might call, though.

He dropped his arm, his muscles screaming. *Arm first. Arm then jaw, then lungs, then jaw again, then hands, then neck.* Everything.

Something's wrong. Some subconscious, quiet part. *Something's wrong with me...*

His shoes squeaked over the tiles as he went to unplug the floor buffer. Done with today. If Desai wasn't going to fire him over their fight, he wasn't going to get fired at all. They were all just waiting it out.

He needed a shower. He needed Tylenol. He needed to finish off the rest of those leftovers, his appetite coming back, hitting him all at once—actually reheat them this time so that they wouldn't make him sick. Cook off the grease.

Reaching for the plug, something caught his eye. It seemed like a trick of the light. An eyelash caught in his sclera. A migraine coming on, its sickle-shaped aura floating through his vision.

But no...

When he moved his head, it stayed in place, and it didn't go away when he blinked.

On his bad hand, rash-covered and bandaged, a thin white line arched against his skin. Touched the first knuckle... straightened itself out again...

Languid and waving...

A worm.

CHAPTER SIX
BRICK BODY COMPLEX

A fucking *worm*.

Xavier dumped a first-aid kit onto the countertop in the staff restroom, picking through it with his good hand. Shaking with a deep-felt disgust. Like a palmetto bug crawling across his hand, legs leaving a ghost itch on his skin.

Too big. Bugs shouldn't be allowed to get that *big*. They shouldn't be allowed to be—

Inside.

It was *inside* him.

A worm.

He braced himself against the sink, tried to get enough stability to grab the thing with a pair of tweezers. After a few attempts, he caught the end of it, pulling its body taught and ceding a few more centimeters.

He didn't feel it. *How long had it been there? How long had he not felt it?*

He pulled—

And it ripped in half. The bit still attached to him writhing.

Did that kill it? Would it rot and turn necrotic and make him lose his whole thumb? His whole *hand*?

This was taking too long.

He repositioned his hand. Broke down the parts. *Know the engine, fix the car.* Nail plate, sterile and germinal matrices, eponychium. He wedged the tweezers under his thumbnail—

And wrenched the nail up with a horrible, shooting pain, one that made his breath hiss out of him like a leaking oxygen tank, the torn nail barely hanging on. *Look at how bad your cuticles are. You should come in more.* Like lifting a rock to find all the pill bugs underneath. *You should come in every week.*

Sweat dripped into his eyes, stinging, and he pulled at the worm again. Slowly this time. Carefully.

He thought of butterfly needles. *Little plastic wings.* This wasn't as bad. More blood than this had been shipped off from urgent care at 11 p.m. on a Monday night. *For five-hundred dollars.* He had to be careful. He had to take care of it. *This was less blood. Less blood and free.*

This was him taking care of it.

In the end, the thing was longer than his hand. Unfurled from his torn-up nail bed. More and more of it, peeled away like a hangnail clinging to a curl of skin. Squirming like a living strand of hair in the sink.

Xavier had seen something like this before. Worms in blood. White and red. Worms where they shouldn't be.

Where? Where was it...?

He curled in on himself on the floor of the janitor's closet. Nowhere else to go. Nowhere with a lock.

Zion hasn't called me back.

He'd tried to go to his apartment, but there'd been somebody waiting by the door. A man in a suit. *Somebody watching you.* Not in the lobby anymore but outside his house. *His house.* They'd be in his room next. They couldn't just leave him alone.

He'd managed to find some antibiotics in the heavy duty first-aid kit in Desai's office, some far off part of his brain wondering where the hell Desai was, an alarm bell going off.

Not his first priority though—he'd downed half the bottle, trying to flush them out. Make them die in his blood. Maybe it worked. That's what it *felt* like, him lying on the floor with his face against the cool concrete. His blood dying.

A panic attack. A conniption fit.

You just get so up in your head sometimes—

He'd seen this before.

A trailer out in the boonies, the whole structure sinking in on itself. The inside had been a straight shot, a line of clear carpet from one end of the trailer to the other, the rest just trash. Smoke and black mold and tooth rot.

And a woman had been waiting for them—him and Unc—perched in her wheelchair like a throne at the end of the carpet, smoking with her oxygen on. It was against company policy and common sense to go in there, a literal bomb waiting to go off. But Rob had anyway.

He'd sweet-talked her some, like always. She'd been afraid of living alone, had been leaving the stove on more and more. Rob had given her his sympathies then had a look at her feet, pulling down her compression socks... Staying remarkably, unshakably calm as he revealed, inch by inch, the cracked red skin and black flesh underneath the nylon. Twitching white moons of maggots.

"Oh, I know it's bad, that's why they covered up," the woman had said, taking another puff. "You ain't gonna call an ambulance, are you? I ain't payin' for that shit."

White bodies twisting in flesh. No pain, all the nerve endings dead. Eaten away.

Xavier found Dr. Michaels's card in his wallet and dialed the number, the red whorls of his fingerprints smudging the paper. Expensive cardstock, cheap blood.

He was put on hold. *Nylon and gangrenous skin, sloughing off like nothing.* Classical piano. *A chugging oxygen machine, a hissing nasal canula.* A voicemail box. *A cigarette burning down, smoke covering rot.*

"You've reached the office of Dr. Brian Michaels. Please leave a—"

Xavier cut the call.

That voice.

Worse than the worm. At least *it* was just an animal, doing what was written into it like rings inside a tree. Growing. It didn't know. Couldn't.

That voice, though... It was intentional. The voice of gray tap water. Of toxins built into the walls. Of maggots under nylon and the murmur of oxygen leaking, threatening to explode. Of a butterfly needle sitting in the crevice of his pockmarked arm. Squeezed dry.

Like Rob, making himself so small. The look on his face a few minutes before he'd died. "You don't need to call nobody, Xav. We ain't about to waste everybody's time drivin' me out for them to give me a Bayer aspirin and bill. I got both of those already. Go get me an aspirin, yeah? I just gotta sit down for a minute..."

Getting our exercise in today, boys.

Another pang somewhere deep. His nostrils flared, abdomen painfully contracting as he vomited stomach acid and blood and worms.

Out of his mouth. His nose. Visible only as a teeming movement. As a shivering, twitching shadow in the reeking puddle. Hundreds of them. He felt something warm leak down his pant leg. Saw his sweats stained red, a dark line running down his calf, then a steady stream. Red soaking through.

Leena and Cyril were arguing—not about anything important like their exit plan or how they were going to get rid of the scraps without being seen. They were arguing about Cam. About how, according to Cyril, *she'd fucked them over ten ways to Sunday like the ungrateful brat she was.* About how, according to Leena, *that wasn't fair, that wasn't fair at all.*

Ari just let them go at it, the casement window facing the parking lot cracked open while he smoked. Nothing else to do. Leena wouldn't let anyone leave, paranoid about the suits seeing them, and Cyril had put all of Rashon Wilkinson's pills in his lockbox, too smart to flush them.

That would be wasteful, and they'd never be wasteful. *No bigger sin in the world.*

Ari hadn't gotten any sleep since talking with Leena, fingers grasping at each other, filling in the details, while Cyril took care of dinner. There was no space to be nostalgic about that, though, not with so many eyes on them.

"Eat first," Cyril had said, already chewing, "Hungry decisions aren't good decisions."

In the end, they'd agreed to wait it out, Ari staying up to keep watch on the parking lot and piece together the valuable moments of surveillance down-time that gave them some breathing room.

His first pack of cigarettes was already gone, him finishing one and immediately going to light the next off the glowing nub. Chain smoking like his dad. *Shit.* Like the cab drivers who parked in the alley under his bedroom window when he was a kid, bitching about rideshare apps and leaving cigarette butts and food wrappers like footprints, proving they were there.

"Wǒ kànjiàn lù biān liǎngpáng dōu shì lù shù," he said. *I see green trees by the road.*

Another puff. "Lù píng—"

Leena appeared from nowhere, grabbing his hand. *Concern. Camille.* Nothing new there, but also... *Excitement.* A desperate urgency. Good news.

The son "around here somewhere" is outside.

She dragged Ari out into the hall, ignoring Cyril's protests, his frustrated face shut behind the door to B4.

Be quiet.

Ari did as he was told, the two of them creeping to the laundry room where the son from 305 was waiting. Where he was *losing it.* Bloody. Blood that smelled like family. Trying to force a wrinkled dollar bill into the quarter machine in the corner. Angrier and angrier as it kept getting spat back. Like a mocking green tongue, sticking out. *Lü shétou.*

This close, Ari could feel it—need turned to hysteria turned to anger... turned into a fist. Hitting the top of an open washer, the metal buckling and popping back into place, then the son's own head. Sharp knuckles cracking against the skull.

"He's gonna hurt himself," Leena whimpered, leaning into him, her mind already turning. *Proverbs 29:15.* Whatever the hell that meant.

Was I this bad?

Ari couldn't dredge up much from that time. Just snapshots. A frog's eyes piercing—two silver dots. Something had been squirming underneath them. A mouth foaming with hydrogen peroxide and metal clinking into the sink. Then nothing. Then Cam, hands in his hair. Whispering empty, comforting words. Had that made him feel any better?

Probably not.

INDIGENT

He watched the son's panic with a growing shame, a painful second-hand embarrassment. Ari let go of Leena's hand and looked away.

The quarter machine was always a piece of shit. The tenants had been asking for years for free laundry—they were already paying rent for Christ's sake—but it never happened. Never *would* happen. Xavier just needed a dollar to get the washer going. Get the blood out of his clothes.

He'd bled so much. From everywhere...

Blood on his hands, his legs, in his shoes, like he'd waded through water. Thank God it was a workday, the lifeblood of Leigh Pierce gone or sleeping. Or at least looking the other way, choosing not to see.

But somebody's still watching you.

Somebody, sure, but not anyone he had to worry about. Xavier was confident about that, though he didn't know why.

And he'd hit himself. *Fuck*, he'd hit himself! A closed fist right to the temple. *Why...?*

A childhood memory, amazing in its sudden clarity, of the *bang* of his forehead against the kitchen table. Him needing to get re-centered quick and easy, to make his frustration a physical thing and give it to someone else. Someone who knew what to do with it.

A memory of Mom, placing her open palm on the table when she caught him working up to it. Reflexive, lightning fast. "What should we do instead, Xav?"

What should he do instead…?

A rag. A T-shirt. A pair of boxers. Something clean stolen from a pile of unattended laundry. So he *was* a thief now, but he'd give them back. He just needed four fucking quarters—

"Somethin' happen with that?" a voice asked, and Xavier stayed focused on the machine, on his multitool *almost* prying open the corner of the back panel. Almost…

"Nothin'. I'm- I'm with maintenance. It's broke. You gon' have to come back later."

"Later when?" *Not from here,* some northern accent with specifics he couldn't place.

Xavier glanced up, saw—*Anemia.* Pale, tired. Not enough blood. An image of Rob pushing an old lady in a wheelchair, dead asleep after five minutes of PT. His fingers pressed against her wrist, checking her pulse. "You watch, just that's gon' give her a bruise," he'd said, patting the hand back in place.

"You're the one who found that girl a few days ago, right? The one who died," the guy asked, and Xavier wasn't surprised, knew already what this was about.

"Why d'you care?" he asked.

The guy scrolled through his phone for a second, holding it out for Xavier to see. *Don't touch him.* The same part of his brain that had panicked at the sight of the worm in his hand. An animal rejection of a poisonous thing—the midbrain, still afraid of monsters and the dark and bugs. *Don't touch him.*

But there was more—the thoughts at the crown of his head, traveling along the gyri and sulci in a self-perpetuating electric wave. Needing, more than anything, to *know.* To be sure.

Xavier reached for the phone. Fast. Touching for less than a second. Less than *half* a second, not even *that*—

Something.

A flicker.

A picture seen through a pinhole. A girl.

A part of a part of a part of a part—

Xavier knew his name. And the girl's name. He *knew* them. And he dropped the phone, vaguely registered the sound of it hitting the concrete. Cracking.

"Are you okay?" Ari asked—*How do I know that?*—stepping closer.

"Sorry, I'm good... I'm good..."

His heart pounded, painful in its insistence, the effort it took to move his blood. He could feel it. Cardiac muscle straining. Veins expanding. Contracting. Blood running slush-like through them.

Xavier reached for the phone again, saw the picture of the girl from the alleyway. Healthier, smiling. "That's Cam?" he asked.

How do I know that? How—

"Camille," Ari answered, staring at him. Expecting something. *What?*

"Was she sick, or—"

"*No.*"

Not offended, but... frustrated. Like Xavier was some hopelessly dumb kid who couldn't get his multiplication tables right. A frustration that Xavier knew—that midbrain again—would turn into something more violent if he let it. If he kept being *wrong*.

"No, yeah. No, sorry. It's fine. *You're fine,*" Ari backpedaled.

Wrong again. Not the North, the Midwest. "No yeah" means yes and "yeah no" means no.

"She's not—she wasn't sick. It's hard to explain," Ari said.

Grit and lint dust floated by Xavier's bare feet, his ruined work boots tossed in the laundry room garbage. Grit scratching as he got up—taller than most people, Ari included, making him feel a bit safer, a little less *wrong*.

He grabbed his wallet, resting on top of the washer where his clothes were waiting. Useless. *Four more quarters.* Inside was Dr. Michaels's card. He handed it to Ari, careful not to touch him again. Relieved to get rid of it.

"They said she's still a Jane Doe. If you wanna call them, maybe they could…"

Xavier felt like an idiot, like that woman sitting in her throne room made of hoarded junk, letting flies eat her feet. He felt stupid and ignorant and *right*, for just this one time. Knew it in his gut. This was better than throwing the card out. Maybe Ari would be smart enough to use it.

"No," Ari sighed, frustration tamped down into something quieter. "We can deal with it."

He knows. He has to know.

"If that's broken, I'm gonna go. Here—" Ari placed a five-dollar bill by Xavier's wallet and turned to leave, not looking back once.

Xavier stayed quiet, unmoving as he listened to the footsteps stop in the hallway, a nearby door opening. Rashon's apartment?

Rashon's dead. Just a statement of fact. *Rashon's dead. Zion's dead. Anthony's dead.*

That seemed obvious now, true on the face of it. Three men who looked like him. Who'd lived here with him and smoked with him—their knees touching—who'd stood by chatting while he changed the pipes out from under their kitchen sink. They were dead.

But were they asking for it?

He clenched his fists—Where did *that* come from?—wanting to feel the impact of his knuckles against his skull. Needing to—

What should we do instead, Xav?

He took a breath and picked up the money, could almost picture Zion leaning against the washers, talking while he worked, Xavier feeling almost normal. Like he had friends. *Three men who look like me, but not me. Not yet.*

He was crying when he fed the bill into the coin machine, the light glowing. *I see a green light.* The words came from nowhere, like a sharp pressure against his forehead—re-centering—as the quarters clattered musically down.

"I see a green sponge," Ari muttered. "*Wǒ kàn dào yīkuài lǜsè de hǎimián.*"

He chugged a cup of tap water, then held the plastic to his burning forehead. A feeling like a fever, about to be sick. Because Cam was both *there* and *not there*, buried in this stranger.

To distract himself, he paged through Leena's pocket Bible, looking for Proverbs 29:15, the verse that had been on her mind as they'd stood there watching the son from 305—*Xavier*, he knew now, *Xav*. He read the line, his shoulders shaking, filled with a dreamy and horrible euphoric disappointment—a ragged sound escaping his throat.

The rod and reproof give wisdom, but a child left to himself brings shame to his mother.

A child left to himself.

Xavier in his borrowed clothes, watching the sputtering spin of the washer's glass face. Half-awake, sure he was about to drop dead. What would happen then? The little red heart on his driver's license said it was okay to cut into him—that he'd agreed to it—so they'd carve him open, and then they'd find too much.

Four lungs. Two hearts. Half-felt, as though an organ could go numb and come alive again, prickling. They'd slice into his eye and find a pupil under the pupil, a lens under the lens. Doubled and doubled and doubled as they cut...

He could see his endlessly duplicating body displayed with other things that were freakish and exotic and not-quite-human. An echo of the times where men who looked like him were displayed with a painted Africa at their backs—an impossible mishmash of landscapes out of a more cultured imagination. Saw himself standing in their place, his face white and red, his thumbs gouging out a pair of blue, blue eyes.

A child left to himself.

Anika Davis's boy stood under the dull overhead bathroom lights while Miss Inez snored through another episode of Jeopardy in the living room. He kept quiet, squinting to make out the cool, weird *thing* squirming around at the bottom of a Coke bottle he'd fished out of the trash.

"Give me 'European Historical Figures' for two-hundred," the TV droned.

He'd found it in the murky runoff dripping from the laundry room pipes, lifting it out of the graywater with a stick.

"This infamous prince of Wallachia was killed in 1477."

It was some kinda worm, smooth and skinny and white.

"Who is Vlad Țepeș?"

He'd never seen a worm like it before.

"*That's correct!*" *Ding, ding, ding!*

He filled the bottle with water and watched, wide-eyed as the worm twisted in on itself, so thin it didn't even make bubbles. Like it wasn't even there.

Cool.

Atlanta was full of hiding places and prying eyes, Leigh Pierce

Estates the focal point, reflected in the city's wide-open pupil. In the lens of a camera trained toward the door. A man with a badge and a gun, chewing a piece of Nicotine gum. Popping.

Xavier wasn't aware of him precisely but knew the feeling of being watched. He felt it in a prickling along his neck. His ears burning. *That means somebody's talking about you.* He borrowed Miss Inez's car, bad transmission and stained upholstery hanging from the ceiling like loose skin, driving first to the corner store to pick up more groceries—the fridge and cabinets back home horrifically empty—and then to the pharmacy.

Mebendazole, pyrantel pamoate, laxatives. Whatever it took. Bought with cash.

Maybe he should go to the ER. But a voice in the back of his head put a stop to that. It sounded like one of Uncle Rob's tirades. "I get paid when people get better, they get paid when people stay bad. And you can *tell*."

Sick people are mean. And stupid.

Did Rob know that he was referring to himself? *Why didn't you notice? You're supposed to be smart.* Or maybe he didn't know, just saw it as an observation, *telling it like it is.* Either way, Rob was right about ERs.

So back to Leigh Pierce, where he left Miss Inez's car key in her mailbox, unwilling or unable to speak to her face to face. Where he went back to the bathroom with a notebook and a timer running on his phone. Prepared this time. Ready.

Step Four—Last but not least, take responsibility into your own hands. Never ask for a seat at the table. Build your own goddamn table. Make it so nice that they ask to sit with you.

INDIGENT

Xavier vomited eleven minutes after taking fifty milligrams of pyrantel pamoate, fourteen minutes after fifty milligrams of mebendazole. Worms came up both times, spilling out with colorless bile. The laxatives worked fine—twenty minutes, then blood in his stool, no worms.

He pictured them hooked into the walls of his intestines, burrowing in like the head of a tick, clamped down. *Ticks have to be burnt out.* Held to the flame of a lighter or suffocated in alcohol and scraped away... He could always stop by Miss Inez's place after all, ask for something strong and clear, one step away from rubbing alcohol.

That could be his last resort, if nothing else worked.

He swished water around his sour-tasting mouth before trying again. Twenty-five milligrams this time. There was a chance that, if he found a small enough dose, he could sneak something past them. Death by a thousand cuts. By ten or five or even a single milligram of antiparasitics slowly pumped in over the course of a day. Breaking them down. He just had to be *systematic* about it, patient, and by the time Mom got back—

A phone call interrupted his timer, making him flinch. Mom.

A flash—Mom leaning over him in the tub, his body submerged in milky white. A pulling at his scalp, combing lice out of his hair. Drowning them.

Hold still, Xav.

"The manager called askin' if you was okay. Said you keep leaving early. You still sick?"

"I'm fine. It just a bug."

Another flash—a bug plinking down on his English textbook in the middle of school, right in front of him. Falling from his scalp. Brown and flat-bodied and twitching. *A bug on top of a word. "Sluggish—slow moving."*

"You coulda told your boss that so they ain't hitting up my phone while I'm at work."

Xavier scratched at the rash on his bad hand, the stitch on his index finger inflamed. His nails broke the skin as easy as tissue paper, making him lightheaded.

Epidermis, dermis, hypodermis.

"Sorry, I just been busy."

"Yeah, with all that work you been doin'."

He didn't respond, his eyes seeing movement by the suture at the joint... a white line. Wriggling. He took a sharp breath, mouthing the words. Noiseless.

"Stratum corneum, stratum lucidum, stratum granulosum, stratum spinosum, stratum basale, papillary layer, reticular layer..."

"Xav? You know I'm joking," Mom said after a second. "I'm just makin' sure you okay."

Xavier turned the hot water on full blast, holding his hand under the faucet. Blood and yellowish discharge and a worm— much smaller than the last one—pulsed out of the broken skin. Pulsing with his heartbeat. Escaping down the drain.

He watched it, eyes wide. Jaw working.

Mom said something.

Hold still, Xav.

He didn't hear her.

An egg. A hypothetical. Nestled into the soft walls of the nasal cavity. A hollow space gone dry and fissured. Denying. A warring home turned on itself.

An egg dispelled outward. Out into the ever-creasing joint of a hand, a fresh house welcoming and warm in the narrow lines of its being. The soft curve of an arching finger.

Water and lifeblood for the taking. Breaking through. Unfolding. Then—

Iron and air. An artery opened up,
                    letting in the world.
Flayed...

By the sharp edge of a fingernail...

Intentional, this body. Purposeful.

Flowing out and out, burning. Exposed. Carried down through a space not unlike a gullet. Dark and humid and churning. Not unlike an intestine with its lines and curves and beautiful directionality—a brilliant forward motion.

But unalive. Ungiving.

Down further, into the cool of the earth. Hard stone a bony carapace surrounding an empty space. Mineral and noxious.

A false esophagus yawning open into an endless stomach. Silt and water and refuse. A dead stomach underground. A current flowing.

Somewhere...

CHAPTER SEVEN
BYGONE

Subjective:

Case History—Beryl Ridge, Missouri was ground zero. Beryl Ridge, Missouri, did not exist anymore. It was burned to the ground.

Objective:

Documentation review including Bulter County police department reports, comparative autopsy of Subject 1 and Subject 2. [5]

Assessment:

Biological connection confirmed between two subjects (1 & 2). Biomarkers under further review.

---

[5] Coroner, M. N. (1989). *Inquest into the death of Jacob Kirk.* (File no. 000783/19327). Court of Sisseton, South Dakota.

Plan:

- Continue low-level surveillance of property
- Debrief surveillance team on acceptable safety measures (non-lethal)

The official documentation was easy enough. What Michaels didn't feel comfortable noting in his report: Beryl Ridge, Missouri didn't have a chance.

"Something in the water," his old man had said once, sitting in front of the TV, watching news footage of some riot they played on repeat for weeks. "What's wrong with folks these days?" *Gotta be something in the water.*

Most of this job was scouring spreadsheets with a fine-tooth comb, excited about some significant data point only to find, nine times out of ten, that it was a fluke, poor record keeping on the admin staff's part making patterns emerge and fall away regardless of reality.

It'd taken him a year to pinpoint the epicenter of a tuberculosis outbreak in Vidalia all because its hick ER staff couldn't keep accurate intake records to save their lives.

Beryl Ridge was Vidalia all over again: a bunch of incompetents covering their behinds and hoping their scope of influence was so small that no one would notice or care to check. No one in Jefferson City had anyway. They hadn't caught wind of it until there wasn't much to do but burn what was left to the ground and hope the bastards weren't fireproof.

Thanks to that, there were plenty of Beryl Ridge lose ends to go around. Unaccounted for men and women and even a handful of children who'd slipped away in the chaos.

Like all illnesses, they left traces. The corpse of a young man in a gay bar restroom, remnants of *Gordacia* underneath his nails. A missing teenager found in Sica Hollow State Park, two hundred miles away from his foster home, a lily clasped in his hands and his face covered. His body a soup of half-digested tissues and worms. Carter's couple out in Wyoming, one of them a nature lover who'd backpacked through... the Ozarks.

And *there* it was. Like a party game—*Seven Degrees of Beryl Ridge.*

Another degree: the Jane Doe from Leigh Pierce had family. The *Gordacia* from her body (amazingly decomposed in a matter of days[6]) matched the sample taken from the Sica Hollow boy. Siblings found over a thousand miles and twenty years apart—the same parasitic strain.

"You know what a group of worms is called?" Carter had asked, yawning in the middle of Michaels's rant about *this lead being what well-kept and well-maintained data could accomplish.* "A clew. C-L-E-W. They're from the same *clew.*"

Of course, Carter couldn't just call it a *colony* or *strain* and be done with it. He had to pick something worse, something more... buggy.

Michaels had called it a *strain* when he debriefed his surveillance team. They had to be measured about this. The observation of

---

[6] Work in progress, pending state and federal clearance for public consumption (2011): "*The rapid decomposition of host cells in humans infected with Gordacia valentulus*"

Metro and Fulton was already slow going, the Estates residents non-cooperative, the property manager a sentient bundle of nerves in designer jeans. Things weren't going much smoother in the Section 8 housing next door either.

What he *didn't* need was a certain someone coming in to make a spectacle of it from the top down. Imagine it, Carter passing out manilla folders of gore and redacted witness interviews, eyes lighting up. "You wanna see some *Hills Have Eyes* shit, boys?"

No. Absolutely not.

It was strange, not knowing everything about a person. What Ari *did* know about Xavier: A sense of pressure against his forehead, the sharp, jolting pain waning into a soothing distraction. An old woman with no feet...

Or maybe there *were* feet, but something was wrong with them, the image tied to a prickling, mildewy dampness and a primal phobia of blood and bugs. Bugs *in* blood. One part of an intense discomfort with many branches, loose associations Ari couldn't catch, not with the time he had.

Less than a second. Less than half a second, not even that.

When he'd first gotten back, Leena had sat across from him, holding both of his hands. Ecstatic in the beginning. Working through food, through names, some part of her still annoyed that he'd gone with something other than her suggestions.

Calvin. Judah. Alexander. Meat. Blood. Offal.

A surge of terror right after.

What would happen to her now that she was the only woman in the house? No one to bounce off anymore, to reaffirm what *woman-ness* even *was* with all their parts so muddled? A fear as she'd stared at him, gripping his wrists, appraising. *At least you know what being touched by a man is like. We know that together.*

Then contempt, the reminder that Camille had never even bled. Too skinny for it. *Never a woman anyway. Not really. What's the difference between now and then?*

All of it suffocated by a long-instilled reflex to bear that cross like every other. *The sacrifices a mother makes. But it's all worth—*

And he'd ripped away from her before he could think anything stupid.

"Don't let them make you feel bad," Cam had said a few months before she'd left. "They don't want *us*. When we leave, they'll find someone else, and they'll be fine."

With Leena's reaction still buzzing through him, Ari knew Cam had been right. *You can ditch us on your own, but as soon as I wanna go—*She'd been right, and he just hadn't wanted to hear it, happy, in a way, to have a mother who looked at him, a father who was more than a dirty dinner plate by the sink in the morning.

He should've listened. Now, he was stuck with Leena's infuriating excitement, Cyril's empty encouragement.

"Let's see if it lasts," the old man breathed, going to each of them.

Ari cleared his thoughts before they touched—wall, *qiángbì*, ceiling, *tiānhuābǎn*, window, *chuānghù*—and Cyril took his wrists. Hands and lips to skin. Engulfing them.

"If it takes, we should plan on goin' shopping sometime soon," Cyril said. "Another mouth to feed."

Xavier staked out the laundry room, back against an old dryer that hadn't worked in months. *Out of Order* in his own sharp handwriting.

He sat on the concrete, working his way through Mom's stash of MoonPies. Two boxes of them kept in the cabinet over the fridge in a fruitless attempt to forget about them and be healthy. The antiparasitics—less than a milligram now, dabbed bitterly onto his tongue—did nothing but empty his stomach, left him reaching for whatever he could to fill it again.

Like walking on the bus as it lurched forward, inner ear sending signals to his body to readjust, he'd blink and find food in his hand, unsure how he'd gotten started. *You're eating garbage,* his body was telling him. *Don't you want* real *food?*

He didn't know what that was, though, his body some separate thing he couldn't read. *Almost* understanding, but not entirely. Like those glances from Lan, like some stubborn patient's face. A thing that detested him.

Xavier slammed his head against the side of the dryer with a dull thud, the metal siding buckling. It cut through the hunger pangs, let him notice the graveyard of wrappers at his feet. Crinkling, gathering lint. *I have to buy more before Mom gets back...*

But no distractions. He had to keep an eye on apartment B4, on Ari and the two other voices, heard with his ear pressed to the door, listening, a man and a woman, older.

They *knew*.

Maybe they knew what *real food* was, or had medicine that actually worked, that didn't leave him feeling like roadkill, violently flattened out. Anything. The only thing left to do was get inside. Invite himself to the table.

It was hours before he heard the door to B4 open. 1 a.m., Ari taking the stairs. Xavier made a note of it and waited for the others to clear out, running out of sweets and forcing himself to stay put with another quick crack of his head against the dryer. And another—

Around 3 a.m., Ari came back to the basement, jogging in and out of B4, two overstuffed gym bags slung over his shoulder. Xavier followed him out to the parking lot, hiding behind the Dumpster with the other feral animals as Ari tossed the gym bags in the back seat of Rashon's rusty Chevy Caprice.

The station wagon's headlights illuminated the alley before angling away, plunging everything back into shadow. A humming darkness, full of mosquitos and cicadas and a single orange bulb by the basement door. Xavier watched until the taillights disappeared down Fulton, waiting for sunup.

Leena's father had been part pig.

He'd known for a long time that his heart was likely to give out before the rest of him, and when it finally happened, no one was surprised or particularly worried. He wouldn't die. Sitting by his bedside at the hospital in Cape Girardeau just pretense. It was the most normal, expected thing in the world when he came back with a new aortic valve.

Strong and young and *porcine*. As tough and splendid as the boars that rutted around the Butler County Fair, snuffling.

They'd had money then, her father *gettin' while the gettin' was good* at the Ford plant and leaving before Ford left them. And after that, hauling rocks—hearts shot through with streaks of blue and gold—to wholesalers throughout the state. A marble man.

All that money had dried up, though. No more Ford, no more rocks, her father's expensive pig heart a vestigial reminder of needs well-met. So far removed it might as well have been a lie or her imagination. Maybe he *had* died that day, and everything after that had just been a dream.

Maybe he wasn't that strong.

Leena always thought of her father whenever she prepared hearts. She couldn't quite bring up what he looked like, but could never forget that pig valve, the shape of him carved in blue-veined marble. *Is this what the surgeon felt like?* Knife in hand, slicing into the muscle fibers.

If only they'd let me watch back then. See them crack his ribs open...

Like most every part of the body, save for the entrails, hearts were better raw, but Leena wanted to be accommodating. Xavier— she'd looked up the name, Basque and Spanish for "new house," which seemed delightfully welcoming, an open invitation—would need to be introduced to things slowly.

No raw foods.

When Camille was young, she'd eaten in the dark. No looking. No thinking about it. Leena would wrap a thick scarf around Camille's eyes before they got started on anything raw. Afterwards, Cyril would add the leftovers to junk food—soups and fried rice and pork n' beans.

He'd coaxed her out of her shell while he taught her the difference between searing and reverse searing. Braising and blanching and broiling. She'd help him haul bags of charcoal out to the grill, uncomplaining, then sleep on his side of the bed, curled up against him. A daddy's girl, always was.

Flesh. Bone. Offal.

This is now bone of my bones and flesh of my flesh; she shall be called 'woman.'

It was easier to think of Camille now, knowing that she was still with them, in her way.

While the heart cooked down, Leena prepared four lunch boxes. Four. A good, round number, a real family. Cyril sleeping in, Ari up before her, taking out the garbage while the spies were away. Back to routine, the portable radio singing quietly from the counter as she doled out their vitamins.

Iron. Vitamin C. Magnesium. Vitamin B12—

A knock, and she froze.

On the other side of the door. *Xavier.*

"Maintenance!" *New house.*

She stayed quiet, willing him away, but he knocked again.

"Just a second!" she called.

She placed an opaque lid over the simmering heart and ran to the living room to grab her wig, patting it down over her thin pony-tailed hair, the balding scalp. Presentable enough. Family could see family on a bad day. What else were they for? Her fingers picked nervously at the hem of her blouse as she cracked the door open, chain secure.

"Hello?" she said, looking out.

He was a handsome boy. Tall, with wide-set hazel eyes and a soft face. Soon, all that cute baby fat would be winnowed down into something more human, more real. Winnowed down until the bones stood out under the skin, dark and radiant with fever.

The fever would break soon, and he'd be hungry. Hungrier than he'd ever been in his life.

Or, the idea pushed forcefully to the forefront of her mind, *it wouldn't break*. It wouldn't break, and he'd just fade away, like a polaroid losing all its color.

Just like my first one. Like Cal.

"We're sprayin' for mold today. You shoulda got an email about it."

Xavier lifted a tank and nozzle, the smell of bleach hitting her nose.

"Can you come back another day? My husband's not feelin' well."

"This equipment's a rental." Pushing in. Insistent. A pup clawing at his mother's breast. She couldn't say no, not to a child who was hungry.

Leena bit her lip, closing the door to slide the chain lock, bleach sloshing as he picked up the tank and stepped inside. She looked at his hands—*callused*. Cy would like that, a son who knew about hard work. It gave her some hope that he would take to Xavier quickly, not the months it took him to get used to Ari, grumbling in private to her about *that boy Camille brought into* their *house, actin' like he's got any right to be that stuck up.*

"So this if for mold?" she asked. Just for something to say.

"Yeah. These basement apartments get real humid in the summer time."

She hovered around him, arms crossed over her chest—*don't touch him, not yet*—a step behind as he surveyed the apartment. Xavier was quiet, not responding to any of her attempts at conversation. Systematic.

Cal had been like that, just a boy and already so serious. Brave. Already reconciled to the fact that the world, as a matter of course, would be mostly unkind to him, accepting it with a kind of puerile stoicism that Leena had found heartbreaking and charming, endlessly charming, as she'd watched him.

And you shall not desire your neighbor's house, his field, or his male servant, or his female servant, his ox, or his donkey, or anything that is your neighbor's...

But she had, feeling it as deeply as she had years ago, lying in that bathtub with warm water gone red, Cy grasping her hand, promising to make up for it. To give her whatever she needed as blood plumed out between her legs. Six months and nothing to even bury.

INDIGENT

Cyril always wanted a boy. She'd followed Cal and figured out he was unhappy, that his house was not a home. That he was running wild. *Daddy always wanted a grandson.* She'd laid out on the sidewalk to watch the sun sinking, tinging South Dakota a deep orange-pink, and he'd gotten there right on time. Seeing her contorted face, her hand clasped around her ankle. Stopping for her, kind boy.

Was this Camille's gift to her, an "I'm sorry" and "I love you" wrapped all in one? Had she taken the time, in her last moments of life, to leave them with a sweet, serious boy like the one they couldn't bring themselves to bury?

Leena wiped her eyes with the heel of her hand, impatient, and followed Xavier into the kitchen. *Let's see if it lasts.*

The woman who answered the door of B4 reminded Xavier of the last landlord, Anne. She'd owned Leigh Pierce Estates since the eighties and, according to Miss Inez, tattooed her lips burgundy red so she wouldn't have to bother with makeup anymore. Xavier had never confirmed that, but he believed it.

Anne was the kind of person who didn't mind tolerating a little temporary pain for permanent convenience. A woman who only acknowledged him when he existed in the space between timidness and aggression—a Black face, gone when times were good and begrudgingly in agreement with her when they were bad, a threat in his presence, in him being *on her side* whenever anyone came complaining.

This woman gave him the same impression, someone who hated any violence that wasn't her own. If she acknowledged what she did as violent at all.

She hung around him like a sweat bee. At his left elbow. His right. Directly behind him. Hardly even there, so pale and thin, flitting in and out of his periphery. She smelled like baby powder and flowers.

Like Zion's apartment, Rashon's place had been cleaned. Deep cleaned, not even the potential for mold left. If he squinted, though, he could pretend Rashon was there, hunched and nervous, leaning on the kitchen counter while Xavier sprayed the corners. "I just wanted to make sure somebody got to it 'fore I breathed in too much. I heard you can get mold in your lungs now, if it too humid. It gives you cancer, I heard. Sometimes I wish I'd just get cancer already so I could stop worrying about almost getting it, you know?"

No sign of him now. Xavier even checked the ceiling, looking for the spots of blood he'd found in Zion's apartment. Nothing.

She finally gave him some space once he got to the kitchen. *What if I got a steak knife from the drawer and stabbed her?* Both carotid arteries were clear along her neck, two thick blue lines branching out of her blouse and winding up to her mandible, sitting on top of loose flesh. She wouldn't be the first person who got killed here. She probably deserved it.

The woman with her hands on her throat, blood leaking through her fingers, eyes bulging—

184

Xavier blinked the image away. Intrusive, like standing at the top of a stairwell and imagining what would happen if he jumped, if he fell in all the worst ways.

He checked under the sink, trying to ignore whatever she was cooking on the stove. Something under a silver lid, a delicious smell escaping in a gout of steam through the vent every few seconds. How was he *still* hungry?

Stomachs under stomachs under stomachs—

"It pops up in dark places," he mumbled, trying to get back on track.

"Oh no, that makes sense. You look close as you need to, honey."

She didn't sound like the old landlord, at least. Anne was all backwoods, sharp and abrasive. This woman's voice was softer. Debutante. So high pitched he suspected her of faking it—an intentional, calculated fragileness. How the world taught her to speak, like the girl calling him from urgent care, like Rob talking to doctors. A voice that was theirs and not theirs.

The steam from the stove found a way to his nose even with his head shoved under the cabinet. Would she be willing to let him lift the lid? Breathe the vapor in. Tasting it with his nose...

He got to his feet. Too abruptly, the woman jumping. Eyes boring into him.

In the hallway, he sprayed down the doorframe of the linen closet, pausing at the picture of Rashon with his niece. He could almost hear the story: "That's up at Lake Burton. She a natural. Got a blue ribbon at the kids' tournament they do at the Y. I got a picture of it here somewhere..." He'd never found the picture. Xavier wondered if it existed at all or if the image had just been held up in Rashon's mind, overexposed and nice. A rare good memory.

Rashon Wilkinson is dead.

"Can I get you anything?" the woman asked. "We have lemonade. It's just the powdered kind, but—"

"No, thanks."

He hurried to the bathroom, closing the door on her before she could follow him there, too. Breathed in. Breathed out.

Nothing in the living room. Nothing in the kitchen—though she hadn't let him into the fridge. Nothing under the bathroom sink. And nothing here either. When he opened the medicine cabinet, he found it starkly and uncharacteristically empty, just a bottle of Tylenol and some shaving gel, a dry blue crust on the nozzle.

Inside the Tylenol bottle—nothing. Behind the medicine cabinet—nothing. A penlight shined through the gaps in the ceiling exhaust fan—nothing.

Before he could stop himself, Xavier's right hand was in a fist, a sharp knuckle drilled squarely into his temple. He stood there, blinking and frustrated, waiting for his ears to stop ringing before he opened the door.

The woman was right where he left her, veiny clasped in front of her. "Nothin' so far?" she asked.

Nothing, the word making him want to scream. He showed his teeth. "You keep the place clean. More than I can say for most people."

"Oh, that's—" She stopped, her eyes flicking past his head then back again with a smile. A nervous laugh that didn't change her face, made for the benefit of someone behind him. "It's okay, hon. They're sprayin' for mold."

A man was standing outside the bedroom, one hand on the doorknob. He was huge, head nearly scraping the doorframe, but sick-looking, just like the rest of them. Anemic, a plaid button down hanging loosely off his shoulders, sitting on top of his protruding collarbones.

More than any of them, the bones of his face stood out—*pterion, zygomatic arches, glabella*—a violent starkness. A man who, unlike Xavier, was familiar with his violence. Who was allowed to be.

"I just got the bedroom left, then I'll leave y'all alone," Xavier explained.

"Go 'head," the man said, unblinking.

The woman nudged him forward, and Xavier brushed past, into the room. He sprayed bleach into the corners, trying to be discreet as he looked for prescription bottles or homemade remedies. *Anything.*

Just another clean room, fitted bedsheets tucked tightly under the mattress corners, two pairs of shoes laid out neatly under the window.

"You're the boy who talked to my daughter before she passed," Xavier heard from behind him, the voice low and deep and careful.

The man standing closer than he remembered.

Xavier wanted to lie but found himself nodding.

The man smiled. Good teeth, straight and white. He closed the space between them in a few steps, walking with a limp—well-hidden, used to it. All his weight off the gastrocnemius and soleus, no pressure on the Achilles tendon. He stood so close, Xavier could see the slight droop of his right eye, the nearly imperceptible difference in definition of the hollow cheeks.

The girl in the alley, her eyelid going slack...

Xavier pictured him leaning forward, just a few more inches, those teeth sinking in, stripping the skin from his face. *I can see it.* Visceral and real—white teeth on black skin, staining the enamel a gory pink. *Blood on teeth.*

The man smiled again, looking at Xavier's injured hand. "She do that?"

"I... got bit by an alligator."

"That's the better thing to happen, believe me." And he laughed, startlingly loud, grabbing Xavier by the shoulders and pulling him into a bear hug, his right arm weaker than his left.

Another *flash*, Xavier forcing himself not to jerk away even with that curdling feeling under his skin. A name—*Cyril*.

"Camille and I... didn't get along as well as we coulda near the end there. But she was my little girl. I'm glad she had somebody bein' kind to her," Cyril said.

A funereal sincerity, like the talk at Rob's service. Too impersonal for it to matter if it was true or not, something written in a card and sent with flowers. *Your uncle was a good man. Your uncle always knew how to make people laugh.*

She was my little girl.

"I'm sorry."

"Nope!" Cyril said, pulling away, clapping him on the back. "That's all the sentimentality you're gonna get outta me today." Then, yelling into the hall. "Hon! We gonna invite him to dinner?"

188

"You don't need to," Xavier, started, but the woman had appeared at Cyril's side, smiling. *What's her name? An "L." Something with "L."* Everybody smiling. The air hot.

"So we can say thank you," she stressed, latching onto Cyril's hand. Another image rising in Xavier's mind, unasked for, of the old man flexing a muscle, the woman's wrist snapping under his palm. Snapping like a twig.

Ari drove without thinking, cutting a twisting line from Leigh Pierce Estates out into the countryside, the radio mostly static. Snippets of country and classic rock. Prescription ads and fire-and-brimstone preaching.

And the Lord in his righteous anger had said to them, I had planted you a choice vine, a completely faithful seed. How then have you turned against Me?!

It reminded him a bit too much of Wednesday nights, Leena and Cyril and sometimes Cam going at the good book with highlighters. He turned the volume down, focused instead on the cicadas and bullfrogs: green-bodied nature and its sounds, kudzu draping down from the roadside powerlines like a funeral veil. A beautiful place.

He'd heard that, away from the cities, Georgia still had sundown towns, a needle of anxiety in the back of his mind. It was anyone's guess whether or not Ari passed that paper bag test, driving alone in the dark. But it'd be a good cover if somebody came across B4 and 205 out here. A story that told itself.

He pressed a cigarette against the car lighter with one hand, driving with the other, window rolled down. *Both hands on the wheel, boy. Nine and three. Can't believe your daddy didn't teach you how to drive.*

Would Xavier be waiting at the apartment when he got back? An angry figure zip-tied to the bathroom radiator. Or would he be sitting placid and understanding at the kitchen table, taking to it like a fish in water? Or still lurking, watching? Not brought in just yet, still... off.

Is he, though? Xavier in the laundry room, that basement smelling like detergent and mildew and blood. Iron under molding flowers. *Or is he just not Cam?*

There'd been recognition, like passing someone on the street. Nodding. *I know you.* But that was it. Only a one-way glimpse through a crack in the door. None of what made Cam familiar— that endless vocabulary, even when there was nothing to think about but food.

Starving, edacious, insatiate, esurient.

"It takes time," Leena had said, determined not to let his disappointment get to her. "We didn't know you all at once either."

Ari hit the brakes, swerving into the grass. He finished his cigarette before grabbing the bags from the back and heading out.

There was a line of Indiangrass sprouting uncontrolled at the roadside, then a steep drop-off into a ravine. *Watch out for poison ivy!* his brain piped in, Leena's voice.

He watched out for poison ivy and slid to the bottom of the ravine, the temperature dropping, almost cool in the shade. Still humid, swimming through the air. Light came in filtered through the tree branches, through the silky film of lappet moth nests. *Invasive*. Ari stared into the silk, searching for the ghostly shadows of caterpillars hiding inside. Children safely eating their fill.

The South was full of invasive things. Lappet moths, kudzu. There didn't seem to be much of a difference anymore between them and the things that were supposed to be there.

He walked until he found a fallen tree at the other side of the ravine. Soft rot and whitecap mushrooms, roots exposed at the base of the slope. Perfect. Crouching down, Ari lifted a handful of dirt to his nose. *You want it to smell like compost. That way you know it has the bacteria we want.*

He shook the dirt in his palms, uncovering the soft brown-white body of a wasp larvae, twitching. He let it fall between his fingers, then got the collapsable shovel from the gym bag, psyched himself up for an hour or two of digging.

Wasp. *Huángfēng*. Mushroom. *Mógū*. Femur. *Gǔgǔ*. Skull. *Tóugǔ*....

Ari had met Cam in a laundry room. He wondered if that meant anything or if it was just a coincidence. It probably was, but he kept falling into a stupid optimism that Cam was still there somewhere, dropping hints at the base of things.

His mouth had tasted like vodka, and a pair of sneakers had been poking out between the washer and the clothes hamper. White legs drawn up. "Are you okay?" he'd asked. A bad trip—just an assumption, a wrong one—and she hadn't bothered to correct him.

Drew had picked them up after they missed the last train for the night, Cam sitting in the backseat drawing on the window glass, the pictures quickly filled in by the fog coming off Lake Michigan. Clinging to everything. The two of them had argued about her in Chinese, like she couldn't tell.

"I'm tryna be nice."

"You gotta stop 'being nice' to crazy white people who treat you like shit."

Drew had been right. Of course. What about Sarah? Scars and DIY tattoos on her inner thighs, telling him that her aura was magenta and his was orange, and "I thought we could make it work, but we just can't," picking her nails. Or Karly, who'd stolen his all-day festival pass and left him stranded in her friend's Winnebago out by Douglass Park, ignoring his texts.

Or Tyler, head in Ari's lap after getting back from the bathroom—third time that night—asking to take a break. "Did I do something wrong?" Tyler's nose had been raw and red. "Are you mad at me?" Glossy almost-blue eyes flickering down and away.

"I'm not mad," he'd sighed. "I just think you like me more than I like you."

Him going after *crazy white people* who liked postpunk and codeine and him, for a while. But only ever for a while.

Except Cam.

Cam, who had pressed a lock of his hair into the pages of her journal to remember him by, *just in case*. Who'd sat in his brother's car, listening—hungry and jealous and angry and *wanting* all at once—considering whether she could reach in and pluck out those words easily or if she'd have to pry them loose.

192

A bit of both, she'd realize later. Happy. So happy.

Cam, who had never wanted anything less than all of him. Every part...

Ari brought the blade of the shovel up in a smooth arch, grit falling into his hair, metal hitting the fallen log with a hollow ring. A sound like a skull splintering open. The bleeding ooze of wood pulp. He watched ants and wasps scramble, their larvae exposed and writhing, and brought the blade down again. And again.

And again.
And again,
And—

I just think you like me more than I like you.

CHAPTER EIGHT
LOOK OUT, KID

Xavier hadn't been on a run in years, not since Shayna left him.

The feel of it—the two of them practicing at the high school track, her pulling ahead, baiting him into blowing through his energy reserves while he held back. Watching the flex of her calves, her ass, her smiling face glancing back at him.

Back then, he'd been able to run to the Checkers clear on the opposite end of Fulton Street in fifteen minutes, meeting Rob there to drive back in the Chevy, milkshakes melting in the heat, pooling in the cup holder as traffic stalled and crawled.

"Ain't goin' to the Olympics or nothing," Rob had said once, patting him on the shoulder, "but not too shabby."

He could beat that time now, belting down the sidewalk from Leigh Pierce with surprising ease, nausea and five years' worth of lapsed training not holding him back. Self-preservation. The *sibylline* understanding that staying one more second in the basement where Zion and Rashon had died would ruin him—the mechanics of it unclear, but not the outcome.

Underneath it all was a cold, resigned fear. Because he *had* to go back. And he would. *That man had talked to him.* Knowing the end did nothing to change it, but it could be avoided for a little while longer.

No car, so he ran. Simple as that.

Teeth breaking skin. A memory. Someone else's memory planted behind his eyes.

He wasn't dressed for a run, and this wasn't a neighborhood where people went jogging, as much as the coffee shops and yoga studios pushing in from the north side of Fulton wanted it to be. Some part of him was afraid of getting stopped—*must've stole something*—but he kept going until the stabbing pain in his left foot caught up with him, the exposed steel toe in his old work boots cutting in.

Bleeding.

He'd go back to the basement tomorrow with an excuse to get them to leave while he gave the place a more thorough search. It was impossible to really look with that Anne-clone following him.

He'd find something. *That pan on the stove, breathing out steam.* He had to. *A steam that smells like barbeque, like the church potlucks from when I was little, back when Mom needed me to know about God.*

Ari got back to Leigh Pierce Estates that afternoon, the lobby buzzing like a hive of wasps. He skirted around the crowd, listening to them get blindsided. Evicted.

"Illegal, isn't it?" "I don't know. I don't know—" a crack in the voice, a silent insistence that *we are not talking about this right now.* Some of them held envelopes. Crushed in a fist. Pinched on the corners between thumbs and forefingers like it wasn't theirs. Like there had to be a mistake.

Envelopes. Something stirred, a sympathy long buried. Buried like the skulls of the men from the basement, like his brother under the frozen ground outside of Indianapolis. *His mother with an envelope, waiting for a man in a blue suit who'd throw them to the dogs faster than blinking if they fell behind.* That came first, before utilities. Before rent. Before food.

His jaw twitched. *Before food?* Sympathy bent into a hungry indignance. *Wouldn't that be nice.*

Leena had called him, elated on the other end of the line as she told him how Xavier had stopped by. She hadn't touched him. *Just to be sure.* She did this on purpose, let Ari get attached while they sat back, took in everything second hand.

Didn't want a repeat of *the first one.*

It was up to him, then, to go upstairs, to knock on apartment 305, and actually set things in motion, burning with a ravenous impatience.

When Xavier answered, though—a *one-way glimpse through a crack in the door*—Ari didn't know what to say.

"What d'you want?" Xavier asked, just an eye in a sliver of light.

196

What do I want...? He'd *wanted* to ask about the footless woman, tease apart all the ideas branching away from it. To understand. To know.

Instead, Ari asked, "You wanna see something?"

An eye, liquid and bloodshot. "I don't think that's a good idea."

"I *need* to show you something," Ari insisted.

Xavier swallowed, Adam's apple moving in a smooth movement of the muscles. "Okay."

They took the emergency stairs to the roof, Xavier following him at a safe, suspicious distance. Again, that image of Cyril, dark hair and corduroy work jacket moving through the birch trees in front of him... The cold, resigned fear of his footsteps.

Will Xavier remember this the same way? Should I stop...?

"What's going on downstairs?" Ari asked as he kept walking. Too late to back out now.

"We're gettin' kicked out."

"Everybody?"

"Everybody."

The doorway to the roof rose into view at the top of the last flight of stairs. "Know where you're gonna go now?"

"No. Do *you*?" Xavier asked, and Ari glanced back at him. "You live here, too, right?" A challenge in his voice, an inside joke between them. Daring him to lie.

"We'll figure something out," Ari answered, shoving the door open against the gravel. Sunlight spilled out, white-yellow like butter. Melted and hot. He walked into the sun, breathed in the heat.

Xavier shut the door behind them and doubled over, vomiting up chunks of barely digested junk food. Sickly sweet starch and chocolate.

"You okay?" Ari asked. Just a reflex. *Yes sir, no sir, please, thank you. Are you okay?*

"You *know* I'm not okay," Xavier groaned, dry heaving. "What's wrong with me? You know. I *know* you know…"

And Ari *did* know. He knew that if Xavier was only good for one meal, he'd be half-dead by now, eaten from the inside out. This meant **they** were hoping to keep him around. Ari smiled. *You're fucked.* He searched his pocket for Cam's cigarettes. *Thank God.* Found the pack half-crushed underneath his boxcutter. *I'm sorry.*

"**Them**," he said, keeping it simple.

Ari broke out the cigarettes. A Pavlovian response. Roof: smoke. He looked away, faintly aware that it was embarrassing, puking in front of a stranger. *But we're not strangers. You know that, don't you?*

Ari drifted to the ledge overlooking the parking lot, stepped up to balance against the railing. Hot metal smarted against his fingers. He jerked away, then, more decisively, rested his bare palms against the metal again until the pain wore itself out.

Waiting.

After a few minutes, Xavier appeared beside him, and Ari pointed to the man in the parking lot. "See him? He showed up a few days after Cam died. He parks down by the road first then moves closer every few hours. Then, he switches out with another guy."

"Really?" Xavier asked, an edge of hysteria cutting through. "They stakin' us out? Why?"

"Why d'you *think*?" Ari snapped, catching himself. Had he always been this impatient? Had things always gotten under his skin so easily? "They're slackin' off, though. He gets here at midnight, then leaves after a few hours to go get coffee or some shit. So I had time to leave today when you were following me all obviously."

"I wasn't—"

"I just thought you should know." Ari shrugged.

Xavier nodded, staring at the spy, the muscle along his jaw flexing. Standing out. A rope pulled taught, so much pressure the fibers would start to unfurl and *snap*. Then, the jaw would go slack, hanging open like a gaping Halloween mask.

"If they know you here, why don't they do somethin'?" Xavier asked.

The answer was obvious, making Ari want to take a lose brick and throw it, either at the man's windshield or his head. Unsure. His arm would decide.

We're bugs in a terrarium. Not being hunted. Just watched.

"They know *Cam* was here. And they know that *you* talked to her," he answered, stomping out his cigarette and picking up what was left. A mangled bit of filter and dead ash. Leave no traces. "You should probably be more careful than me, honestly."

"What'll they do if they find out I'm...?"

Ari looked at him, deciding to be honest. No reason to not be. "They cut Cam open."

A pig or a squid?

Xavier just nodded again, sweat beading on his forehead, while Ari went to light another cigarette. Dirt was pressed underneath his fingernails, and his hands were shaking. Fumbling with the lighter.

Xavier's turn to look away, scrolling through his phone, through the call history. He pressed a number, and Ari's phone vibrated in his pocket.

"She called you. When I talked to her," Xavier said.

"I know. I shoulda answered it."

Ari blew out smoke, his mouth moving on its own. A memory—one that might help. "When we first met, she didn't have an ID, so I was the one who had to pick these up for her. I wasn't even old enough to get them. I used my brother's license. We didn't even look like each other, but..." he laughed. "It pissed her parents off that she smoked so much, but she said it helped with stress."

Another drag, another breath closer to regaining his composure. He held out the pack, offering Xavier one. If Cam was in there, she'd never pass up a cigarette.

"I'm straight," Xavier said, shaking his head. "Got caught smokin' *once* and my mom whooped my ass. She gets worried about that kinda stuff."

Ari bit back the disappointment. Maybe it was just a cover, Xavier's round-about way of saying it'd be a bad idea to move too quickly. That he'd have people looking for him. *Lucky you.*

"My mom's... happy to have an extra room in the house," Ari said, and when Xavier looked away, embarrassed, added, "I played drums instead of piano."

They stood watching the day drinker for a while, saw him amble over to the curbside where he climbed into a waiting car, switching out with a stranger in an identical hoodie. An identical brown bag in his hand.

"Your parents want me to have dinner with y'all tomorrow," Xavier said, his eyes glued to the man in the parking lot.

"You comin'?"

"Is it a good idea?"

Ari felt a laugh coming up his throat and forced it down, his chest aching. Xavier's expression got to him, though—worried, wide-eyed. It reminded him of Cam, her face floating over him, white hands pressing a cup to his lips.

Don't worry. It's good for you. The voice people used with a child. He laughed, the sound delirious in his ears, like a mirage in the heat, making him laugh even harder.

Xavier left the rooftop alone, half-worried that he'd take the trash out tomorrow morning and find Ari's body crumpled in the alleyway, bones broken over the staircase where Camille died.

Blood and worms.

He was worried because Ari had considered it, fleeting and unserious, as the two of them stood there looking over the city. Hands brushing in another flash. This time:

A girl seen through a pinhole.

Teeth breaking skin.

Gray trees against a pale sky.

Talking wasn't the right word for it: *Communicating*. Getting an idea across.

Ari holding out a cigarette, letting the ash catch in the breeze, his eyes following the spots of smoldering gray as they floated down, wondering absentmindedly if a fall from this height would kill him and deciding with relief and disappointment intermingled that it wouldn't.

Xavier had wanted to say something, but Ari had just kept on smoking. The thought unacknowledged. Unimportant. He was like Zion in a weird way—sneaking around where they shouldn't, a mutual trust that no one would tell, Xavier's anxieties waved off with a smile and a puff of smoke.

Different smells, though—weed and tobacco.

"I'm sorry about Rob," Ari had said after they'd been communicating for some time, like it was normal. And Xavier had to leave. One of those stomachs under stomachs under stomachs rupturing.

He went back to his apartment lightheaded and hungry, a renewed urgency to the sour taste in his mouth. *Chemical communication.* He'd read about it as a kid, after he'd caught a moth bigger than his hand with owl-eyed wings in the woods out by Rob's place. He'd kept it in a little plastic terrarium on the porch. "You ain't bringin' no bugs in my house."

The two of them had woken up the next morning to find his moth belly-up, legs curled into its soft body next to a cluster of bright yellow eggs, Rob's yard covered in hundreds of moth corpses. Brown and orange and many-eyed.

Dead wings bristling. Getting picked up in the wind like leaves.

Was that all he was? An already-dead moth responding to a chemical lure? Weren't people supposed to be smarter than that?

Apparently not, with Ari pulling Rob's name out of a hat like a hack TV psychic. *I'm hearing a name that begins with R.* Those worms in his hand with a signal running through their bodies like free-floating neurons. *I'm sorry about Rob.* A hungry curiosity, consuming everything. Stomach and brain.

Dredging up things he didn't want to talk about.

It dredged up enough that the spies outside were an afterthought, a fear in the back of his head, so much like what had always been there—there since his mother stood in from of him, hands on his shoulders, patting down his backpack straps. *You shot up too fast. They gon' think you grown, and they'll treat you like it.* How long would they stick around? *Just don't give them a reason.* Were there cameras or mics in the hallways, hiding behind his bathroom mirror? *Yes sirs, no sirs, thank you sirs. Always.*

He wasn't thinking when he opened the door, looking over his shoulder to see any miniscule changes in the hallway. Any spots where an eye or ear could be hiding, drilled into the plaster. He didn't notice Mom sitting on the living room couch until he'd locked the door behind him. Triple-locked.

She was still in her uniform, black tie crumpled on the coffee table, and she had his laptop, scrolling. She'd been crying.

Wasn't now.

"You see the letter?" she asked, not looking at him. Just scrolling and scrolling. "Fuckin' sixty-day notice like that's enough time to find anythin'."

Xavier sat beside her, hiding his bad hand. The laptop fan was whirring, its ten-year-old hardware straining under the million tabs she had open. Apartments, room rentals, income-based housing, lawyers, tenant forums...

"They can do it if we at-will tenants, but not if we got a lease. I'll go ask them about it," she explained, still staring at the screen. "Lived here how goddamn long, and they just..."

He squeezed her hand. One of her nails was gone, four sky blue ones and a plain pointer finger, rough with nail glue. Nail biting—a bad habit she'd made sure he never picked up with a few well-placed slaps on the hand. *Don't be nasty.*

Nothing there when he touched her. No thoughts, no worries, no daydreams. That didn't matter. Everything was clear on her face. His too.

"What you not tellin' me?" Mom asked, closing the laptop.

"Nothin'."

"Xavier James, I swear to God."

"They don't want us to get a lease. They want us to leave."

"You don't know that. And stop cryin', it ain't the end of the world."

Was he crying? When did that start?

He blinked, no energy left to lie. "It's gettin' torn down. Even if we had a lease, it don't matter."

He'd spoken too little too late, but it was still a weight off his chest—a second of relief before he saw Mom's expression, a new heaviness pressing down on his lungs.

Diaphragm. Intercostals.

Contract...

Release...

"Just how long'd you know about that?" she asked.

"Like a week, it's not—"

"A week's a long time when you lookin' for a *fucking house*. And you just weren't gon' tell me? You were gon' wait for me to get a letter in the mail. And then what?"

"I'm sorry. I didn't want—"

Mom got up, ripping her hand away. She grabbed her keys from the kitchen counter.

"Mama, where you goin'?" he asked. A whine, sounding like a kid. And, like a kid, he followed after her, breathing in through his teeth as she shut the door in his face.

Alone.

They'd see her out there, keeping tabs. *Just don't give them a reason*—But he stayed put, knowing not to go after her. Turning instead to punch the doorframe. His knuckle split painlessly against the wood, only noticed at all because of the blood. A single smudge. Fresh. Dripping.

He stared at it. Fixated.

Shanice thought about most things in terms of driving. It was how she wrapped her brain around everything, kept it consistent. The time it took to get from Atlanta to Marietta was the same time it took to get her nails done, as long as they were simple. Just a manicure and some polish.

In the time it took to get from Atlanta to Athens, she could clear her head. *Think.* She'd been sitting in a bus for thirteen hours and was already driving again. Back aching.

The hatchback handled easier, though. She could take the side roads, going nowhere. Maybe she'd pick up a milkshake. Something sugary. Her eyes were on the look-out for *Now Leasing* or *Welcome* signs as she drove.

Before she knew it, she'd bitten off another one of her nails. The right thumb this time, the acrylic popping off between her teeth with a painful squeak.

Xavier would be going to college in the time it would take to make sixty drives from Louisville to Miami, if the traffic was good. Closer to fifty-five if it was bad. Sixty thousand miles. Two months. No time at all.

No time. And now he was lying to her.

Just like Ro—

How could she even *start* to think that? Rob—only getting all the bad parts from the men in their family. Onery, bad with money, a bad heart and none of their daddy's inclination to complain about it, saying everything was fine. *Everything good, 'Nice, everything's good!* A lie they should've carved into his headstone.

Dishonesty that did fuck all for nothing and no one. Passed down like garbage in their blood. Impossible to get away from even when she'd tried to filter it out, forced herself through a sieve to leave only the good parts—

Think she too good to even tell us she leaving. Too good to say goodbye. Triflin'.

206

INDIGENT

She pulled to a stop at the light on Peach Tree Street, turn signal clicking. She waited and waited with the cars lining up behind her, honking. Waiting... It took her a while to realize that the light was stuck on red, that it was broken.

Leena didn't believe in coincidences. She believed in a plan laid out, a game of One with purpose beyond her understanding. That didn't stop her from trying, though, mulling it over with Ari's head in her lap, combing the hair out of his face. Fingertips brushing over his closed eyelids.

"Such good eyelashes. I feel like I'm losing mine," she murmured.

Another headache, one right behind their eyes. What did he expect, taking all those pills knowing they'd run out eventually?

Of course, he probably didn't think Cy would cut him off, either.

He'd let Camille do most anything she wanted in that area of her life. *Spare the rod, spoil the child,* flourishing under a soft, guiding hand. Not boys, though. Boys needed more than that. "Tough love," Cy had told her, putting the lockbox key in his back pocket, the pills rattling around inside the black shell.

Leena didn't have the stomach for that, necessary as it was. Even if she did, she was preoccupied. Thinking about Xavier, about the perfect symmetry that confirmed, like so many things, her convictions.

Five years ago, Ari had been brought into their family. Five years ago, Xavier had lost a member of his. An uncle. Beloved and sick, held in some hallowed, unattainable place in his memory. A place with reaching branches, creating the right conditions for **them**.

A connection and a path planned out from the beginning by Someone who knew better.

She pictured them side-by-side like a gear turning. One space closing, blood filling a stomach, and another opening up, a stomach emptied with grief. A yawning nothing of a feeling. *New house.*

Maybe somewhere right now, the next part of their family was being made empty—unsated and *wanting*, ready for their first meeting another five years from now.

Ari, eyes still closed, half-asleep, was listening in on her musings. They were *bullshit*. His word, not hers.

"Quit bein' ugly," she said, leaning in to kiss his forehead, her fingers lingering on his lips.

◈◈◈◈◈

"Guess what I'm cookin'," Cyril said from the kitchen, turning down whatever Tom Petty was singing about.

At first, Ari didn't register that Cyril was talking to him, just went on reading.

"No guesses?" Cyril asked, louder this time.

Ari dog-eared his dollar store book, the plot dropping out of his head as soon as he closed it, staring up at the turning ceiling fan blades. A shadow growing and shrinking like flexing fingers.

They hadn't done this in a while—an excuse to talk about food, that inexhaustible topic.

"Lasagna," he said after a moment. After the past few weeks, the normalcy was easy to sink into. Nice. "With ricotta and mascarpone and parmesan and mozzarella."

"Hmm. Sounds good. But try again," Cyril said, something popping on the stove.

"Pizza."

"In an Italian mood? How 'bout pepperoni and mushroom? Lots of red pepper."

He heard Cyril's footsteps on linoleum, muffled as he stepped onto the carpet. Then, Cyril draped his bad arm around Ari's shoulders, holding a fork in his good hand, some green *thing* hovering by his mouth.

"I need a more refined palate here," Cyril said, a smile in his voice.

Ari took a hesitant bite, fibers slick against his teeth as he chewed, just once to break it down before swallowing. Disgusting. Cyril laughed.

"What I thought. We got some belly left. Might could make it taste better..." The fork disappeared, replaced by an open palm. Rough, an orange pill waiting. Ari stared at it.

"Before Mom sees. Want you in a good mood tonight," Cyril urged, and Ari knocked the pill back, hearing it click against his throat as Cyril's lips brushed the top of his hair—h*ungry and getting hungrier*—still, despite everything, drinking in the affection, kicking himself over it.

Dad. *Yuèfù.*

When Leena finally emerged from the bathroom, she had a full face of makeup and a strawberry blonde wig. A sundress and a waft of perfume, both floral.

"What d'you think?" she asked. "The wig's not too... *wig*? I can change it."

"You look beautiful, hon. Besides, there's no time for that," Cyril said as he headed back to the kitchen, nodding toward the door.

Xavier knocked—7:01 p.m., fashionably late—wearing the same outfit from Rob's funeral. *A distorted reflection in the side of a car door, bulbus suit stretched over shining, polished black.*

Ari'd mentioned Xavier's uncle yesterday, on the roof, though maybe he shouldn't have. But it was *right there*. A ghost reaching his fingers into everything. Leena was at least right about that.

Xavier handed Leena a bouquet, and she breathed them in, smiling with her whole face. "How sweet! Let me get these in some water... Ari, say hello! Be a *welcoming* presence. Please."

Ari plastered on a smile. When would the Valium kick in? Just one. He'd be lucky if it did anything at all. "Hello! *Shalom*! *Mi casa es tu casa*!" he said, pretending not to notice Xavier's hand going to his jacket pocket, a hidden one inside the lining.

A knife? A gun? Whatever it was, Leena and Cyril would be indignant about it. *Like we'd hurt a hair on his head!* Ari started giggling while Leena waved Xavier over to bother Cyril in the kitchen.

Dinner came not long after, Cyril and Leena at opposite ends of the table, Xavier in Cam's spot on Cyril's left. Almost normal. Leena clasped her hands, and they followed her lead, heads bowed, Xavier off by just a beat.

"Lord," she started, "be with us today as we give thanks for times past. Grant us courage to embrace the present and grace to share the future in memory of our loved ones..."

Ari glanced up, meeting eyes with Xavier, neither of them praying. They shared a smile, a mutual moment of embarrassment, went back to bowing their heads...

"Thank you for food in a world where many know only hunger, and for friends in a world of loneliness. We ask you to bless this meal we share. Amen."

"*Amen*," they all said, Leena and Cyril digging in.

Xavier just watched them, poking at his steak, well-done on his insistence. Ruined meat, all the blood gone from it. He looked like he might be sick, and Ari nudged his foot, encouraging.

Xavier cut into his steak with a paranoid deliberateness. The knot of his Adam's apple hovering at the base of his throat as he held the meat to his lips, took it in.

Chewing.

That knot bobbing like a fishing lure hooked on a set of gills.

Ari felt Leena's hand on his knee underneath the table. Tensed... and released as Xavier took another, less tentative bite, and she pulled away. Instead of staring, Ari occupied himself by picking over his vegetables, tweezing apart the fibers inside the stalk. Green and translucent. Barely edible. It was better to think about what it broke down into.

Vitamins, potassium, iron. Could always use more iron, even if it meant grease and grass and dirt in his mouth.

"Where are y'all from?" Xavier asked once most of his plate was clean, going into the obligatory small talk that no one else had bothered to start.

"St. Louis," Cyril said. "We're both Southern boys, it looks like."

"Very many people would resent it being called the South, hon. It's not quite…" Leena corrected, giving Cyril a tight smile, a stickler for details. "Cy's from North Carolina, though, so he can make the good ole' boy claim if he wants to," she added, smoothing it over.

"We're technically rivals in the barbeque game, but I can put that behind us for the greater good," Cyril said, and Leena rolled her eyes, took another bite.

Pink and bloody.

When their plates were cleared, they cracked open some of the beers that had been sitting in the fridge since they'd moved in.

Leena took a sip, making a face and passing the can to Ari. He downed it, and Cyril passed him another, rolling the can across the faux-woodgrain, aluminum *tinking*, a liveliness in his face. And Ari was sure that, with the four places occupied at the table—Cyril's children sat on either side of him—he could reach out, their skin touching, and something would *be* there. He didn't do it, unsure how long it would last, something like grief sloshing around his gut.

The people in the basement. Cyril. Leena. Ari. *Cy. Hon. Sweetheart.*

Cyril in the kitchen, mouthing the lyrics to songs Xavier had heard before but didn't know, songs coming out of a little plastic radio. Lovingly re-seasoning a cast iron pan. Like Mom, the movements automatic.

Leena sitting on the living room couch, sharing a beer with Ari, head on his shoulder. She'd asked about Xavier's hobbies, about school, and he'd tried to talk about physical therapy, but the words were coming slower and slower.

Now, it was all her. Talking about how surprisingly nice Georgia was compared to a litany of other places—Nebraska, Maine, Florida—a tangle of tangents that Xavier had trouble keeping track of, content just to listen to her voice. A voice from a storybook, or the woman who'd read off the names at his high school graduation, melodic and clear.

Next up, Xavier James Coates...

Ari between them, sixish beers in and not seeming any worse for it, the faintest red flushing his cheeks, piping in every now and again as Leena talked. Arm over her shoulder, twisting strands of her synthetic hair absently between his fingers. Her hand reaching up, brushing his wrist...

Touching, always touching.

Xavier sat on the other end of the couch, his fingers wrapped loosely around the penknife in his jacket pocket, lulled into an uncomfortable restfulness. They'd taken down the picture of Rashon and his niece. He didn't know where they put it—not in the garbage, where Xavier'd stood for too long, scraping the dregs off his plate. Hardly anything left. If he'd been alone—he was ashamed to admit—he would've licked it clean.

Nothing in the bedroom, where he'd searched for a nerve-wracking minute while everyone found a new place to settle down after dinner. He'd found a lockbox that was promising, but no key. No picture, no meds. No nothing.

A failure then.

But for the first time in days, he wasn't hungry, the food going to his stomach and staying there. Rich and heavy and satisfying. Making him sleepy. *Stomachs under stomachs under stomachs.* His fingers slipped from the penknife. He wouldn't need it... Hopefully...

A part of a part of a part of a—

"I'm so happy you could come," Leena said, putting a hand on his knee. Warm. Over the clothes only. No communication. He could hardly hear her even in the quiet.

Was something in the food...?

Sleeping pills, poison.

He couldn't think... met eyes with Ari, who seemed to get it, to see the panic rising dull and slow. Getting warmer. *Something wrong. Something—*

"Xavier should get goin'," Ari said, loud enough for everyone to hear. "He's got..."

"Work," Xavier croaked.

"He's got work."

"Oh, but I want to show him pictures first," Leena said. She was on her feet, wobbling once, righting herself.

"We don't need to see—" Ari started, but she was already gone, disappearing into the bedroom and rushing back a few seconds later with a small book, a finger to her lips.

"Cy doesn't like me taking pictures. 'Live in the present' and all that," she whispered, nodding toward Cyril, still in his own world in the kitchen, ignoring them entirely.

She leaned close, the book open on her knees, turning quickly through the pages.

Maybe it was just drowsiness, but the pictures were surprisingly uninteresting. Leena posing next to a state park welcome sign. Camille flashing a peace sign. A man about his age who Xavier didn't recognize, a beanpole of a person with long hair pulled back, standing next to Camille with his arm around her waist, awkward. Camille wearing oversized sunglasses and posing in front of the Chicago bean sculpture. The city warped in an endless convex behind her, trapped in silver.

"This one was right before she met Ari. It's a nice city. Have you been?" she asked, and Xavier shook his head, signaling his exit as politely as he could. Head swimming.

"*Mom.*" Ari took the photo album, closing it.

"Camille was so lonely, having to hang around Mom and Dad every day. She wouldn't say it, but you know. Mother's intuition. It's good she found somebody. And Cy *let* her have somebody... But I guess I'm bein' unfair. He used to be better about that kinda thing. He really did..." She looked at Ari, smiling. "Maybe it's been enough time that we can go back, sweetheart. We could take Xavier to—"

Ari jerked away, Leena nearly falling off the couch as he stormed out of the apartment. Xavier wanted to say something, horribly aware that he shouldn't be left alone with just the two of them. Cyril and Leena. *Cy and hon.*

Cyril came to meet them, sweating up a storm, wiping the burning red skin of his neck with a dishrag. "Not scarin' you off, are we?" he laughed. "Don't worry 'bout him throwin' a hissy fit. Calms down fast enough."

"It's gettin' late," Xavier said, his tongue thick, struggling to get up. His entire body had fallen asleep. Pins and needles.

Cyril followed after him, blocking the door.

"If you ever need anything—*anything*—all you gotta do is ask." He went in for a hug, skin touching skin as Cyril spoke directly into his ear. "Careful now. They're watchin' us out there."

Xavier nodded blindly and hurried out the door. Not remembering the walk back, the collapse onto his bed, still in his outside clothes, his shoes. Mom giving him the silent treatment from the living room. He dropped to sleep faster than blinking, before he'd even closed his eyes.

A dream. Of a room full of water. Of sea foam touching bare toes. Foam crawling with worms.

"Hey."

Mom was on the other side of the bathroom door, her voice strangely flat. Watered-down. Even that hurt Xavier's ears. Her voice, the knocking, the light, the exhaust fan, water moaning through the pipes. Leigh Pierce complaining at him, *accusing* him of something…

"Yeah?" he said, his voice sounding alien in his ears while he stared at the number on their bathroom scale.

He was down over five pounds since yesterday. Scales could be wrong. Rob told his patients that all the time. *You just have to use the same one every time. Consistency.* Xavier had been using this scale since he was a kid, an artifact from Mom's life before him.

Will I have patients anymore? Did he see that right, the scale needle twitching down another notch? *Or will I disappear before then?*

"One of the ticket girls is pickin' me up today," Mom said, growing quieter. "I'm running to the store before I head out. Want me to pick you up somethin'?"

Xavier stepped off the scale and went to the door. Her shadow moved in the strip of light underneath. He said nothing.

"I'm gon' be gone for a few days, up to Louisville. I'll get in a few more shifts so we can start savin' up. We'll figure out this rent shit when I get back, okay?"

Xavier put his hand on the doorknob. Stared at it with surprise. A dead hand attached to a dead arm. Not his. Lifted and placed there, guided by strings. His jaw hurt.

"Okay," he said, feeling for the muscles in his tongue and throat, trying to connect them to the sound. But he couldn't.

"You still sick?"

"No, I'm—"

"Stop lyin', I'm not stupid," she said, still soft. Worn out. "If you not gon' call the guy, at least go to urgent care. I'll leave you my debit card." She didn't say anything for a while, still standing there. That warm shadow. "I love you."

He heard her breathing, heard the soft creak of a body against the door. *I love you, too.* But he stayed silent, terrified to speak.

Xavier waited to hear the front door close, saw a body in the mirror that looked like his but felt somehow different. Insubstantial. He could take a shaving razor to the skin and it would open up like scissors slicing through paper. He could cut the arm clean off and wouldn't even feel it.

It was fake. It wasn't his. Wasn't his—

A fist hitting his head, against the temple over and over.

Over and over and—

But he had an ache in his right tooth.

The posterior superior alveolar nerve. Connected to the maxillary nerve. Connected to the pterygopalatine ganglion. A tooth, two nerves, the ganglion. Four things that were his. That was something. He lowered his fists.

That was something.

Xavier tore through the kitchen, starving, looking for anything he could keep down.

He landed on a pack of chicken thighs, tearing the plastic with his nails, water and blood running down his wrist as he threw the thighs into a frying pan. Hand to his mouth, absently licking the blood from his fingers.

He caught himself after a second, gagging at the idea of it. Just the idea, though. The *taste*—

"Room service!" Desai called from the hallway—a knock like a sledgehammer, drilling through Xavier's skull—and Xavier cursed. Desai's voice was wrong, too. A recording of a recording.

He opened the door, found Desai and Dr. Michaels waiting, Michaels in the same suit as before, or one exactly like it. Gray like bad water. Like the inside of that woman's trailer.

"We're doing a wellness check today," Michaels explained, giving his car salesman smile, hands on the silver clasps of his briefcase.

Xavier let them in, feeling like he was about to fall apart, the strings laced into his muscles straining. About to snap—

"I wanted to run a quick test, too, if you don't mind," Michaels was saying, case clutched to him like the geriatrics who sat next to Xavier on the city bus, angled away...

"What d'you mean?" Xavier asked. *Run.*

"Saliva samples. We're getting one from everybody, but staff first, with manager approval."

"I already did mine, it takes like a second," Desai piped in.

"Still lookin' for tapeworms?" Xavier said, trying to infuse his voice with nonchalance, a harmless lightness—*Hello, this is Robert Coates calling from Serenity.*

"Among other things. Public health's a bear. Gotta keep an eye on it."

"Can I say no?"

"Of course." Dr. Michaels's smile faltered, less patient. "That's the smarter thing to do anyway, I mean, *this guy* was cooperative and missed out on a gift card," he added, nudging Desai with a forced laugh. "Later then. It's fine."

It's not fine.

Xavier didn't say anything, Michaels nodding toward the kitchen. Toward the smell of burning. "So. Making anything good this time?"

Coming in here, eating our food—

"Just bachelor stuff," Xavier answered. It gave him an excuse to put space in between them, going to throw some random spices into the pan.

"Too bad." Michaels said. "How're you? You haven't been into work lately. Schedule changes?"

Watched. Always watched. *Probably stole something.* "Don't know if he told you, but we're gettin' kicked out. Mom's taking some extra shifts while I pack up, look for another apartment."

Dr. Michaels looked almost embarrassed. Almost. The chicken popped. Grease and fat flying, hitting the smooth white knobs of the oven.

"...Besides that unfortunate news, how're you doing?" Michaels asked.

"I'm good." The chicken was burned down to the marrow. Smelled disgusting.

"Well. I guess I should leave you to that then..." Michaels put a hand on Desai's shoulder.

Desai stared at it like bird shit that had dropped out of the sky, a dirty white splatter on his expensive shirt. His voice didn't match it, though. Deferential. "Do you mind, sir, if I have a talk with Xavier? As an employee?"

Sir.

Making himself small. No different than him or Rob or anyone at Leigh Pierce, no matter how much he played pretend. No matter how many of them he threw under the bus. The birds shitting down on them, untouchable, from a blue, blue sky. Michaels gave him the go-ahead before leaving.

"My condolences. I'm so sorry to hear that. Remember, you can always call—"

Xavier flipped off the stove and went to the peephole, watching the doctor sweat in his suit, step inside the elevator. The smell of him still here.

In *his* house—

"Holy shit, dude. *These people.* They won't get off my ass!" Desai hissed, spitting strawberry fumes. "They're gonna put cameras up. In my office, in the units. Not just the hallways. They won't piss off."

"They can't do that. It's illegal."

"They had a lot of paperwork that made it seem legit... *It's not my fault!* I keep telling them no, but—" Desai said, close to hyperventilating. "Look, you need to delete our texts. Dude heard the guy in B12 is gone and freaked out. If they find out we pawned everything, it's gonna be a clusterfuck."

"So I'm gettin' paid now?" Xavier didn't bother waiting for the answer. Shoved him backwards, Desai's knees bumping against the coffee table. Nearly buckling.

"It's not like I don't want to. But that guy didn't have shit—"

"*He didn't have shit,* and you took it anyway, and he's still gone!" Xavier barked, voice tearing out of his throat.

Desai scurried away, like a cockroach, a rat, and Xavier moved with him, alien muscles twitching. Closing the gap. "Have you wondered for even half a fuckin' second what happened to him? Did you bother even *tryin'* to figure that out?"

Desai was at the door, eyes rolling, the dismissiveness stabbing at Xavier like a needle breaking skin. A needle between his fingers. He grabbed the first thing within reach—

The alligator head, grinning. *Zion's.*

Desai threw up his hands. "Oh, what happened to the crackhead living in my basement? I wonder if it has something to do with crack—"

Xavier slammed the alligator into Desai's temple, and he crumpled. A paper man.

Friable.

The taxidermy skull fractured, half of the head skidding across the floor, marble eyes watching. In his hand—a hand, **their** hand— just the bottom jaw and the wooden base. A line of teeth cresting a glint of copper.

Desai got up, sputtering, blood soaked into his pricey dress shirt.

A hand braced against the wall.

An arm swinging with another *crack*—

Blood arching upward. *Three drops of blood on the ceiling. Dried. Soaked into the paint.*

Blood on his face. In his mouth.

He could taste it.

CHAPTER NINE
CYMOTHOA EXIGUA

Lan had forgotten her fabric softener, last week's laundry already shoved full to bursting into a single washer. *Shit.*

This wasn't her usual laundry day, but her cousin Tham had shown up to gift some expensive chocolates—like her life, luxurious and sweet—and wound up crying into Lan's shirt instead, pressing her baby bump down with her hands like she could iron it out.

Tham had fallen asleep before Lan could tell her about getting evicted. Sixty days. Some part of her had hoped her cousin would be able to help, but Tham had her own problems. Like always.

What bullshit.

Lan hurried back upstairs and grabbed the jug, prepared to wait in the laundry room all day. Anyplace that wasn't her apartment—Tham snoring on the couch, pretty nose crusted with snot—was a good place. The property manager and one of the cops from the lobby were standing by Xavier's door, Lan lowering her head as they said their good mornings, the bad feeling sticking with her as she headed back to the basement and dumped the fabric softener into the machine.

"Excuse me?"

An older woman stood in the doorway, one arm in a Velcro brace held limply to her chest. "I'm sorry, but can you help me get my laundry?" She held up her hurt wrist, flustered, looked like she'd been crying.

Join the club. What about Tham, who only ate grapefruit and soda crackers and stopped eating even *that* when the baby pushed her over a hundred pounds? What about the letter on her kitchen counter, the envelope torn open? Where was she supposed to go? She'd never lived anywhere else. *Join the fucking club.*

"Where is it?" Lan asked, polite.

"Oh, just across the way here," the woman said, drifting back out into the hall. "I got a rolling basket just for this, but the handle broke already," she rambled, running her good hand through her hair. It was fake, shiny blonde plastic, and she looked sick. Cancer or lupus or something that made people's hair fall out.

Lan followed her into the hall, reaching for the white curve of the plastic laundry basket propped against the doorframe of B4.

"Thank you for helpin'. You're so sweet," the woman said.

Lan hooked her fingers around the edge of the basket and started dragging. She heaved it over the rusted metal door bar, off the carpet and onto the concrete. Plastic scratching. Strangely heavy. *When was the last time this lady did her laundry?*

But, unlike Tham, *she* actually bothered to help someone besides herself every now and again. "Is this the only one?" she asked, but the woman hadn't followed her.

Lan frowned, wandering out of the laundry room to check and nearly crashing face-first into some guy as he barreled out of B4. *That's not his apartment.* Down the hallway. *Where've I seen him before?* A dead sprint to the stairwell. She flinched as the door slammed behind him, the sound echoing through the basement.

Ari's family had always shown up at the worst times, his brother especially. Some sixth sense for how to be as inconvenient as possible.

"I can't believe you ran away for a fucking girl," Drew had said, sitting in an Indiana diner, Cam perched on the hood of their car outside, smoking. Gray. Everything gray.

"Ma's gonna have a heart attack. An actual, literal heart attack. You're gonna *kill Mom* over a girl. A white girl."

"That's not what happened."

"That's what it looks like from here."

Why am I thinking about that now?

The lack of words, maybe? The same feeling rising out of his stomach. Ari had tried not to look at Drew back then, had focused on the feeling of glass against his skin. Ice-cold condensation. White flecks floating in water. *A white girl.* Swirling. Waiting.

He tried not to look at Xavier now, no idea how to even start. Cam would've had the words for it...

What it looks like from here: Karma coming back to bite the property manager in the ass.

Ari placed his foot on the manager's neck. He saw a finger twitch. Still alive then. Xavier would have to get better at that. Pressing harder with no change. Alive but not conscious. *Hope it hurts.* A few minutes of digging, hands brushing on the roof, was all it took to understand the visceral satisfaction that must've come with bashing this specific skull in.

Xavier wasn't acting like it, though, panicking. Pacing.

Ari breathed out through his nose, trying not to smell the blood. "Xavier. Calm down."

"Fuck off! *You* calm down!" Xavier snapped.

"Okay," Ari said, no right to get mad. This *was* at least partly their fault. *His fingers curling around the hammer, Leena's voice getting closer. "Thank you for helpin'. You're so sweet." Footsteps breaking away, leaving an open space to swing*—leaving Xavier with all the steam and nowhere to blow it off.

Maybe this was for the best. Xavier wouldn't have been happy if the girl from 311 got hurt. And Leena would *know* that if she'd just—

Ari bit his tongue. Refocused. Tasting blood as he steered Xavier to the couch and forced him to sit. Squirming. "Okay. Breathe in and look around. What do you see that's gray?"

Gray like dirty snow, kicked up by flailing shoes. Kicking out. Like dead grass under ice and the molted bark on a birch tree. Like the sky in Indiana in winter.

Ari grabbed the sides of Xavier's face, looking him dead in the eyes. "Breathe in." He waited for the give of Xavier's chest, the whisper of air through the teeth. "Hold it. Gray carpet..."

"That blanket's gray... The TV's gray," Xavier said, eyes flooded with black. Nothing but pupil.

"Now breathe out."

Ari exhaled, and Xavier followed his lead, their lungs moving together as he pulled away and shook two white pills out into his palm. Just a snippet under his hands: Xavier sitting at the foot of a bed, smoking and lightheaded. A shadow beside him. Warm insides. Warm throat. Already drifting. A good memory.

Two pills—enough to knock out a lightweight.

"How're you feeling?" Ari asked.

"I... I have a toothache," Xavier said after a second. "The posterior superior alveolar nerve. That's mine, isn't it? Still?"

"Let me see."

Xavier opened his mouth, let Ari tilt his head back and look inside... Straight down into the throat, bloody and raw. He found the bad tooth on the right side, a dark cavity in the molar, flush with the gums. Ari reached in, slowly pressing his fingertip against the rotten spot.

A *wince*. But Xavier stayed put, trusting, as Ari released the pressure on the tooth and placed the pills on the center of Xavier's tongue. Watched them begin

to

fizzle

and

dissolve.

Xavier woke up on the floor, his shoulders cracking. Sharp plastic cutting into his wrists, his ankles. Talk radio murmuring, meaningless. Speaking in tongues.

Next level sharpness and boosted physical performance all in a single daily supplement. He felt the fibers of the carpet scratch against his cheek. *Healthy is a choice.* Eyes rolling, catching the ceiling fan in their periphery, turning and turning. *Take your heart into your hands.* It could be his floor, his ceiling fan. Identical in all sixty-three units of Leigh Pierce. His house, or anywhere, no difference…

A pair of white socks, crossed at the ankle, at the sharp knob of bone. Pink heels and toes…

In a rush, he remembered Desai. *His eyes two perfect circles*—Desai crumbling. Blood in black hair…

There wasn't blood on this carpet. This carpet smelled like baking soda, a bubbling scent right against his nostrils.

"Are you comfy, sweetheart…?" A voice like music. "I don't think he hears me."

"Knocked him out but good."

The feet moved out of sight. "Wait…" he groaned.

Desai falling. Hands and knees on the floor, then his face…

A hand. Dark skin and white gauze—Xavier's hand, *his* hand? —holding tight to Zion's memory. *Our knees touched.* Two pieces of a mouth. Two smiling curves. Smiling because Desai was dead. A death smelling like strawberry vapor and burnt chicken and hot blood.

If you ever need anything—anything.

When did he get here? He had a memory of walking down the basement hallway. Soft hands on his wrists. In his mouth. Then... nothing.

"Wait."

The socks came back. A piece of thread was poking out of the toe, pointing at him.

"Let's get you up..."

And Leena was eye to eye with him. Brown irises and clumped mascara. She kissed his forehead with an image of a boy through a water-spotted window. Dark hair, red bike. Hangers scraping along a rod, parting to show blue eyes in a white face. *Such a pretty girl...* Toes poking out of red water gone cold. *Nothing left to even bury.*

Then her lips were gone, the sensations leaving with them. He watched her pull up a kitchen chair, setting it down directly across from him, and Cyril took a seat. Spine curved like a gargoyle as he leaned in, the toe of his shoe brushing Xavier's leg, a taunting, impossible closeness.

"We're leavin' tomorrow. Woulda *liked* to have more time to ease you into everything, but that's not how it worked out..."

He waited for a response, but Xavier said nothing, noticing this close that Cyril was missing part of a finger. His left pinkie lopped off at the second knuckle. A mangled hand resting on a knee.

"We could do New Orleans. Fun place. Somewhere you can slip up and it'd be fine," Cyril said, trying to smile, one side of his mouth not quite managing it.

Xavier's stomach spasmed, and he tried to relax—*pyramidalis, external obliques, internal obliques...*

Cyril put a hand under his chin, at once repulsive and relieving, and he listened in. *Rectus abdominus, transversus abdominis.* Cyril was full but could eat, making Xavier realize that he was empty. Starving.

Steam like summer barbeque. A steak under fork and knife, flesh sliding apart. Blood in my mouth. Her blood, body popping, collapsing. His blood, like tree sap. Dried onto my shirt—

"It'll get worse," Cyril said. That same lopsided smile. Not happy, not unhappy either. "They start eatin' you alive after a while, if they don't get what they need."

They...

They.

The expanding stomach in his stomach, the brain folded into his brain. **They.**

Cyril held out his hand, a worm emerging from the nail of his pointer finger. *Pellucid*, the word rising in Xavier's mind. Familiar and unfamiliar. *Pellucid, crystalline, translucent.* Xavier felt his eyes go wide, a midbrain panic, as Cyril cupped the worm in his palm.

"Greedy little bastards. Have to keep up with them." With a gentle motion, he pressed the worm down.

"Is that what happened to Camille?" Xavier asked, transfixed by it, watching it disappear into the ridges of skin. Pulsing. Shifting into the calluses. "She *didn't keep up with them?*"

"We thought she could manage it. We were wrong. So it goes," Cyril said, and Leena made a sound somewhere out of sight, a noise coming from the corners of her body.

Cyril cleared his throat. "We got a part of her here at least."

His hand was under Xavier's chin again. Suffocating. The hunger between them collective and compounding—*You just get so up in your head sometimes.*

The front door clicked opened, and Xavier craned his neck to see Ari in the doorway, heaving a trash bag over his shoulder. Black plastic. Like what they'd zipped Camille into. And Rob. Like dead, moldering skin.

Ari dropped the bag on the kitchen tiles and went out for more. Six of them by the end, laid out with a ritualistic care. One after the other.

"Ari," Xavier pleaded, not sure why. Expecting help? Expecting someone to see him on the floor, bleeding and starving, and *do* something. *Something* before he died here. A moth following a pheromone trail that ended with its body carried away on the wind. Light as paper.

Ari locked the door.

Doorknob—

Dead bolt—

Chain lock—

"I'll text your mom so she doesn't get too worried," he said, staring at Xavier with a cold, useless sympathy.

Xavier slumped, his eyes burning, too dehydrated for tears. Nothing left inside. And he lurched forward, cracking his forehead against his knees. A noise in his ears.

What should we do instead, Xav? What should we—

Cyril grabbed him by the hair, forcing his head back. "None of that, now."

"Cy—"

"He's *fine.*"

Another noise from Leena. And Ari watched them, taking a drag off Desai's vape pen. Strawberries wafting, sucked up into the AC going on high in the window. Freezing.

"Your mama's gonna be lookin' for you?" Cyril asked, looking him in the eyes. *Dad's gone crazy.* Xavier nodded, his mouth moving. No stopping himself.

"Mom's stuck with me. She wanted so many things. She says she didn't, but she did. And she got me instead. Just me. I'm all she ever got..."

Cyril stroked his hair, comforting, and turned to Ari. "Think of somethin' good. We need at least a week."

A nod, another sweet-smelling puff.

"If you get addicted to those things, I'll be very cross with you," Leena said from across the room, her voice muffled. Strained.

"I only do it socially." Ari slumped against the door, refusing to look at any of them now.

"Make yourself scarce," Cyril ordered, giving Ari and Leena a hard look. "Both of you. Don't need any distractions."

They didn't argue, going to Rashon's old bedroom. Hands all over each other, muttering. Leaving him alone with Cyril.

Was he going to die now or later?

Will I feel it at all?

"It's my responsibility to manage my children and my household. Manage it *well*, you understand?" Cyril asked.

Xavier nodded, and with a surprising strength, Cyril grabbed the collar of his shirt and dragged him to the kitchen, Xavier's bound ankles screaming as he was dropped onto the linoleum. Dropped hard.

A knife roll was already laid out on the counter, Cyril choosing a large butcher knife to cut Xavier's hands free before pulling the nearest garbage bag close. He gestured with the blade, serrated and gleaming. Not a suggestion.

It was difficult to undo the knots, Xavier's fingers numb. Slipping. Cyril waited patiently for him to get the bag open. Waited patiently as Xavier processed what he was seeing—

A leg.

He jerked away, but Cyril grabbed the back of his neck, forcing him back down to uncover the arms. Another leg. The torso. A head.

Desai's head—looking at him with eyes half-open and glassy.

Cyril lowered himself to the floor, sweat pouring down his face. He leaned against the kitchen cabinets, breathing hard. "Good, now come sit," he said, pulling over the nearest piece—an arm—and patting the space next to him.

Xavier crawled over, a dog, feral and stupid and hungry. Hands shaking as he stared at Desai's arm, hacked off at the shoulder.

"I want you to think of it *academically*, understand? Hands-on practice. That's what you want, isn't it?" Cyril asked.

A hollow spot in his stomach. Something moved in Xavier's mouth. Under the thin skin along his fingertips. Twinging.

Cyril guided his hand—gentle, like Rob walking alongside his patients, gait belt keeping them steady—placed Xavier's open palm on the exposed bone of the shoulder. "Where should we start? Tendons, bones...?"

"Bones," Xavier heard himself say. Both their voices so far away. "I been studyin'..."

Maybe he hadn't spoken aloud at all, but Cyril nodded, twisting the knife to cut through the skin, the muscle, the fat... Down to the pink-white center.

"Good. Show me."

And it seemed like a very good idea, permission for Xavier to open the cut wider, worms sprouting from under his nails. Roots plunging deep, spread flat and red and blood-fed over the bone. He watched, absorbed in **their** movements, in the calm **their** eating sent through him...

"Humorous. Radius. Ulna," he choked out, tracing down until he got to the wrist. He tore at the flesh for a better look. Peeling it back.

"Scaphoid, trapezium, capitate." His mouth was swimming with **them**.

"Hamate." Making it difficult to speak.

He stopped. *Flexor carpi radialis. Flexor digitorum profundus* flexing—his and not his. A dark, twitching hand coming away with a hunk of flesh. Tendons and muscle and lean meat.

In the mouth. A teeming, starving mouth.

Wrapped in a blissful, gratified blankness. The feeling of a stomach full. Of Shayna's head on his chest, rising and falling. Of his mother's hand against his forehead, sheltering. Soft...

A step through a threshold. Reaching out

into this

new house.

Speaking with it. Speaking into it. With a voice echoing and re-echoing. Ringing with a sharp edge that pries open the world. Hands tearing.

Not this body's hands.

Our hands *our* teeth *our* tongue.

Our tongue tasting for the thousandth time and the first time. A cherished memory like a current rushing in and retreating.

Teasing. An old taste glutted with unspoiled senses, new muscles spasming. *Wanting.*

Our stomach. Newly full.

Our voice sputtering

thank you thank you thank you it's okay you're okay I'm here with you

You're alive.

Leena moved through the rooms of 305 with a desolate feeling in her chest. A pitcher with its insides poured out.

She went through the motions, told herself that was why she was there—cleaning blood from carpet, throwing out two halves of a bloodied reptilian mouth. But really, she savored the opportunity to take it all in.

There'd been no chance with Cal or Ari, plucked from a full house, and the place where they'd found Camille didn't even have the suggestion of a child. Not a trace. Apartment 305, though, was a reservoir of information. An open obituary.

Xavier James Coates, she read from the framed high school diploma. Xavier James Coates: a track star—shame it wasn't football, Cy would've liked that better—a silver medalist in the Fulton County Science Olympiad, a volunteer at the Bankhead Senior Center.

There was a picture of him standing with a man who was not his father. A man whose words—she knew, Xavier's world opening up to her under her lips that morning—could uplift and maim in the same breath. A man who didn't know or care to know the impact of these things... And there was a *mother*.

A mother whose presence was in the bus schedule on the fridge, in a bedroom closet divided down the middle. A memory of her soft hand shielding from pain. She looked young in the one picture that existed of her, smiling at his graduation, an almost manic happiness.

The Coates, Leena surmised, were a family that ended after that photo, happy to pretend the last handful of years hadn't happened. It was encouraging, an assurance that **they** were righteous in taking him in, a sheep separated from goats. A hand outstretched with feed in the palm. Faith through works.

Leena sat at the foot of his bed, the sheets rough under her fingers, her chest still yawning, waiting to be replenished, refilled, her face turned upward.

INDIGENT

Anika Davis's boy darted out of the dollar store, still angry that the ancient old cashier wouldn't let him buy a Roblox gift card without a grown-up. Even though he was *rich*. Fifty dollars cash. And all he had to do was help get a bunch of trash down to the basement in one trip instead of two. Easy.

He'd grabbed Miss Inez's big laundry basket with the wheels and waited on the third floor, heels bouncing, while the guy from the roof stuffed the basket with garbage bags.

"What's in there?" he'd asked.

"A dead body."

"That's what you actin' like. Is it *drugs*? Do you deal *drugs*?"

"No," had been the answer. *No* in a puff of strawberry smoke.

That had made Anika Davis's boy as aware as he'd ever been that adults could do all the bad, unhealthy shit they wanted, but *he* couldn't even try weed once—maybe more than once—without everybody acting like it was the end of the world.

"Ask *who* it is," the guy had said after a minute, smiling, letting him in on a secret.

"Okay. Who is it?"

"The property manager."

"Oh, my mom would *love* that."

And the guy had grinned. Huge. Like what quiet Miss Davis in apartment 101 thought of his dumbass joke mattered more than anything.

Don't talk to strangers.

But they weren't strangers, were they? They were neighbors. A neighbor who'd handed over five brand-new ten-dollar bills with a *promise not to tell*.

"I'm not a snitch," Anika Davis's boy had said proudly, lugging the laundry basket down the stairs. God, the thing was heavy.

Shoulda asked for sixty *dollars...*

Xavier stood in front of the bathroom mirror, his reflection a blurry silhouette. An outline unfilled.

Someone had drawn a flower on the glass, the phantom lines of petals and leaves appearing in the shower steam, over his face, while he tried to cry quietly. One hand pressed to his mouth, his nose, forcing the sobs back.

A fading orange light washed over the parking lot outside the casement window. So he must've been asleep all day, or maybe more than that. Asleep for five hours or five years. The only indication that it wasn't the latter was that Leigh Pierce was still standing, him squirming around its insides. A parasite in the gut of an animal trundling along, its head slowly, unknowingly lifted into the crosshairs of a rifle.

He dug a spool of floss out of the cabinet and went at his teeth, thinking of **them** twisting up from between the molars. He flossed until his gums bled and a worm was drawn out of his bad tooth, clinging to the plastic string before falling into the sink with a loud *click*.

The sound made him freeze, terrified he'd lost the tooth entirely. But no, it was just a worm—part of its body gone opaque, hard and pebble-smooth to the touch. A facsimile of enamel that he poked at with fascination and a dull disgust.

Cyril's hand had been on his. The whorls of the palm shifting.

How much of his hand was real…?

There and gone, the thought.

Because there was blood in his mouth.

A tongue skimming along teeth. Head lulling back… Sucking the wells of his gums dry, blood coaxed out with a pulsing of the muscles.

Hungry again. What had been a shiftless and drifting ache, a need without direction, now given a target. A *taste*—

"Knock, knock!" Leena said from out in the hall, her voice full and close, the door opening. "Sorry! I thought you were in the shower still," she said, a bundle of clothes hugged to her chest.

His clothes. A T-shirt and plaid cotton sleep pants from his room. They'd been in his room. *His* house.

Xavier took the clothes, something clean at least, changing in front of her without hesitation. It'd taken almost a year of dating Shayna before he'd been even remotely comfortable with her seeing him that way, self-conscious every time. But that had been *his* body.

Not this one. This body that could've been Leena's for all he knew.

Leena looked at him, at the tears gone cold on his cheeks. "Everybody has tribulations," she said quietly, sitting on the counter. Xavier didn't say anything. Didn't look at her.

"Cy can be... overdramatic sometimes. But tomorrow, we can sit down at the table and eat breakfast and have conversations like normal, civilized people. And *that* will be what it's really like. I promise."

It sounded like a lie. Mom telling him they weren't poor. Uncle Rob in that woman's trailer, pulling her socks back up and grinning like nothing was wrong—"Well, no wonder y'all need some new shoes."

Leena reached for his hand, and he flinched away for a moment before sighing, letting her take it. Was that his hand or hers pulling back a flimsy curtain, looking out to see a boy ride past on a red bike? *Stopping for her. Kind boy.*

Did it matter?

"We were in a bad way before. Cy wanted us to move,"—hands on her stomach, subconscious and quickly corrected—"But we could never make enough even with me working. I had nightmares where I'd come home and find him with his head blown off... I emptied out the shells in his gun and kept the whole box of them with me in my purse. I brought them with me to work every day."

Under her hand, Xavier saw a younger Cyril. A first-born son, uncomplaining, coming home six days a week smelling like chlorine and silt and a growing, all-consuming exhaustion. He saw Cyril with a shotgun, peeking out of that gauzy curtain, the whites around his eyes showing.

Where're the shells, hon? The look of a man realizing that he'd been promised something that never materialized, that never would.

The slow realization—a bitter, bitter remedy to all his problems—that food was like *gold*. It was a job with a retirement plan and a boss who gave a damn. It was a house built with his own hands. A craft room and a hobby farm with a boy and a girl and a dog tending to a flock of spoiled goats. Bleating. It was golf with the boys on the weekends. Food was every promise. Every*thing*. It was something he could provide.

A realization, desperate and gasping, relayed to Leena silently through the skin, years and years ago back in the Ozarks, his hand over hers. Crushing it.

"Can I at least leave a note or somethin'?" Xavier asked. Nothing else to say, knowing that it was settled. No point in arguing, in pretending like he didn't understand what this was.

Leena gave him a tight-lipped smile and left him with his thoughts—her thoughts, Cyril's thoughts, **their** thoughts—rattling around his head, blood in his mouth.

Ari wanted to say he hadn't had a roommate since Drew, two beds pushed to opposite sides of a tiny bedroom overlooking the alleyway. That wouldn't be right, though, because Drew had left him—or moved out, same difference—and then there was detox.

A month of buprenorphine and vision boards and sweating out the second-worst fever of his life, watching Turner Classic Movies in the common room with all the other burnouts whose families were sick of dealing with them.

At night, he'd shared a plain white room with some plain white hick from Gary, Indiana, got called "Chong" on good days and "Chink" on bad ones. Ari couldn't be too mad about it—wasn't like he ever retained Gary, Indiana's real name either.

Sharing a room with Xavier felt the same way: two people trying their best to avoid the obvious questions. "Ever shared a room before?" he asked.

How'd you wind up here?

"Nah." Not looking at him.

How'd you let it get this bad?

"Get used to it. They think you need a babysitter."

Are you gonna do it again?

Ari grabbed a blanket from the futon and tossed it on the floor, figuring he should let Xavier keep the couch. An olive branch. Xavier still wasn't looking at him, and that was fine. All their time belonged to something else, and there was food in the fridge, and there was no hurry anymore.

He balled the blanket under his head, fingers tracing the laminate. Plastic pretending to be wood. Cheap.

It was probably better that Xavier didn't want to talk. Dealing with the property manager had taken something out of him. He *still* didn't know what the guy had said.

"What?" he'd asked, hands gripping the edge of the tub, his ear to the bloody mouth. He couldn't make out anything, though, just a groan of air and spittle.

Then, he'd slid the blade of a hunting knife between the base of the skull and the first vertebrae, where he'd been taught, pressing down until he heard a wonderful *crack*. As he'd taken the saw to the major joints, humming over the jagged start-stop of metal on bone,

242

he turned up his music and tried to focus on that instead of the blood.

Verse.

Instead of the skin parting to fat parting to muscle parting to bone.

Chorus.

Verse.

He'd done a pretty good job—only a single piece missing by the time he'd packed the property manager away. A paring knife slipped past the yellowed teeth. Twisting until the tongue could be ripped free from the dark cavity of the mouth. The tongue, scarfed down in seconds. He hadn't even tasted it. Not really.

Bridge.

Verse.

Chorus.

And back in the room, the sky darkening outside— "Is it always like that?" Xavier asked.

Ari twisted around, but Xavier still had his back to him, talking into the couch cushions.

Cyril had been thinking about it: Xavier pulling away from an opened chest. Reflective and serious. "The bronchial tree is black. Look. It got struck by lightning." *Sure, son. Of course.* They'd all said crazier shit than that, in the middle of it. Cam had recorded them once, playing it back when Cyril and Leena were out.

Is it always like that?

"No," Ari lied. "It woulda been better to wait 'til you were starving. Makes it easier."

"I *was* starvin'."

And all Ari could think of was blue-tinted snow on windows. The delirious ache of his own teeth sinking into his forearm. Gnawing.

Laughing while Leena grabbed at him. Screaming. Lapping up his insides. Cam curled up like a cat on the floor. Like chili oil, that beautiful, translucent sheen on her teeth. His mouth over hers, sharing the taste, fighting not to bite through her tongue like he desperately, desperately needed to...

Cyril with his left hand mutilated, standing over her. Even now, they didn't know if it had been an accident, a moment of weakness, or if Cyril had done it on purpose. Fed his daughter from his body like Athena sprouting from the skull of Zeus.

Starving.

"No," Ari said. "You weren't."

CHAPTER TEN
GIARDIA LAMBLIA

Xavier dreamed about his body suspended in cool, flat water. At once floating and watching himself from the shore. He saw the white body of a worm twisting by his hand, like the extended tentacles of a jellyfish. And another and another.

He watched them, deathly frightened, in all the peacefulness, of what would happen if he disturbed them. If he swam to the water's edge and met eyes with himself—

And he woke up, taking the world in.

Light leaking from underneath the door, winking off the coiled dryer vent in the corner. The AC humming—Rashon's utility bill running into the stratosphere—a snoring down the hall, cars passing outside...

And he was on the floor, legs tangled in the blanket trailing up and onto the futon. His hand was draped over Ari's body. Fingers touching.

Xavier jerked away, but Ari didn't move, hardly seemed to be breathing at all. After a moment, Xavier crept forward again, filled with a bitter curiosity. Tired already of this body that wasn't his, that moved and spoke and ate when he didn't want it to.

A lifetime of keeping a safe distance, of understanding what that *meant*, only for him to be flayed open every time they touched him. His insides laid out to get gawked at.

He could do it too, though. *Pry*. He could cut them open and look inside.

His hand rested first on Ari's shoulder, then the curve of the neck. Down to the throat... He could probably crush Ari's windpipe and make a break for it. *But what then?* Leigh Pierce would still be bulldozed into nothing. There would still be eyes watching him, waiting for the moment he fucked up.

What should we do instead, Xav?

Xavier didn't know, just traced over the arc of Ari's neck, thinking about Zion, his hands and the rhythm under his voice, a performance to it. Not like Rob performing for the doctors. *That voice.* The opposite. Zion, hands sweeping, taking up space—

"He was dying anyway," Ari said, eyes still closed, an image of black lungs seeping up under Xavier's hands. Of disease gone unacknowledged and unchecked. "I'm sorry we were the ones to find out, though."

Quiet. He could've been talking in his sleep, except Xavier knew better. He could feel the spark of wakefulness, the gears turning behind the eyes. Wanted, more than anything, to reach in and grab them. Grind everything to a halt.

"You can try if you want." Ari's voice was flat, calm at the prospect.

"I don't really," Xavier lied, creeping away, his back against the door. "I didn't mean that."

"You didn't?"

"No. I'm just hungry."

Ari opened his eyes, giving Xavier a conspiratorial smile.

They raided the kitchen, Xavier's stomach in knots, picturing in brief, disjointed pieces his hands sliding underneath skin. Fingernails scraping bone. Cyril's voice low, steady as a metronome. "There you go. Good boy, you're doing good. You're okay..."

Any food is good food.

Once he was done eating, he found a steak knife in one of the kitchen drawers and hid it in his waistband, the edge pressed cooly against his skin. He watched Ari pack everything back into the fridge, wanting to be ready to run. If things came to that.

It seemed stupid—the knife, the secrecy—once the two of them got on the roof, backs against the rusty water tower supports, Xavier's hand white-knuckled around the knife while Ari smoked. Not touching. Trying, Xavier assumed, to give him space.

Ari rolled the cigarette between his thumb and forefinger, the glowing cherry reflected in his eyes, illuminating the slim lines of his hand. *A hand in the dark, disembodied. Floating.* Like Zion again, reaching out, offering him a puff.

"Shit's bad for you," Xavier refused.

"So's cocaine. I'm not doin' that."

Xavier sighed and held out his hand to take the cigarette while Ari shook another one out from the pack. Different brand, same CAM <3. Camille wasn't picky, apparently.

The cheap lighter sputtered in Ari's hands as he tried to get a spark going. "Help me out?"

Xavier leaned forward so Ari could light his cigarette off the glowing ember of the last, held it there for a dizzying moment—*vertiginous*, his brain said—**u**ntil the paper started to smolder and Ari pulled away. Xavier let smoke leak out from behind his teeth, tasting like nothing. Just a warmth, a heat.

The packs had definitely been pilfered from someone's house, from dead pockets. Some private place. Stolen. *Thought he was going to steal something—*

Xavier crushed his cigarette in his palm.

If Ari noticed, he didn't say anything, too preoccupied with some self-given distraction of trying to blow a smoke ring. Smoke passing over his lips.

Are those clothes his? The phone? The cigarettes?

Xavier's palm itched, and he opened it to see that the skin had already blistered, a raised spot of fluid. On closer look, there was something moving inside it. Pulsing. Another confirmation of what he already knew, what he'd known the second he'd touched Ari in the laundry room: he had no room to judge. He didn't own this body either. Might as well not own anything at all.

Ari's cigarette had burnt down to almost nothing by the time he finally managed a single smoke ring, elated for a second. Smiling a real smile that Xavier remembered seeing before.

A hand-me-down memory, not his either.

"The key to happiness is setting *attainable* goals," Ari said, leaning his head against Xavier's shoulder. Sharing the good mood.

Xavier didn't move, resigned to the lack of personal space, to his body breathing with four lungs instead of two.

"Think it means anything?" Ari asked. "Your dream with the room filling up with water."

"My dream?"

"Well, it wasn't *mine*."

They'd been touching. Of course. Not a second of privacy.

Xavier shifted, pulling away. "I don't know. But I've been havin' it a lot."

"Cam took it really seriously," Ari said. "If you dream about a white dog in the woods, it really means your middle school gym teacher is gonna get hit by a car. That kinda thing."

"It's just pattern recognition," Xavier said, sensing Ari's relief and finding himself relieved too, the feeling doubled, sitting warmly in his gut.

So used to having to suffocate that part of himself for Mom, for Uncle Rob—people who believed because they *had* to that there was a bigger meaning behind everything. Being told time and time again not to ruin it. *You just get so up in your head sometimes.*

"It's just our brain tryin' to make sense out of things while it processes information in our sleep," he continued.

"So you're processing the same thing over and over, then."

"I guess so."

"I have this recurring dream," Ari started, settling in against him again, subconscious, a magnetic pull between them. "I'm in a theater, I think, behind the stage, and I'm walking up a set of stairs. And I'm totally sure that once I get to the room at the top, the projection room maybe, somethin' bad's gonna happen. I just keep walking up, though."

Xavier could almost see it, like a passing reflection in a window. A red staircase.

"Cam figured it was about 'bridging the gap to my shadow self' first, then she thought it was about me wanting a new hobby. Then, she thought it was just... *stairs*."

Xavier *did* manage to laugh at that. A small one, but still. "You never see what's up top?"

"No. But it's recurring, like I said, so you'll see it eventually. Maybe you'll figure it out."

A promise through a puff of smoke. Like Leena with her photo album, not a doubt in the world that he'd be with them next time, that they could take him anywhere they wanted.

Xavier shot to his feet, kicking up gravel as he drifted over to the edge of the roof. Ari watched him.

"If I give you a note for my mom, can you leave it in my apartment?" he asked, looking down into the alley. *Watching ash float down. Relief and disappointment comingled...* He'd have to fall in all the right ways. Land on his head.

"You don't wanna do that."

"I kinda do."

"*Kinda*," Ari scoffed, and Xavier ignored him, staring down and down to the spot where Camille died, to where her memories bled out onto the concrete. Leaking into him.

I can't do it.

He stepped back, feeling a drop in his stomach. It'd been ground into him for too long—by Mom adjusting the straps on his backpack. *They gon' think you grown.* By Rob giving a sickly sweet smile to every patient and secretary and doctor who looked at him funny, introducing himself with *that voice,* and by Marius beating him to a pulp, hearing in his inner ear one of his ribs cracking. By the indifferent silence that came after Rashon's death. After Zion's...

Ground into him since he could remember that he couldn't keep himself small and have his dignity. That he had to *pick one.*

Xavier sank down, resting his head against the safety railing, a scream building up. *I have to stay alive*—the realization riding on a wave of giddiness, a lightheaded sort of confidence, like going to Zion's bedroom after they'd smoked. *Our knees touching.*

He closed his eyes. Still hungry, off balance because his stomach was empty. Too hungry to even have a center of gravity holding him down...

Ari's hand was on his shoulder, stabilizing. "D'you see anything green?"

"I don't know. The trees," Xavier said, finding his voice after a frantic second of clambering.

"They don't look green in the dark, though. What d'you *actually* see?"

"Nothin' then."

"Sometimes, you havta look harder," Ari said, hand running along the railing as he moved away, finding a patch of moss. A creeping, nauseous green under the rooftop lights, tucked into the nooks of a ventilation unit. He took a piece and held it out for Xavier in his palm.

Xavier stared at it until the soft blur of color sharpened, tiny green sprigs standing out.

"Green moss," he said, taking it.

A ripple under the skin. Ari sympathetic to the feeling of existing—miraculous and violent and bitter—where he shouldn't, long past the time he should've stopped. Xavier rolled the moss between his fingers until it fell apart, fibers unwinding.

"I have an idea," Ari said, helping him back to his feet, their hands touching.

Desk. *Zhuōzi*. Window. *Chuānghù*. Cabinet. *Guìzǐ*.
New house. *Xīn fángzi*.

They got into the rent office with Xavier's key, scrounging up some paper and an envelope from the property manager's desk. Leena would have some—she hoarded stationery, a holdover from her old job—but she'd notice if something went missing. They couldn't go back to 305, either, *absolutely not*, so petty theft it was.

Ari waited in the doorway while Xavier wrote his letter, deciding not to ask. Not to *pry*, the word floating to the surface of his mind.

252

Pry. A jaw after rigor mortis, hands under lips. The ribs, heart and lungs behind fingers of bone. A lockbox, a few hours of peace hidden inside the metal. *Pry.*

Instead, he focused on the memory of Leena standing at the edge of the bus terminal. Blue dress. Waving. "Sweetheart, what'd you do to your hair!?" Her hands running over his face, over his shaved scalp. Prickling. He'd hated the feel of it. But his cheap bleach job had been stained a permanent pink-red from what had happened. The smell clinging to him. The color.

"Why you people always do that with your hair?" Gary, Indiana had asked when they'd first met. "Poppin' percs like every piece of trailer trash in the county didn't make you white enough?"

The memory of Leena's white hands clasped around his, pulling him closer to that blue dress. "Don't worry. We'll do better. We'll fix this. I promise." Cyril sitting across from him, hands interlinked, apologizing. Cam's arms draped over him. "I'msosorryI'msosorryI'msosorry. It'll never happen again."

Ari watched Xavier now, head bent over the desk, the stuttering of the pen over paper. *It'll never happen again.*

"What'd you tell my mom?" Xavier asked, looking up at him.

"That she'd havta find her own ride back 'cause you were staying at a friend's."

"A *friend's*? Fuck, she's gon' think I'm avoiding her. Or doin' drugs."

"Or both," Ari joked, and it did *not* land, so he turned his attention back to the lobby, hoping the suits hadn't set up cameras yet.

If he focused, Ari could hear the pen cap crack under Xavier's teeth, feel the ghost of pressure against his molars.

"What'd you tell your people when you left?" Xavier asked.

"Nothing."

"You didn't have nobody looking for you?"

A gray sky, somewhere in the past. *I can't believe you ran away for a fucking girl.* Grime floating in ice water.

"No."

"Maybe if they *knew*," Xavier started, going down a dangerous road. "My mom... wouldn't get it, but she'd help. I know she would."

The memory of birch trees in winter. Red spilling out into a colorless expanse, spilling out over his fingers. Searing. Steaming. Black plastic over a face. Teeth cutting through.

"If you tell her too much, she's gonna look for you, and that's not gonna work out for anybody. We just need to... to drop off the face of the earth," Ari said.

"What if—"

Ari glared, put a stop to the idea. What was he supposed to say? *Don't worry, it gets easier. You'll remember every fight you've ever had, and every awkward conversation, and every time someone yelled a slur at you while you were walking down the street. And you'll forget your mom's face and what your favorite food tastes like. You'll forget your own name if it's not taped onto everything you own. It gets easier.*

"It gets worse," he said, and Xavier only nodded. No more questions.

With the rent office locked up tight behind them, they went upstairs, where the girl in 311 answered after four knocks. Just a voice. American and tired. It had to be past midnight by now, Ari lingering in the stairwell, listening, telling himself that it wasn't *prying*. It was necessary, in case Xavier got carried away.

He was doing fine enough for now, trying to convince the girl—*Lan*—to hold on to the letter for a week or so then get it to Miss Coates. Enough time for them to be long gone. She was preoccupied with the eviction, more worried about that than anything he told her.

Would she be this unsure if she knew she'd been a hairline away from something worse?

"I'm movin' in with my aunt soon..." Ari heard her say.

"Just sometime before you leave, then. *Please*."

"Xavier. Are you in trouble?"

Are you?

"Yeah," Xavier answered. "Look, I gotta go. You can read it if you want, it's nothin'- it won't get you in trouble."

It took her a moment to answer. Unbreathing. "I'll give it to her. Just be careful, okay?" she said, closing the door.

Ari backed away before he could get caught eavesdropping. He heard the exhale, the half-running footsteps. Once Xavier got to the stairwell, he collapsed against the wall, hands to his mouth. *Grime floating in ice water. Spinning...* Ari crouched in front of Xavier, hands on his face, hit like a sledgehammer with panic.

Not mine, not mine.

But it *was*, a sharp-edged memory cutting through—

"Something gray?" Ari asked through his teeth, the nerves tearing through them. There was no other color to choose from, the stairwell closing in.

Gray sky. Gray branches. Huīsè de yún.

"Somethin' was wrong with her—"

"I know. Something gray. It's an easy one."

"I can't breathe- I can't—"

Ari dredged the words up from somewhere, knowing and not knowing. "Diaphragm... Intercostals."

Release. Xavier breathed out, air shuddering through him. *Contract.* Chest expanding...

Drew had said a name he couldn't quite make out. Glass clinking. A heater had been going. Too much noise...

"Contract, release," Xavier breathed, hysteria still right under the surface.

Drew had hugged him. That almost never happened, but it'd been too long. A hug, a realization—slow, goosepimples rising on his arms underneath his winter jacket. An empty body. Horrifically empty. Walking. Talking. *Touching him—*

As Xavier's breathing leveled out, Ari stood up, wiping his eyes.

Gray. Trees against old snow. *Xuě.* Diaphragm. *Contract.* Gray like bad water and the inside of that woman's trailer. Intercostals. *Release.* Gray stairs. *Lóutī.*

"Four gray walls," Xavier said, rising shakily to his feet. "A thousand gray steps."

Ari started down the stairs. Back to the basement. "We should probably count them, too. Calm down some," he said, not looking behind him, knowing that Xavier would follow.

"I'm sorry about Drew."

Ari wasn't sure that he'd heard it at first. It could've been in his head. Or maybe it'd come out of his own mouth. A rich, resonant sound emanating from the inside, humming through the bones of his skull. His voice and not his voice.

"It's okay," he said, feeling his tongue move, the quality of it different, though he couldn't place how.

My voice. Wŏ de shēngyīn.

"It's okay," Ari said again, to no one in particular.

Wŏ de shēngyīn. His voice coppery. Getting caught in his throat. A mouth full of mouths—

Leena tried not to think too hard or too long about the *whys*. Why had this happened? Why did some people take to **them** like tomato vines growing unchecked in a window box when other people withered away to nothing? Why, why.

Someday, they'd figure out that it was blood type or cholesterol levels or some discontinued allergy medication they'd all taken once that had made them more open. Pure chance, some wholly unsatisfying, meaningless answer.

It was better to think of it as a hand outstretched.

So she would take it. She would walk through the fire, coming out, through His grace, not smelling like smoke. She would kiss her family. She would let them rest their heads in her lap while she tweezed out wriggling bodies from bloody pockets underneath their tongues.

She would do all these things gladly.

For over an hour, she sat on the kitchen floor, metal clinking on teeth as she leaned over Ari's mouth, digging. She'd told Xavier to go back to bed, but he stuck around, propped against the counter and looking deliberately away.

By breakfast—the sky still pitch-black—the overflow had mostly cleared up, Ari stirring a spoonful of salt into a cup of water and taking a drink. Swish and spit.

Leena didn't touch him, afraid she'd make it worse with all her worrying. Cal on her mind, his tongue eaten and worms swimming in the cavity like a dark pond, a hunger surpassing anything they could provide.

"You *have* to know the trick to keepin' **them** happy by now," Nial had asked her at the end of his first visit, Leena still marveling at his age. His health.

"What trick?"

"God blessed Noah and his sons and said to them: 'Be fruitful and multiply,'" he'd told her.

Still so young in her mind, that sweet little boy with his mother's hair at First Glory Sunday School, Leena writing his name in all capitals for him to trace over in crayon. *N-O-A-H* back then.

When had he changed his name?

When had he stopped being sweet?

But that happened with all children, didn't it? If it wasn't this, it'd be him disappearing from her classroom and popping up years later at his parents' auto shop, acne ridden, all the good leeched out of him by shameless public-school girls and marijuana. Was this really that different?

Be fruitful and multiply. She'd done that hadn't she? So why were things still like this?

Why, why, why—

Xavier was still having growing pains, sitting in Camille's spot to her left at the kitchen table, trying to be invisible. What could she say to smooth things over? *How'd you sleep? Are you hungry?* She settled for nothing, passing him a Tupperware container with Camille's name smiling lovingly up at her from the lid. CAM <3. She'd have to change that.

"Cy, where's the label maker?" Leena asked, opening her own container. Breakfast was always junk food—vitamins, a boiled egg, apple slices and peanut butter—and her body was always disappointed.

"It's 'round here somewhere. Stop jumpin' the gun, he hasn't even picked yet."

Xavier poked at his apple slices, frowning.

"Sweetheart, what would you like to be called?" she asked, touching Xavier's hand, just enough to get his attention. Tired. Like her, he'd stayed up fretting. *A kind boy.* He blinked at her, comprehending but disobliging.

Understandable. "Xavier" was a good name. *New house.*

"You could go with 'Cam,' and we wouldn't have to change any of the labels," Cy mused, sensing their reactions without looking up, using his good hand to peel away the lid between him and his breakfast. "Just a thought. Ignore me."

Ignore me. And she would.

Leena focused on the breakfast prayer, voice clear and slow. She looked at her boys. *Amen. Amen.* Looked at Xavier, her eyebrows raised. *Amen.*

They ate quickly, Leena feeling a pleasure not in taste but in routine. In regularity. Cy always took his pills first, swallowing one after the other with a sip of water, his chin tucked down, then onto proteins and starches. Leena started with proteins, saved the pills for last (bad to take them on an empty stomach). Ari worked clockwise around his plate until everything was gone. Camille had gone counterclockwise.

Xavier only watched them.

"Your brain might not want any of it, but the rest of you *does*," Cy explained, noticing after a few minutes that Xavier still hadn't touched his food. "If we only ate what we wanted, we'd be dead in a month."

"Bite with just your front teeth. You won't even taste it," Leena added.

Xavier followed her advice, grimacing his way through. But he'd get used to it, like they all did. Chalky yolks, apple slices oxidized and slug-like, peanut butter like a lump of silt pulled from the lake.

Leena closed her eyes as she took a bite, conjuring in the absence of any taste an impossible picture. Impossible, but so clear: all her kiddos, alive and dead, sitting at Noah's table at First Glory. Cal, Camille, Ari, Xavier. Little and sweet, sitting together at the kiddie table while she passed out cups of applesauce, their fingers peeling with Elmer's glue. So real, so *right*, that by the time she was done with her breakfast she was sure it could've been true.

260

INDIGENT

They left before the sun came up, Cyril flipping through news stations from the passenger's side of Rashon's station wagon while Leena drove. "Road maintenance operations on I-20 Westbound. Left lane blocked."

Xavier sat behind him, legs already beginning to cramp. His knees pressed against the seat, backpack resting on top of them. Everything he owned. The trunk was dedicated entirely to the communal and the morbid. "An air quality alert is issued until noon." A blue cooler. A plastic-lined, duct-taped storage tote. A toolbox, two gym bags.

Two hands clasped over the center console. White fingers.

"Road construction on I-185 Northbound. Right lane blocked."

Xavier was dimly aware that they were fleeing Atlanta for good, a hazy sadness churning under layers of hunger and exhaustion, like water under ice.

"Smog alert for highway drivers this morning."

He was dimly aware that he probably couldn't be a PTA anymore, that touching *anyone* was out of the question. All of his practice, of filling his head with Greek and Latin and putting up with Uncle Rob's jabs, his disappointments, wasted.

"It's gonna be another scorcher today, lows in the nineties..."

Wasted. The worst thing in the world.

Wasted now that he was leaving.

But *was* he though? When his blood was still congealed on the floor of the first-floor janitor's closet? His hair in the shower drain of

305, caught in mineral grit and soap scum. Collating. The oil of his skin lingering on the pen in Desai's office desk, imported cigarettes and bad cologne and *him*, still there. Persisting.

Besides, he was hungry. A prion unfolding proteins in his brain, unraveling down to the midbrain, the brainstem, the spine. Down to the web of nerves taking in the world, an endless relay of reminders of his empty stomach.

A part of a part of a—

They would find out Desai was dead soon. The sun would come up, and a few hours after that, people would start to get worried. A few hours after *that*, Dr. Michaels and the spies—insulting and infuriating in their carelessness—would nose their way in.

Xavier didn't want to think about what Mom would do, but he couldn't see her. Wouldn't. A creeping terror prickled over his skin at just the thought, remembering Lan's hand on his, a thing he'd dreamed about. *You should come back every week.* Something wrong. Numb. *Did she think anything at all?*

It had already started with Mom. A watered-down voice on the other side of a door. Some part of her already dead, floating away from him like an amputated limb trailing blood.

He wouldn't let it get any worse. He'd stay away. He'd leave the parts of him that were safe. Parts of him that would stay encased in Leigh Pierce Estates until the day it was demolished, going up in a plume of asbestos and dust.

And then it wouldn't matter anymore.

The Caprice made good time down the Georgia backroads, winding southward toward the Florida panhandle, driving until the gas tank was empty. Refilled. Taking off again. Leena thanked God they didn't get pulled over with how distracted she must've looked, drifting wheels and missed turn signals all the way down.

Tomorrow will be anxious for itself. Sufficient for the day is its own trouble.

She had Xavier's phone tucked away with her things, every part of her body itching to get back to it. So she kept her hands to herself. None of her boys would appreciate her being nosy.

She'd been polite about it, hadn't she? Listening when the boys were asleep—only ever then—to the woman who had been Xavier's mother. A pit chiseled out of her like marble. Hers were wayward children.

Not this one, though.

A quiver of arrows, loosed and discarded and reclaimed.

She's looking for him.

Leena looked at Xavier in the rearview mirror as she drove, trying to see if he was angry with her. With them. With **them**. But Ari's hand rested on top of his—welcomed, accepted—and she hoped that the pattern would hold, that food and family would override any hard feelings. At least for a while.

They stopped for the night at a motel near the Florida border. Their cooler was tucked safely away into the offset wardrobe and their bags rested against the wall, Ari and Xavier disappearing somewhere while Cy rested. His body curled in on itself like a sleeping bear on top of the comforter, breath slow and rumbling as Leena watched him, unblinking.

"We passed a thrift store a few miles back. A nice one," she said absently.

"You take the boys," Cy said, his eyes still closed. "I'll hold down the fort."

And while the Caprice pulled out of the motel parking lot once more, into the still heart of Dosa, Georgia; while Shanice climbed out of the elevator and Lan listened for the sound of 305 opening, Xavier's letter tucked inconspicuously into her bookcase, unread; while Anika Davis's boy stuck the tip of his pointer finger into the tepid water of his makeshift worm tank for the thrill of seeing it shoot toward him with surprising, terrifying speed; while Leigh Pierce sank into itself—its various parts collapsing together, pulling away, collapsing again—

Cyril got out of bed.

Arms stretching up and over. Shaky but getting better, stronger.

Once he was sure he could keep his balance, he pulled the larger pieces from his storage tote—two legs, an arm, the intestinal tract, one staring head—noticing with a distant pride the nice, clean cuts.

Confident, his boy. Not in everything, but in *this*, in what was important. Camille would've been taken care of after he was gone, had things turned out differently. Had she been a good girl and minded her business.

If she hadn't reviled him—

Whoever reviles his father or mother must surely die. It was a commandment. A *rule*.

He laid everything out in the tub and flipped on the light—some old part of him still afraid of being left in the dark—and locked the door. The other bodies would react. They would *revile*. Not ready yet.

So he had to be quick.

With some difficulty, he stripped off his clothes and lowered himself down, straining as he came to a rest on top of the viscera. A yearning in what was once his flesh.

Knowingly, deliberately, he brought up his hands, thin nails digging into thick skin as he opened his chest. Bloodless and clean as flesh parted.

Easy, like butter under a hot knife.

No pain. None for a long, long time as **they** writhed out of him, his head falling back, gray eyes staring blankly out as the matter and mass of his body left him. Twisted out in a hungry flood around his wasted legs to gorge.

"I'll hold down the fort," the mouth says. Lips open, releasing warm,

tongue-shaped air.

Words from Father. Him. Now come from me. A full circle. A body looping and looping and—

I'm so proud of you, son. The head of the table. *Proud of me.*

Us. I. Mine. Ours. My... my home well lit. Electricity flitting through an invagination in the mind, deep-felt. Moving through us. Pulsing in the shape of a...

Fort. Fort-ified. A building. Safe.

Roof eaves walls ceiling floor. Tar, bone char black.

We understand.

No, they didn't—

Eat. While it's safe. Fort-ified.

He wasn't hungry.

Eat.

He wasn't—

Rest. We will... hold down the fort.

INDIGENT

Stop. Please—

Eat.

Rest easy.

We are a father aren't we.

A blue boy.

I'm so proud of you, son.

Aren't you...

so proud?

PART THREE

CONFLICTUAL COCOON

"Anger's my meat; I sup upon myself. And so shall starve with feeding.

William Shakespeare

Things should've gone differently.

The trooper had dropped her off at the Grady Memorial emergency room. "Get yerself checked in. Yer a good girl, don' want nothin' ta happen to ya." She'd taken a second to consider it. More than a second—she'd even walked inside.

In the end, though, she'd just waited for him to leave before climbing onto the hospital shuttle, giving the driver the address for Leigh Pierce Estates.

There was a penny in the corner of the bus window, stuck between the glass and the sill, and she tried prying it loose as the bus got moving, the effort leaving slender indents on her fingertips.

It was tails-side-up anyway. Not worth it.

The driver was a kind older woman who, at another time, Camille would've felt safe and irreproachable and right following out to the parking garage at the end of her shift. *Excuse me, I need some help gettin' my mom into the car, I can't lift her by myself...* Kindness an open vein exposed.

Was she asking for it?

But her stomach felt like a rock in the center of her body, never hungry—never even the idea of being hungry. Boiling in sweat and gasoline and sewer run-off. *This is the day that the Lord has made.* Weighing her down. *Let us rejoice and be glad in it.*

Her phone was close to dead, the charger back at the Peach Pit Motel where, right about now, Derrick-or-Darren was probably waking up disappointed, voiding his frustrations out into the motel sheets. Pervert.

Was this a mistake? Even if it was, did it *matter*? This was a consequence of a consequence of a consequence. It was *telic*. The only way things could go.

If she didn't want to be here, she shouldn't have pried. *Honor thy father and mother. Honor them so that your days may be long.* She always skipped the second part. A warning built in.

She should've taken it to heart, Exodus 20:12 and the way she felt, watching with bile in her throat as Ari had paged through her mother's photos, violating the little privacy they were afforded. She should've left Dad alone.

She should've treated it like every other memory she had of someone she'd loved once and forgotten it.

JULY 19, 2011 — TUESDAY

After midnight. A new day.

Moths fluttered around the light above her head. Soft and orange. Dust motes and wings throwing shadows over her face. Her hands. Soft shadows.

Resplendent...

Throwing shadows while Camille lay on the steps outside of Leigh Pierce Estates, her body deserting her. *What did he do?* She could feel them on the other side of the wall. So close... But maybe this was right. Maybe she was born to burn bridges—some fundamental facet of herself passed down from that first woman standing barefoot in the driveway or the deadbeat who'd fucked her. Impossible to stomp out. Some part of her that could only end things if she did it absolutely.

Such a pretty girl.

A body on the bedroom carpet. Sandalwood, tobacco, musk. The shape of a woman looking in at her, blotting out the lights. *Look at those curls.* Black plastic pulled over a half-familiar face, her boy but not her boy. Plastic sucked tight against the teeth, a thrusting tongue, hands going slack.

And those freckles. Sleeping pills in the vegetables, knowing they wouldn't taste it, wouldn't notice. *I can't believe you tried covering them up...*

Her legs twisted underneath her, numb and useless. *What did he do? What did he—*

She hadn't even gotten to say goodbye to Ari before getting thrown out. Hadn't gotten to really explain things. All he'd seen was that last night, the night she'd left, trying to absorb the calmness of his heavy, dreamless sleep as she decided on a pillow or a knife.

The knife had seemed bestial, like butchering an animal. But the pillow hadn't felt much better. She knew what suffocation looked like. That was a lie that people told, the obsession with bloodlessness.

Like Dad's body in the bathroom, ribs open and gleaming like a carnivore mouth. Not a drop of blood. His eyes open and blank with her hands on his face, his shoulders. Unresponsive as **they** squirmed out of him.

Dad sitting at the foot of the motel bed when she'd gotten back, kissing her hair, a tear wiped away under his thumb. *It made him go crazy*. Feeling nothing. *What's wrong, Camille? You look like you've seen a ghost.*

She felt it in her gut even now, the horrified certainty that they would all die quietly while their bodies kept going. Stolen. A lie from the very beginning that **they** wouldn't take everything eventually.

She'd smiled at Dad and gone to the medicine cabinet and told them she'd make dinner, an anger building. Directed in, directed out. Because Mom had killed her that night. And a decade later, Camille had killed Ari in the same way, with the same soft lies. Just like Mom.

Telling herself that all she'd wanted was to reach out. Telling herself she couldn't *be* him, but this was the next best thing. The closest she'd get.

She should have burnt the bridge, standing over them, sunk so beautifully into a drugged sleep. But she could never hurt someone who was alive, whose skin spoke to her.

That was probably a lie, too, **them** whispering into her family—deeper than blood, felt within every fiber of themselves—that they were the only real people left in the world. And if *that* was a lie...

Murder fell right underneath dishonoring one's parents as one of the worst sins imaginable. So here she was, her body breaking down under her father's hands. Unmade by him—his *right*. His responsibility. A consequence of a consequence of a consequence.

Camille searched her pockets and came up with a lighter, fingers raking through the litter in the alley until she found the abandoned stub of a half-smoked cigarette. She relit it, blowing smoke through her teeth. She didn't taste it. Didn't taste anything.

She felt her right hand, parts of her face, her lungs rising and falling. Pieces of her floating, disconnected. How much of her was already gone? Just **them**, not even a person anymore.

If I'm not a person, what am I?

They'd killed a dog once, a black mutt with docked ears that wouldn't stop barking. Dad had cracked it over the head, and Camille, crying, the blindfold already over her eyes, had asked if God would be mad at the poor thing for attacking them. Just an animal, stupid and scared, protecting its house. She remembered Dad's arms around her. *Succoring, solacing, assuaging.*

"No, sweetheart. Animals are innocent." Mom's voice a warm sigh, breathed into her hair...

Did that mean **they** were innocent, too? Animals growing, looping after each other. Natural and blameless. Camille lay down on the steps, feeling the shape of them, the jutting angles, through her jacket. Breathing in. Breathing out.

Animals are innocent.

Maybe, if **they'd** taken enough, if the imbricating rings of her body were more **them** than her, some of that virtue would rub off on her. Maybe He would understand.

Animals don't go to Hell.

CHAPTER ELEVEN
HAMILTON'S RULE

The apartment was as clean as it'd ever been when Shanice finally got back home. That was the first thing she noticed, a queasiness starting up as she breathed in the powder-fresh air.

Was Xavier trying to apologize…? This wasn't his way of doing it, though. Too much of his day was cleaning.

Their last real fight had been over GSU, him being pigheaded about the tuition like taking out one more payday loan was the worst thing in the world, leaving Rob's old textbooks at a Salvation Army donation box and taking off somewhere.

He'd shown up later to give her the keys to Rob's hatchback, spotless in the parking lot, tank full and a new lumbar cushion for her back in the driver's seat. "He shoulda gave it to you, I think."

All that. But he hadn't cleaned.

Something's wrong.

She'd gotten a short text saying he was with a friend, but it felt like a lie. Even if it wasn't, she had no idea who. Nobody to call. She hadn't been in the apartment for more than a few minutes, scouring it for anything, when someone knocked. Nerves in the sound.

"Miss Coates?" came the voice on the other side of the door, and she hurried to open it.

The queasiness doubled as she met Lan out in the hall. All the girls at the Queen Nails wore makeup and tight-fitting clothes under their aprons—a look Shanice figured got micromanaged down to the color of their eyeliner. She'd never seen Lan with glasses or a baggy T-shirt. She tried not to look surprised at the difference, the completely different shape of her.

"I- I think Xavier's in trouble," Lan said.

She had an envelope, held with both hands like some fragile thing, the same yellow paper of their eviction notice. "He left this with me. He didn't want me to give it to you until later, but... I don't know. It doesn't feel like something that should wait."

Shanice took the letter, feeling the bad news weighing it down, and invited the girl inside.

"I can for a little bit," Lan said, running a hand through her hair, the strands sticking up at wild angles. "As long as I'm back on time to make breakfast for my cousin. She's pregnant."

Said like a confession, something to get off her chest. "Good?" Shanice asked.

Lan just shook her head, and Shanice gave her a tight smile, could practically smell that old buffet bathroom where she'd sat waiting for a cheap pregnancy test to soak in her piss. Years ago, the scents of anxiety and meat and old sat-out salad dressing and shit mingling...

INDIGENT

Something's wrong.

Dosa was a nowhere of a place. It fed off the overflow of tourists who wouldn't shell out the money to stay closer to the beach, streets lined with coconut palms, fronds dripping with neon string lights. Pink stucco facades that would never, despite all their attempts, hide that this was still, in fact, *Georgia*.

The dreamy white beaches of the Florida-side Gulf were still an hour out, and all Dosa had to offer was a facsimile. Exotic views for cheap.

And their motel was the cheapest of them all, the last of Desai's cash gone to that and a new tank of gas. Xavier had waited in the car, watching Leena pay at the front desk with a crushing finality. After all his work, Desai was worth two hundred dollars and some change. Desai was gone.

Once they were checked in, Leena and Cyril unwinding in their room, Xavier let Ari drag him to the complementary tiki bar for "practice." No arguing. It was just some half-assed excuse to get away.

Stuck in one room again.

A newfound claustrophobia, never given the chance to grow in a previous life of comfortable shoebox apartments and packed train cars and familiar crowds. A claustrophobia that sprouted under Camille's lips one night.

It had been raining. *Lights and water...*

Xavier knocked back a shot of coconut rum—much easier to do when he never liked the taste in the first place—and blocked out the awful karaoke and memories that weren't his to focus only on the hand—*his* hand—on the weight of the glass. Isolating, with effort, the dorsal interosseous muscles, the hypothenars.

Squeezing.

"You gonna pay for that when you break it?" Ari asked, reaching out.

Xavier looked up, shocked to see Ari's face so similar and so different from what he remembered. The lights were just right. *Winsome, pulchritudinous.*

He imagined the beautiful, focusing crack of the Formica tabletop against his head and ripped his hand away. "We in bumfuck Georgia. You can't be doin' that. Unless you want piss in your drink."

"Not like we'd be able to tell," Ari shrugged, downing another shot, looking at him over the glass with what? Pity? *A charity case.*

Xavier could scream—or find out exactly how much force the shot glass could withstand. If not against his own skin, then against the head of the man struggling through "Margaritaville" at the karaoke stage, not even 7 p.m. and already shitfaced.

Asking for it.

Ari took his hand again, nails digging in. Melding. "Try to relax," he whispered, and Xavier almost laughed. *Try to relax,* coming from the guy who, five minutes ago, was told he couldn't smoke inside and who'd daydreamed about stubbing the offending cigarette out in the busboy's eye. All the gory details.

278

Relax," Ari said again. Leaning in, dizzyingly close. "Colors to be together. But if you need to be alone, you'll havta find something that's yours…"

On the table, one of the thumbs twitched. "*Mǔzhǐ,*" Ari said.

Xavier took a second to think. "Extensor pollicis longus," he said, envisioning it without looking, the flex of the thumb. Like magic, he felt the tensing along a wrist—h*is* wrist. Next, the pinkie: Extensor digiti minimi. *Xiǎo zhǐ.*

Different labels for different hands. Coming back to himself.

"Cam used words. SAT words, I mean. Ones people don't just throw around all the time," Ari explained, their hands still touching and Xavier gratefully, miraculously, able to feel the boundaries between them.

Gratefully, miraculously, able to think of something else for a second.

"What's 'pulchritudinous' mean?" he asked, a Camille word for sure. Like a weed growing out of the sidewalk.

"No idea," Ari laughed.

"Me either."

"*Look at my boys bonding*!" Leena's voice cut through the tinny tropical music, reaching his ears crystal clear.

She plopped down next to Ari in the booth, leaning into his shoulder. "Dad's napping, so I thought we'd go to the Goodwill before it closes, see if they have anything nice," she said, her hands balled into fists on the table, jealousy flitting across her face when she saw Ari's hand on his.

"Oh, did you know that '*dosa*' is Cherokee for 'mosquito'?" Leena added, smiling.

"No, Mom, I didn't know that," Ari said—automatic, call and response—as he slid out of the booth, taking Leena's hands.

She swayed against him, half-twirled into the open crook of his arms with a loving familiarity. Not-quite dancing in not-quite Florida.

Would Zion like this place?

Xavier's finger traced along the rim of the shot glass, cool and smooth. He closed his fist around it and dropped it in his jacket pocket, getting up to follow them outside.

Xavier couldn't get to sleep, crammed onto the twin bed with Ari, backs pressed together, listening to Cyril snore on the other side of the room. Drunken conversation floated past their window, setting his teeth on edge, eyes glued to the curtains.

Any second, someone would come bursting in. *Knowing.*

How could any of them fall asleep?

But they did, slept like the dead, and he resigned himself to staying awake, chewing over what had happened at the thrift store like a cow with its cud. A bloated stomach, set to split open.

He closed his eyes, seeing the station wagon's headlights cut through the dark. That deep South darkness, trees pressing in, a sharp cone of asphalt stretching out endlessly. The rattle of air through Cyril's lungs like tires on the road.

He saw the junk aisle, the metal shelves under hard white lights. Surrounded by ceramic angels, just like the glass cabinets at

Bankhead Senior Living, staring at him while they'd practiced arm lifts in the common room. Up and over. Up and—

What had the man said? *Look, this don't need'ta turn into somethin'...*

It hadn't, but it was *close*, this body shifting so happily into a long-buried violence. That man staring at him. Accusing. What was even worth stealing? Worth *turning this into something?*

Then Leena's touch, her voice. The words lost in the roaring of it all, nothing left but the tone, endlessly apologetic. *Diffident, verecund, pathetic.* Her hands filling him with a tenuous calm as she'd led him away to the furniture section, to one of the ancient, sagging couches.

That smell—death and dust and Marlboros.

His head lulling back to stare up at the lofty warehouse ceiling with Ari's finger on his lips, a torn cuticle welling blood. Just a few drops, enough to bring him back, disoriented. Ashamed.

Ari's blood in his mouth. Liquid iron held underneath his tongue, lapping...

Removed from it all, tucked into the scratchy motel sheets, it seemed ridiculous. Even on his bad days, he could deal with it—get through his job with brief, obligatory *yeses and nos. Pleases* and *thank yous.* So quiet. So serious. *That way.*

But he'd always managed, going days without speaking, without being spoken to. Without asking anyone for anything.

Self-contained. Unlike Rob, who had all the friends in the world but couldn't go a week without asking Mom for something, driving her up the wall.

Was that gone, now...? Razed from him like a layer of sunburnt skin. Would he go the rest of his life *needing* them? These people he barely knew, as much as his mind wanted to say otherwise. These people who had promised, settling into bed a few hours ago, to get him more and better "practice" tomorrow.

The thought filled him with an uneasy dread, an even more uneasy relief. The relief of *instruction*, of real, functional learning. The light, weightless dread of Desai's eyes widening, his skull bleeding years of bile onto the carpet—

Someone laughed outside, and Xavier held his breath until the sound died. *One Mississippi. Two Mississippi. Three...*

Breathe.

How would he get word to Mom once he was far enough away to be someone else's problem? Their address wouldn't be there forever. The green-tinged copper mailboxes were doomed for a pile of rubble, set to be excavated from the remains of Leigh Pierce like evidence of an ancient civilization.

He couldn't call. *Her voice. That less-than-a-voice they all had.* Texting from a burner phone, then, or the email she never bothered to check. Worst-case scenario, he could send something down to Barnesville and hope the country folk didn't hold on to anything with her name on it out of spite.

It was natural for Ari to think it was a bad idea—a learned expectation. The cards just didn't fall that way for him. But that didn't say anything about Xavier's chances. All he had to do was stick around people with more experience than him until he got used to it. Shadowing.

Then, he would go back. He'd manage like he always had.

INDIGENT

Or maybe Ari was right and it'd be better to cut ties entirely. *To drop off the face of the earth.* Mom would understand, wouldn't she? She'd done it before.

From the bedside table, the cheap vinyl stamp on the shot glass stared at him, tinged a sickly green in the clock light. Kitschy glassware: the first thing he'd ever stolen. Something to hold Zion inside. His breath hitched, and he focused on the soft breathing at his back until it leveled out again, nudging Ari awake.

"You ever been to Atlanta before now?" he whispered.

"No? I don't think so..." The voice bleary and close. Real.

"Not for like a quiz bowl or a track meet or nothin'?"

"You think I did *track*?" A yawn, a tensing of the intercostals and diaphragm. "Were you in my senior calculus class? Sixth period," Ari asked. Xavier shook his head. "Didn't think so," and Ari pressed the pillow over his face, dropped almost immediately back to sleep.

"Just checkin'," Xavier said quietly, watching him.

"How're you liking the weather?" Michaels asked, taking a seat across from Carter on the patio.

The wrought-iron chair burned against his back, a bead of sweat rolling from his hairline and down his spine. He shifted, trying to get comfortable. Ten in the morning and already almost a hundred degrees.

"Mimosa weather," Carter said, pushing the carafe across the table. He'd discarded his suit jacket, two dark rings of sweat already soaking the pits of his shirt. "I ordered you the eggs Benedict. 'Course we're *here*, so it's some pretentious thing with caviar and avocado."

"Thanks."

"Didn't want to keep you waiting," Carter said, dabbing at the sweat along his neck with the thick cotton napkin. "So your Jane Doe's got a name, I heard?"

Michaels handed over the folder and poured himself a drink, watching Carter's face as he read. Eleven-year-old Emily Dunn and her father were reported missing from a mobile home park in Alabama over a decade ago. Good ole' dad must've been a kidnapper, the report concluded. This, despite the mother's insistence to the contrary.

"The man's a sperm donor," she'd told them. "Can't hardly get him to watch her for a day. He didn't take her nowhere."

It was easy—the easiest thing in the world—to assume the worst of Patrick Dunn and call it a day. Another one of the million unfortunate domestic disturbances taking place in every trailer park across the state, unavoidable in places like that. [7] Not overly interesting.

What *was* interesting, though: a connection emerging. Emily Dunn and the Sica Hollow boy, fifteen-years-old when he was found, five years before the alert for Emily went out. Two high-risk minors disappearing and turning up again miles from home as corpses with worms in their blood.

"You listen to the interview I sent you?" Carter asked.

"Nuttier than squirrel shit, like you said."

---

[7] Price, Marcia S. *Reframing domestic violence in low-population rural regions of Alabama as a health epidemic.* Berry College, 2002.

"A *sack* of it. Don't misquote me, now," Carter laughed. "How many times did he mention the number of steps it took to get from Point A to Point B?"

"Almost every sentence."

"A hiker. Got his pedometer back in quarantine, and it calmed him down some. Not enough to matter, but you know." Carter tapped the folder with his free hand, finishing off his mimosa. "Looks like the bugs pick one thing and stick with it."

"A pattern of behavior." Michaels nodded.

"Remember that Fox commercial they used to play back in the day? *Do you know where your children are?* I'd start asking that, if I were you."

"Somebody's already missing one," Michaels said after a second, embarrassed.

His assistant was transcribing Miss Coates's panicked late-night voicemail as they spoke, an explanation between sobs and nose sniffs about the letter her son had left.

Should've caught it while I was there. But he'd been too preoccupied, the air in that place hot, a defiant curtness in everyone he spoke to that had seemed perfectly justified, given the circumstances. No one at Leigh Pierce Estates had an excuse to be in a good mood.

So he'd missed the obvious, and now Xavier Coates was either already dead or on the fast track to it.

Could he be the third piece confirming the pattern? Twenty-five was hardly a child, not the best fit, but these things were relative. He'd be replacing Emily, after all, who was around the same age.

Children didn't stay children forever. Not that it made any difference to Miss Coates.

You need to find him. My baby, my baby—

Michaels took another drink, the liquid dropping into his hollow insides. Groaning. This was why he worked in R&D. He never had the stomach to sit there chatting with doomed patients, making small talk while they fell to pieces in their hospital beds, the elephant in the room.

Carter shook his head, the picture of distant, refined concern. "Gone already, you think?"

"I'm not sure. But it's what we needed to call a quarantine, so…"

"You're speaking my language now, Doctor," Carter said, waving over their waiter. Michaels nodded absently, breathed in the stifling humidity as a plate of eggs was placed in front of him.

A neat pile of translucent orange orbs was perched on top, shivering in a puddle of hollandaise. Under the red-filtered light of the patio awning, they looked disturbingly like viscera. Like dissected bronchioles under a microscope. Michaels swallowed, his appetite gone.

"It was *salmon roe*, not black caviar. Shoulda clarified," Carter said, spearing a sausage link with a spirt of grease. "Hope you don't mind."

Píláo de. Tired.

INDIGENT

They needed a new car. Cyril insisted, waking them up early that morning for one last shopping trip before heading out. It wasn't a lie, but it wasn't the whole truth either. The whole truth was that they needed a new car and Xavier needed a lesson in *detachment*.

"Detachment is a virtue," Leena had preached, back when Ari still went to their Bible studies. "The gate into Heaven is narrow, and we need to let go of all worldly things to get through it. *All* of them." Then, turning to her book. "'Whoever does not hate father and mother, wife and children, brothers and sisters, *even life itself*, cannot be His disciple.'"

Cam had looked at her mother, unblinking, squeezing Ari's hand under the table with pent-up excitement. Relieved and reaffirmed. With God's permission, she'd thought, happy to the point of delirium, she could hate them as much as she wanted.

"Of course, it's idiomatic in the original Hebrew," Cyril had added. "Not *hate*, really, just realizing that nothing takes precedent over Him, even things you honor."

And her relief had vanished, squashed like a bug.

Xavier didn't need that lecture, but he *did* need to know that not every meal came with ill will. They couldn't all be Desai's.

Sometimes, it was all they could do to hate life itself for just a few minutes, enough to get the job done. Xavier would learn that and settle into this life more, its expectations.

Hopefully.

Now, Xavier was still convinced that this was temporary, a wavering optimism underneath all his thoughts, underneath every brief touch, and Ari wasn't going to argue. It'd be hypocritical. He'd thought about going home just yesterday, really considered it for the first time in a while.

Standing in the Goodwill glassware section, half his attention on Xavier the next aisle over and the other half on a box of artisan snuff bottles nestled in between the chipped coffee mugs. Each small enough to fit in his palm, tiny landscapes beautifully painted on the inside of the frosted glass. An entire set of them.

Someone's Nai Nai must've died. What was she thinking, dying here?

Beautiful glass bottles just like those got sent to his home every few years with a letter, and Ma had read each one of them aloud, her finger tracing over the characters on the page that he could never hope to read, single words jumping out at him. *Safe. Family. Work.*

He should've taken one of the bottles, sent it to Ma as a kind of apology. He could even deliver it in person. *I'm sorry I don't call enough.* He wouldn't stay. Just a visit to refresh his memory of her face. *Are you mad at me?*

It was an option now, with Xavier here. An older son—somebody to take care of Mom and Dad, who was *obligated* to, leaving his life wide open... Ari didn't entertain the thought for long, wished more than anything that nobody knew the stupid, impulsive things that popped into his head.

They'd find out soon enough, but for *now* Ari had an intense need to keep the nostalgia lodged painfully in his chest private, even as Xavier sat beside him. Reaching.

They cut a straight line out of Dosa and into the countryside, Ari smoking out the window while Xavier glanced over every few minutes, confused and put out by the distance. Xavier would understand. Later.

How long would Ari have to avoid Leena, though? Driving and fussing over Cyril wouldn't preoccupy her forever, and then she'd want to talk.

She'd figure out he'd been thinking about home too much and stay with him, touching—touching until they agreed that it really *did* feel too much like a sin to think of those things, until there was no telling where one of them ended and the other began.

Dosa, *mosquito*. Xavier, *new house*. Leena, *light*. Cyril, *lordly*. Camille, *priest's helper*. Calvin… Maybe reusing it was in poor taste, but they hadn't gotten much mileage out of it the first time…

Leena spent most of the drive enjoying the country and mulling over names, keeping her mind off the voicemails. Xavier's mother had been calling nonstop since last night, texting once the voicemail box had filled up.

There'd been no chance to go over them all, her eyes squeezed closed and the phone, almost dead, gripped in her hand under the pillow, feeling the smooth edge of it and the buzzing notifications under a layer of lotion and rubber. She could hear Xavier's breathing—not slow enough. Still awake. There'd even been a few maddening minutes of whispering between the boys.

But it was done. The voicemail box was full. She'd absorb it all and finally throw the thing out. No harm, no foul.

As soon as Xavier picked a more suitable name, it'd be less of a problem, less of a need gnawing at her gut. She could listen to those voicemails to *Xav* or *Xavier* or *Xavier James* in the angrier ones—b*aby* in the most desperate—without feeling guilty. She could listen to them and know that her boy was not the one this woman was after. That voice was simply making a mistake.

She'd be patient. She'd let him pick this time. It would have saved her and Camille a few arguments, especially near the end. But it was so perfect, wasn't it? Her girl's angelic blonde head nestled against Cyril's ribs, breathing together. *Priest's helper.*

Listen to your father, who gave you life, and do not despise your mother when she is old.

Maybe if she'd had more of a say, Camille would've listened. Wouldn't have despised her—

Best not to think about that.

Besides, she didn't need another Ari. She'd wanted to go with Zachary for him. *The Lord recalled.* But she'd let him say no, and all that got her was a child with too many holdovers from that first mother. Her *tongue.* Clinging onto it to spite her. Putting up walls. Teaching Camille how to put up walls.

She should've put a stop to it early, like how her mother had jabbed her at the dinner table whenever she'd held a fork in her left hand instead of right. Correction.

But she'd lapsed in her responsibilities. She wouldn't do that again with Xavier. Couldn't. Gabriel, then. *Strength of God.* A good name. Not a hand-me-down. Xavier deserved more than that. She would float it by him a few times, insisting. Get him used to it.

He would understand.

INDIGENT

Forty minutes out, they came across a smattering of trailers out in the boonies with miles between them, that country privacy she knew and loved. They drove past one and circled back, making sure it was the kind of quiet they wanted before Leena pulled off onto the narrow gravel shoulder. Cy guarded the car while she and the boys took the long way through the trees, avoiding the driveway.

The cynical part of her knew this was going to go poorly.

Ari was in one of his moods, not speaking to anyone since waking up that morning, and Xavier had hardly been given any time at all. But Cy was adamant about throwing him in head-first. Seeing if he could swim. *I don't think that works, hon. I don't think that's ever worked,* she'd wanted to say. But there was little point in arguing. Cy was bullheaded, just like her daddy.

It was early, the leaf-light dusky and cool. Peaceful. The ground crackled brittlely under their feet, everything parched and yellowed. Camille could've been with them right now, a beautiful, beautiful distraction, walking along the decaying barbwire fence that marked the property line. Running her fingers along the wood. Splintering...

As the trees began to thin out, Leena spotted the single-wide on its crumbling cinderblock foundation and took Xavier's hand. "I'm gonna go in, and I'll text when it's a good time."

She squeezed, caught flashes of a trailer similar to this one, an old woman with bleeding, rotting feet. "It's alright, sweetheart," she said, smiling at him.

There was a truck out front that seemed to get a lot of use, the wheel wells caked with mud. Just one row of seats in the cab. It'd be a tight fit, but they would make do, like always. Maybe the boys could lay in the bed of the truck, like they used to do when she was younger.

Back then, fresh out of high school, she'd watched the boys—so like men to her—pile out of their truck beds, back from a hunting trip, dragging out their proof of an exquisite death. Showing it off. A young six-prong buck or sometimes even red-furred foxes trussed together at the feet.

Did boys still do that these days?

Either way, the truck felt like a good omen. This was a place where men killed for food. For sport. A place where it was acceptable.

She waited for her boys to crouch under the trailer's largest window a few feet away from the door, their bodies hidden by the rotting wooden railing of the porch. When they were out of sight, she walked up the trembling porch steps and knocked. Quiet at first. Then frantic. Letting herself feel some of Xavier's nerves, working herself up until it was hardly a lie when the door squealed open on its hinges.

A man stared at her from the other side of the screen. He could be Noah's—*Nial's*—father. The same beard that never grew in quite thick enough along the jaw, that same tired look she saw every time he picked the kids up from First Glory. The expression she'd left him with years ago, clinging to Cy's arm and praying for their families to be safe as they parted ways at the rest stop off I-70. Too many mouths to feed. Too conspicuous.

292

This man, though, was empty, living in a filthy trailer out in the woods without even a dog to miss him. Disgusting.

"Oh, thank God!" she gasped, her eyes burning. "I was driving out to see my daughter and got a flat, and I don't have a spare, and I've been using the GPS on my phone all night, and it died as soon as I got out here, and I just need to call for a tow or, or- I don't know…"

"There's a shop in town, but they ain't open yet," he said, chewing the inside of his cheek. "I could drop you off at the McDonald's to wait. They're close."

"Thank you so much! My daughter hates me driving alone," she said, letting herself smile even though she didn't feel it. It felt more like showing her teeth.

He rolled back on his heels, still chewing. "Come in for a sec. Mosquitos'll eat you alive if you stand out there…" Still tired, a frown on his face, a victim of begrudging obligation.

No, this man wasn't like Noah's father at all. That man had been a *good* neighbor, happy to help. Never complaining.

She stepped inside, kept the smile plastered on. It was close and stuffy, body odor and long-unwashed carpet washing over her. Like where they'd found Camille. Where they found so many hopeless people. She stood by the door, listening for signs of anyone else as the man pulled on a fresh T-shirt. Nothing. She texted Ari.

"Alright, let's head out," the man said, brushing past her and out the door.

"This is so nice of you," she said, a beat too late, turning to see his body lurch into the screen door, buckling the wire mesh.

A low, animal sound escaped him. Wheezing. Hands to his face.

The second blow didn't come soon enough, giving the man time to right himself, the whites of his eyes shining. Dumb and stunned. A young buck. But she was frozen, staring at the awful shape of his jaw, the bone out of place.

He lunged out of view, and Leena heard the *thud* of bodies. On the stairs. On the dry, hard ground. She rushed forward, her foot touching a hammer.

She saw a pale, sure hand.

Ari grabbing the hammer—

Bringing it down in a smooth arc against the man's head as he bent, fists colliding against Xavier's face once. Twice—

A perfect, wet crack as the disgusting, empty body gave out, collapsing on top of Xavier.

Her poor boy sputtering through a broken nose. *Not ready*.

Leena hurried down the steps and pulled Xavier to safety while Ari took care of the rest, sharp cracks of bone devolving into the dull, wet squelch of metal against unresisting flesh.

Xavier stayed by her side, didn't move. Only his eyes twitching, pupils following the arc of the hammer as it raised up and came thundering down in a bloody pulp. Up and down up and down up—

"*Ari*," Leena warned, her hand on Xavier's cheek, trying to turn his eyes away.

His adrenaline was dying down, replaced with that same fear, that same horrible, disgusted reluctance. A growing awareness of pain. "It's okay, sweetheart. Let's go..." she urged, hugging Xavier close, dragging him to his feet and into the trailer.

She sat him down on the couch to take a look at his nose, a thin white line writhing inside the split bridge.

"I'm so sorry, sweetheart. We'll tell Cy you did it," she said, pressing the worm back in without comment. "Won't we?" she called, feeling Ari getting closer, within earshot.

At that, Ari decided to join them, soaked. Ghoulish and red. He had the hammer in his hand, marching up to them—still with that agitated intensity—to place the claw against the side of Xavier's head.

"*Temple*," he said simply before giving Xavier the hammer, not letting go entirely. Guiding Xavier's hand to place the hammer this time against his own head. The sweet spot. "Temple."

"Sorry. I missed," Xavier said blankly. A lie. Leena could feel it, him shying away from a killing blow with a deliberate twitch of the *flexor digitorums*.

The words didn't mean much to her, rose to the surface of her mind like driftwood on water. Debris from another place. Xavier was focused on them, though. Scientific. *Think of it academically*, Cy had said, the most helpful way he could think to frame it.

Not helpful enough. So impatient.

Ari knew he was lying, the anger broiling in her stomach, kicking up a sour taste. Leena put a hand under Ari's chin, palpating, loosening his jaw against her fingers. There was a bad mood with a curdling disappointment underneath it, the ghost of bitter blood on her tongue.

She wiped some blood from his face, leaving a clean white line along his cheekbone, and popped her finger into her mouth.

"The kidneys probably aren't great on this one," she said, trying not to make a face. "Any food is good food, you know."

Anika Davis's boy turned circles on his bike between Leigh Pierce and the Quik Stop—Mom never let him go any farther, not since a girl younger than him got hit by a stray bullet over by the public housing—watching the blockade from a distance. Cops waving through traffic, leaning into car windows.

He'd never seen so many cops in one place. *Who got in trouble?* Hopefully not his neighbors. *His* neighbors would never be that stupid. Leigh Pierce was a place for smart, good people. People who'd let him into their apartment for a cup of water or to use the bathroom when Mom was out and Miss Inez was sleeping too deep to hear him knocking. It was *not* a place for dumbasses.

In the Leigh Pierce lobby, he skirted past people in white coveralls and masks, like the painters who re-did the walls in his apartment once. They didn't have paint, but they were hanging up tarps like painters did sometimes, when things were gonna get messy.

The lobby was cut in half again and again by heavy plastic curtains, tiny squared-off rooms where they moved, where they talked. Low voices whispering.

It made him want to curl up in his room. Somewhere normal and safe.

INDIGENT

Miss Inez was standing in the hall, leaning on her walker, a cop's hand on her shoulder. Across the way, his apartment door was wide open, ghost-like shapes inside, going through all his mom's stuff. Wrecking it—

"*Hey*! What you doin'?" he started, but Miss Inez cut him off, grabbing his wrist.

"There you are, boy!" Angry. Not the normal kind. It sparked a far-away memory, everything seeming so tall, Mom shrieking as he ran too far ahead and the world disappeared out from under him, his body tumbling down the apartment stairs.

Angry and scared.

"What's happenin,' Miss Inez...?"

She didn't answer.

"D'you live here, son?" the cop asked instead, his hand still on her, his voice muffled behind a face mask. Only the eyes visible. Blue-gray eyes.

What did Mom say? *Yes sir, no sir, always show your hands, don't argue.*

"Yes, sir," he said.

"Come on in. Let's get you checked out."

Anika Davis's boy balled his hands into fists—he was getting invited into *his* house—but Miss Inez looked at him, warning. He shut up and followed the man inside, sitting down on the couch with Miss Inez's walker squeaking behind him.

The people in plastic suits were busy in the kitchen, letting the sink run, water collecting in the basin while they took leftovers from the fridge to hold under a flashlight and pack away. His stomach growled.

"How're you feeling today, bud? Sick at all?" the cop asked, but Miss Inez put an arm around his shoulders, knowing what to say.

"His mama ain't home. We have to wait for her before you go askin' him anythin'."

"Teenagers can give medical consent without a parent present. You up for that, bud?"

"I'm eleven. *Sir*," Anika Davis's boy said, his stomach groaning again. Leg bouncing, the energy ripping through him. He felt the spit pooling in his mouth and swallowed.

The cop waved him off and wandered over to the kitchen, watching them empty out the fridge, hand resting on his gun. A guy trying to look busy. *Why's he just standing there...?*

The cop, the gun. His skinny, drumming fingers tapping his knee until Miss Inez yanked his ear. "They lookin' at you. Stop twitchin'."

Anika Davis's boy nodded, sitting on his hands, not moving them even as his glasses slipped down his sweat-slick nose.

❧❧❧

Shanice stood deathly still while they swabbed the inside of her cheeks. Cotton scraped dryly across her gums, leaving them twinging even as the Q-Tip was dropped in a vial of liquid. The doctor, a woman in white plastic, flicked the bottom, saliva and cotton fibers floating. Spinning.

"We want it to stay clear. Blue means something's up."

She nodded, her eyes fixed on the policeman leaning against the doorframe, on his gun—"just a precaution, we don't want any trouble"—trying to ignore the sounds of plastic suits tearing through her bathroom.

They'd found something, *traces*, which meant the gun was already drawn, pointed down at the carpet with a finger on the trigger. She waited and waited for the vial to tell them she was okay. That her spit was clean.

That they shouldn't be *pointing that thing at her*—

"Looking good," her doctor said after a few minutes, holding up the vial. A beautiful, safe clear. "We're going to insist on a blood sample, though. Just to be sure."

The gun didn't move. Still ready to go. *Just to be sure.*

Where was Xav? "I'm in a bad way," he'd written. "I'm sorry." Maybe this wasn't helping him at all and it'd been a mistake, her bringing all of this down on her neighbors' heads. On *her* head. If she'd known *this* would happen—the roadblocks, the police, the ultimatums—she would've just tracked down Xavier on her own.

That was always the better option, at the end of the day, no matter who she tried to trust: her parents who raised a hand to him over nothing, her dumbass brother, the schools that let her boy get picked on, or the doctors who told her to *wait and see,* or the police here now, holding a gun in her face.

Always better to just do it her goddamn self. *What the Devil meant for bad, you can get meant for good,* Granny used to say—

And a shot rang out. A snapping of air that reverberated through the bones of Leigh Pierce in an instant. Died just as fast.

CHAPTER TWELVE
ANSCHLUSS

It could have been anything, really. A car engine, a cooling unit conking out. It took Michaels a long moment—a drop of sweat trembling on his nose and plopping onto his clipboard, ink bleeding as heat rose off the cracked Fulton Street pavement—to realize that it was a gunshot.

He took in the sound with a strange calm. Almost a relief. Atlanta's finest were prepared for the worst after Carter got the bright idea to tell them how the "bugs" could power through riot gear.

"These people, *if* we even find them here—*if*—are having a major psychotic break," he'd explained on the way over, waiting for them to nod along. "Don't shoot unless you absolutely have to."

So here was the shot. The inevitable sound he'd been dreading all morning, now behind him. Now just another thing to contend with instead of anticipate.

Michaels hurried inside with the medics, pulling on his PPE as he moved down the hallway alongside their stretcher. A high wail was coming from one of the ground-floor units. Like an animal stuck in the walls, little more than background noise as he trailed after them into 101. A body lay obscured on the carpet, an old woman kneeling, legs crumbled like she'd fallen there, her voice hardly audible.

"Isaiah—Zay, Zay—it's okay, you okay. Breathe, *breathe*..."

Another scream, the senseless crying of a child. A *child*...?

His eyes wandered around the room, landed on the officer standing stock-still in the kitchenette, mortified as the boy was lifted onto the stretcher, face streaked with tears and snot. A boy who Michaels would've pegged as a high schooler if it weren't for the crying, how high-pitched it was.

"Get him to isolation!" Michaels ordered as they hurried the boy out, turning to the woman. "Ma'am, are you his mother?"

"Babysitter," the officer clarified when it was clear she couldn't speak. A mess.

A mess that both of them had to help onto the sofa, the officer endlessly apologizing. Michaels could punch him, this idiot twenty-year-old who probably couldn't even read the safety manual they'd given him with that gun. He could see the lawsuit now.

"He came at me. We found one of—one of those *things* in his room, and soon as he saw it, he jumped up. He came at me, *I swear*..."

Michaels just nodded. The calm was starting to wear off, some-thing happening in his gut. He stepped over the spot of blood on the carpet, ignoring the officer's excuses and the woman's crying as he went to the kitchen...

To the tub waiting for him on the counter. "Vanilla Bean" in big letters on the side—a gallon bucket with a few inches of water in the bottom.

And in the water, a nearly invisible strand. *Gordacia valentulus.*

He looked closer, and the worm twitched. Twisted. His breath caught in his throat as, in one shivering instant, the worm dissolved into nothing. Fine white particles suspended. Sinking down...

A horrible quiet had replaced the boy's crying, a quiet running underneath everything. Michaels stepped back, the heat pressing against him. Humidity and blood.

Still sweating, still focused on those white particles, *floating,* he moved to the kitchen sink, pulled down his mask, and vomited his empty stomach out.

Subjective:

Location report—Leigh Pierce Estates. Quarantine in process. Adherence to preventative measures low.

Objective:

Subject (ID) sustained GSW to abdomen. To be treated at GM Hospital.

Assessment:

Continue previous recommendations.

Plan:

...

INDIGENT

They wouldn't eat—*really* eat—until nightfall. An exercise in self-control. Xavier couldn't help but be grateful for that, having sunk into a humiliation nagging at him all morning.

Had he really attacked someone? A stranger? *Any food is good food.* Had he really been that *bad* at it? A muscle isolated, one that seemed very much like his when the rest of them didn't, latching onto that feeling in a second of desperation—the *flexor digitorum.*

And what did he get for trying to keep a piece of himself, a finger, not even important? A broken nose—the sneezing, squirming ache as Leena reset the bridge. A bad haircut—locs hacked down once he noticed the blood soaked into the ends, thick and cloying. *Whose was it?* Ari and Leena trying their best to keep their disappointment to themselves and being God awful at it. At least they had the sense to leave him alone, letting him float between them as he pleased, not expecting anything more.

"You've done about all you can do for today," Leena had said, touching his newly trimmed hair with a frown.

For a while, Xavier stayed inside where the air was cold and the body was far, far away, watching Leena piece together a decent lunch. Protein powder and expired packets of instant oatmeal, vitamins doled out over small talk: Georgia was the largest state east of the Mississippi. Did he know that? "Gabriel" meant "strength of God." Did he know that? "Ozias" meant the same thing, if he wanted something flashier.

"What d'you think of those?" she asked.

At the mention of names, Xavier drifted off to the bedroom to watch Cyril, finally awake, practice sit-to-stands. The right hip flexors were the problem, all weaker than they should be. Xavier showed him how to do lying leg raises, picturing the woman in the trailer.

Picturing Rob's anatomy books piled on their coffee table, the way the words sounded when read aloud. *Iliacus, psoas major, rectus femoris, sartorius.* Those melodic Latin roots, mysterious and still strangely understandable, easier to wrap his head around than the two years of Spanish he'd taken and nearly flunked. Something warm to sink comfortably into, to know everything about.

He listened to Cyril's breathing as they worked, hesitant to reach out, to share the slow rise and fall of the lungs. *His* lungs. A part of him still shrank away from Cyril, certain that any contact for too long would get him swallowed up entirely.

It made him go crazy.

A light touch on the wrist was all he could do, but it was enough to convince Cyril to do ten repetitions, Xavier watching on, proud. Accomplished. He felt himself smiling, not bothering with those scripted encouragements and congratulations he could never make sound natural. Cyril knew.

Out of the corner of his eye, though, Xavier saw Leena watching them—hovering in the doorway, looking for a split second like she wanted to burn the place down with all three of them in it. Then, she smiled at them, and Xavier got up from the dirty carpet to head out into the heat.

The backyard was overgrown, consumed by the tree line, the trees offering shade and not much else. Xavier swam through the air, no way to tell the difference between sweat and humidity, following the sounds of compressed guitars and grainy vocals. He found Ari farther into the woods, phone speaker blaring, hair plastered to his forehead as he stood knee-deep in the hole where they'd dump the *inedibles.*

That was what Cyril had called them, going over the basics while they exercised. Inedibles.

"I don't think Leena wants me here," Xavier said over the music, watching Ari drive a shovel into the earth, heel on the blade. Leaning into it.

"She does," Ari replied, not looking up. "She's just not used to you."

"Probably a good thing."

Ari shrugged and went back to digging, working silently until Xavier cut in again, offering to take things over. A thank you for Ari picking up the slack for him again.

He remembered crouching in the shadow of the trailer, Ari handing him the hammer with a flash. An image of Desai's body on white porcelain. Still breathing. *Aim better,* Ari had thought. *Aim for the temple.*

Twice now—*twice*—Xavier couldn't quite manage it. So this was fair, taking over the job of boring into the ground like a mole. Like a worm. After a while, it reminded him of long-distance running. Of muscles burning in a pleasant letting-go of energy and warm asphalt underfoot and citrus ice cream. Of deferred satisfaction.

For a few weightless hours, Xavier could see himself staying here. He could still put all the Greek and Latin roots in his brain to good use, helping Cyril's right side... helping cook. *You a goddamn encyclopedia, you know that?*

In the heat, muscles burning and stomach aching with an almost-pleasant emptiness, a need that knew it would be sated, and with Ari sitting nearby—music and the low hiss of turning pages as he read, a companionable silence that Xavier had yearned for so often—it was easy to see all of this uncertainty as growing pains.

Cyril speaking from the head of the table, slow and deliberate; Ari working clockwise around his lunch plate, their feet touching; Leena humming as she rose from the table, her hands on their faces... The rituals of the day a slow-dripped treatment for a convalescence that would soon be over.

And when it was over... what then? What would he be when he could aim for the temple without flinching?

What should we do instead, Xav?

It was an almost happy idea, until—

"Do I *have* to change my name?" Xavier asked.

They were sitting in the grass, sweat-damp shirts drying in the fading sunlight, their silhouettes thrown against the side of the trailer. One of the shadows was... *off*. It took Xavier a moment to realize it was his. When he raised his hand, the shadow moved along with him, and when he touched a finger experimentally to the bridge of his nose, wincing, that alien profile against the ticky-tacky did the same.

But the shapes were all wrong. *Anamorphic.* Not him.

"I guess you don't need to," Ari said with a prickling discomfort. Xavier glanced uncertainly at his hand, interlaced with Ari's in the grass, decided to leave it there.

"Leena was talkin' about some of the names she likes. But it's just... I'm named after my dad. And that's pretty much the only thing I ever got from him, you know?"

"Just tell her to fuck off." Ari pulled away, agitated, but Xavier pressed on.

"What's *your* name?"

"Ari," he said as he fished a stray cigarette from his pocket, lighting up. Just an excuse to keep his hands busy. Away.

"What'd your mom call you?" Xavier asked. *Prying.*

"Ari."

"Your *actual* mom who put an actual name on your actual birth certificate."

Ari smiled. "*Wǒ kàn dào yī kē lü shù,*" he said after a moment, and, for Xavier's benefit, "I see a green tree."

"Do you *know*?" Xavier asked, wanting to strangle him. If it had been anyone else, someone empty, there'd be nothing to stop him from trying.

Another smile, smoke curling out of the nostrils, a gleam in the eyes. Resentment. The same *look* Leena had given him while he was running through new exercises with Cyril. That same inherited feeling squirming through him, flinching at Cyril's touch and Leena's *sweethearts.*

A rot chewing away at them. Turning everything good bad, eventually.

He watched Ari, the frowning profile gazing out over the woods while the cicadas stirred in the evening heat, screaming.

"*Wǒ kàn dào yīpiàn lüsè de cǎo yè,*" Ari muttered, not looking at him. "I see green grass."

It was a good night for a bonfire.

Cicadas and crickets. Blood and smoke.

It would've been a good night for anything, though, with how many oxies Ari had taken. "I can quit codeine anytime. I just wish it would quit *me*," he'd heard once in his group session, a joke from a nurse determined to keep things unserious. "Hospitals on my day off. Hospitals on my day on. Tell codeine to leave *me* alone!"

And everybody had laughed. Haha.

I just wish it would quit me.

Ari knew he'd be disappointed in himself later—the last six years down the drain. But those familiar blue pills were sitting right at the top of the lockbox after he'd swallowed his pride and asked Cyril for the key, the two of them getting a fire going while Leena and Xavier rummaged for more kindling.

"Dad," he'd started, watching the old man snap a twig in his hands. *Snap* like a rib, the iron-rich sponge of new blood in its center.

"Now, I *know* you want something," Cyril had said, grinning.

Ari wasn't entirely sure if he'd taken so many pills on purpose or if it had just turned out that way. Just like he wasn't sure if Cyril had left the oxycodone there by chance or on purpose, hoping for something convenient to happen.

As far as Cyril was concerned, Xavier had excelled at the one thing they needed a younger body for. Leena didn't have the heart to tell him otherwise, keeping her hands to herself, and she'd asked Ari to do the same.

He didn't have to be told twice.

Had he been right after all, bracing himself for a killing blow as he walked ahead of Cyril through the cold? Waiting and waiting for years. Maybe he shouldn't have stopped.

Sitting in front of the bonfire, the flames rippling, Ari thought about Nial. That revolving door of friends and lovers attached to him at the hip until they suddenly, conspicuously weren't. Leena whispering, "Don't mention it."

Was that normal? Were *they* the weird ones, ignoring that it was better for them—for **them**—to run through people like water? Like blood...

Had he taken five pills or ten? Less?

More...?

He felt this body blink, its feet too close to the fire, yellow heat seeping in through the toes of the shoes. In a haze of smoke, he watched Cyril eat a finger, sucking the marrow from the protruding bone. He watched Xavier's mouth move and Leena throw up her hands, laughing. He felt like laughing, too, but he also felt like a marble rolling around in this body's head. Spinning down and down and down.

A marble that was *named*...

He could probably guess. His brother's name was Andrew, which meant his parents wanted something traditional and sufficiently white: *John, David, Eric, Matthew.* Names rolling around in the braincase along with him, all equally right and equally wrong. He watched Cyril put a hand on Xavier's shoulder.

"Thank you, son. Really. I- I can't do everythin' I used to. So, this is good. It's good." Convincing himself.

Xavier didn't respond, and Ari saw a space to speak, felt the urge to ruin it. He saw his muddy reflection, his eyes in a pool of food oil. Saw himself glancing up to see Ma's paint smudge face. The happy, gushing lilt of her voice. He could have ruined that, too. He could've told her that Drew was a straight C- student who'd spent the night before his first day at Northwestern panicking, begging for Adderall. He could've told her Drew was dating some Honduran DREAM Act girl with a septum piercing.

He could've told her that their dream of having a neurosurgeon son—tall and important and American—had been tragically misplaced, and they'd suffered all this time just to get stuck with two fuck-ups whose biggest claim to success was being born *here* instead of *there*. Why hadn't he...?

Because you're selfish.

Because Drew being the one his parents bet on meant that he was as good as invisible, resigned to become his father eventually—some glaring absence in someone else's life—but not *now*. Not anytime close to now.

And he was still selfish, so he kept his mouth shut and let Cyril go on believing that Xavier would stick around, even though the gears were already turning, Xavier already running through the script in his head of how he'd leave them.

Cam would never leave me.

He daydreamed about the possibilities of being as good as invisible again—of falling asleep by the fire and not waking up. Of walking back to Chicago on foot, like a pioneer or the men who'd looked like him going West for gold.

310

INDIGENT

They ate outside, the night sticking to their skin. Blood steaming and congealing, the smell of it grotesque in the heat. But any food was good food. At some point, Ari found himself broken away, a satiated dizziness clutching at his insides.

There were three bodies bent together by the fire. Was he there with them? His senses projected outward? In his skin and out of it, the fire at his back and on his face, a stomach hollow and wanting and full and splitting open all at once. A stomach in his mouth, in his chest, in his fingertips.

The porch steps scraped against his legs, and he was happy that they'd crept up to him without his asking, sitting down. Feeling the weight of everything. Heavy. Watching.

He watched two of the bodies move by him, up the steps, into the trailer. Unsteady. Their voices, their white skin soaked yellow and orange in the flickering light. Xavier's body or his body was by the fire, stirring in the blood-damp grass and coming to sit on the steps for another brilliant moment. A *penetralia*, Cam would've called it, a dislocation of their innermost places.

A counting of stomachs…

After coming back to themselves—my legs. *Wǒ de tuǐ.* My eyes. *Wǒ de yǎnjīng*—Ari and Xavier stood outside and washed away the worst of the blood with the garden hose. The water seared his skin, brought with it that familiar, lingering sadness, the familiar relief.

Mine.

Then, they walked together into the woods, carrying the waste between them. Ari had assumed he'd be filling the grave alone, that Xavier would feel the need to retreat back into himself. But Xavier hung around, distant at first, then beside him, lugging the remaining pieces to their resting spot in the trees. Ari laughing, giddy with company, with rushing blood.

Laughing as he tossed the overripe kidneys, the bones, the mess between the legs, the brain. *Dànǎo*. Its pale folds were infinitely recognizable even in pieces. Appetizing.

He caught Xavier hesitating, moving his finger along the ridges held in his palm. A small movement Ari recognized: fingers subconsciously searching for a weak spot to peel, to *pry*...

"There's diseases in the brain," he explained, his words slurring together.

Diseases, and associations that bothered them in ways they couldn't put into words. Or wouldn't. Only felt in touches. Briefly and childishly mulled over in one of Cam's journals—the first one, given to him in confidence. "Just burn it when you're done. Not 'throw it away.' Burn it," she'd insisted. A hope in a kid's messy, uneven handwriting: *The head's off limits. Miss Leena says so. That's where the soul is, right?*

Ari waited for Xavier to drop it, gray matter falling through dark fingers, listened for the wet *plunk* of it falling into place.

"I'm probably gon' leave tonight," Xavier said, either a few minutes or a few hours later, the hole covered in fresh dirt and the two of them heading back to the fire.

"I figured," was all Ari said, fingers interweaving, explaining what he couldn't. "Mom had your stuff. In her bag if she didn't get rid of everything…"

"Thanks."

Ari nodded, focused all his energy on that flickering spot of brilliant yellow in front of them. *Huáng huǒ.* "I think I'll sit outside for a while," he said, waiting for Xavier to break away.

This was a mistake, leaving so soon. *Telling* someone about it. If he didn't say it, though—r*eally* say it—Xavier knew he risked backpedaling, sinking into a warm, full-stomached complacency.

He could already feel it, four bodies melding peacefully together like clotting blood under the stars, next to the fire. Stumbling closer to the trailer where Ari had laid across the porch steps. For a second, he'd seen Ari crumpled in the alleyway, bones broken over the staircase where Camille had died.

Then it had gone, and Xavier sank down beside him. Falling into each other. Mouths and mouths and mouths, red-crusted. *Wanting—*

And then he was himself again.

Not a single thing left that he could claim as his. Not his tooth, that reliable, *personal* twinge. Not the finger, the twitching muscle that had spared a man's life for a few seconds longer.

They were *eating* him. All of him.

Everything was gone, and, terrified, he had to claw it all back out of a mound of flesh—

A shoulder attached to an arm attached to a hand. Metallic water burning over the palm, over the lines of his future, running dark then clear onto the porch slats.

He couldn't find his voice for some time. The smaller muscles, the more discreet ones, were difficult to nail down. Intercostals up to the cricopharyngeal up to the palatoglossus, flesh tightening behind teeth.

"You okay?" he'd asked first, though the second-hand fuzziness still pressed behind his eyes. And the aftershock of Cyril's anger over it, Leena's sadness.

It made things safer, saying his plan aloud while Ari was only half-there and they buried what was left of the man from the trailer, staring down at the remains with a knee-jerk, visceral loathing.

Was he asking for it?

Xavier wanted to feel anything else—tried to—but couldn't. Nothing but that resentment that lived in all of them, fused and squirming. It was just another reason to leave while he could.

Even now, he jerked away from the idea like a hand ripped back from a flame, because he *knew*. He knew that leaving would be like a hammer cracking against his skull. Disorienting and painful. Pulsing...

But not inherently lethal if it only happened once.

Not once. Twice.

He thought he understood, then, what it took for Mom to escape Barnesville all that time ago, drive away with a gaping, bleeding spot between her and her kin. He'd just have to follow her example, be strong. Be *himself*, no matter what the family wanted—*because* of what they wanted. Back to basics.

INDIGENT

Step One—Every man needs to ask himself, "What is holding me back?" Eliminating those things from your life without prejudice is the first step to accruing value.

The grease-flecked oven clock read 2 a.m. by the time Xavier crept inside to find his phone and wallet. Cyril and Leena were asleep, arms and shoulders and the soft swell of Leena's hair peeking over the arm of the couch as he moved past them into the bedroom.

He found Leena's suitcase, a wig resting on top of it and looking for a heart-stopping second like some kind of vermin. Curled up and breathing. Xavier held his breath, straining to pick out any sounds from the living room... Nothing but the rattling box fan in the window, hotter inside than out, suffocating in a dead man's room as he dug through Leena's clothes, lavender and linen filling his busted nose.

In a hidden pocket at the bottom of the case, he found Leena's photo album. The one from their first night as a family. The night they'd fed him. Flayed him open.

He regretted paging through the pictures—they did nothing but muddy the waters—but he couldn't help it. A snapshot and a memory that could've been his tumbling after it...

The image: Ari driving, a sliver of orange rock and blue sky seen past him, through the window, his eyes glancing over at the camera. Then *Ari's face, almost unrecognizably fuller, haloed in a noisy, watery light.*

The image: Leena smiling next to the world's largest ball of twine. Then *pale hands parting fabric.*

The image: Cyril, dark-haired and imposing, standing on a patio, looking away. Then *teeth breaking skin. Breaking bone.*

Staring through slit eyes at the anguished line of Cyril's mouth. Bone of my bones and flesh of my flesh—

Last: Camille draped over a park bench, stretching, the feline arc of her spine. Then *the sensation of a head turning, seeing a freckled nose in the mirror underneath blue, blue eyes.*

An iris circling and circling. Layers of color. A lens under a lens under a lens under a—

A handful of cards slid out of the book jacket and onto the carpet, touching his bare foot. *Clacking.* Names and faces, IDs. He recognized his face among them, staring, the only thing of his that he could find. Leena must've thrown out his debit cards, tossed the phone while he'd been busy trying not to kill that guy in the junk aisle. A driver's license was better than nothing, though.

He slipped it into his back pocket, staring at the other cards, at the names he'd never heard and faces that had wormed their way into his memory, chewed holes in it. Heart in his throat, Xavier dropped the IDs back where he found them, zipped up the suitcase, and hurried to find his shoes.

The work boots bit into Xavier's skin as he walked, extensor hallucis longus screaming. *That* was definitely him.

He wished he'd had more presence of mind to get some better shoes at the Goodwill, couldn't bring himself to try on anything from the pile of old boots and sneakers thrown against the wall by the screen door. Still too disrespectful, upsetting someone's space after they were gone. Changing the way they'd left it.

No one else had that issue; he found Ari smoking on the back porch, wearing a stolen T-shirt and jeans. Earlier that day, he'd watched Ari grab a belt from the man's bedroom and punch a new hole in the faux leather with a nail, slipping it around his waist.

Xavier had gone to the bathroom after that to look at this body in the mirror, staring with muddled awe and disgust at the round cheeks, the softness of the abdomen. Animal excess. The same feeling hit him again now as he leaned against the porch railing, watching curls of smoke get lost in the sharp shadows of Ari's face. A *person's* face.

If he left, he might as well be the only person in the world. He'd be totally, profoundly, *alone*—

"Eric," he said, a proclamation. A way to keep himself on track, keep those second thoughts from getting too loud.

Ari glanced back at him, cigarette hanging from his teeth as he took in the backpack slung over Xavier's shoulder. "*I knew it*," he said. "It was one of the options, anyway."

"Where'd you get 'Ari'?"

"I stole it from Ari Marcopoulos," he answered. Reluctant, like pulling teeth. "I knew this girl once. She was rich, and she really liked artsy, pretentious bullshit. So I *also* liked artsy, pretentious bullshit. His photos are pretty good." Ari stubbed out the cigarette. Tobacco spitting against paint and dirt and mold. "Think of yours yet?"

"I don't know... Goku?" Xavier shrugged, and Ari laughed. Maybe a real one. "Sorry, I ain't as bougie as you."

"You'll think of a good one eventually..." Ari said. "Find everything you need?"

"Just my ID. Wish I had my phone, but I don't know who I'd call anyway."

"What if you wanna come back?"

"They don't want us."

Why did he just say that? But it was true, wasn't it? Ari's reaction cemented it. Blinking like he'd been slapped, eyes watering. *They don't want us.* It felt good to hear, something he'd been yearning to let out, like an animal scratching at the door.

They'd had this talk before. This fight. He'd felt this body like a house rotting, trying to hack his way out of it—now or never at all—certain that Ari would stay until the eaves fell in, and there was nothing he could do about it.

He'd known that ever since he saw Leena at the door, glowing in that blue dress he'd let her borrow, talking about nothing as she returned from the bus station. "Okay, Mom," Ari had said, rolling his eyes, making everyone stop.

That *word*. That name given freely, unasked for. And she'd thrown her arms around him, kissing his face, his hair.

"You know we love you. You know your mom loves you—"

"How much longer you think Cyril has?" Xavier asked, back to the present.

"He'll live forever with my luck."

"I give it a year," Xavier said. It could be true—true like the two of them standing on a train platform in the rain. All just perception. "You see it all the time at the old folks' home. With people who've been together forever, one person dies and the other goes right after. They plan two memorial services by default, just in case."

318

Ari didn't respond, but Xavier could sense him mulling it over. A germinating seed. "We could plan on meetin' somewhere...?" Xavier pressed, trying not to sound too desperate.

"Okay," Ari said, and he lit another cigarette. *A hand in the dark, disembodied.* "Wanna do that lame-ass tourist trap bar from yesterday?" he asked. "I'll buy you another drink."

"A year from now?"

Ari nodded, holding smoke behind his teeth. Xavier could taste it, faint and warm as he tongued at his bad tooth, found it smooth and painless. It was so humid, as damp as rain, like the night they'd met. A girl seen through a pinhole.

What had he been thinking back then? *I don't know you. I want to know you.*

He stood there for another moment. Breathing in.

I want to hold you under my skin. I want to scratch away at myself and find you underneath.

Breathing out.

I want to tell you those things and watch the confusion on your face.

Letting go of the taste of burning.

I want to watch you begin to understand.

"I understand," Ari breathed, not moving even as Xavier walked past him, down the creaking porch steps and into the grass. Away.

CHAPTER THIRTEEN
NEGATIVE RECIPROCITY

Leena woke up before the sun. Something was wrong, her gut full and chest oddly hollow. She stood in the shower—water pressure low, dribbling over her skin as she scrubbed and scrubbed—dreading whatever it was, unwilling to face it just yet.

A little slumber, a little folding of the hands to rest, and poverty will come upon you like a robber.

If she had to face the day, she was going to do it clean and soft, her skin glowing with fresh blood and fingernails painted, two spots of blush high on the cheeks. She would give that robber Poverty her best face.

There was a splinter underneath one of her nails from yesterday, helping Xavier haul sticks and branches and slabs of dry bark out of the woods, ready to burn. Such a sweet boy, holding out his arms to her while she bent, hands combing through the leaves.

She'd spotted a cluster of mushrooms and plucked one from the bunch. "This is a good spot to bury the leftovers. The ground's already breaking something down."

"Okay..." He'd looked away from her. Nervous? Ashamed?

"D'you know what this is called?" she'd asked, spinning the stalk of the mushroom between her fingers. "Honey fungus. You can tell because of the little five o'clock shadow it has on the cap. Isn't it cute? It's edible, too."

"For *us*?"

Leena had brushed off the dirt with her blouse and popped the mushroom in her mouth whole. It was always a better idea to cook honey fungus or risk an upset stomach later, but it had helped Xavier relax a little, a promise that the body waiting for them by the firepit wasn't all there was or would ever be.

It had felt good, biting the cap off between her teeth. A primal kind of feminine, real and close, that foraged in the trees and delighted at the rich gills of a mushroom flayed out on its tongue, that wrung the necks of chickens and plucked them clean of feathers, ready to eat. Dirt and violence and uprootings turned into a loving gesture...

And then they'd walked back to the fire.

She knew that Xavier was gone the second she looked out the tiny bathroom window and saw Ari sitting on the back porch. Alone. A desolation she sensed through the walls.

She always wanted to leave me.

Leena finished her makeup and went to the kitchen, quietly gathering the last of the offal from the fridge while Cy slept on the couch, dead to the world.

What would he do when he woke up abandoned? He would take it in stride, surely. *Definitely.* But her surety wasn't turning out to be worth much lately. She took the cool pile of innards and went to sit with Ari outside, ready to face the uncertainty of things.

"Good mornin', sweetheart."

"Morning."

"...How long's he been gone?" she asked, letting him rest his head on her shoulder. Her boy.

"A few hours. He's not comin' back."

Just being pessimistic. But her gut told her it was true. She started portioning out their breakfast. Kept her hands busy, pink nails slicing through the silverskin, leaving wisps of it clinging to her fingers, to the glass bowl, revealing the soft gray-pink organ meat.

"Here, eat," she said, holding a section of liver to his lips, pressing it against them until they finally opened. She placed her hand against his jaw, urged the muscles to move, to chew and swallow, her chin resting in his hair.

"You just can't stop leavin' me, can you?" she said after a moment, when the sound of teeth grinding against teeth died down, when there was nothing left but the drone of the cicadas.

"*I'm* here."

"You're gonna leave soon enough, I know that. I've known that for a while."

His jaw tensed, and she listened in on the lies he considered telling but didn't, opting for nothing at all. "The day Camille brought you home, I knew what she wanted. I would stay up and cry over it. I was so happy when you came back to us, you know that?"

"I know, Mom," Ari said. "I just don't think anyone else can say that."

"Have I been that unkind to you?"

Yes. It was under her hands, the real answer. "No," he sighed. "But there's more to it than that."

"All I've ever done is keep you alive. That's been my life."

"*Your* life, and we're living in it, right?"

"Ari... Do you want me to apologize? I can do that."

"No. It's okay, Mom."

Leena peeled away another section of liver, chewed it over until it was nothing but paste in her mouth. She had an urge to lock her lips over his, to push the paste into his mouth with her tongue. *I would feed you forever. I would give you the world if I could.*

"Cy's gonna be angry, I think," she said, a relieving change of subject.

Ari nodded. "*We* could leave, you know?" His voice was neutral, quiet, but she felt the pleading underneath. A hopeful, forgiving hand outstretched. And that *we...*

"Cy can't be on his own anymore," she sighed, seeing in her mind an open door closing. "'Sickness and health,' and all that."

He didn't move away from her, not physically at least, and she was grateful for that. Repeating it in her mind over and over, even though it wasn't what he wanted from her, flowing out. *I'm sorry. I'm sorry.*

Repeating it even as he closed himself off from her, thoughts in a language she couldn't understand. Intentional.

She should've learned it. She should've let Camille call herself Gwen or Kelly like she'd wanted. She should've put her foot down and insisted on easing Xavier in, like dipping a toe into water, instead of drowning him.

Cy wanted to go after Xavier, pacing from the living room to the kitchen and back again like a caged bear. He hadn't even cleaned up, his shirt stiff and creased with blood, his hands nearly black with dry viscera. Gray eyes bulging from a red face while he kept pacing...

Pacing...

Leena watched and listened, her fingers woven in front of her on the kitchen table and a growing revulsion bubbling in her gut at the odor of stale blood, at the black-red smears Cy tracked over the carpet.

Like Judah tracking blood through the hills, his eyes blazing as he struck down the Canaanites. God Himself exalting and exalted in Judah's beautiful, righteous violence. What color had Judah's eyes been? What was seen from above as he tilted his blood-slicked head upward towards the sky?

"Not like he's gonna get anywhere fast, but we could still lose him if we wait too long," Cyril was saying, more to himself than them, her at the table and Ari standing silently in the doorway. His nails were biting into his palms, and Leena felt it in her own skin, cherished it.

324

"You don't need to go chasin' anyone down in the woods, Cy," she said at last, staring at the knobs of her knuckles. "We're leavin'. Just leave it be."

"*Just leave it be*," Cy repeated, bitter and far away.

When Camille'd left them the first time, the three of them waking up groggy and sleepy-eyed in their motel room, he'd reacted the same way.

He'd insisted. He'd ripped the telephone from the wall and thrown it to the floor like an infant dashed against the rocks, the spiral cord trailing. They'd piled into the car and circled the surrounding neighborhoods, looking for any trace of her as Cy sat in the passenger's side. Fuming.

Is this about Camille? Leena wanted to ask, but she didn't dare mention it out loud. Now wasn't the time. But would there ever be a good time, really...?

Cyril stormed past her and grabbed Ari's arm, pulling. "Let's get to it."

"Mom's right," Ari said, not budging.

Leena got up, instinctive, her eyes taking in the small changes. The line of Cy's back shifting. *Where're the shells, hon?* "Cy...?" she asked, and he turned to look at her.

"What was it, hon?" he said, his jaw twitching. "'He must manage his own household well, keeping his children under control with all dignity.' Is that right?"

"That's not—"

"Is that what it *says*?" A horrible desperation in his voice. Pleading.

She hesitated, stepping closer. "There's nothing *dignified* about any of this, Cyril."

He moved towards her and took her hand, kissing the knuckles, apologizing. An apology she wanted dearly to accept as she watched him go back to Ari with a sigh, his exhaustion pulling down at her eyelids.

She watched Cyril cup his hand under Ari's chin, and she watched as her boy accepted the touch, drank it in. *We've got to be a united front. We have to be on the same page.*

"What d'you think?" Cyril asked, looking Ari in the eyes, his wrist flexing. "Think we should just let him go? Let him get caught and cut open in a lab somewhere? Or just starve to death? Starvin' isn't dignified either."

The hand moved down in a blurring of skin—

Those suffusing bodies—

Eating—

And Ari fell to his knees at Cyril's feet, a blank shock in his eyes. Like the chickens' whose necks she'd snapped as a child. His hands went to what was once, just seconds ago, his throat. Now a ragged hole bleeding out from under his fingers.

The wet gurgle of a drowning body, of liquid dropping hot and viscous into lungs.

Leena took it all in, her chest too tight to breathe—Cyril's red body swaying, dreamy as he stared at the blurred lines of his hand, his fingers, pressing **them** back into his broiling skin. Ari with his mouth opening, closing, gasping for air.

And she screamed, pushing Cyril away.

His bad leg twisted underneath him, and he fell back onto his tailbone with no reaction. Still watching her and **them** in a daze. Leena heard some high-pitched sound in her ears that may have been her voice. Talking, reassuring, dictating, while she searched for something to stop the blood. A dishrag, a towel, a blanket—all soaked through in short order, Ari's eyelids fluttering.

Is it my fault? Am I a bad mother, after all this? Couldn't even keep an eye on my own little girl. On my own boy—

"There's a hospital in town," she remembered, her hand on Ari's cheek, urging him to stay awake.

"No—" Cy croaked out, but she was already in the kitchen, grabbing Rashon Wilkinson's car keys, metal indenting skin.

She tried to get Ari to walk with her, watched the bleary blink of his eyes as she urged him upright, still conscious, but he couldn't stand, lulling against her. She grabbed another blanket from the couch and laid it out on the floor, dragging him onto it while Cyril struggled to his feet.

"You can't. Anyone's gonna be able to tell something's up. And we got Xavier wanderin' around, just askin' to get caught," he said, finding his voice again, the soft croak slowing smoothing over. Getting louder. "I'm tryin' to protect you—"

"Don't talk to me like I'm stupid. This is your fault!" she screamed, grabbing the ends of the blanket and heaving the dead weight out the door.

"This is not my fault!" Cyril yelled after her, still unable to find his legs, knees buckling as he tried to follow.

"All any of them've ever done is give us trouble," he sobbed, unable to get up. "And you've been makin' it worse. Coddling them.

I didn't say nothin', even when I *knew*—If Camille just keeled over in a ditch somewhere like she was fuckin' supposed to, I wouldn't have to do this. But she just had to tough it out for the first time in her goddamn life and ruin it!"

Leena stopped on the porch stairs, her mind turning, working out the safest way to drag Ari down. What did she look like, the muscles in her face twitching in every imaginable way, unable to settle on one reaction?

"You never wanted any of them?" she asked, quiet.

His face softened. "I just want you to be happy. It's always been you...."

A line of blood ran from his right nostril, dark black against the red-stained skin. And she closed the door on him, slowly easing Ari's body down the stairs.

⁂

When Cy proposed to her, Leena had thought the wedding band looked like a scar on her knuckle. She'd thought it, felt awful, and immediately took it back. But she'd kept thinking it in the days that followed, and had to eventually settled on the compromise that scars weren't inherently bad. Some of them had meanings, stories.

At night, she'd slip it off her finger and place it on her bedside table, the tiny diamond in its center winking at her, him breathing slowly at her back. There'd been a comfort in the flat steadiness of his company, in the voices at First Glory gushing about his good looks and his good job. It wasn't until **them** that she grew to love him, *really* love him.

It's always been you...

As she sped down the backroads to Dosa, chewing her bottom lip to shreds with Ari bleeding out in the backseat, she tried to think back. She conjured up an image of Cy standing there, a seething disapproval in his eyes when she brought in Cal, presented him like a prize pig.

But was that right? Had he hated the idea *that* much, or had he just stood there quietly, no comment?

There'd been a certain amount of righteousness when Cal passed, a smugness—*I told you so.* But he'd been *right.* Wasn't that warranted when he was right? Camille was different. He was a man born to have a daughter. A paper tiger. He'd wrapped his arms around her while she slept. He'd fed her from his body. That couldn't be a lie.

I just don't think anyone else can say that.

The lights of Dosa were just ahead through the trees, a shimmering pink-white haze against the sky, slowly graying at the horizon. By the grace of God, she managed to make it to the little shoebox hospital without the police chasing after her, and she dragged Ari out onto the pavement in front of the ER, into the sweltering air.

Gasoline and burnt rubber and blood swimming in her nose.

He was still breathing, but she couldn't see it—could only feel it, that phantom sense of four lungs moving together. Air a bubbling red.

"I'm so sorry, sweetheart. I am. I guess it doesn't mean too much, now," she said, gravel biting into her knees as she crouched beside him. "You loved Camille, right? Didn't you? You had a good reason for bein' here...?"

Leena waited for an answer under her hands. Didn't get one. Every ounce of the consciousness focused on willing life into the lungs. In her periphery, she caught a flash of green, a pair of scrubs lingering on the other side of the glass sliding doors to the ER. A young man looking out, gesturing, rushing toward them.

She leaned in, her lips brushing Ari's forehead.

And she was gone—

Back behind the wheel of the old station wagon, driving with the sun in her eyes. With water in her eyes. Half-blind as she blew past the turnoff for the trailer out in the woods and kept going.

Xavier's phone was still in her pocket, pressing against her flesh. Pressing like a spear into her ribs that she dislodged with a wail from deep inside.

She drove with one hand and unlocked the phone's screen with the other, her thumb dialing the correct code on her first try, brand-new but still remembered, down to the muscles. The battery was nearly dead. It didn't matter. She knew the number by heart because Xavier knew it by heart. The voice that picked up on the other end was familiar and beautiful and lush with fear.

"Xav, baby, where are you?! What happened?" *Baby*. Desperate, then, still looking.

"Hello? Is this Xavier's mother?" Stupid question. *Stupid*. Of course it was—

"Who is this?"

"I understand bein' worried. I've had five children. They're like blessings, aren't they? Like God coming down and sayin',

'You're worthy of something *important*. I know you, I *trust* you to do it....' He trusts you, I can tell. Not me, though. He never told me that."

"D'you know where he is or—"

"Dosa, Georgia. D-O-S-A. It means *mosquito*. Did you know that?" Leena asked, the weight coming off her chest. The mother *knew*. His mother knew. Xavier was safe. She'd kept them safe.

Empty noise crackled in Leena's ears. "Miss...?" came the voice at last.

"Leena. My name's Leena."

"Leena. Are you okay?"

"No," Leena said. Mint sweet and simple, that word. *No*. "I've never spoken to one of them before, their mothers. Thank you for talkin' with me. I'm gonna let you go, now."

She hung up, the phone sliding from her hand and clattering to the floorboards. The road sloped down, swallowed up on either side by a crop of rock, and she eased up on the pedal for a second before pressing her teeth together, feeling it in every inch of her skull as she floored it.

She could find someone new. A new husband. A new child. A family that aligned more closely with what she wanted. She could be a mother again, a better one. *Be fruitful and multiply.*

It would be so easy to be *fruitful*...

Or—

Or she could just be herself for a moment. She could put all her energy into her roots, encased. Grow in other ways. Grow down and out.

The station wagon groaned all around her, and she unbuckled her seatbelt. Thinking of the Bay City Rollers and Cyril and the Ozarks, those thin-trunked pines dark and unforgiving. Not like these trees, bursting with green and scattering leaf light across her face, her hands.

Thinking about *shale and limestone*, about Camille's blue eyes widening as Leena stood in front of her like a magician, snapping a shale stone in half with her bare hands, proving rock could be weak.

Thinking, as she let the car careen closer and closer to the cliff-face, foot on the pedal and hands in her lap, about how the brittle pieces of her would be brought together again by an all-loving Hand. That they'd be arranged in some better formation, the cracks repaired with gold.

Xavier didn't know where he was —Alabama, Florida, or Georgia still, the state going on forever. Inescapable.

He'd run through the night until he couldn't. Then he'd jogged. Then he'd walked, not stopping. Not trusting himself to stop. He'd curl up to sleep on the side of the road and wake up at the trailer, by the burnt-out fire, his body crawling back despite him, picked up by the wind.

He walked down the highway, dead on his feet by sunup, a homesickness in his gut and a limp in his left foot as he kept his eyes peeled for Rashon's station wagon or that dead man's pickup. What way was Leigh Pierce? What way was home?

INDIGENT

Would he be able to hitch a ride? Or maybe he'd find a bus stop, run into a Greyhound with one of Mom's friends behind the wheel. His eyes followed the cars, trailing after them until they were out of sight. What was it? *Colors to be together. Something that's yours for when you wanna be alone.*

"Black Toyota, black Dodge, black Ford," he said, counting the cars that blew past him without pause.

He felt like those people at the old folks' home, wandering off on his bum leg, looking for husbands and wives and parents and children who didn't even exist anymore. Maybe that's what he needed—a locked door, tired nurses in thrifted scrubs keeping him in his place.

It wouldn't be too bad. He could walk and walk until these shitty shoes cut off his toes entirely, and someone like Uncle Rob could come visit him in his locked room, make him feel optimistic about his chances while he balanced on his good foot and ate through a tube in his stomach. Safe.

And then something hit him, the wind ripped clear out of his lungs—

He collapsed, the skin of his knees, on the heels of his hands, scraped open on the pavement. It should sting, but he couldn't feel anything. He couldn't *breathe.*

We can't breathe.

He made his way off the road, into the dry grass and brambles along the shoulder, digging his hands into the earth. A quiet place to decompose. The blue of the sky was pushed back, bleak. Some element of color he could no longer make out. *Somebody's dead.* But who? Who—

"Hey, bud!"

Who—

Flashing lights. Red and blue glinting off a candy wrapper in the dirt by Xavier's face. They gave him a headache, and he squeezed his eyes closed. *Who?* But this body couldn't ignore the voices. It wasn't made for that.

"Come on, man... On your feet."

Empty hands touching him, grabbing at him. Heaving.

"What's your name, man?" the mouth was saying, not unkind. A mouth with a blue shirt and a badge. *Yes sirs, no sirs, thank you sirs. Always.*

Xavier felt his jaw moving, soundless. He'd done this before. He'd shoplifted that lip gloss and gotten a talking to. Nothing worse. It was fine. He could be a sweet, smiling distraction.

But, no...

This body could never. It had different eyes, different hands. *Show your hands, don't argue.* But where were his hands? Where were they?

The badge gave him a look he couldn't read, couldn't see clearly.

"It's illegal to walk on the highway, you know, 'specially when you're not facing traffic. Gonna get somebody hurt."

"Somebody's hurt," Xavier heard himself say, latching onto the words, watching the lips in front of him, repeating the movements they made.

INDIGENT

There was his mouth, that mouth with lips too foreign to say anything that could help him. But where were his legs? His hands? Did he even need them, dark and rough and conspiring against him?

"Somebody's dead," he said.

"Easy... You on somethin' right now? You take anythin'?"

Touching him again—

Xavier shoved him away. What were these ears hearing now? Yelling? Birdsong? Passing cars? It could've been anything.

All he could be sure of was that, at some point, his mouth was pressed back into the dirt, and this body couldn't move, even when he found the muscles for it. Pressure drilling into the back of his neck. He couldn't move and somebody was dead.

He closed his eyes.

The drive to Dosa was infuriatingly slow. Shanice just about had an aneurysm worrying. But, three hours into a five-hour drive, her nerves couldn't keep up that energy. She just had to assume no one was following her.

This old lemon she'd borrowed from one of the ticket counter girls wasn't made for speeding. Eighty on the highway was all Shanice could coax out of it, getting passed by minivan moms and spotless pickups with nowhere important to go.

It was probably for the best with all the speed traps down here. If she had to talk to one more cop today, she was going to scream.

They wouldn't even let her in her own house. She'd been staying at Lan's place ever since they found *traces* in 305, Dr.

Michaels sitting across from her in a face mask and plastic coveralls, only his eyes visible. Run ragged.

The basement was off-limits entirely, and they'd shut off the water. Telling everybody to clear out. Telling everybody to stay put. That there was nothing dangerous. But if there *was*, it'd be in their blood. Shanice's fingertips ached from the tests they ran every time she'd gone out to the Porta Potties set up outside, every time she went down to the lobby to get a brown-bag meal or jugs of clean water. A single red dot welling out of an invisible needle-prick. Over and over.

"That thing tell you your blood sugar?" she'd asked once, waiting for the result in the curtained-off lobby.

"No, sorry," they'd told her. "It doesn't."

They didn't appreciate questions like that. The not-even-really-a-riot that had broken out in the lobby after what happened with that boy put most everybody in a bad mood. Gossip all over. *Anika's boy was sick and crazy and alive at Grady. He was sick and crazy and shot dead. He wasn't sick at all, but they'd gunned him down anyway.* Tall like Xav had been.

Lingering outside the bathrooms, eavesdropping, she'd learned that they were looking for worms. She'd learned that those worms made people violent, and that they were awfully worried about how it would look, any news about *that kid who got hurt.* Got hurt, like he'd fallen off a bike or touched a hot stove. She'd learned that she couldn't afford to sit on her ass and wait for them to find Xav.

"Found two of them down by the state line a few hours ago," one of the masks had said, a woman's voice, tired and matter of fact.

"Still on our side of it?"

"Yep, still our problem 'til they get flown out to Carter's place."

"Of course. Of *fucking* course."

Flown out? The same men that'd shot Isaiah Davis in the stomach were going to fly *her* son somewhere? And if she couldn't ask about her own blood sugar, she wasn't even going to try to ask about *that*. Lan and her cousin agreed to help, scared as they were about getting on the doctors' bad side.

"You don't got to if you're too worried," Shanice had told them on the elevator ride down to the lobby, her emergency credit card and Xavier's birth certificate stuffed in her purse alongside her good dress. Just in case.

Lan had only shrugged, fidgeting with her glasses, cleaning the smudges. "We're neighbors."

It was easy enough, two cute little girls like that—one whose stomach was just starting to show—shouting about "My baby!" and heat stroke and every other complaint under the sun while Shanice slipped behind the Porta Potties and across the street.

Shanice didn't want to think about what kind of trouble they were in by now. Instead, she thought about that *other* call, that other drive to that other hospital to see what was left of her brother. More of the same, no matter the smaller details.

When was the last time you saw Rob? What did you say to him? She wouldn't let that happen again. It didn't matter how grown her boy thought he was. *Do you even remember?* She gnawed on one of her nails, glanced in the review to see the comforting ribbon of highway stretching out behind her.

Just a body walking alone. A hand clutching a case, dragging it behind. Scraping. A push-and-pull. A nice pressure there in the hand. Right there.

A body that waited patiently, that listened to a fleshy skull in a car window. To the talking meat idling on pavement. "You break down or somethin'? I can give you a lift into town," it offered.

A body that showed its teeth. "I appreciate you."

And what was a body? Just a house for something more clever than itself.

We are clever. We'd like to be clever.

A body that rejected **them**. A rot in the limbs. There was a word for it...

Downsizing. To be made small-er. Smaller.
Are you small?
Leena.

I am sorry. We are downsizing—

Leena.

I am sorry. We are downsizing. You will always be a part of our family.

Where was she? He didn't—

INDIGENT

We'll find them.

Rest easy.

We are a husband

aren't we?

339

part of a part of a part of a part of a part of a—

CHAPTER FOURTEEN
NEED COMPLEMENTARITY

When would he be cut open? Had it happened already?

Ari couldn't feel much of anything, so for a few seconds or minutes or hours, he could've been nothing but a brain. A nervous system free-floating. For a few seconds or minutes or hours, he was ecstatic. No more mouths, no more stomachs. He'd never have to eat again. Never even have to think about eating.

Wǒ kàn dào báisè de tiānhuābǎn...

But this body came back to him eventually, like it always did. Chest. *Xiōng kǒu.* Lips. *Zuǐchún.* Throat. *Hóulong.*

The mouth cut off and made useless. New holes bored into the skin. A foreign hand working the lungs. Concave and convex again. Reaching in—

He heard it before he felt it, the hollow scrape against his throat. Inside and outside. Teeth grinding in a parched mouth, dry as bone. *Shuǐ...* The skin of the lips splitting as the jaw opened... But there wasn't any water, and even if there was, his hands were stuck.

Maybe they were just too heavy, two dead things bolted to his wrists. But, no, there was something pressing cool and smooth against the skin. It was official, then. He'd been strapped down and cut open.

Cyril had been right.

A pig or a squid?

The hand that had torn out his throat, a violence under the skin that he'd breathed in with something close to relief, had been loving and merciful and right. *I'm sorry.* And he'd fucked it up again, living through a fortunate death like a roach scurrying away after being crushed, dragging its guts. *Are you mad at me?*

He'd cut Drew's throat open, too, Cyril guiding his hand. *Quick, while the blood's still movin'.* His brother's face had pressed out from underneath black plastic, the lines of it shuddering as the blood had run out and out and out.

It seemed very fair, for him to share the same fate as his brother—surrounded by white and gray, his neck gaping open—and as Cam, what little was left of him destined to be thrown out with the used needles and medical waste.

When would they be done with him? Would they just let him waste away slowly or would they be kind—take him out back to be put down like the family dog? Just an image. A stereotype from some other person's life, not his.

"You no have dog, Eric, landlady say no," Ma had told him once.

And he could almost bring up her face, if he tried, but it was mostly just frustration. Frustration with her bad English and the fact that she felt the need to use it whenever they were out. Frustration that these people made her feel that way. Frustration that *he* made her feel that way, probably. Frustration that he'd never apologized for that.

If he latched onto the feeling long enough, he could see it, her small mouth turned down, unhappy or concentrating, a beauty mark just underneath, on the chin. Trembling, her hands grasping a phone as she waded through the English language, slow and clear and so unlike her real voice. Her real English.

Erasing herself—

Someone opened the door, and he lost it, her face falling away as the tumblers clicked loudly back into place. Back into obscurity, his mother, who had spoken Chinese.

Gone.

And they touched him with those empty hands. And went for his neck. And he wanted to scream but didn't have the air for it. Instead, he settled on opening his mouth, **their** cornsilk bodies waiting on his tongue, and twisted his head to bite down.

Biting until he heard the music of a thin bone snapping, resonating through his teeth, until ice-cold skin gave way to hot blood and the person who'd ruined it, who'd ripped the memory from his head half-formed, was screaming enough for them both.

Subjective:
Location report—Brighton County Medical Center. Rural. Three stories, handicap accessible. Quarantine (no negative pressure space) located on third floor.

Objective:
Subject EZ apprehended. Medical history available and pending review. Subject LC expired on arrival, autopsy pending.

INDIGENT

Assessment:

Contact precautions at all times. Psychiatric regimen recommended pending medical case history review

Plan:

- Maintain quarantine at BCMC.
- Transfer patients and remains of patients to secure location in XXXXX.

Michaels had worked with Brighton County only once, back when he'd addressed a zoonotic disease outbreak at the Florida/Georgia line.[8] It'd been a rundown place when he was there, and it was no better now that he'd circled back to it. He had every reason to be pessimistic. Why would they know what they were doing? Why would any of this go well?

The DON explained in between nervous giggles about the young man who'd been dropped off at their ER in the early hours of the morning and who, by this retelling of the story, had hemorrhaged enough parasites to fill an entire sharps container before he'd even been intubated. More strained laughter. More explanations about the woman they'd pulled from a car wreck not an hour later, a pile of worms and bones by the time the EMTs arrived.

I told them to call y'all right away. This ain't our pay grade to deal with.

True. But the closest facility with anything resembling an isolation ward was in Tallahassee, so it was little ole' Brighton County's

---

[8] *See:* Brighton County Medical Center case reports #1763-3870. Overseen by Michaels, B. (2008). Exotic pet trade (alligators and snapping turtles) impact on communicable disease.

problem until they could arrange safer transport to Carter's quarantine facility. They'd roped off a few units reserved for psychiatric emergencies, BIOHAZARD decals stuck hastily to the doors, and gotten to work.

Slow going, but Michaels couldn't complain. He was still thanking his lucky stars that they'd found a live one—the only thing potentially saving him from being let go, with the quarantine of Fulton Street going so poorly.

An eleven-year-old. An eleven-*year-old*—

He'd never been fired before. He'd only ever discarded an outgrown position for something bigger. His one hope was to latch onto this case study and let it float him down the river.

Hell, maybe he'd even have time now to make a pivot to his first interest. COPD—chronic obstructive pulmonary disease, the thing that had made his father and his father's father miserable for half their lives before putting them both in the ground before they hit seventy.

It hadn't been the main thing according to their physicians, but Michaels knew better. He knew that people could power through almost anything if they saw a point in it. If it was *worth it.* And, for his old man, it simply wasn't. Not after a while.

It'd be much easier to make that pivot with one last strong paper under his belt. And *that'd* be much easier to do with a subject who was alive, living and breathing, barely, through a tracheostomy tube jutting out of his mangled throat. *Like a dog got at him. Or a bear.*

No one wanted to get too close after some unlucky nurse's thumb had been bitten clean off in the middle of a routine gauze redressing. The *Gordacia* had burrowed into the severed digit and started eating away before they could even think of reattaching it. Unlucky, but good for Michaels's report—proof that they were well within their rights to be jumpy. Trigger-happy.

"Acute agitation. Physical and chemical restraints (haloperidol, 20 mg IV before wound care, ALWAYS)"

Of course. Chemical restraints always seemed barbaric, but what else was there? It'd be weeks before the subtler psych meds did any good. All Michaels could do now was put on his PPE, have a sedative ready, and hope that a few hours' rest put this one in a less homicidal mood as he entered the isolation room.

Dim lights. Standard four-point restraints at the chest, wrists, knees, and ankles. The whispering exhale of the ventilator—so different, so much more refined, than the noise of his father's old CPAP machine, the grinding mechanical wheeze that meant his old man was breathing.

Without context, the restraints seemed excessive, a twinge of pity stopping him dead in his tracks there in the doorway. All this fuss over nothing but a shockingly thin body lying still, skin nearly as white as the bedsheets.

He would've thought it was a corpse if it weren't for the face. Dark eyes set deep above the hungry, staring cheekbones. Dark eyes following him as he closed the door quietly at his back. *Awake, alert.*

Eric Zhang was twenty-four but looked younger, only identified because he'd been arrested a while back[9], over nine hundred miles away from here. A name in the system, a face hardly recogniz-

---

[9] State of Illinois v. Zhang, schedule two violation of Illinois Controlled Substance Act, possession and distribution (I.L. Crim. Circ. Ct. 2005).

able but fingerprints that worked well enough. A pattern confirmed. Eric looked away as he came to a stop at the foot of the bed.

"Good morning, Eric." The eyes flicked back to him, then away again. Staring at the ceiling. *Oriented times one.* "My name is Brian Michaels." *You're just some guy. Never say you're a doctor.* "How're you feeling?"

He held out a pain scale in pictures—a bright red face, agonized, on one end, and a serene green face on the other. Eric didn't bother looking at it, his jaw working, and Michaels filed it away.

"I heard there's a valve they can put on your trach tube for you to be able to talk. Don't ask me how it works, but I know they need to get close enough to hook it up."

The mouth moved again, soundless. Two syllables. *Okay? Thank you? Fuck off?* Michaels could never read lips. "Would you like us to get a hold of your family?"

A white lie. He'd already spoken to Jie Zhang, had sat on the other end of the line as she cycled through what sounded like confusion, shock, relief. A mother's relief. Frantic Mandarin punctuated by his translator's monotone: "I'm coming to get him. I'm leaving now. Is he okay?" The translator calmly relaying his useless, fear-inducing words: *"No, you can't." "No, he's not."*

The lie was probably obvious, but he couldn't backpedal now. "We'll let them know that you have to stay in isolation and that you probably won't want to talk to anyone for a while. Anything else you tell them—or don't—is up to you."

Eric didn't respond. Maybe there was more of a language barrier than Michaels had assumed. But if the arrest transcripts were any indication, Eric spoke perfectly fine, very combative English. Something else, then.

Maybe he wasn't even cognizant at all of what had happened to him, of what he possibly had to hide.

How many bodies had piled up?

Were they disgusted with themselves or too far gone for that? What was even the point—pumping them with antipsychotics until they had the presence of mind to feel ashamed of what they'd done? To feel disgusted.

That seemed cruel, too. Out in the sticks where Michaels had spent his childhood, everyone knew good and well that it was better for a rabid dog to be put down quickly.

"None of this is your fault," he said aloud, reminding himself. "You're sick. It gets into your brain, makes you not trust anyone who's trying to help you. But that's all we want to do. Think about whether you want us to make that call."

He turned to leave, pausing as he stood there, grasping the door handle. No interrogations, just casual. Something he'd remembered off-hand. "Oh, I had a quick question for you. Do you know a young man named Xavier Coates?" he asked over his shoulder.

He watched those clawlike fingers scratch at the bedsheets. Four points—chest, wrists, knees, and ankles—the body pulling against the restraints with a growing animal panic. Michaels took that as a *yes* and left the room without another word.

When they'd first moved to Leigh Pierce, Xavier had ridden the elevator with Mom, up and down, learning the right buttons to push in case of an emergency. Third floor for home. Ground for school. Basement for laundry and tornados.

He'd sat in a sandbox in the courtyard—before it had been removed, too full of bugs and cat shit—watching tiny red mites crawl over the blue-stained woodgrain.

Mom's body had curled around his in the bathtub, a blanket over their heads and wind roaring outside. Roaring like a freight train right by his ear. The basement had already flooded. No other option.

When it was over, he'd gone out in his too-big rain boots to help clean up the tree branches and shingles and glass from the liquor store down the street... Or that'd *used to be* down the street. Just gone, like it had never existed.

Some of the neighbor kids had found bottles that were still good and hid them underneath their shirts to sneak inside. Xavier had followed their lead, stashing a full bottle of strawberry gin and juice under his mattress. Pink-red and sweet tasting, leaking out of a thin crack along the bottle's neck.

No water and no power for over a week. They'd eaten dry cereal and Little Debbies and heated bottled water in pots balanced on top of Mom's car cigarette lighter. A few days in, Mom had sent him outside to pick a switch from all the debris after she'd found the gin. *If you don't go get one right now, Xavier James, I'll pick one for you.* So he did.

She'd cried afterwards, holding him on her lap in the dark bathroom—awkward, all legs and elbows—a candle flickering as she kissed the top of his head, apologizing. The candle was white. It had smelled like baking bread. That had smelled good back then. Bread and cocoa butter lotion.

He had a mother who was tired. He had a mother who brought food and water to their neighbors. *Nobody else showin' up to help, are they?* He had a mother who took life out on him, but only once. He had a mother who learned from her mistakes quick.

Where is she...?

Not here.

Not on this hard cot under hard lights, no different from the concrete floor. He was alone. He was alone and someone was dead, Cyril or Leena or Ari. He didn't want to think about who, about what must've happened after he'd walked away.

Selfish. Ungrateful.

Instead, he stared at his hand, right in front of his eyes. The stitches, those pig guts poked into his skin, were gone. Eaten or dissolved. He wondered if that would happen to him, too, if he waited long enough. If he just lay here, curling in on himself.

The layers of skin would go first. *Stratum basale, stratum spinosum, stratum granulosum, stratum lucidum, stratum corneum, dermis, subcutaneous fat...*

The door opened, slow and heavy, metal scraping against concrete, the sound sending a jolt of pain through his ears and along his jaw.

Then the muscle. Epimysium, per-
imysium, endomysium, and fascia.

"Xavier Coates?" a voice said. Not the one that had pressed down on his spine, his face in the dirt, until his vision had gone black around the edges. There was still dirt in his mouth, the grit settled there, tucked against the gums.

Then the bone. *Periosteum, cortical, cancellous, bone marrow.*

He'd tasted bone marrow. Saw the layers splinter out under his fingers, leaking...

"Drunk and disorderly, we thought. We were gonna send in a req to put him in protective custody after he sobered up. Looks like he's got a few injuries."

That was the voice. The one that had seen this body, the face and the hair and the skin, and treated it accordingly. This body weighing him down. *They cut my last one open.*

From the cot, unmoving, Xavier watched a pair of feet get closer. Dark shoes, squeaking in plastic shoe covers, connected to the legs of a plastic suit.

They cut Cam open.

And in no time at all, a storm of white suits hung around him. In a car, out of it. In a white room with white lights as they forced him back onto a white bed.

There was blood in his mouth. It tasted like his. It tasted like someone else's.

And as quickly as they'd arrived, they were gone, this body stuck, suspended in a room that he'd wanted to work in once. A room that seemed foreign now. Dangerous. A heaviness in the long,

long limbs that were his and not his. He could feel the styloglossus muscle flexing, tongue soaking the blood in as he drifted off...

A body drifting and drifting through a floating room. Up a red staircase. Into a filthy trailer that smelled like smoke and mold, oxygen wheezing. The heavy metal of a rooftop door, safe and familiar. Out of it and into the fresh air...

Shanice stood at the admissions desk at Brighton County Medical Center, nails clacking against the Formica. Only two blue ones left on her ring finger and pinkie. The rest had been bitten off.

She'd changed into her best outfit in a gas station bathroom once she'd finally hit Dosa, had gotten good at looking presentable even after hours on the road. Hopefully, it would be enough for the woman at the front desk to take her seriously. Probably not.

She watched the attendant, the gloss coming off on her teeth as she chewed her lip. Tacky and sweet.

"You're sure he got here today?" the woman asked. Annoyed, like this wasn't her entire damn job.

"He might have. I just know he called and said he had to get to the hospital. It'd have to be this one, right?"

"And the name was 'Coates'?"

"*Yes*, Coates," Shanice said, wondering if she should smile, if it would make things go smoother, but she couldn't.

She didn't have the energy for it, and it was already 11:32 a.m. according to the waiting room clock, almost eight hours after the phone call that had led her here. No time for smiling, for buttering people up.

"I don't know if we can help you right now, Ma'am..." the attendant said. "A clinician will meet you out here if you wanna wait."

"Wait for what?"

"That's all they told me, Ma'am."

Shanice straightened her skirt and went to sit down in the waiting room with the old ladies and colicky babies, a little boy sniffling behind her.

She put her hands on top of her purse and pressed her heels together. *Presentable.* She thought of the social worker visiting them. *Are you hungry?* She thought of Granny tugging at her nose. *Be presentable.*

She half-expected Rob to come barreling out of one of the hallways, scrubs tight on his arms. Laughing. He'd always hated hospitals, treated the job he'd lucked into like the worse thing in the world.

Undeserved favor.

He'd made a good paycheck and lived like he didn't, like he was still back in Barnesville flipping burgers, spending his money on scratch-offs and girls, living out in a mobile home in the middle of nowhere. Maybe he'd kept all the money under his trailer. No way he'd pissed through all of it. But if anyone *could* do that, it'd be Robbie.

Thank Jesus her boy was smarter than that. *Better* than that...

Did Xav hate her? Was that why all this was happening?

Maybe, for all her trying, it'd just turned out to be more of the same. Like Granny, given a shit hand—being stuck in the South back when things had been worse, getting matched up with some spineless man who had her pop out child after child until her body gave out, slapping them around until they knew better. Quick and hard.

Shanice had hated her until there was enough time and distance for her to make out the reasons, to forgive it as much as she could. And wasn't that all Xavier ever wanted? Distance.

Once he got it, what excuses would he make to forgive her for everything wrong she'd ever done?

If he was here, if she found him, she would accept it all. She wouldn't argue about a single damn thing.

Shanice sat there stewing, fingers gripping the faux alligator skin of her purse, eyes searching the room. They landed on a man walking in from the parking lot, older and limping but no cane—s-*tubborn man*—pale, except for his face and hands.

They were a raw, painful red, like he'd scrubbed the top layer of skin clean off. He went to the desk. Stood where she had stood with his red hands on the counter, just as she had.

"I'm here to see my wife," he said.

"Name?"

"She's not a patient. She dropped someone off at the ER last night. She'd be waitin' for him…"

Someone was screaming outside. Long and high and far away. Shanice's back tensed. But this *was* a hospital. Somebody was hurt, getting dragged out to the ER. That was it.

"Sir, I don't think—"

"It's crucial that I see her," he said, already angry, and Shanice stiffened.

White men like that always felt like they had the right to start something. The same kind of man who caused problems when the bus was late, like she could control traffic. The same kind of man who her father had dished up chili for overseas, never looking him in the eyes.

She looked away—dealt with enough of that in her job—turning as the hallway's double doors swung open.

It was Dr. Michaels.

She recognized him even with half his face covered, nervous and excited. This was the right place, then. Had to be.

The doctor locked eyes with her, a clipboard tucked under his arm, and started in her direction. Obviously not happy to see her, but that was his problem.

Shanice kept her eyes on him and her ears tuned toward the desk, sure—more sure than anything—that it was about to get bad. She could hear it in their voices. Somebody in this redneck hospital was going to make everybody South of the Mason-Dixon line look bad and start yelling or throwing punches, and she just had to be ready to get out of the way fast when it happened.

"Miss Coates! What a surprise to see you here," Dr. Michaels called, closing the gap between them. At her side, now.

In her periphery, the man collapsed against the counter. Then he was staring at them. At Dr. Michaels. At *her*. Shaking. Eyes glaring out from a skin-and-bones face.

"Sir?" the desk attendant asked, touching his hand.

And he grabbed her. Fingers around her neck—

INDIGENT

Dr. Michaels took Shanice's arm, rushing her to the double doors, safe behind a keycard lock. People screaming. Sprinting for the exit. A boy with a busted arm falling to his knees, a red handprint smeared on the floor—

Glancing back, Dr. Michaels nearly yanking her arm from its socket, Shanice made out the woman's hands going to her neck, clawing. Blood sprayed from her mouth, across the table and onto the man's shirt. His face.

Blood streaming down his arm—

And as she was pulled into the hallway, the doors swinging closed, Shanice saw a body drop out of sight behind the counter, the head still lifted up and up... She saw the man rip away at the severed stump of the neck. Bring his hand to his mouth—

Chewing.

"What's happenin'?! What the *hell* is happenin'?!"

Subjective:

Objective:

Assessment:

Plan:

What's the plan? What's happening?

Michaels wanted to answer Miss Coates but couldn't yet, had to focus on deep breathing, on the *pranayama* they always touted at wellness seminars. In and out.

The secretary at least had the good sense to hit the panic button before things escalated, all the staff on their side of the doors scrambling. Locking themselves and their patients away in designated safe zones. Michaels watched their frantic bodies, a rainbow of scrubs and white coats.

"We have to go," he said, still breathless, forcing the words out.

Miss Coates was still by the door, looking through the tiny square window into the waiting room. It had quickly emptied out, the secretary's body just visible. Two small feet in pink flats, toes pointing upward, pantyhosed legs soaking in a growing pool of blood.

The man was crouched over her. Eating.

But Michaels could handle this. He'd pulled worms from ankles and elbows and rib cages, tweezed them out inch by inch. He'd watched from an observation deck as a cadaver was cut open. He'd *been watched* from an observation deck.

That girl had an access card, though, and if he had any mind left at all, the infected man would find it and get in here eventually.

Who was it? Someone from Beryl Ridge? One of the Brewers or the Drummers or the Clarks? He had the names in his phone, encrypted, the most recent pictures they had.

The walking skeleton outside wasn't immediately identifiable as any of them, but it was possible, especially now that they'd identified the corpse from the car crash. The plan was to show the pictures to Eric Zhang today, get to the bottom of things. He still had time to do that if—

"We have to go," he repeated, more force behind it.

"Xavier's here, isn't he? My boy's here?"

"Miss Coates, we have to go—"

"What were y'all gon' do with him?"

She ducked away from the window as the man shifted, his head rising above the counter. He'd turn and he'd see their shadows under the door. Any second now...

"Now's not the time," he whispered. "We have a facility for hospice care. It's safe, I prom—"

"*Hospice?*" she hissed, keeping her voice down. "If you not gon' take me to him, you better tell me where he is right now, so I can do it my goddamn self," she said, not moving away from the door until he nodded. It was nearly impossible, the muscles in his neck tense, straining.

Like a good public servant, though, like someone who caught outbreaks *before* they happened and consoled families and kept children safe, he squared his shoulders and grabbed a few gowns and masks and gloves from the nurses' station.

He and Miss Coates rode the elevator up to the third floor. Silent. Still in shock. He tried explaining the safety protocols for when they got to the isolation room, but he couldn't hear his own voice and couldn't tell if she was listening.

In the end, the two of them flinching at the shuddering elevator doors, he led her through the makeshift isolation ward to Xavier's room, entering the code and hoping that'd be enough to keep them safe until back-up arrived.

Xavier was on high alert as soon as they got inside. Four points—chest, wrists, knees, and ankles—just like the one next door. He wasn't as thin as the others, but he was getting there, shadows under his eyes and a thin white scar running across his nose—busted cartilage recently healed. Michaels didn't remember that from their last meeting. It hadn't been that long, had it? Only a few days...

Only a few days.

Maybe he'd managed to track Xavier down before he'd done something unforgivable.

He watched as Xavier shrank away from his mother, her hands fluttering over him, finding the hitch for the restraints. "Mom...?" he rasped.

Oriented times two, Michaels's brain chimed in, making him pause. Making him stand back as Miss Coates got the first wrist free.

Not too late after all. Not beyond saving.

"We gotta go, baby. Let's go—"

She got his hands free first, shaking off Michaels as he tried to pull her away.

After the first one, she was able to quickly release the rest of the straps, metal and plastic clacking to the floor. Four points of safety, gone.

"It's okay. It's okay.... I ain't mad at you. I'm not," Miss Coates cooed, like she was talking to a baby. A baby or a dog.

She hugged him close, and Michaels almost stepped in, seeing the tensing of Xavier's shoulders under her hands. "I'm just a little mad at you. That's okay. We'll deal with it later," Miss Coates was saying, not letting him go.

There were tears in her voice. Michaels wondered if that would set one of them off, if they responded to *that* as violently as they responded to blood. What would they find if he asked them to pump Xavier's stomach? Would Miss Coates be as cavalier with safety SOP if she *knew*?

After a long second, Xavier hugged his mother back, his hands draped loosely over her waist. Afraid to touch her.

Miss Coates pulled away, trying to take his hands, and he *jerked*, teeth bared, as though she'd sent an electric shock through him.

Michaels put himself between them, and Xavier glared at him, a flash of recognition and contempt.

"Mom—" Xavier started, and he rose to his feet, stumbling on the numb limbs before righting himself, skirting around them with his back to the wall, eyeing Michaels.

"I didn't steal nothin'," he said. Insistent.

"What?" Michaels choked out.

"I saw you write it. *I saw it*," Xavier said, voice cracking. "I didn't steal nothin'."

"Okay, I believe you."

Michaels nodded, not sure what else he *could* do, what would help, not sure if he'd ever helped a day in his life. And he felt himself get smaller, falling back against the bed as Xavier fled the room without looking back, his mother calling after him.

Someone real was in the room at the end of the hall, and Xavier's only plan was to find them and figure things out from there. He was too tired to think beyond that. Couldn't do it on his own.

He found the door locked. Then, he found a fire extinguisher hanging on the opposite wall and used all his strength to bring its metal edge down on the door handle until it gave in. Hanging loose and useless like a broken jaw. Cracking.

He opened the door and—

Something.

A flicker.

A part of a part of a part of a part of—

The world crashed into him as he saw Ari lying there, saw through a pinhole. *Consumptive, exsanguinous, spectral*—bubbling to the surface of his mind as he choked, trying to make sense of the endlessly branching bronchioles shared between them.

Expanding, contracting. *Kuòzhāng, chéngbāo.* The punctures in their skin. Their neck unpeeling, layer after layer, down to the vertebrae—

The body fell to its knees, taking Xavier along with it. Gasping. Pulled along until it was on its feet again, hands and hands and hands against the rough cotton sheets. Fibers pressed into the infinite whorls of their fingers.

It took him too long to find the latch for the restraints. Mom had done it just minutes ago, but he wasn't able to grab onto the picture of it, where her hands had snaked in and unclasped. All that was left was the lingering repulsion, skin still hot where she'd touched him.

Where she had *forced* herself in—

But he loved her, didn't he? He thought so, or he'd like to think so. They'd shared a body before. Once.

He spoke to Ari through their skin—felt the hopeless resignation as he finally got the restraints free. There was still the problem of the IV, the trach tube, all the machines they'd hooked into him, siphoning him away.

"You can't give up," Xavier said, finding his voice. "You wanna figure out what happens to us if we stay here?"

He already knew the answer, didn't wait for Ari's response before leaning closer, finding the fissure between parts in the tracheostomy tube and disconnecting it from the ventilator with a *snap*.

Ari's eyes went wide, and Xavier found his hand. *Don't freak out. Just breathe.* Lending his lungs, melding. Diaphragm, intercostals. *Kuòzhāng, hétóng.* Lungs under lungs under lungs—if one died, another sprouted up from the remains.

Breathe... You're okay...

"Xav?"

Mom.

Mom in the doorway with Dr. Michaels beside her, two faces hidden behind masks. "What you doin'?" she asked.

She took a step forward, just one, leaving Michaels standing in the threshold, fidgeting. "Just listen to me. *Listen.*" Another step. "I know you think they wanna hurt you, but I won't let them, you hear me?"

"You can't promise that," Xavier said.

Another step.

"I'll figure it out. It don't have to be here. We can go wherever you want." She was close now. He could reach out and touch her if he wanted to. If that wouldn't be the end of the world. "I just want you to be safe. You know that."

She raised a hand, saw him flinch subconsciously away before putting it back down, hidden in the folds of her hospital gown. An armless woman.

"I'll get us home. I promise," she said.

What should we do instead, Xav? Her hand had pressed against his head. Protecting.

Ari didn't trust her, a distrust tinged with jealously, with resentment, flowing through their veins. Xavier could talk him into it with a little time, though—

"We need to move to one of the safe rooms," Michaels cut in, stepping between them.

Mom nodded, a sheen of sweat on her forehead, the smell of skin and salt hitting his nose, and Xavier felt himself dragged back down.

She's listening to him, *trusting him—*
Why?

"There somebody out there," she said. "I saw what he did..."

"*He's* what happens when this gets out of control," Michaels said, looking at them with those flat gray eyes. Bad water gray. Dead lung gray. Xavier felt a movement in his jaw, under his teeth.

Michaels put his hand on the bedsheet. Too close. A cockroach. *Clicking.* "We just have to—"

INDIGENT

And Ari lunged forward, moving out from underneath Xavier's hands as he ripped the IV needle from his arm, a shining arc of blood and fluids springing from the brachial artery.

Ari stabbed the needle through Dr. Michaels's cheek, scraping teeth.

Smog-gray eyes finally closing as Michaels stumbled away, hands to his face, beautiful-smelling blood running down his jaw. Dripping onto his paper gown.

Relief flooded through them even as the roach skittered away, even as Mom screamed and screamed. Xavier took Ari's hands again, could feel the lungs faltering. So back to breathing. To control. To melting together.

And they both turned at once, their senses blossoming out to the limping footsteps in the hall. Sensed before Mom, backed into the corner of the room, whimpering. Before Michaels, fumbling blindly... headlong into Cyril in the doorway.

Xavier could see it: Red skin. Black blood overflowing. Over Cyril's hands. Over the panes of his face as he knelt down, gnawing. A red face by the fire. *A red face flickering.*

A red face standing in front of them now, grabbing the Good Doctor by the jaw as writhing bodies detached from his skin like stray tendons. Rushed into the mouth, the nose.

Screaming drowned in a gargling wetness as **they** ate the doctor's tongue, borrowed through the palate and into the soft flesh of the nasal cavity and the throat. Teeth came away under Cyril's hand as he dropped the twitching body to the floor. Teeth skittering over tile like music. Like bugs.

Xavier thought Cyril was trying to smile, but something was off, the droop worse, pulling down his lips. "Everybody's here..." he slurred.

Not everybody.

Just the three of them. Leena was dead, then. Camille's mother was dead. His mother was dead, and he felt a surge of joy and grief that he thought would kill him—

But his mother was also *alive*, as small as she could be, face buried in her arms as Michaels's skull turned to mulch in front of them. Xavier watched as the crown of the head sank in, like fresh bread deflating, fascinated.

Not s'posed to eat the brain. Don't they know?

"Xav, what's..." his mother whimpered, and Cyril twitched.

Unwelcome. Unwanted. Xavier felt the echo of it, felt it in the grinding of his teeth. But that couldn't be right.

We shared a body once.

Cyril staggered toward her, death in his face, in his outstretched hand. Blurring. Xavier didn't let him get close, breaking away from Ari to slam Cyril against the wall. It knocked the wind out of all of them, Xavier and Cyril collapsed and wheezing, Ari focused on nothing but counting his breaths.

"Mom! Go!" Xavier yelled, afraid to meet her eyes.

But he heard the soft hiss of her Velcro back brace as she stood up. Heard her shoes squeak. Saw a flash of beach-blue nails fly in and out of his vision like a dream as she ran.

Cyril let out a sound from deep in his chest, a sound that morphed without pause into sobs as he lay there against the tiles, hitting his fists against his temples until Xavier took them in his hands, forced them back down.

"I knew you'd get us caught," Cyril wept.

Attritional. Contrite.

"I didn't—I didn't mean for that to happen," Xavier said, crying, unable to stop himself, their tear ducts overflowing.

Ineludible.

"Well, it fuckin' *did*!" Cyril screamed, rising, through sheer force of will, back to his feet, both nostrils bleeding red-black.

The strength was leaving their limbs. A pressure building and building and building.

"She's gone. My girls are gone..." Cyril sighed, watery eyes lifted, finding only the cold, white ceiling. *Wanting.* "Now, all I got is you..."

Xavier reached out. "Dad—"

And Cyril exploded.

Coated the room in blood and worms.

I never liked hospitals.

It was a stupid thought, the most useless thought she'd ever had. But it was the only thing buzzing around Shanice's head for those long seconds immediately after she watched the man who was there and who suddenly *wasn't*. Just a pile of nothing by her son's feet.

Seen through a crack in the door—her little boy. Taller than her, much taller. *You shot up too fast. They gon' think you grown.* The outline of him blurring. Breaking down.

There was an awful sound in her ears. *Teeth.* Her entire body rattling like she was back behind the wheel of her Greyhound, coaxing it back into working order, shuddering and vomiting black smoke. She shrank into her gown.

Why don't you go get him? Can't even tough out some blood for your own son.

But it wasn't just blood, was it? It was *moving*. Moving—

Xavier looking at her with liquid hazel eyes, covered in a slick and shining red. Like the day he was born. Like the day she'd watched, delirious with exhaustion and something better than happiness, as his tiny body had been lifted up and out, the cord between them tugging. *Snipped.* But mothers carried their baby's cells inside of them even after the baby was born.

She'd read that in a pamphlet from the women's clinic the same day she'd decided (against her mother's advice, against all her threats and screaming) to keep him, this little crying body in her arms, so small and red. Seeing her for the first time and recognizing her.

Same nose, even now. The family nose. Perfect on him. Same strong hands.

He is an on-time God, she'd thought back then. Thought over and over as she'd held him against her and felt her body leaking out onto the sheets. But that hadn't mattered. *He is an on-time God.*

Shanice pushed through the broken door. It swung on its hinges behind her as she braved the teeming walls. She stepped closer. And closer. She reached out to show her son that he would always be a part of her, the best and smartest parts of her. Always.

They were on him.

On his clothes. His skin. A wonderful feeling of the world ripped open, of sensing himself from every possible angle. He blinked and the world blinked with him. He took in the world and the world took him in. Finally, *finally* knowing.

A thousand arms open and wanting. A thousand mouths saying *yes yes yes yes.*

They were hungry. His hand, that had once been part pig, was being eaten down to the bone. Bright pink and white peeking out of his split skin. He didn't feel it, and he felt everything. He would consume and be consumed, and everything would be alright.

He heard a laugh and realized it was this body laughing, bouncing from every corner. Echoing—no, *reverberating*—back.

Xavier turned and saw from every angle Ari on the edge of the bed, a beautiful picture in red, watching, enraptured, as the lines of his palms split open, blood pouring from them like a well never-ending. Blood poured from the re-opened gash in his neck as he sat there laughing. *Laughing.* Silent, but felt.

"Xav! Xavier! Are you okay?!" His mother's voice heard with **their** ears.

She was there, coming toward him. Beautiful, too. He could see all the pieces he shared with her from here. The eyes, the nose, the slope of the chin. The thin cotton mask couldn't hide it, the lines of her face etched in water and heat.

"Don't come in here, Mom," he warned, horribly disappointed. *Wanting.*

She could be a part of this, too. Whatever *this* was. But she wouldn't want to. He knew that.

She wanted so many things. She says she didn't, but she did.

Her body stopped just an arm's length away. Limbs and torso swimming in a gown, still bright white. Spotless.

She's safe, some part of him thought. *Safe.*

"I'll- I'll get help. I'll find somebody—"

"Can you just stay there?" he asked. "Wait with us. With me? Please."

He couldn't feel his face—couldn't tell if he was smiling—but he tried. It would be good for her to be safe and to know that he was safe. Submerged.

She nodded, her eyes wet, and the scent of it was perfect. Right. Wet brown eyes that followed his every move as he sat with Ari, leaning together. No difference between their two bodies now, no breaks. He looked around, suddenly determined to bring her in just partly, if the entirety of her was too much to ask.

Don't be greedy.

He touched Ari's wrist, felt the warmth of it. Felt the skin give sweetly away under the slightest pressure as his fingers hit bone. Rested comfortably there against it. "I see a green button," he said, spotting the call button hanging by the bed.

Ari nodded, settling against him. He held up his hand, showing Xavier the green light on the pulse monitor still clinging to what was left of his thumb. A green light blinking. Hypnotically bright. *Lüsè de.*

"You see anythin', Mom?" Xavier asked, deferring to her now, hoping that she'd find something new, something too small for him to notice. She was good at that.

She didn't answer, tears welling over. He could tell she was trying to hide that. But the salt was in the air. Welling up. She'd find something eventually. He knew she would. So he just leaned back on his hands, let himself cheat for the next one.

"The trees outside are green..." he breathed, and something in his throat *popped*.

Green. What else?

Collard greens, fresh okra, ripe plantains. The mailboxes at Leigh Peirce—copper and verdigris. The beer bottles in Zion's fridge, and the stars glowing on the ceiling of his childhood bedroom. A snuff bottle with trees painted inside the glass. The spidery veins in a block of marble...

Green...

There was Uncle Rob's class ring. August. A peridot. His uncle dead in the ground in Barnesville, under green grass. Rotting away just like the green rolls of fifties that were tucked in an old lockbox buried two miles from his double-wide at Escénico Mobile Home Park.

A plot of land just above the waterline where turkeys foraged through the green, green grass, looking up at them with dumb blinks as he led Xavier to the right spot in the weeds.

Xavier had watched his uncle dig, springtails hopping around his feet. Not an ounce of fear in them.

Mom should've come with them, the three of them together. She'd be happy, and no one would bother her, and Xavier could see all the way out to the road. All the way out to the treeline. He could protect her and Uncle Rob easy.

"Why d'you hide your stuff here, Unc?" he'd asked, holding a jar of twenties in his hand. Rob's last payday.

"Because this place, little man," Rob had announced, hands sweeping over the field with a flourish, never anything if not confident, "is *safe*."

At that, his shovel had hit metal with a hollow *thunk*, and he'd stopped, sweating in the Georgia heat, to give Xavier a smile.

A NOTE FROM THE AUTHOR

A *medically indigent adult*, in the United States, is defined as a person who does not have adequate health insurance and is unable to afford the costs of healthcare on top of daily living expenses.

Half of the US population is reported to struggle affording healthcare and medical expenses, while ~68,000 Americans die each year due to lack of healthcare. The current (as of 2025) changes at the HHS are stoking fear and distrust in these institutions and in medical professionals.

Healthcare is a multifaceted monster, and money isn't the only thing stopping people from receiving help. Medical trauma can be historical (such as the frequent abuse and exploitation of Black Americans by healthcare institutions) or based in personal, intersectional experiences. Oftentimes, it's both. And that learned distrust is a killer even generations out. Addressing medical trauma is tantamount to overcoming it.

As an author, healthcare worker, and human who has lost friends and family to medical trauma and financial inaccessibility, this is an issue close to my heart. Healthcare is a human right. *All* people, especially those from marginalized backgrounds, should feel safe with their doctor(s).

It is my goal as a healthcare worker, writer, and human to work to turn that *"should"* into a reality.

DISCUSSION QUESTIONS

1. Who or what is the villain in this story? Did they win or lose?

2. What are the most prominent themes in *INDIGENT*?

3. How is the theme of medical trauma portrayed throughout the story? How do different characters contend with medical trauma?

4. The phrase "sick people are mean" appears multiple times throughout the narrative. What is its relevance to the story and the themes?

5. Why do you think the characters made the decisions they did? What decisions would *you* make in a similar situation?

6. How does the writing style of this book contribute to the themes or tone?

7. How did this book challenge or change your perspective(s) as a reader?

8. What symbolism did you spot in this narrative, and what does it mean?

ACKNOWLEDGMENTS

Books, no matter how much my introverted writer self wants to deny it, are a collaborative effort. *INDIGENT* wouldn't exist without a lot of help. Thank you to...

My medical issues for posting me up in bed and giving me nothing to do but work on this.

Kelley and Hannah for supporting this weird little book.

Adam Novak for encouraging me to turn this screenplay into a novel.

Yi Lin Zhou for the fantastic cover art and Mandarin translations. (Never trust internet translation apps, folks! That would've been bad.)

Chess, Robin, and Reid for reading the roughest of rough drafts and dealing with my nonsense.

Dominique Lassalle Escallón, Kelly Ragan, and Jane Thompson for taking on the unenviable task of editing the roughest of rough drafts and dealing with even more of my nonsense.

My husband and my person, Alex, who supported me every step of the way.

ABOUT THE AUTHOR

Briana N Cox (she/they) is a queer, Black author, screenwriter, and playwright based in Nashville, TN. She is the oldest of seven children and a first-generation academic, with a BA from Swarthmore College and an MS in speech-language pathology from Purdue University.

She was a Playwrighting Fellow with the TN Playwrights Studio in 2019 and has been featured on the 2024 Next List highlighting up-and-coming screenwriters. Her script "To the Family of Verlean Banks" was produced in 2025.

Briana writes genre stories from the margins, illuminating the experiences of often overlooked demographics with authenticity, dignity, and dark humor.

Find them here: brianancoxwriter.com